A Child's Voice Calling

A Child's Voice Calling

MAGGIE BENNETT

ARROW

Published by Arrow Books in 2002

1 3 5 7 9 10 8 6 4 2

First published in the United Kingdom in 2001 by Arrow Books

Arrow Books Limited
20 Vauxhall Bridge Road, London, SW1V 2SA

Random House Australia (Pty) Limited
20 Alfred Street, Milsons Point, Sydney,
New South Wales 2061, Australia

Random House New Zealand Limited
18 Poland Road, Glenfield
Auckland 10, New Zealand

Random House (Pty) Limited
Endulini, 5a Jubilee Road, Parktown 2193, South Africa

Random House Group Limited Reg. No. 954009

www.randomhouse.co.uk

A CIP catalogue record for this book
is available from the British Library

Papers used by Random House are natural,
recyclable products made from wood grown in sustainable forests.
The manufacturing processes conform to the environmental
regulations of the country of origin

ISBN 0 09 941574 7

Typeset by Deltatype Ltd, Birkenhead, Merseyside
Printed and bound in Great Britain by
Cox & Wyman Ltd, Reading, Berkshire

In loving and respectful memory of my aunt
MABEL ANNA COATES
(1891–1979)

And with grateful acknowledgement to
Judith Murdoch, literary agent.

Prologue

Anna-Maria's first baby was conceived in a golden Hampshire meadow beneath a hedgerow of tumbling wild roses, in an ecstasy of loving and giving; the confinement took place at 23 Macaulay Road, Tooting and she was completely at the mercy of her mother-in-law.

Mrs Court stood over her, arms akimbo, sleeves rolled up to her elbows. 'Ye've got a fair way to go yet, Annie. The head's still high, so ye'd best get up off that bed and walk around for a bit, to bring it down.'

The girl winced as another contraction began, tightening her abdomen to board-like hardness. Surely this could get no worse!

'Come on, ye'll do no good lyin' there, my girl, get up an' take a turn round the room. Yer can lean over the bed rail when yer get a pain, an' breathe hard in an' out.'

Anna-Maria had to obey, as she had done ever since she'd met Jack's mother. Ever since she'd run away from her home, broken her father's heart and estranged herself from her sisters. Ever since she'd jilted young Eric Drummond who'd told her he loved her. Only last summer, but a lifetime away.

'Sit down by the window for a bit, an' get a breath of air,' said Mimi Court, pushing up the sash an inch or two. 'Nobody'll see yer through the net curtain.

I'll get Elsie to bring a cup o' tea – be back in a minute.'

Anna-Maria sat down heavily and looked out on Macaulay Road. Oh, how she had hoped and longed and prayed to be out of this house and into a home of her own before the confinement! It was almost seven months since Jack had first brought her here after their elopement and her thoughts went back to that September afternoon.

It had all been so romantic, her first sight of London: the River Thames and Westminster Abbey, the Houses of Parliament and the big clock, just as in the pictures she had seen. She and her beloved Jack had mixed with the fashionable throng in St James's Park, the gentlemen in pearl-grey top hats escorting ladies bedecked and beribboned in silk and lace, topped with enormous feathered hats and carrying dainty parasols.

But then they had to get a motor-bus, something Anna-Maria had never seen before, and travel down to Clapham, where they boarded another bus, this time a horse-drawn one which set them down beside a large stretch of common land. Jack paid threepence to a man who carried his portmanteau on a handcart down a wide, unpaved lane with trees on either side, turning right into Macaulay Road. Number 23 was one of a row of solid gabled terraced houses with small front gardens bounded by privet hedges and iron railings.

Jack had told her that his widowed mother was a midwife and also took in lodgers, so Anna-Maria pictured a woman who was kind and hard-working. Nevertheless she felt increasingly apprehensive as the meeting approached and hung back when Jack inserted his key into the front door.

'Here we are, sweetheart. Yer mustn't mind me mother, she's bound to be a bit surprised at first.' He opened the door and called out. 'Helloo-oo! I'm home again!'

Anna-Maria put on a demure smile to greet Mrs Court.

The figure of a woman appeared in the passage. She was in her early forties, short and round-bodied, not fat, and wore a gown in a deep plum colour, buttoned up to the neck and lace-trimmed. As she stepped forward Anna saw sharp brown eyes and a jutting nose like Jack's, though her colouring was much less dark. Her hair was styled like the Queen's, drawn smoothly to the back of her head where a short length of fine black lace fell to her shoulders. For one brief moment she stared at Anna-Maria who involuntarily drew back.

'Mimi!' cried Jack, holding out his arms.

Mimi? Was this a pet name like mamma?

The woman smiled and allowed Jack to embrace her. 'And about time, yer young rascal. What're yer been up to?' She looked past him at Anna-Maria. 'Yer didn't say yer was bringing company.'

Her way of speaking resembled Jack's, though she made an attempt at superiority, carefully sounding her aitches and drawling over the vowels; this was her company voice and likely to be completely discarded in times of anger or emotion, as Anna-Maria soon discovered. 'And who is this young lady?'

'This is Miss Anna-Maria Chalcott and I've brought her back with me from Belhampton,' answered Jack with just a slight hesitation. 'Miss Chalcott, this is my mother.'

Anna-Maria gave a slight bow and was about to

say 'How do you do?' when the woman forestalled her: 'Why, Miss Chalcott, what was yer parents thinkin' of, lettin' yer leave yer home in the country?'

Anna-Maria looked to Jack for aid and he hastily answered on her behalf: 'Miss Chalcott'll write to her father and let him know she's safe and well. Meanwhile she can stay here, can't she, Mimi? She can have my room.'

'Not with you in it, she can't, whatever next? My goodness me!' Mrs Court sounded very shocked. 'Ye'll have to stay at Bill Williamson's down the road. Anyway, ye'd better come in.'

Jack stood aside to let Anna-Maria follow his mother into an over-furnished living room where she was told to take a seat. Mrs Court went through to a kitchen beyond, beckoning Jack to follow her. Although the door was shut, Anna-Maria picked up some of their heated exchange.

'I tell yer, Mimi, I'm not askin' yer to do anythin'! As far as I know she's not even—'

'But she could be, yer mean? Once is enough, think o' that Hackney girl.'

'An' anyway, it don't signify because I love her, if yer can understand that, an' I've said I'll marry her.'

While unable to hear much of what was said, Anna-Maria heard *that*, spoken boldly by the man she adored, and she sighed in sheer relief. Dearest Jack!

Mrs Court was speaking again: 'The mother's dead, yer say. Any money there?'

Jack muttered something about a nice line in draperies and upholstery, a big house and a decent little two-wheeled gig.

'Oh, tradespeople. Nothin' to give herself airs

4

about. And no son to take the lot when the father goes?'

Anna-Maria closed her eyes, suddenly tired and feeling slightly sick. A few minutes later Mimi bustled in with a tray of tea and cake. Jack followed with a hot-water jug and winked at Anna-Maria from behind his mother's back as she put down the tray.

'A cup of tea, thank you, that's all, Mrs Court,' said Anna-Maria quickly, conscious of those sharp eyes upon her, and longing to be alone with Jack.

But that was not allowed her, not for a whole week, during which Jack slept at a neighbour's house and met her only in the company of his mother and when he took her out for walks and to the Sunday morning service at St Nicholas's church. This was followed by a lavish dinner at which Mimi Court presided and carved the joint.

There seemed to be two permanent lodgers, a thin, worried-looking woman called Miss Lawton who went out to give piano lessons and her elderly mother who seldom emerged from the room they shared.

'The ol' girl's lost her wits and don't know what day it is or where she is,' Jack explained. 'Mimi took 'em in because they'd lost their home and were almost starvin' – she's got a good heart that way, y'know. Some o' Mimi's patients stay here for a while, like that one.'

He nodded towards a heavily pregnant young woman called Ivy who sat down with them to Sunday dinner and hardly uttered a word.

Elsie was a sullen maidservant who seemed to occupy a special position in the house, though it took Anna-Maria some time to discover what it was.

Under Jack's guidance – and he was under his mother's – Anna-Maria wrote a deeply penitent letter to her father, begging him to forgive her for running away, and telling him that she was happy and comfortable at the home of Mr Court's mother until they could be married and have a home of their own. She sent her love to her sisters Kate and Nell, and said she looked forward to visiting Belhampton again as Mrs Court, accompanied by her dear husband who also sent his deepest respects and kindest regards.

A whole week passed with no reply, then came a black-bordered envelope from Miss Chalcott, the eldest sister. It was short, cold and carried dreadful news. There was to be no happy return for the prodigal daughter. For George Chalcott had suffered a severe seizure while returning home in the gig and in spite of the best medical attention had died without regaining consciousness. 'You have brought shame and disgrace upon our family, and the shock has killed our poor father,' Katherine had written. 'Your presence at his funeral service or at this house will not be welcome, and neither Elinor nor I ever wish to see you again.'

Mrs Court found Anna-Maria lying on the floor where she had fainted and a doctor was sent for. He confirmed what Mimi already suspected, that a child was expected in the following spring, about the beginning of April. A quiet wedding was hastily arranged at St Nicholas's church between Miss Anna-Maria Chalcott and Mr John Masood Court.

Thankfully back in his own bed, Jack's eager anticipation of his wedding night received a setback when his young wife wept uncontrollably in his arms. 'Papa, oh, dearest papa, forgive me!' she

6

sobbed over and over again, until at last she fell into an exhausted sleep.

Which left Jack no choice but to turn over and fall asleep also.

When a letter arrived from the Chalcotts' family solicitor with the news that there was no bequest for Anna-Maria, at least not for the time being, Court's brow darkened. Chalcott Draperies was to stay in the family with a manager in charge and George Chalcott's capital, mostly invested in bonded stock, was to be transferred to his daughters' names in equal shares and not to be withdrawn by one of them without the consent of the other two.

'They're tryin' to do us out o' what's ours by law,' Jack muttered angrily to his mother. 'I've a good mind to go and confront that crook of a lawyer meself.'

But Mimi counselled patience. 'Could be all for the best,' she said with a knowing nod. 'The longer it's left the more it'll grow. *And* it can't be squandered, neither.'

Soon after this Jack took his portmanteau packed with haberdashery samples and the photographic equipment that was his sideline, and went off on another business expedition, leaving his new wife to be taken in hand by his mother.

'Ye'll have to learn to pull yer weight, my girl,' Mimi declared on finding Anna-Maria still in bed at nine. 'I can tell ye've always had it easy, what with bein' the youngest and yer pa's pet an' all, but cryin' won't bring him back, neither will layin' around bein' waited on.' Tying a long white apron over Anna-Maria's black mourning dress, she added briskly, 'Ye're a married woman now and ye'll have to learn how to keep house for my son. Now, then!'

Dazed by the changes that had overtaken her, Anna-Maria obeyed with a docility that would have astonished her sisters. The child growing within her seemed to have taken over her mind as well as her body and half the time she seemed in a dream. Under Mimi's supervision she prepared vegetables, grated suet for puddings, washed fruit for cakes, kneaded dough, trimmed meat and fish for roasting and baking. Her hands roughened and she was often extremely tired, but at least she had no time to mope under the burden of sorrow and guilt that Kate's letter had laid upon her.

Mimi advised her to take note of the work that the maids had to do: sweeping and scrubbing, raking out ashes and laying fires, emptying chamber pots and boiling up water for the washing that had to be pushed through a mangle and hung out on the line or draped over the wooden beams of the 'airer' with its rope on a pulley. 'Ye'll 'ave that to do an' all, when yer get yer own home,' Mimi told her.

Her own home with Jack! Anna-Maria could hardly wait, but as yet there was no sign of it.

As autumn advanced, chill easterly winds blew across the sprawl of south London suburbs where marshes and market gardens had been rapidly swept away and replaced by bricks and mortar. Jack remained away on his business trip, though he promised to be home for Christmas and ready to start house-hunting.

One night in early October Anna-Maria was awakened by a series of agonised screams and sat up in terror: it sounded as if somebody was being murdered in their bed. She heard footsteps running along the passage and Mimi's voice calling out, 'Stop that bloody racket, ye'll 'ave the 'ole neighbour'ood up!'

Anna-Maria got out of bed and opened the door to peer into the passage. The screams were coming from Elsie's room and a great clamour was going on behind the closed door, which suddenly opened to reveal Mimi with an apron tied round her black house gown. 'Go back to yer bed, Annie, an' stay out o' what don't concern yer!'

Trembling, Anna-Maria obeyed, though she lay rigid in her bed as the noise went on. Mimi's voice could be heard giving orders and telling Elsie to fetch this and that. Then there was a last, long, blood-curdling shriek, followed almost immediately by a high-pitched squealing.

The explanation dawned. The young woman called Ivy had been giving birth to a baby. Anna-Maria knew the basic facts about childbirth, but had not realised that it was so painful. In fact, there were a lot of things she did not know . . .

Next morning there were bloodstained sheets soaking in the galvanised iron tub and for ten days Ivy stayed in her room with her baby girl who could sometimes be heard crying. Then one morning she left quietly, leaving the baby with Mimi for a further two days until a man and a woman came and took it away, handing over a large envelope in exchange. Nobody talked about it and Anna-Maria hoped she would be well away from Macaulay Road when her own baby was born. She did not want Mimi as her midwife.

Yet here she was enduring pain the like of which she

had never known was possible. At some time near to midday she was lying on her back and Mimi was bending over her, pushing her legs apart and probing with her hard fingers, and saying something about breaking the waters; Anna-Maria thought she would faint clean away with the agony of it. Somewhere there was a sound like an animal in pain, an agonised howling – and she realised it was herself making the noise.

Mimi straightened up and covered her with the sheet. 'The pain's goin' off now, Annie, so stop 'ollering an' make the most o' the rest before the next one comes on. Let yerself go loose an' floppy like a rag doll.'

Anna-Maria sighed, closed her eyes and at once fell into a doze. She thought Jack was beside her, his eyes looking deep into hers – ah, those bold black eyes of his that had stolen her heart and swept her to dizzy heights of joy! It had been love at first sight between the young photographer and the fair-haired, blue-eyed girl whom he called his English rose; and it had all happened so quickly, their meetings in the summer woods and fields, his avowal of love and her passionate response; everything else was forgotten in this all-absorbing obsession – her father and sisters, her home, Eric Drummond the vicar's son – all the life she had known in her eighteen years was nothing compared with what she felt for Jack Court.

Another pain began with a twinge, a hardening of muscle, a knife thrust in her back, a mounting crescendo of agony, tearing her body apart, or so it felt – again the animal in pain, no room in her head for anything else until the slow, merciful descent into another interval between contractions.

Again she drifted into a short, sweet oblivion, but

this time her memories were more recent. During the past winter she had shed some of her illusions about her adored husband who spent such a lot of time away. As Christmas approached she longed for him to return, to cuddle up to him in bed, to feel his hand gently stroking the round bulge of their child while they discussed names for a boy and a girl.

But when Jack came home he was preoccupied and unsettled. Sales had not been so good, it seemed, and when she asked him about the photography he snapped at her impatiently, 'What's the use o' takin' pictures when I got to pay another damned photographer to develop 'em? Yet need a studio to make it a payin' game.'

'But as soon as we've got our own home, Jack, you can have a room to yourself in it.'

'Oh, for heaven's sake stop goin' on about a house, Annie! A man gets tired after workin' the hours I put in every day. 'S'all right for you, layin' around on a sofa.'

Tears sprung to her eyes at such unkindness – and it was so unfair, too. She turned from him, biting her lip and putting his crossness down to tiredness, though she was deeply hurt.

On Christmas morning he refused to go to church, so she went with Miss Lawton who dressed all in black and carried a worn prayer book. After Mimi's enormous dinner of roast goose and plum pudding Jack spent the afternoon smoking cigars and drinking port wine with Bill, the friend with whom he'd lodged before the wedding. With their heads together over a newspaper, they studied form, whatever that was, and talked of Kempton Park where something important was due to take place on Boxing Day. When the two young men left the house together Anna-Maria got out her embroidery and sat with Miss Lawton, a nervous, fidgety woman who flushed and stammered when spoken to; she was the sort of boring spinster that Anna-Maria would previously have shunned.

At the end of the evening, weary and dispirited, and needing to empty her bladder again, she heaved herself up out of her chair and lit her candle to go to bed, there being no gaslight above the ground floor.

She was fast asleep when Mimi woke her to help get Jack up the stairs to his room, where his mother expertly pulled off his boots, coat, jacket and trousers, and put him to bed. 'There y'are,' she panted, 'he'll lay like a log till mornin'. Get in an' turn yer back to 'im, 'e won't be no trouble to yer, 'e's too far gone.' She spoke with a certain spiteful relish at Anna-Maria's horrified expression. 'Ain't yer never seen a chap bottled before?'

Lying awake and staring into the darkness while the bed vibrated to his tumultuous snores, Anna-Maria felt utterly alone; this was her *husband*, mindless and shameless in her presence. She was trapped and there was no way out.

The baby kicked inside her as if to remind her that it was there and she was comforted by it. Placing her hands on her abdomen, she told herself that everything would be different when she held her child in her arms.

In February there had been that strange encounter on the train.

From time to time Mimi would send her daughter-in-law out shopping for her in Tooting or Balham when she wanted her out of the way. On this particular day Anna-Maria decided to take a bus to

Battersea and go from Clapham Junction on the train to Waterloo. It was fine and clear, with a hint of spring in the air, and Anna-Maria enjoyed looking again at the Houses of Parliament and Westminster Abbey where she spent a few minutes sitting and remembering her first sight of it with Jack. Arriving back at Waterloo, she got on the train and found an empty compartment where she sat in a corner seat and covered her bulge with the evening newspaper she had bought.

The door opened and a man looked in. He was wearing clerical black and carried his hat in his hand. 'Er, I beg your pardon, madam, is there room for—?' he began and then stared blankly. She looked up and froze at the sight of Mr Eric Drummond. What would he say? Surely he'd retreat at the sight of the girl who had thrown him aside so heartlessly: but he came into the compartment, his eyes fixed on her face. 'Anna-Maria! Is it really you? May I sit down?'

She nodded and he sat on the edge of the seat opposite her. 'Forgive me, I've heard nothing about you since—'

She did not want this conversation. 'I'm married, Mr Drummond. I am Mrs Court. There's nothing to say now.'

His pale features flushed. 'No, of course.' There was a long pause and then, not knowing what else to say, Anna-Maria turned to face the window. As she did so the newspaper fell from her lap.

He saw. 'A child,' he whispered. Still she neither spoke nor looked at him as he sat crushing his black hat between his hands.

What he said next took her breath away. 'I'd have married you, Anna-Maria. I'd have married you and called it mine.'

13

She flinched and closed her eyes, such was the impact of the words. A conflict of emotions raged within her, regret for all that she had so heedlessly thrown away, the harm that had been done. But now there were her marriage vows, the promises she had made to the man she had chosen. And he was not this man. There could be no going back, nor was there anything more to be said. Anna-Maria sat absolutely still and silent, gazing out of the window until the train slowed at the approach to Clapham Junction.

When it stopped she stood up awkwardly and Drummond rose to help her. She shook off his arm and got down from the carriage without assistance, walking away without a backward glance. He never saw her tears.

Back at Macaulay Road she found Mimi occupied with a visitor who had been put in the back bedroom, so Elsie dourly warned Anna-Maria. Which meant keep away.

On the following day a silent, white-faced young woman departed in a hansom cab, all alone, and watching her go, Anna-Maria realised that Mimi Court not only delivered babies, but she also got rid of them. And would have done the same for Anna-Maria if Jack had wished it. Ah, but he hadn't, she thought with satisfaction. Jack had chosen to marry her and for all his imperfections she knew that he loved her in his way. And she loved him – far, far more than she could ever have loved Eric Drummond.

At last an upturn in Jack's business deals allowed him to secure a house to rent furnished, a small, narrow-fronted terrace ready for occupation from the first of April. After waiting so long it was difficult to believe that finally they were to have their own home. Sorrel Street was in north Battersea, one of a maze of residential thoroughfares between Queenstown and the Wandsworth Road, and theirs was number 12. Jack took his wife to see it and told her that it would be an ideal first home. She was overjoyed.

But his mother insisted, and Jack of course agreed, that they should stay at Macaulay Road until after the confinement, so that Mimi would be on hand to deliver the child.

It happened on 30 March 1894.

'Jack, are you awake?'

'Huh – mm-mm – what?'

'What time is it?'

'What? Dunno. It's pitch-dark still. What's up?'

'I've been lying awake. Oh! There it is again, another pain.' She moaned and buried her face in the pillow.

He slowly surfaced from sleep. 'Is it the baby, d'ye reckon?'

'I don't know. I'm not sure, but it's hurting a lot. *Oh!*'

'I'll call Mimi.'

Anna-Maria was in labour and the next twelve hours were remembered only as a blur of pain, with Mimi bustling around the room and Elsie's raw-boned features appearing at intervals as Mimi demanded fresh water and towels. Morning passed into afternoon and at about two o'clock Mimi told her to start pushing down when she got the pain. '*Push*, Annie, come on, *push*, an' again, *push!*'

And push again. And again for countless more times, until she thought she would die before giving birth. The agony was indescribable.

'An' once more, Annie, one more big push down – come on, take a big breath an' *hold* it, grit yer teeth an' *push – an' push – push – push – push – push*!'

She heard herself screaming as she stretched and split, and something burst forth from between her splayed legs. There was a gasp, a choking sound and then the room was filled with the piercing cry of a newborn child.

'Oh, it's a girl, would yer believe. Well, time enough for a boy.' Mimi sounded rather flat and out of breath. 'Elsie, go down an' tell Mr Jack it's a girl at ... er ... a quarter past three.'

When the baby was wrapped in a towel and placed in her arms, Anna-Maria was filled with wonder and something she had never known before. A great surge of love welled up like a fountain within her, directed towards this new being who had so changed her life, right from the moment of its conception. *It* had become *she* and was hers to hold, to keep, to cherish for the rest of her life. She thought of her own mother, the loving mamma who had died ten years earlier: her name had been Mabel and this child would be called after her.

'You're my little girl,' she whispered, gazing at the sweet round head covered with golden down, the clear blue eyes, the rosebud mouth. And those tiny hands, each finger so perfect, tipped with its delicate nail. Anna-Maria touched the baby's hand with her forefinger, which was at once encircled by the little clinging fist. 'My daughter,' she whispered. 'My own beautiful little Mabel. You'll make such a difference, my darling. All the difference in the world.'

Chapter One

'Come *along*, Albert, never mind about dilly-dallying with them Paddys,' Mabel called to her brother outside their school. 'It's my piano lesson today and Mum'll give it to me if I'm not home when Miss Lawton comes. Why're yer shuffling along like that? Oh, just look at yer bootlaces, ye'll trip and fall for sure – here, let me do 'em up!'

She stooped down at the kerbstone and quickly laced up his boots while he fidgeted, conscious of the grins of the Irish boys. 'I ain't got no lesson,' he muttered.

'You mean you *have not got a lesson*,' Mabel corrected him, straightening herself up and taking him firmly by the hand.

'Ah, de poor liddle feller, see, he has to go wid his big sister!' jeered the tousle-haired boys forced to attend the London County Council School in Hallam Road for lack of affordable Catholic education.

'Shut yer faces, yer dirty Paddy-whacks, hope the boat sinks that brought yer over!' retorted Mabel, whose tongue could be versatile when required. Breaking into a half-run she dragged the protesting six-year-old through the streets. There was no time to stare up at the high windows of the Women's Rescue just off Lavender Hill with its iron gate through which the children could sometimes see the rescued women and girls sitting out of doors hemming sheets; today she had to hurry, for there would be

17

trouble is she was not at home when Miss Lawton arrived on her bicycle.

There would be trouble anyway when her mother saw the white card she had been given to bring home. Better wait until the lesson was over and Miss Lawton had gone, not that the timid spinster would be likely to pass anything on to Grandmother.

Mabel enjoyed her piano lessons and the daily practice was no hardship either, except that there was rarely time for a full hour at the keyboard. At seven years old she already had her responsibilities in the house, especially in helping with the care of the younger children.

'There you are at last, Mabel, and about time too,' scolded their mother, standing at the door of number 12 Sorrel Street with four-year-old Alice and little Georgie who was not yet two. 'There's Miss Lawton just coming round the corner, so hurry up and get your music out. Oh, Albert, what a dirty face – here, let me wipe it – and your hands too. Just *look* at you, you little gypsy!' She dabbed vigorously at the squirming, sun-browned boy whose black hair and eyes proclaimed him Jack Court's living image. 'Georgie must go into the kitchen while Mabel's playing, otherwise he'll be into everything. Alice can sit and listen to the music if she's good and keeps quiet. Good afternoon, Miss Lawton,' Annie continued, raising her voice as the black-clad lady dismounted and leaned her bicycle against the low railing. 'Mabel's all ready for her lesson.'

Georgie gave a frustrated howl as his mother hoisted him up to carry him into the kitchen. Beneath her apron a fifth child was beginning to show, drawing on her reserves of strength, already drained by four children and a miscarriage.

The years had taken their toll of Anna-Maria Chalcott; there was now little trace of the headstrong girl who had become Annie Court. The once bright hair was pulled up into a knot on the top of her head from which stray tendrils hung and the blue eyes were surrounded by a network of fine lines, the result of a continual struggle to survive on an income that could never be guaranteed from one week to the next, though the overall trend was downwards.

Yet she smiled and her face lit up as Mabel's nimble fingers began to play a scale on the second-hand upright in the front room. She often said that her eldest daughter was her chief comfort, for the beautiful baby had become a sunny-tempered child whose grey-blue eyes were always bright with interest in the world around her. Her heart-shaped face, which reminded Annie of her own mother, was framed with abundant light-brown hair that hung down her back in shining waves. By contrast Alice was dark like her father and Albert, with the same strong white teeth, while Georgie was fair like Mabel. It was often remarked that the combination of Jack Court's swarthy looks and his wife's delicate fairness had produced some uncommonly fine-looking children.

While the music trickled through, interspersed with Miss Lawton's gentle directions, Annie got on with preparing supper. It was mutton stew this evening, ready to serve at any time. She never knew when to expect Jack who liked to have his meal on the table when he came in; otherwise it had to be something that could be quickly done in a pan, like rashers of bacon fried with onions and potatoes. Eggs were an expensive luxury, for there was no room to keep chickens in the backyards of Sorrel Street.

The piano lesson finished with quiet praise from Miss Lawton who proclaimed Mabel the best pupil in her grade. Annie smiled proudly and patted her daughter on the shoulder, which made Mabel all the more reluctant to produce the shameful white card from the newly appointed school nurse: for her lovely fair hair had been pronounced *verminous*.

Mabel could not ever remember seeing her mother so angry. 'How *dare* they! I've never heard of anything so disgraceful!' It was a relief to know that her indignation was directed against the school, and the nurse in particular, for labelling her daughter a dirty child with head lice, when in fact the school itself was so obviously the source of the infestation. 'I've a good mind to go and speak to that head teacher myself and tell her what I think,' declared Annie with a flash of her old spirit. 'Sassafras oil indeed, the sheer, barefaced *cheek* of it! Talk about adding insult to injury – your father will have something to say when he hears of it, I shouldn't wonder!'

But Jack Court had other matters on his mind when he got home just after seven. 'Haven't much time – got a couple o' blokes waiting at the Falcon, a dead cert running tomorrow at Goodwood,' he muttered, striding through to the kitchen and frowning at the sight and smell of the stew Annie was ladling out. 'Is that all yer can do for a man who's been workin' all the bloody day? Mabel, go down to the corner for a jug o' beer – here's tuppence, that'll do.'

'But she's just sitting down to her supper, Jack!' protested Annie.

'It won't take her five minutes there an' back, and there're still plenty o' kids playin' out, so why worry?'

'You know I don't like ours mixing with that rough lot. It lowers the whole neighbourhood, having children running around and yelling till all hours. And I don't like Mabel being seen going down to the public.'

Annie looked prepared to stand her ground, but he dismissed her with an impatient gesture. 'Run along, Mabel, there's a good girl – for yer daddy.'

Mabel half rose, while glancing anxiously at her mother who threw down the ladle in a rare gesture of defiance. 'No! I'll go myself, rather than send Mabel to that place. You see to the supper, Mabel – there's some bread on the table to dip in the bowls.' And Annie put on her jacket, hat and gloves, for she refused to wear a shawl like some factory worker or laundress; she picked up an earthenware pint jug and marched out of the house.

Jack frowned, glancing round at their faces. Georgie had fallen asleep and Alice was busy with her spoon, but Mabel and Albert met his eyes accusingly.

'Poor ol' Mum,' said Albert with a most unchildlike scowl.

Jack Court shrugged, frowned and turned his attention to little Alice. 'Who's Daddy's best girl, then?' he asked, taking her upon his knee at the table and ruffling her dark head. Even at her tender age Alice was well aware that she was specially favoured by her father.

She smiled up at him artlessly. 'Poor ol' Daddy,' she said.

The ongoing battle against head lice became part of

daily life. Mabel was by no means the only sufferer and several mothers had marched to the school to complain rather than to make excuses for the outbreak revealed by the nurse's inspection.

A toothcomb was bought, and after Mabel's hair was washed her mother pulled the comb through it strand by strand, searching out the offending black insects and their greyish 'eggs' or 'nits' that stuck to the hairs and would hatch out another generation if not removed. Oil of sassafras was rubbed in and a cotton cap worn overnight, followed by more hairwashing and combing until Annie was satisfied that Mabel was free of lice and nits; but how the girl's heart went out to the persistent offenders who had to sit in a separate group in class, threatened with the ultimate disgrace, a shorn head. The smell of sassafras continued to linger, forever associated in Mabel's mind with the school nurse's visits.

Sunday tea at 23 Macaulay Road was a time for clean pinafores and best behaviour. Jack's mother received her son's family with matriarchal formality, though she very seldom appeared at Sorrel Street. At fifty she had put on a little weight and now wore her hair curled like Queen Alexandra's, with a fringe.

Everybody had been warned not to breathe a word about the head lice.

Jack kissed his mother as soon as she opened the door, though Annie who was carrying Georgie kept him firmly between herself and her mother-in-law.

No sooner had Mabel, Albert and Alice crossed the threshold than their grandmother gave a suspicious sniff. 'My word, Annie, I hope that horrid smell isn't what I think it is, else yer neighbours'll draw their own conclusions.'

Annie sighed deeply and mumbled that there had been an outbreak at the school for which all the pupils had had to be treated. Mimi looked entirely unconvinced. She never lost an opportunity to criticise or contradict her daughter-in-law in front of Jack and the children, thereby implying that Annie was a poor manager.

When it became apparent that another child was expected, Mimi had rolled up her eyes as if unable to believe that such carelessness was possible. 'I'd've thought ye'd've had enough sense to wait a while after the last time, Annie – give yerself a chance to build up yer strength a bit.'

Annie had answered her with unusual sharpness: 'You'd better have a word with your son, then.'

'Oh, shame on yer, Annie, in front o' them innocent children! Whatever next?' had come the shocked response, followed by a very pointed change of subject.

They all trooped after her now into the living room, a veritable Aladdin's cave to the children, being stuffed with furniture, pictures, ornaments and bric-a-brac of all kinds. A dining table was covered with a purple velvet tasselled cloth over which a white lace-edged one was spread. There was a sideboard, a sofa, a piano and a glass-fronted cabinet crammed full of china and crystalware. A minefield of footstools and pouffes littered the floor space, which delighted the children, but for Annie the room was full of potential trippings-up and breakages; she was on constant tenterhooks for fear of a disaster.

'Well, then, Mabel, how're yer getting on at school?' asked Mimi Court condescendingly. 'Yer mother seems to think ye're uncommonly forward.'

'Miss Thomas asked me to stand up and read from

23

my exercise book to the whole class,' answered Mabel promptly, catching her mother's eye and smiling.

'Did she indeed? And what was this masterpiece all about?'

'Well, there was this Salvation Army meeting, y'see, and these two men came out o' the public and they were shouting an' making fun o' the man who was speaking, see,' said Mabel eagerly, warming to her subject. 'Some o' the people laughed, but the band picked up their, er, oompahs or whatever they're called, and started to play this hymn, ever so loudly, "Onward Christian Soldiers" I think it was, an' so these two men had to shout louder – and then some other men came along an' told them to pack it in and clear off. "Shut yer great gob!" one of 'em said – "Stow it, Bill Wilkins, d'ye hear? Unless yer wants a clip round the—"'

'That's quite enough, thank yer very much,' interrupted her grandmother with a pained air. 'For a child o' your age, Mabel ye've got far too much to say, an' a most unfortunate way o' sayin' it.' She looked reproachfully at Annie as she spoke.

'*Most* unfortunate,' mimicked Albert in a squeaky voice just loud enough for his grandmother to hear. She turned sharply and was struck once again by his resemblance to Jack at that age. She would have loved to make a fuss of him and favour him with little treats like the new silver threepenny piece in her purse or a chunk of her home-made toffee; but the boy was quite ridiculously attached to his elder sister and he was now whispering something into Mabel's ear, holding up a not very clean hand to cover his mouth. Less than a year apart in age, they were as different in character as in looks, yet there

24

had always been this special bond between them, which Mimi distrusted. As babies in the same pram, Albert had scowled while Mabel had smiled; as a toddling bundle of mischief he had crawled into every cupboard, pulled out drawers and pee'd into them, clutched at saucepans on the kitchen range and only escaped a scalding through Mabel's prompt grabbing hold of him. Yet he always responded to her smiles or frowns; she alone could persuade him out of his sulks, while he never failed to tease her into laughter when she was downcast. In Mimi Court's opinion, the pair had never learned their manners and she blamed Annie.

Mabel caught her mother's eye, adding to Mimi's irritation.

Alice saw her opportunity. 'Please, Grandmother, may I play with Humpty-Dumpty?' she begged in the sweet little good-girl voice she knew would contrast well with Albert's unsatisfactory behaviour.

'O' course yer may, yer dear little soul,' replied Mimi approvingly, taking down the painted wooden eggshell character from his shelf; he always landed the right way up, no matter how hard or how often he was pushed over. 'Grandmother likes good children who mind their manners – doesn't she, Georgie? Let yer little brother play with Humpty-Dumpty too, Alice – but Albert can keep his grubby hands orf. I can't understand why yer don't take that boy in hand, Annie.'

Albert assumed an air of bored indifference and murmured something about babies' rubbish, though Mabel burned with indignation and when tea was served she infuriatingly refused the fruit cake.

'Why, what's the matter with it, girl? Ye've always taken two slices before,' snapped her grandmother.

'If there's anything I can't abide it's a child who sulks.'

'Well, I'll leave you ladies to yer gossip,' said Jack who had seen a couple of old drinking pals going past the window. Ignoring the tightness of his wife's mouth he added, 'If I'm not back by five, ye'd better get the Clapham omnibus from outside the new hospital down the road.'

By which Annie knew that he would not be home till late.

Autumn came in with cold, damp weather, bringing the Court children their share of coughs and colds. Annie grew more tired and depressed as the months went by and much as she disliked keeping Mabel away from school, she made the coughs and sneezes an excuse for demanding her elder daughter's help on the dreaded washing days. Mondays were particularly miserable in wet weather when the sheets, towels and clothes hung draped over wooden 'maidens' in both kitchen and living room, keeping the air chill and moist. If the range fire was kept in all day it made the washing steam, causing the walls to stream with condensation. Even by getting up at six to light the copper to heat the water by seven and get the washing done by nine and mangled to flatness by ten, it would still not be properly dry until the next morning, sometimes not even then. With Mabel to mind Alice and Georgie, Annie was better able to get through a wet Monday, though she was exhausted by evening, and the coughs and running noses of the little ones sorely tried her nerves.

'You're my greatest comfort in the world, Mabel,' she murmured as her daughter brewed a pot of tea for them both. These words were reward enough for

26

Mabel, though her mind was on Albert who was due home from school.

Annie stirred her tea and went on talking, or rather thinking aloud. 'If Jack doesn't come up with ten shillings by the end of the week, I don't know how I'm going to feed us all.'

Mabel was dismayed by the anxiety in her mother's face and voice. The use of Jack's name instead of 'dad' or 'your father' had the effect of distancing him while drawing her into sharing her mother's troubles. 'Don't worry, Mum, we'll manage,' she said reassuringly, though with no idea of what could be done if the money was not forthcoming. She knew from things she had heard at school that there were poor children who had not enough to eat, and went ragged and barefoot, foraging for whatever they could find by begging or petty thieving; but this was usually because one or other of their parents had become ill, or perhaps had even died. Mabel shuddered involuntarily at the very thought of losing her mother, the loving centre of her world. As long as she was there to kiss and comfort them all, the family was surely safe. And yet here was that same mother talking of poverty and not having food enough to go round.

They were drinking a second cup of tea when Albert arrived home from school, his trousers torn and his hair unkempt.

'Albert! We told you to stay with Lily Finch and her brother,' said Annie, horrified at his appearance.

He stuck out his bottom lip. 'She kept 'angin' about wiv daft girls, an' Jimmy went to play football,' he muttered in a surly tone.

'Have yer been in a fight?' demanded Mabel.

He shuffled his feet. 'Yeah, but I kicked 'em 'ard up the yer-know-what, an' they let me go.'

'Heavens, he talks like a guttersnipe,' groaned Annie.

'Why couldn't *you* take me, Mabel?' he asked reproachfully.

Mother and daughter exchanged a guilty look; the washing hung damply and depressingly around them.

'I'll go over and see Lily Finch about this,' said Mabel grimly.

'But we didn't pay her to take him, did we?' Annie reminded her.

'Yer won't 'alf cop it from Miss Thomas for stayin' away,' added Albert with a meaning look at his sister. 'She didn't 'alf go on about it, worser 'n last week.'

Annie put her head between her hands. 'You'll have to go to school next Monday, Mabel. It isn't right for you to fall behind with your lessons. I'll just have to get through it, that's all – other women have to manage.'

But the sight of her mother's weariness and knowing her worries about money had made a deep impression on Mabel, and she began to form a plan to earn some money and keep the family supplied with whatever cheap food she could find. Her small face hardened as she summoned up the necessary determination to carry it through.

First she needed a few pence to get started, and an idea came through seeing one of her classmates taking and fetching a neighbour's two young children to and from school every day. She had to take care of Albert, so why not another one or two? She began to look out for an opportunity to offer her services and a few days later she found one.

One of Albert's classmates and his five-year-old sister had been brought to school by a neighbour because their mother was about to give birth to a baby. On the way home Mabel called with Albert at their house in Darnel Street to find the household in chaos. The baby had been born but the mother was very poorly, so the neighbour who was preparing the tea said. Mabel's offer was accepted and it was arranged that she should call the next morning at half past eight to take the two children to school, returning them in the afternoon, for which she would be paid two pence per day. It meant that she and Albert would have to leave home a quarter of an hour earlier, arriving back that much later in the afternoon, and on this particular Tuesday Mabel was only just in time for her piano lesson; but after earning her first two pence on the Wednesday, she was ready to put the second part of her plan into action.

She had heard from some of the poorer children at school that their mothers or older brothers or sisters got up early and lined up outside certain shops which sold perishable goods cheaply before the official opening time. So on Thursday morning she quietly got up at six and hurried through the dark streets to the bakehouse on Wandsworth Road. The first batch of loaves was just being taken from the ovens, and one of Mabel's pennies bought two stale loaves from the previous day. She then crossed the street into Victoria Rise where a shabby queue of women and older children were standing outside the butcher's, waiting for him to take down the shutters. They were after the 'trimmings', the beef and mutton

scraps that could be stewed with onions and potatoes to make a meal. Mabel took her place behind
them and her other penny bought a bagful.

Of course this new regime had to be carefully
presented to her mother and a few little white lies
told; for example, that she had been specially asked
by the family in Darnel Street to take the little boy
and girl to and from school while their mother was
recovering from the birth. As for the bread and meat,
Mabel put them down on the table with such a
flourish that Annie could not possibly object to the
early shopping trip, though she shed a few tears in
private at the thought of Mabel feeling so responsible
for the whole family. The food was put to good use
and if Annie half regretted burdening her little
daughter by speaking her fears aloud, she was
touched beyond measure by Mabel's response.

'Oh, Mabel, dear, to have a daughter like you
makes up for everything,' she said as she hugged her
close; but when the girl had gone to school, and Alice
and Georgie were playing on the rag rug, she
whispered to the empty air that Mabel deserved a
better life than this. How different life would have
been in the healthy country air of Belhampton ...
She remembered Eric's words on the train: '*I would
have married you, Anna-Maria. I would have married you
and called the child mine.*' Her beautiful, fair-haired
daughter could have been Mabel Drummond.

Yet Annie Court could not imagine her life without
Albert, Alice and Georgie, her children who were the
reason why she carried on the day-to-day struggle to
bring up her family respectably while living on the
poverty line. They helped her to repress her memories of the past, that other life which was now never

spoken of because of what had happened to her poor papa and the unforgiveness of her sisters.

Encouraged by her success at early morning shopping, Mabel next decided to try her luck at the Friday night stalls in Nine Elms Lane. Albert begged to come with her and so, with Thursday's and Friday's earnings in her pocket, and promising her mother that they would come straight home, they set off to walk over the railway bridge and along Battersea Park Road to the line-up of stalls and costers' barrows beneath the gas lamps in the late October dusk. A mist curled up from the river, which mixing with the pall of chimney smoke gave a greenish tinge to the lights. A barrel organ was playing on the corner of Tideway Walk, and a crowd of rough-looking children had gathered to listen and caper to the music while workers from Price's candles and Doulton's pottery had come over to spend their pay, rubbing shoulders with gasworkers, laundrywomen and clerks. Newsboys shouted the headlines and racing results, and flower girls eyed the better-dressed men strolling between the stalls.

Holding tightly to Albert's dragging hand, Mabel surveyed the busy scene, though with so many street sellers competing for trade she wished she had somebody to advise her on how best to spend her four pennies.

"Ad a good look, 'ave yer? I'll turn rahnd, so's yer can see me backside an' all.'

Mabel started, realising that she had been staring at the ragged girl who had just spoken. She was wrapped in a long, grimy shawl which she drew around herself and the baby she carried in her arms. Her features were sharp, her hair lanky and uncombed, and her toes stuck out of her worn shoes. She was about the same size and height as Mabel, though her face appeared older and in better circumstances she might have been quite pretty. Jostled by the crowd, the two girls found themselves standing next to each other and Mabel was unpleasantly conscious of the smell of the girl's unwashed clothing. 'I'm sorry,' she said awkwardly. 'I didn't mean to be rude.'

The girl nodded towards Albert. ''Im yer bruvver?'

'Yes – and is that *your* baby brother or sister?' asked Mabel, just to show that she too could ask questions of a stranger.

'Yeah, bruvver. Bleedin' 'eavy 'e is, too. Got any more at 'ome, 'ave yer?'

'A sister younger 'n me, and another brother. What about you?'

'We've 'ad two bruvvers an' a sister kick the bucket – only me 'n' Teddy left.'

Mabel was so horrified by this that she had no answer and the girl shrugged. 'Yer from rahnd 'ere, then?'

Mabel nodded. 'Are you?'

The girl gestured with her head. 'Over Vaux'all way.' She looked curiously at Mabel. 'Don't s'pose yer got a spare copper on yer?'

Mabel's fingers curled protectively round the coins in her pocket. 'Not to spare,' she said very definitely.

'What yer after, then – cheap grub? If I wasn't weighted dan wiv this 'un, I'd soon be under some o' them stalls, not 'alf I wouldn't! 'Ere, come an' 'ave a gander.'

She led Mabel to a greengrocer's barrow and advised buying one pennyworth of speckly apples and another of four squashy oranges, both items being sold off at half price; potatoes cost another three halfpence and then, moving on to the roast chestnut man's glowing brazier, Mabel spent her remaining halfpenny on as many as he would let her have. Turning to the girl she offered her a chestnut and a choice of an apple or orange.

'Cor, ye're a lidy – I'll 'ave the orange, ta! Orf 'ome now, are yer?'

'Yes, my mother'll be waiting for us. My father'll be home later tonight,' added Mabel, hoping that this week's business would have made him a decent profit and put him in a good mood.

The girl grimaced. 'So'll mine, drunk as a pig an' nasty wiv it. That's why Ma sends us out o' the way Friday nights.'

'Oh, how *awful* for yer!' exclaimed Mabel, who had absorbed much of her mother's horror of drunkenness, not without reason; sometimes Dad had to be helped to bed when he came home from the public, which was no joke for Mum, who always seemed to be tired these days. 'And when . . . when will yer be able to go home, then?'

'After 'e's 'ad a good knock arahnd an' passed out on the floor, most like. Then Ma'll go frough 'is pockets an' take what ain't bin taken orf 'im already.'

Mabel had heard terrible stories of men who beat their wives and ill-treated their children, but not at first hand. Not until now. 'Can't yer mother take you an' yer brother to go an' live somewhere else away from the man?' she asked.

'Cor! Couldn't we jus' grow wings an' fly, eh? Where to – the work'ouse? Fanks for the orange, anyway. What's yer name, 'case we meets up agin?'

'Mabel Court – and my brother Albert.'

'Maudie Ling – an' my bruvver Teddy.'

'Goodbye, Maudie – an' good luck when yer get home.'

And so began a friendship that was to outlast many changes in both their lives.

That evening ended on a high note for when Jack Court arrived home he was in a good humour and, as he himself said, quids in. Business had taken him to Epsom, where his natural flair had stood him in good stead. Having long discarded his hopes of a career in photo-portraiture, Mabel now gathered that he was considering going into books; there was a fortune just waiting to be picked up if he made his own book, or so he eagerly told them, kissing Annie and chucking Alice under the chin.

As often happened when he'd had a windfall, Jack was open-handed and had brought presents for them all. Annie had a new brooch shaped like a horseshoe, as well as an incredible *five pounds* towards house-keeping. Albert had new boots and Georgie a large red and white striped ball to bounce. Mabel gave a whoop of joy at receiving a family songbook with piano scores for each one, both simple and more elaborate accompaniments; and Alice had the best surprise of all, a doll's house with a front that lifted off to reveal an upstairs and a downstairs with two rooms on each floor, complete with beautiful tiny furniture and fittings.

They had fried fish for supper that Jack brought with him, and pork chops for dinner on Saturday. For afters they had a jam suet pudding that Mabel had helped her mother to make, which Jack said was the best he'd ever tasted.

As the young ones frolicked around and Albert thumped the roof of the precious doll's house – a thunderstorm, he said it was – the mother and daughter exchanged smiles.

'There, what did I tell yer, Mum? No need to worry about money – or anything.'

'Yes, dear, your daddy can be very kind when he's had a good day. But I'll never forget what you've done for me this week.'

If only Dad could always be as lucky! But Mabel was soon given an ugly reminder that his family did not necessarily share his good luck.

Only two weeks later, on a Friday night at the beginning of December, Mabel was awakened by the sound of stumbling steps and her mother's voice raised in protest above another sound – her father singing in the silly, tuneless way he had when drunk. Mabel's heart sank in dismay and she felt a shiver of fear. She'd seen how weary Mum was, being now big and unwieldly with the baby she was nearly due to have, and yet here she was struggling to get Dad up the stairs and into their room.

'She's my lady-love – she ish my love, my baby dove –' warbled Jack.

'Careful, Jack, for God's sake don't fall and send up both flying!' cried Annie, and Mabel jumped out of bed and ran to the top of the stairs, scared as she was.

'What's the matter, Mum? What's he doin'? Are yer all right?'

'Oh, Mabel, this is no job for a child – I can manage him, dear. Go back to bed and don't wake the others,' pleaded Annie, while Jack sang romantically: 'I know she likes me – I know she likes me, because she says sho—'

At the top stair he stumbled, and Annie shrieked.

'All right, Mum, I've got him – come on, Dad, this way,' ordered Mabel, taking hold of his arm with both hands and pulling with all her strength, though she was trembling with cold and a kind of horror at seeing her dad in this state. She knew that she had to brave and overcome her repulsion for Mum's sake, but her instinct was to get as far away from him as she could.

'Because she says sho – because she says sho – whoops!'

Together the heavily pregnant woman and the seven-year-old girl pulled and pushed the man through the door, whereupon he fell across the bed. Annie was out of breath and clutched at her bulge: Mabel stood barefoot in her nightgown, regarding him as she would a drunken man lying in the gutter. Her own *father*!

'She ish my lily of Laguna—'

'I'm not going to bother with undressing him, he can sleep in his clothes,' panted Annie. 'If we could just get his boots off to save the quilt – I'll hold his legs and you pull, Mabel, first this one – ah! Now the other. Good girl.'

'She ish my Lily and my rose!'

'He's had a good day on the course, but he was with that Dick Sammons and they've drunk the lot between them – and no doubt he's treated half a dozen others,' said Annie with a sigh.

The boots were slung into a corner and Mabel began trying to turn her father round on the bed so that he was lying in his usual place on the right side.

'Not yet, dear, there's something else he'll have to do first,' Annie sighed. 'Can you pull the chamber pot out from under the bed? Come on, Jack, you've got to have a wee-wee before you go to sleep.'

But Jack was too drunk to stand without support and Mabel had to hold the pot while Annie fished in his trousers and pulled out his male member, which immediately rose in her hand to a half-erection.

'For shame, Jack, it goes down, not up – here – I'll hold it for you while you go. Hold the pot higher, Mabel, don't let him miss it. Careful, Jack – you can go now.'

And go he did, a streaming torrent that hit the chamber pot and splashed up in Mabel's face. Annie directed the flow as he tried to kiss her.

'Wheee-eee!' he giggled, gushing like a waterspout and swaying between wife and daughter. 'She ish my lily of Lagooonaaah – she ish my lily and my rose!'

Mabel forced herself to grip the sides of the pot until the stream had finally dribbled to a stop and Annie tucked the spout into his drawers, leaving his trousers unbuttoned. 'Your grandmother Court taught me that,' she said, her face white with fatigue. 'Always make a man pee out the drink before sleeping, she told me, or you'll have a flood before morning – but oh, Mabel, you little dear, what a sight for you to see!' And she burst into tears.

Mabel rushed to throw her arms round her mother. 'Poor Mum! Don't cry, Mummy, please – oh, I just *hate* him when he's like this, he's not like Daddy at all.'

Annie hastily wiped her eyes on her apron. 'Don't mind me, Mabel, your father gets very silly when he's drunk, but he's not a bad man like some. He's never deliberately hurt me. Not like poor Mrs Finch, Lily's mother – her husband's a brute when he's drunk, and hits out at her and the children. And I know for a fact that he's wet right through a feather mattress till it dripped on the floor beneath – ugh, just imagine it.' She shuddered, then smiled and patted Mabel's cheek. 'As your grandmother says, it's a man's world, Mabel. Now get back to bed, dear, or you'll catch cold.'

Mabel returned to the bed she shared with Alice, thankful that her little sister had not been woken up by the daddy she adored. But she lay awake for some time, thinking of her mother lying beside Dad with his sour-smelling breath and his heavy snoring. And how *rude* he had been, showing his great big *thing* like that, and laughing while he wee'd in front of her and Mum like some dirty boy who didn't know any better. Albert would never do a thing like that, even though he was often naughty in other ways. Before she finally fell asleep Mabel vowed that she would never get married; she simply couldn't understand why any woman would want to.

As Christmas approached Annie drooped, and the care of the younger children fell more and more on Mabel's shoulders; yet she still found time to escort children to and from school as the need arose, delivering them to their classrooms and fetching them as soon as the bell sounded for the end of lessons. Mothers recommended her for her watchfulness, the way she kept the children from straying, and they all liked and trusted her. For her part she enjoyed being with her charges and loved the little clinging hands in hers, the anxious eyes of five- and six-year-olds looking out for her – and the way their faces brightened when she appeared to collect them from their homes or their classrooms. Teachers would call out, 'Who's waiting for Mabel Court?

Don't worry, she's on her way' – or, 'She's just seeing to a little boy who's lost his cap.'

'There's a children's nurse in the making,' she heard one of them say as she went off with her flock one afternoon as the light was failing.

'As long as she's not worn out before her time, like so many of those girls,' came the reply.

Mabel also became much more adept at spending her earnings to the best advantage, knowing exactly how much bread, tea, sugar, or offal could be had for her halfpennies and farthings, carefully counted out; she learned to bargain with street traders and when she managed to save a few coins she hoarded them for Christmas in a small canvas bag she kept under the mattress.

There was no time to linger at the Friday evening stalls, now darkened by December fogs, but Maudie still lugged Teddy there, coughing as she pulled the malodorous shawl more tightly around them both.

'What'll yer get for Christmas, Maudie?' asked Mabel as they shivered beside the chestnut man's welcome blaze.

'Chris'muss? Don't make me larf – the ol' man'll be canned the 'ole time, an' so'll me muvver an' all.'

'*What*?' Mabel thought she had not heard right. 'Did yer say yer *mother*'ll be drunk too?'

'Lor' bless yer, she puts up wiv 'im pissed every Friday, so she reckons it's 'er turn for once,' Maudie explained as if this were quite reasonable. 'Yeah, they'll bofe be rollin', same as last year. Glad when Chris'muss is over, I am.'

'Oh, Maudie – oh, *Maudie*, yer poor thing – and little Teddy too – oh!'

Mabel did not know what to say. Since she had begun to earn and spend a little money of her own, she had seen much more of the darker side of life, the daily drudgery endured by women and children, especially when the man of the house was brutalised by habitual drinking. She saw the burden it placed on families already short of the basic necessities of life.

But the thought of *mothers* getting drunk truly upset her, and her heart ached for her friend and the poor little baby brother, the only survivors of a family of five children. What had happened to the other three, what kind of lives had they had and how had they died? Mabel thought of how horrible it was when her own father had come home so drunk and she hardly dared think of what might have happened to the helpless little Ling children. She longed to be able to help Maudie and Teddy in some way, and other children in need of love and care, and the thought came to her that one day she *would* be a children's nurse as the teacher had said; but for the time being it seemed that there was nothing she could do, nothing she could give.

Only the fragile friendship of a child.

Annie had insisted that she didn't want Mimi to deliver her fifth child and had booked Mrs Lowe, one of two midwives who attended most of the women in their neighbourhood. A Mrs Bull two doors away had agreed to come in and look after the family while Annie was lying-in, and all the preparations had been made. Georgie was moved into the children's room to share Albert's bed next to Mabel's and Alice's, and the cot was made up ready beside Annie's bed for the new baby. Clean cotton rags, towels and newspaper were stored in an orange box, along with a cake of soap and baby clothes. A washing bowl and jug, a chamber pot and two buckets stood in readiness.

When the pains started on a blustery night five days before Christmas, Jack was away and the younger children in bed.

Annie gritted her teeth and pressed her palms into the small of her back where the pain was sharpest during contractions. It's strange, she thought, how you always forget how bad it is until the next time comes and then you remember. Whatever happened, she must not frighten the children; in a small house every sound carried. 'Mabel! You'd better call Mrs Bull and then go for Mrs Lowe. I don't think this one's going to be long.'

While Mabel went to call the midwife, Mrs Bull arrived and busied herself in the kitchen, relighting the range fire to heat water for the midwife's use and to brew tea.

Mabel came running in, her face red with the exertion and her hands cold from wearing no gloves. 'Mrs Lowe's out with somebody else, but Mrs Clements'll be comin' as soon as she can!'

Annie groaned. 'She'd better be quick, then – oh! Aah!' She bit the sheet and gripped the bedhead topped with its brass knobs.

'Go back to yer bed, Mabel, this ain't no sight for a little gal,' said Mrs Bull, but Mabel was reluctant to leave her mother's side. When they heard the knock at the door she ran down to let in Mrs Clements who was short and stout, and carried a black bag that matched the hat and coat which she removed and hung up in the narrow hallway.

Once in the bedroom, her sharp button eyes took in the situation at a glance. She opened her bag and took out the first requirement, a bottle and an enamel mug. 'Come on, Mrs Court, come on, dearie, 'ave a swig o' this to 'elp yer pain an' settle yer, like,' she said firmly, holding the mug to Annie's lips. ''Ere we go!'

Standing outside the door, Mabel listened wide-eyed as her mother was made to drink, choking and gagging on the potent liquid. 'It's gin, isn't it?' she gasped. 'Ugh, I never touch it.'

'Drink up, pet, it'll 'elp yer more than anyfin' else will. One more little drop an' yer won't care if it snows. Good gal!'

Mabel heard her mother moan and make a retching sound in her throat.

'Hey, don't go fetchin' it up again – take some big, deep breaths in an' out, that'll 'elp keep it down – good gal!'

Annie hiccuped and moaned faintly as another contraction hardened her belly.

Mrs Bull came puffing up the stairs with a jug of hot water. 'I told yer to go back to y'bed, Mabel – this ain't no place for a little 'un.'

Mabel reluctantly returned to her roon and got in beside the sleeping Alice. Georgie snuffled and whimpered beside Albert, then cried out in sudden panic, 'Ma-ma!'

Mabel got out of bed and went to kneel beside her frightened little brother, enfolding him in her arms. 'All right, Georgie, it's all right, I'm here,' she whispered as he clung to her in bewilderment. 'Yer Mabel's here, an' ye'll see Mummy again in the mornin'.' Kneeling on the uncarpeted floor in the icy room, she stroked his forehead and soothed him until his breathing took on the soft and regular rhythm of sleep. Slowly she released her arms and tucked the covers around him. Albert and Alice had not woken. Stiff with cold, she got to her feet. A sound of women's voices could be heard in the other room, urgent but indistinct. Mabel stepped out on to the landing again and listened.

Mrs Clements seemed to be giving orders to the neighbour. ''Ave that bowl 'andy, Liza, and spread the towel down there, see? That's the way – and 'ere it comes, see, I told yer it'd push its own way out, di'n't I? And afore midnight, too!'

There followed some confused exclamations, panting and the smack of a hand on flesh.

'There we go – and it's a boy.'

'Is 'e all right? 'E ain't 'alf blue.'

'Fill that bowl wiv warm water to dip 'im in – quick, that gets 'em goin' as a rule.'

'Is 'e breathin'? 'E's ever so limp, just as if 'e was—'

'For Christ's sake, Liza Bull, shut yer trap an' do summat useful! Fill me a bowl o' water!' Mabel heard the note of panic beneath Mrs Clements's irritation and shivered in fear. Why didn't her mother say something? Was she – oh, please, our Father who art in heaven, let her not be dead . . . *Oh, Mummy, Mummy, don't leave me, don't leave us all on our own, Mummy, please! Please!*

'Look, 'e's givin' a few little grunts, an' 'is chest's goin' up an' down, thank Gawd,' muttered the midwife in relief. 'I'll jus' tie the cord off an' cut it, an' then 'e can go down in the cot.'

'Shall I make a pot o' tea?' asked the other woman.

'When I got the afterbirth out yer can. She won't want any, she's out for the count, but we can do wiv a cup – an' a drop o' summat in it, an' all.'

The door opened and Mrs Bull nearly collided full tilt into the child cowering behind it. 'Mabel! 'Ow many times 'ave I told yer to go back to bed? Ye'll catch yer death o' cold out here.'

Mrs Clements looked up. She was holding something like a big chunk of raw meat, which she let slide down into one of the buckets. Her florid features wore an expression of satisfaction. 'Is that the little gal who came for Mrs Lowe? All right, pet, yer can come in just for a minute and see yer little baby bruvver. Come on in, don't be frightened.'

Mabel stared into the room lit by an oil lamp on the chest of drawers. Her eyes went straight to the bed where her mother lay with flushed cheeks, her hair clinging to her forehead in damp wisps. Her mouth was open and she was snoring heavily. Mabel could have cried with thankfulness.

'Fast asleep, quite worn out, poor thing,' said Mrs Clements. 'Look over 'ere, pet, see, in the cot, there 'e is, yer new baby brother.'

Mabel dragged her eyes away from her mother's unconscious form and turned to the cot, which had seemed so small for Georgie but now appeared huge for the tiny scrap of humanity lying wrapped in a towel and blanket. A little bluish-white face peeped out: he was making weak, gasping sounds as if every breath was an effort.

''Ad yer ma got a name for 'im?' asked the midwife.

'She said he'd be called Walter if he was a boy and Daisy if he was a girl,' faltered Mabel.

'Then Walter's 'is name.' The midwife nodded.

'Is he all right?' asked Mabel fearfully. 'I thought babies always cried when they're born.'

''E'll be all right after a bit, when 'e's 'ad a little sleep.'

Mabel glanced at Mrs Bull who did not seem so

convinced that all was well with Walter. ''E's one o' them little angels, come down from 'eaven,' she said with a doubtful shake of her head. 'An' maybe 'e'll stay an' maybe 'e won't.'

''E'll perk up after a bit,' insisted Mrs Clements.

Mabel leaned over the cot. She knew that this baby was going to need lots of looking after, more than Albert or Alice or George. Their mother would need all the help that Mabel could give. 'Hello, little brother Walter,' she whispered. 'I'm yer sister Mabel and I'm going to take ever such good care o' yer.'

But Annie saw and heard nothing at all.

Chapter Two

It was August and the schools were out.

'Hey, Maudie, d'ye see? It's the music man comin' our way! Let's get all the little 'uns into the pram where we can keep an eye on 'em, an' give the others a shout, will yer?' Mabel's eyes sparkled in anticipation.

'Yeah, but 'e won't stop long if 'e don't get some coppers in 'is 'at, an' I ain't got a bleedin' farthin'.'

'Neither have I, but Alice has got a bit o' change in her pocket and somebody's bound to have some more. Come on, let's ask him to play "After the Ball"!'

And with a hop, skip and a jump Mabel Court led half a dozen girls to start dancing on the asphalt surface of the road. Others heard the barrel organ and ran from adjoining streets to join in; in no time a score of girls surrounded the organ grinder and gleefully danced to his tune.

Dr Henry Knowles had never cared much about the kind of image he presented to the public at large. He found it convenient to do his rounds on a bicycle now that the roads were becoming so congested. His father had driven a little two-wheeler gig and he had no doubt that his son Stephen, now in the first year of his medical studies at the London Hospital in Whitechapel Road, would eventually own one of these noisy motor-driven contraptions, as smelly as they were unreliable and a real hazard to horse-drawn vehicles. On his 'bone-shaker' the tall, lean figure of the doctor could regularly be seen dodging between milk carts, coal vans, street sellers and the hordes of children who swarmed the streets when school was out, as now; boys playing football and girls with skipping ropes competed for space on the paving stones. Knowles frowned at the sight of children being sent into public houses with jugs to fetch beer for their parents and probably taking a sip or two on the way home, for it was a hot day; he had seen too much of the ruinous effects of drunkenness on family life and health.

He was now on his way to Sorrel Street to see little Walter Court. The family was on his panel and it was his habit to make quick check-up visits for which he did not charge, on the principle that prevention is better than cure.

But a wave of music broke upon his thoughts this morning and rounding a corner, he found his way blocked by a large crowd of children, mainly girls, dancing in the sunshine, filling the whole width of the street, so that the doctor had to dismount and lean his bicycle against a wall. He stood and watched, finding himself unexpectedly moved by the sight of their booted feet skipping lightly, their pinafores twirling; a few wore straw hats but most were bareheaded, their hair flowing loose or plaited. Some danced in pairs, some in circles, while others gyrated alone. And all were happy, all were smiling as the shabby Pied Piper turned the handle of the cylindrical barrel on its wheeled stand, grinding out a popular music hall tune. Some of them knew the words and all were soon gaily singing the refrain: 'And her golden hair was hanging down her back!'

The doctor picked out the Court girls, Mabel and Alice, but there were some he had never seen, like the scrawny, barefoot girl dancing with Mabel. The music had brought together the rough and the respectable in a shared moment of freedom from the lurking shadows that waited to claim their young lives. How many of them would fall victim to TB and infectious fevers, Knowles wondered, and what lay in store for the survivors? Poverty, endless childbearing and poor health in too many cases, as he well knew.

At the kerbside was an ancient perambulator that had seen better days, probably once pushed by a smartly dressed nanny, wheeling out her charge in Kensington Gardens or some such fashionable park. Now it was battered and rusted, lacking many of its parts, including the hood, and it was crammed with young brothers and sisters of the dancing nymphs, their little faces goggling at the scene. Knowles recognised Walter Court, twenty months old, his dull eyes gazing up at the sky. The doctor knew that he'd be called out to see Walter as soon as winter returned with its cold, damp air and fogs.

And that Mabel would miss more school days as a result, Knowles thought, frowning. That girl was a rare treasure and it was due to her unceasing care of Walter that the poor child had survived as long as this, in the doctor's view, though neither parent truly appreciated her worth. Mabel was one of those 'little mothers' who had the potential to make something of her life if she ever got the chance and Knowles wondered what she would do on leaving school. If he could ever help her by a word in the right quarter, he most certainly would.

Suddenly Mabel caught sight of the spectator. She

stopped dancing and glanced towards her little brother in the old pram.

Dr Knowles waved his hand and shook his head. 'Keep on dancing, Mabel! I'd much rather watch you all enjoying yourselves,' he called out to her.

But the tune had come to a stop and the music man was preparing to move off to more lucrative suburbs. A murmur of disappointment rippled over the crowd and Mabel's eyes watched wistfully as he counted the few copper coins in his greasy cap.

'Wait a minute!' shouted Knowles and all eyes turned towards him as he strode forward. 'Aren't you going to give them another tune?'

'Sorry, guv, but I bin 'ere 'alf an hour an' I've come to the end o' me repertaw.'

The doctor dug his hand into his pocket and pulled out a shilling. 'Will this be enough to start it up again?'

'Cor!' The man's face registered delighted amazement. 'Thanks, guv – not 'alf it won't!'

'The show's worth it,' replied Knowles.

To cheers and shouts of 'Thanks, Dr Knowles!' the music and the dancing began again, and the doctor turned and wheeled his bicycle away. He could always call back later, and meanwhile Walter was getting fresh air and sunshine, and Mabel was enjoying a brief respite from her responsibilities.

The old pram belonged to Maudie Ling who used it to push her brother Teddy around; other children's younger siblings also got dumped in it, especially during school holidays.

Mabel called to Alice and Georgie. Albert had gone off somewhere with a gang of boys and a go-cart. 'Can I wheel Walter home in the pram, Maudie?

My mother'll be lookin' out for us and I dare say there'll be a cup o' tea going.'

Maudie eagerly agreed, but her hopes were dashed when they arrived at Sorrel Street.

Annie Court was furious at seeing Walter sitting up in the old pram with Teddy Ling and other grubby passengers. 'Whatever were you thinking of, Mabel? I trusted you to take proper care of him, not to let him mix with ragamuffins and pick up all sorts of nasty complaints!' she cried, holding out her arms to gather Walter to her heart.

Mabel stood uphappily aside, feeling the slight to Maudie who was longing to be offered tea, as on former occasions when she had come home with Mabel. 'Wait there, Maudie, I'll see if there's some lemonade left, and then ye'd better go,' she apologised, though like Dr Knowles she felt that Walter had benefited from the outing, and when he arrived a little later he sensed the troubled atmosphere and backed her up, assuring Annie that the airing could do Walter nothing but good.

She refused to be persuaded, her anxiety aggravated by the fact that she was expecting again, in spite of all her warnings to Jack to be careful. The trouble was that after he'd had a good day on the course and did not get drunk but came home in a mellow mood and ready to share his winnings with his family, he also expected to enjoy the connubial bliss that Annie had come to dread. While she could hardly confide these intimate problems to Dr Knowles, he had a fair idea of her situation and pitied the plight of women who could do little to prevent conception, other than to refuse their husbands and so cause marital disharmony. The use of rubber sheaths for the penis was something he could only speak of to men and then only when consulted by them; to give that kind of advice to women would soon attract suspicion. It was a constant chagrin to him and he privately applauded the movement among some of the better-educated women to make birth-control information freely available; a great deal of prejudice would have to be overcome before that day dawned.

It was the same when he talked about healthy food: milk and butter, fresh fruit and vegetables: Annie could only see them in terms of money – money that she had not got. Jack had not been home for a week and there was no guarantee that he would be in funds when he reappeared.

Which was why she had decided to do something she had never done before in ten years of marriage. 'Mabel, I'm going over to Tooting to see your grandmother tomorrow, and I'll take you and Walter with me,' she announced. 'Mrs Bull will keep an eye on Alice and Georgie for me, and Albert's out every day with that gang of his – but I daren't let Walter out of my sight, and – well, I'd like you to be with me.'

'All right, Mum,' replied Mabel. 'But why are we visiting Grandmother on a Wednesday?'

'I need some money,' replied Annie bluntly. 'More than you can earn, Mabel. She gets paid plenty for whatever it is she does and it's time she helped her only son's family.'

Mabel stared in surprise, for there was no love lost between the mother and daughter-in-law. Then she supposed that it was Walter's needs that had forced Annie to pocket her pride.

The next morning they dressed as if for church on Sunday. Annie fiercely thrust a long pin through her brown broad-rimmed hat trimmed with velvet flowers, and Mabel put on her best pinafore and her straw hat with the blue ribbon. They had a little pushchair for Walter that folded up when they boarded the motor-bus, where Mabel sat with her brother on her lap to avoid creasing Annie's outfit. Little was said during the ride and the walk up the familiar half-mile to 23 Macaulay Road, but Mabel sensed her mother's nervous tension.

The first thing they saw when they got there was a smart hansom cab standing outside the house.

Annie frowned and clucked her tongue. She had not considered that Mimi might have company. The family usually visited on Sunday afternoons when they were expected, and determined as Annie was to confront her mother-in-law with the facts of Jack's improvidence, it would be awkward if there was somebody else around to hear. But she had worked herself up to such a pitch of indignation that she would not be put off. 'We've come all this way and I'm not going back without saying what I've come to say to her,' she declared, marching grimly forward. 'Come on, Mabel, get Walter out of that chair and fold it up.'

She opened the wrought-iron gate and raised the polished brass door knocker as Jack had done when he first brought her to this house. Was it really ten years ago? Ten years of struggling to keep up appearances with a growing family and shrinking resources. And now at twenty-eight Annie told herself that she'd had enough of it. Mimi Court was going to hear what she had to say and what's more, she would have to do something about it.

Her reverberating knock-knock-knock-knock sounded like the knell of doom to Mabel whose heart was sinking by the minute while they waited for the door to open.

A pert maidservant whom they had not seen before stood before them in a snow-white apron and frilled cap. She raised her eyebrows at them.

'I want to see Mrs Court,' demanded Annie in an unusually loud voice.

'Mrs Court's engaged at present, ma'am. 'Oo shall I say's callin'?' squeaked the girl, obviously reciting what she had been taught to say.

'I'm Mrs Court, her son's wife – her daughter-in-law and I want to see her *now*,' replied Annie. 'And I don't care to be kept on the doorstep.'

'Excuse me.' The maid withdrew into the dimness of the passage behind her. They heard a brief exchange of voices and then she reappeared. 'Will yer wait in the livin' room, Mrs Court? Mrs Court's in the parlour wiv a visitor, but she'll see yer in a minute.'

'Thank you,' said Annie shortly as they followed her into the middle room where Annie sat down and removed her gloves. They could hear a man's voice in the front room where Mimi interviewed her special clients and their relatives.

Annie looked around at the damask wallpaper, new since she had last visited the house. The old stone fireplace had been replaced by a marble surround and mantelpiece, its side columns carved with vine-leaves and grapes. Mimi Court was clearly doing well at her profession.

After ten minutes that seemed like an hour, they heard Mimi showing her visitor out. The hansom departed and Mabel saw her mother bracing herself.

When Mimi entered the living room, resplendent in a maroon silk gown with heavy lace trimming at the neck and wrists, she looked none too pleased. 'Yer might have let me know yer was coming, Annie,' she said in her company voice, sounding all her hs and gs. 'It so happens that I have had important business to deal with.'

Annie had risen and stood rigidly facing her. 'Well, *I've* got important business, too, Mimi,' she retorted, the words tumbling out in a breathless rush. 'I've come to tell you that I can't manage any longer on what your son gives me to live on. Little Walter needs proper food and medicine that I can't afford to give him, and the other children go short. *And* we're behind with the rent for the house. Mabel does her best, poor child, earning a little money to help out—'

Annie glanced at Mabel and in that moment of hesitation she lost the thread of her rehearsed speech, giving Mimi a chance to cut in. 'So ye've come here to plead poverty, is that it?' she said with a sneer. 'And ye've brought young Mabel to back yer up.'

This had the effect of taking the wind out of Annie's sails, for she could not deny it: she had needed Mabel's presence for moral support. 'Well, you are Jack's mother, after all,' she returned. 'You brought him up to be what he is and so you ought to know – you—' Annie's words died on her lips as she began to tremble all over with the suppressed resentment of years. It now rose up within her and overflowed in a torrent of rage and frustration. 'We hardly ever see him, he spends his whole time going from one racecourse to another, everything he earns ends up in other men's pockets, he can't keep it in his own – I can't put up with it any longer – I'm not going to. I haven't even paid Miss Lawton for Mabel's piano lessons this week!'

Walter let out a wail, clinging to his mother's skirt

as he sensed the tension in her body, the unfamiliar high pitch of her voice.

Mimi's eyes narrowed and she turned to Mabel. 'Take that poor child out round the back, Mabel,' she ordered. 'I'm not having scenes in front o' children. Go on, take him out directly. And *you'd* better sit down, Annie, and take a hold on yerself.'

Mabel glanced at her mother's flushed, angry face, then picked up her little brother who whimpered in protest, and took him out through the kitchen and scullery to the backyard where there was a wooden seat. She sat him down beside her and put her arm round his thin body. 'Don't cry, Walter, dear, I'm here – your Mabel's here,' she whispered. Then she noticed that Miss Lawton was hanging out some washing on the line and smiling nervously at the children.

Since her elderly mother had died she had remained at 23 Macaulay Road, a woman with no status in the household, largely ignored by Mimi and despised by the maids. 'Er, hello, Mabel. It's a lovely day, isn't it?' she said.

'Yes, Miss Lawton. Say hello to Miss Lawton, Walter.'

Walter's only response was to hide his face against Mabel's shoulder, and she shrugged apologetically at her piano teacher who bent down to stroke a black-and-white cat sitting on the path. The seat was placed below a wide sash window and through its open top came the sound of upraised voices from the living room beyond the kitchen.

Mimi was berating her daughter-in-law and Mabel listened in growing dismay, knowing that Miss Lawton could also hear. 'And what did *you* bring from yer fine Hampshire home, eh?' they heard

Mimi demanding. 'Not a penny. Them sisters o' yours grabbed the old man's money and yer never once went back to fight for yer fair share. Yer let yer husband an' children lose the lot, just 'cause yer was too proud – huh! Too ashamed to show yer face there again, more like!' As always, Mimi's refinement was forgotten as her anger rose. 'Yet yer got the barefaced cheek to come 'ere expectin' *me* to fork out from me own savings, just 'cause ye're hopeless at managin'!'

'Oh, yes, and suppose I *had* brought money with me, what would've happened to it?' cried Annie shrilly. 'I'll tell you – he'd have gambled it all away on the damned horses, every last penny of it. Any cash in Jack's hand is a bet, nothing more. His wife and his children could starve to death for all he cares. Tell me, Mimi Court, what kind of a man was Jack's father? Was *he* a hopeless gambler, too?'

'You mind yer tongue when yer speak o' Jack's father, Mrs Somethin'-or-nothin',' retorted Mimi. ''E was a *gentleman*, better 'n any jumped-up country draper, but that's neither 'ere nor there. Let me ask *you* a question: what've *you* done to keep 'im at 'ome an' away from all this bad influence? All 'e comes 'ome to is an 'ouseful o' mouths to feed, no idea o' discipline, an' yerself lookin' as if yer was dressed from a Jew's second-'and clo'es shop!'

'And why is that?' screamed Annie hysterically. 'Who is it gives me the children year after year, and doesn't pay me to feed and clothe them properly? Oh, it was a black day for me when Jack Court crossed my path!'

'I'll tell yer what, Anna-Maria bloody Chalcott, it was even blacker for Jack – the biggest mistake 'e ever made, marryin' a useless creature like you. Can't even use a needle and thread to make clo'es for yer children! Oh, 'ow I wish I'd tried 'arder to make 'im change 'is mind an' look out for summat better – though Gawd knows I did me best.'

Mabel gave a gasp of shock at hearing these bitter words and when they were followed by the sound of her mother's pitiful sobbing she could listen no longer. It was not to be borne. She jerked up from her seat. 'Come on, Walter, I must go an' help poor Mummy.'

'Oh, but Mabel—' began Miss Lawton, white and scared-looking. 'H-hadn't you better leave the little boy with me while you go and—'

But Mabel had already picked up her brother and marched indoors, through the kitchen and into the living room. If they were going to leave, she did not want to have to come back for Walter and besides, he would be frightened if she was out of his sight. She found her mother sitting and weeping inconsolably. Mimi had turned contemptuously away from her, but as Mabel entered she raised her head and seemed about to speak; Mabel brushed past her and went straight to Annie. 'Come on, Mother, let's get out o' here and go home,' she said, ignoring Mimi. 'We won't get anything out o' *her*, she's as hard as nails. Come on.'

Annie's face was streaming with tears and her best hat was askew as Mabel gently pulled her to her feet and smoothed down her skirt and jacket. She put Walter into his little wheelchair where he sat grizzling dolefully. 'Let's go, Mother,' said Mabel again, taking Annie's arm. 'Sooner we're out o' here the better.'

'Just a minute, young miss, I want a word with yer,' interposed Mimi, seizing Mabel's other arm. ''Oo gave *you* leave to—?' But she stopped in mid-sentence when Mabel angrily shook off her hand and spun round to look straight into her eyes. The burning fury in the level blue-grey gaze was more accusing than any words and Mimi recoiled from it, biting her lip and clearly disconcerted. She cleared her throat and spoke in an almost conciliatory manner. ''Ere, I can let yer have ten shillin's to see yer through till Jack turns up again,' she muttered, taking the lid off a ginger jar on the mantelpiece and extracting two banknotes. ''E'll be 'ome again on Friday, I shouldn't wonder. An' yer can take another ten for Walter, what with 'im bein' sickly an' all. An' I'll settle with the, er, Lawton woman for the piano lessons, rather 'n let 'er think yer can't pay.'

The suddenness of this concession took both mother and daughter completely by surprise and much as they would have liked to throw Mimi's two ten-shilling notes back in her face, they knew they could not afford the luxury of refusing money. Annie kept her eyes lowered as she pocketed the notes and Mabel said 'Thank you' with cold dignity on behalf of them both. Mimi saw them to the door without uttering another word.

It was a victory of sorts, because they had got what they went for, albeit at the high price of Annie's humiliation, for which Mabel thought she would never forgive her grandmother. And yet she had shown that she was not afraid of the formidable woman, in spite of being beholden to her for money; nor would she ever be bullied into submission by anybody in the future. On reflection Mabel realised that she had grown up in some way today and it was a good feeling, though her heart ached for her mother.

On the silent bus journey home, Mabel took Walter

on her knee and pondered on some of the things she had heard said, certain mysterious references that had been made. What had her grandmother meant by the 'fine Hampshire home' and the 'sisters who had grabbed the old man's money'? What old man? And why had her mother not denied any of it? Mum never spoke about her own family and had only said that both her parents were dead; she had not mentioned any sisters, or a fine home or money. Yet Mabel had noticed certain things about her mother that did not seem to belong to Sorrel Street. She spoke differently from her neighbours, in a better kind of accent, like Dr Knowles or the vicar at St Philip's church. Mum was more like a *lady* than Mrs Bull or Mrs Finch, and certainly Maudie Ling had been impressed, declaring Mabel's mum to be 'ever so posh'.

Mabel glanced towards her mother sitting on the bus with her hat pulled forward to conceal her red, swollen eyes. Now was not a good time to ask, but Mabel longed to know more about the – what was it, the Chalcott family? – because any sisters of Mum's would be her aunts, and Mabel longed to have an auntie, as so many of her school friends had.

There was little opportunity for finding out more about her mother's history in the weeks that followed. Dr Knowles's predictions proved to be only too true, and as soon as summer gave way to September's chillier days and early frosts, Walter developed a cough that racked his small frame and left him wheezing and blue round the mouth. Mabel's time was taken up in looking after him and the others as Annie's pregnancy advanced, and only she could get him to take Dr Knowles's medicine from a teaspoon, bribing him with promises of sugary drinks, rubbing embrocation on his chest and back, and wrapping him in flannel for the winter. His constant coughing and whining got on Jack's nerves, and Mabel had to comfort her mother when her son's illness and husband's ill temper reduced her to tears.

Mimi Court began to visit Sorrel Street more often than formerly, bringing extra food and comforts, though she had few encouraging smiles for her grandchildren. She stood over Walter and shook her head gloomily – and rolled her eyes upwards at the prospect of yet another child. This time she had said nothing to her daughter-in-law: it was Jack who had been taken aside and scolded so severely that he'd quailed before her, and for a time appeared to turn over a new leaf, which is to say that he spent more time buying food for the family and handing over the greater part of his earnings into Annie's keeping.

But Walter's condition steadily declined and he lay passively in his mother's or Mabel's arms, his hollow eyes pleading as if for help that none of them could give. It was heart-rending, and Dr Knowles worried about Mabel as the inevitable end approached. She had not been to school for a month and her piano lessons had lapsed. Her fair hair hung in rat's tails and the dark smudges under her eyes told of disturbed nights; she wore a perpetual anxious frown and even snapped at Albert when he tried to tease a smile from her. He shrugged and slammed out of the house, returning later with a Cadbury's chocolate bar for her, which so touched her that she did not ask where he'd got it.

The doctor eventually took Jack Court aside and spoke seriously to him. 'The boy's dying, Court, and it can only be a matter of days. If it's any consolation to you, I don't think he'd have grown up to be a normal child.'

'What d'yer mean – that he'd've been an idiot?' asked Jack gloomily.

'Well, let's say a bit on the slow side. My impression is that his brain's damaged, possibly at birth, or there may have been a fault in development. Be grateful for what you have, Court, the rest of your children are healthy and sound – and you have a real treasure in Mabel.'

'Yeah, we don't want *her* to go down with anythin',' said Jack wearily. 'She's the only one of 'em with any bloody sense.'

Knowles turned away from him in despair and tried to have a word with the grandmother; but when he met her on one of her visits to Sorrel Street he distrusted her on sight. She nodded graciously to him, raising her eyes heavenward to indicate both Walter's destination and the unsatisfactory household at number 12. She wiped her eyes on a lace-edged handkerchief, but the doctor suspected that she felt no real grief for her grandson. Something about her repelled him, though he could not say exactly what.

The end came a few days later, on a raw November day. Mabel and her mother had had a terrible night with the little invalid who had alternately burned with fever and shivered with cold. His face took on a pinched appearance like a shrunken, wizened old man, and Annie had held him against her breasts until she had fallen into an exhausted sleep and Mabel had taken him from her.

Now it was afternoon and Mabel sat by the living-room fire nursing Walter on her lap, wrapped in a blanket and mercifully asleep at last. Annie was in her bed, completely worn out, and George was quietly playing on the hearthrug with a bundle of kindling sticks that did duty as soldiers. As the room darkened in the winter dusk, Mabel's head began to droop.

She was roused by the banging of the front door and the clatter of Albert's and Alice's boots in the hallway. They had returned from school and Mabel was at once alert.

'Hey, Mabel, d'yer know what?' shouted Albert. 'Yer friend Maudie's been caught thievin', an' the coppers've taken 'er away!'

'Oh, *no*, poor Maudie!' cried Mabel in dismay. She had not seen her friend for some time. 'Was it from a market stall?' she asked, remembering how Maudie used to crawl under the street traders' displays to pick up fruit and whatever scraps might have fallen.

'Nah! She was 'elpin' 'erself from the kitchens o' toffs' 'ouses up Belgravy way – y'know, them posh places!'

Mabel clasped Walter more tightly as she asked, 'And what about her poor little brother Teddy?'

'Dunno. She was after summat to feed 'im on, I s'pose.'

Tears filled Mabel's eyes at the thought of her friend's desperate plight. What would happen to Maudie and her brother now?

'What's the matter with Walter, Mabel?' asked Alice suddenly. 'His mouth's open an' his eyes are all funny – oh, Mabel, *look*! Is he . . . is he dead?' Her voice rose to a scream of fear. 'He's dead, he's *dead*!'

'Sh, Alice, *sh*, be quiet, ye'll wake Mummy. He's . . . he's just asleep, that's all.'

But her fingers trembled and she felt sick at heart as she carefully pulled back the blanket from the little grey face. The body was still warm against hers but limp and lifeless. It was true. His heartbeat and breathing had stopped. Walter Court lay dead in his sister's arms, five weeks before his second birthday.

Alice and Georgie began to wail in unison, while Albert stared open-mouthed at Mabel's stricken face. She stifled the cry that rose to her own throat, knowing that she had to be brave for the rest of them and especially for her mother. 'Albert! Run next door and fetch Mrs Bull – tell her to hurry up and get here before poor Mummy comes downstairs – oh, quick, be quick! And Alice, you go for Dr Knowles!'

'Hush, Mabel, hush, hush, my child, you mustn't blame yourself, I won't have it. You did all that a good nurse could do for him.'

'But I promised I'd look after him, Dr Knowles, an' he died – he *died*, an' I couldn't save him!'

Dr Knowles had never before seen Mabel Court give way like this, and he was touched to the heart by her grief and self-reproach. 'My dear, there are times when nothing can be done – when there's nothing *anyone* can do to save someone we love. Listen! I'm certain that Walter would not have lived as long as he did if it hadn't been for your devoted care. No sick child was ever better served. Hush, Mabel, hush, my dear.'

At the little gathering after the funeral the doctor tried to emphasise to Jack and Annie Court the importance of Mabel's immediate return to school. 'She's an exceptionally bright girl, and must not be allowed to waste her time doing chores and running errands, however willing she may be,' he told them, but Annie's only response was to burst into helpless tears once again over the loss of her baby and Jack Court's sullen mutter was hardly encouraging. Mrs Mimi Court shrugged her plump shoulders at the doctor and told him that he had better speak to Mabel herself, or he'd be wasting his breath in this house.

The doctor stared at her for a moment, wondering why she made him think of a case he'd had a couple of years back, a single girl who'd threatened to kill herself because she was expecting a child; he'd directed her to a Salvation Army refuge for girls in her condition and when he'd met her a few months later she was no longer expecting. She'd told him about a woman . . . and he had decided not to know. Mabel's grandmother had seen him looking at her, because she quickly took her leave, saying that there was nothing more she could do.

Knowles found Mabel in the kitchen with Mrs Bull who was telling her that Walter had always been a little angel and not long for this sad world. 'I said as much, soon's I saw the poor little mite, di'n't I, Mabel, my duck? And now 'e's gorn back to 'eaven agin to be wiv the other little angels, so yer mustn't cry.'

Mabel's eyes brightened at the sight of the doctor who smiled and beckoned to her. 'I've got some news for you, Mabel, about your friend Maud Ling,' he said.

'Oh, Dr Knowles, what've yer heard?' she asked, clasping her hands together, half in hope, half in dread. 'Tell me please! Is she in prison?'

'No, no, no. After she was questioned by the police, she and her brother were put into the care for a society run by the church for children in need of care. It's called the Waifs and Strays Society, and

Maud and her brother are in a home at Dulwich for ... well, for waifs and strays, where they'll get enough to eat and won't have to roam the streets any more.'

'Is it a ... a workhouse?' asked Mabel fearfully.

'Oh, dear me, no, children aren't sent to work-houses any more, thank heaven. No, dear, this is quite a good place, homely, not too large, and Maud and her brother will go to school and be trained for useful work. The society will take good care of them, something which their parents completely failed to do.' He hesitated, then added, 'Not like your little brother Walter, who was always loved and cared for, wasn't he?'

Mabel nodded, remembering Maudie's shocking accounts of violent drunken quarrels and the deaths of three other children. 'Yes, but isn't it *wicked*, Dr Knowles, all the poor children who *aren't* loved and looked after, like Maudie and Teddy!' she cried with a sudden fierce passion that took the doctor by surprise. 'Oh, how I wish I could take care of them all!'

The doctor looked very thoughtful. 'Not yet, Mabel, and not all of them,' he said after a pause. 'But one day I think you're going to be able to help *some* of them, my dear. You're a born nurse and you'll have to train at a hospital, but for now—'

'Oh, Dr Knowles, d'ye really think so? Did yer mean what yer just said? I want to be a children's nurse more 'n anything else in the world!' Mabel's whole face was transformed as she told him of her dearest wish.

'And so you will one day, I'm sure, Mabel, but first of all it's very important that you learn all you can now while you are still at school. I don't want to hear of you missing any more school days, do you understand?' His words were stern, but his face so kind that Mabel smiled and promised to work really hard at her lessons and regain her place at the top of the class.

'Take that gin away, woman – out of the room, out of the house!' ordered Dr Knowles. 'I won't have the vile stuff near a woman in childbirth!'

Mrs Lowe indignantly denied all knowledge of the offending jam jar on the window shelf and a flustered Mrs Bull hastily removed it from the bedroom. It had been her contribution towards Annie Court's ease in labour and having decanted the colourless liquid into an innocent-looking jar, she thought it would escape notice. Knowles had detected it as soon as he entered the room.

Annie's pains had begun on an afternoon halfway through February and Dr Knowles had asked to be notified as well as the midwife. On arriving at Sorrel Street he found Mabel in the kitchen seeing to the children's tea and keeping the kettle on the boil for Mrs Lowe. 'Mm-mm, something smells good. What is it, Irish stew? Any chance of a taste, Mabel?'

She dipped the ladle in the big blackened saucepan, but as she lifted it up a shout and a bump was heard upstairs. 'It sounds as if me mum might be having the baby, Dr Knowles.'

'Then I'd better go up and see what Mrs Lowe's doing,' he answered with a smile. He knew that the midwife was sensible and reliable, better than some of the untrained handywomen like Mrs Clements who still practised as midwives among the poorer neighbourhoods. The new compulsory registration would eventually phase them out, but he knew it would be some years before registration could be enforced.

Apart from banishing the gin jar, he stood aside and let Mrs Lowe go ahead in her own way while he held Annie's hand and talked her through the contractions. They had not long to wait and a baby girl was born within twenty minutes. Her lusty cries greeted her father as he arrived home in no happy mood.

'A daughter for you this time, Court, and your wife's due for a rest,' said the doctor pointedly. 'If you'd care to come and see me we can talk about preventive measures.'

Jack nodded, frowned and finally forced himself to smile upon the newcomer who was to be called Daisy.

What had gone wrong with his life, Jack Court wondered. Take today, three consecutive races won by the favourite and Dick Sammons swanking at the wheel of his own motorcar, while he, the best bookmaker between here and Goodwood, had come home to a houseful of chuntering women, bawling children, yet another baby and God only knew what mess being ladled out at the kitchen table and masquerading as a man's supper – talk about a bloody workhouse! And now this old know-all of a doctor telling him what he should and shouldn't do with Annie in bed. Huh! Chance would be a fine thing these days. If she wasn't having a child or feeding a child or bleeding or moaning about being tired or sighing over that poor little imbecile whose life had fortunately been snuffed out – God! Here he was at thirty-four, in the prime of his life and stuck with this lot. He could hardly be blamed for sometimes accepting what was on offer elsewhere . . .

*

Mabel's days were now filled with housework, running errands, going to school and escorting younger children to and from Hallam Road with her – and always hurrying back to her darling baby, her little Daisy, a dark-haired little thing who cried a lot but always responded to Mabel's soothing voice and touch. The first word she spoke was not 'mama' or 'dada' but 'Maby', accompanied by a broad smile and holding out her little arms to be lifted up.

'I loves 'oo, Maby – I loves 'oo!'

Albert too was a favourite with his youngest sister and would pull comical faces to make her laugh. One of his tricks was to get under the table and then pretend to bang his head on it. Out he would come on his hands and knees, loudly boo-hooing and rubbing his head, which made the little girl shout with laughter and beg him to 'Do it again, Alby!'

'Nice to be appreciated.' He grinned at Mabel who was glad to see him in a good humour. A lot of his time was spent out with other boys who found ways and means of making a sixpence or two. One way was by discreetly taking scrawled notes from back doors and bringing them to Jack Court with small sums of money. 'Running messages' they called it and Jack gave a warning frown if they ever opened their mouths.

It was during Daisy's first year that Mabel found an opportunity to ask her mother about something that had long been on her mind. They were in the kitchen together. 'Mum,' she began, 'yer told me I was named after yer mother.'

Annie stiffened slightly. 'Yes.'

'If I was named for her, who was Albert named for? And Alice and George and Daisy?'

'Albert was named after Queen Victoria's husband and Alice after the little girl in Mr Carroll's story of Wonderland. And your dad and I both liked the name o' Daisy.'

'And Georgie?'

'He was named for my own dear father, George Chalcott. A better man never lived. Mabel, have you put those peas in to soak?'

'Yes, an' the ham bone's simmerin', doesn't it smell good? Mum, what was yer mother like? Yer never talk about her or any o' yer family.' Annie Court's face seemed to close up, though her tired blue eyes softened at some far-off recollection, which encouraged Mabel to persist. 'And did yer live in Hampshire with her an' yer father?'

'Yes, but I lost them both before I married your father and came to live in London.' Annie spoke abruptly, with an edge to her voice, and again Mabel sensed a mystery of some kind.

'Did yer have a big house to live in, Mum?'

'Oh, yes, it was a beautiful house.'

'Bigger 'n this?'

'Much bigger, yes.'

'Did it have a garden?'

'What a lot of questions, Mabel – yes, we had quite a large garden.'

'And did yer have brothers an' sisters, Mum?'

Annie hesitated. 'Two sisters, quite a lot older than I was.'

'What were their names?' asked Mabel eagerly, for this was what she really wanted to know about, these sisters of her mother who were her aunts.

But Annie made an impatient gesture, pushing past Mabel to get to the range oven. 'It doesn't matter, Mabel, I don't have anything to do with them now. Just put this saucepan to the back, will you?'

'But Mum, yer must think about them sometimes,' said Mabel, unable to imagine forgetting Albert, Alice, George and Daisy – and poor little Walter.

'Why should I? They didn't want anything more to do with me after I married your dad.'

'P'raps they were jealous 'cause ye'd got married and they hadn't.'

Annie shrugged and did not answer.

Mabel took a big breath and asked the question that had been on her mind ever since that unpleasant exchange with Mimi when she had talked scathingly about the Chalcotts' money. 'Mum, was yer daddy rich?'

Annie glanced at her sharply. 'Why do you ask that? Have you been talking to – oh!' She seemed to remember something and her eyes hardened. 'Listen, Mabel, if you've heard your grandmother Court saying anything about my family, don't take any notice; she doesn't know anything, she never met them. And I don't wish to speak of it any more, Mabel, it's all in the past.'

But Mabel longed to know about those sisters and their big house in the country. 'Mum, your sisters – they're my aunts, aren't they?'

Suddenly Annie covered her face with her hands. 'Oh, Mabel, don't bother me any more, it breaks my heart to remember – it's all in the past, and – and—'

Mabel was all penitence and went straight to her mother's side. 'I'm sorry, Mum, I really am – I promise I won't talk o' the Chalcotts again. Don't be upset, Mummy, please, I'm sorry.'

George became old enough to start school and

trotted along after Alice who resented being put in charge of him, although he was no trouble, as Mabel pointed out, not half as much bother as Albert had been at that age.

After Daisy's birth Annie never completely recovered her strength and was constantly tired. She seldom ventured far from the house alone, and it was left to Mabel to take Alice and the younger children down to Tooting on one Sunday afternoon each month to visit their grandmother. They travelled on the new electrified tram that now went from Westminster Bridge straight through via Clapham to Tooting, where Mimi received them regally at Macaulay Road and gave them a lavish tea. She and Mabel maintained a polite relationship in which there was no love, more a wary mutual respect, avoiding confrontations.

There was little time for Mabel to read or practise the piano, but because of her promise to Dr Knowles and her determination to become a nurse one day she tried not to miss school, and did her best to keep up with her studies by going over the lessons in the evening after Daisy and George were in bed. Sometimes she could hardly keep her eyes open, but she knew that she must learn to write fluently and legibly in order to take lecture notes and sit for her nursing examinations in time to come.

It was at last becoming recognised that the persistent poor school attendance of older children, especially girls, was due to their being kept at home to look after the under-fives when the mother was ill or having another baby – or having to go out to work as the breadwinner. One London borough after another began to respond by setting up nurseries or 'babies' rooms', usually attached to a school where for a minimal charge babies and toddlers could be cared for while their older brothers and sisters were taught their lessons next door.

Dr Knowles added his voice to the long campaign to provide this service at Hallam Road and when the idea eventually got taken up by a public-spirited woman with some money, he immediately thought of Mabel. For the scheme would be set up by the time she left school and of course he would warmly recommend her as an assistant nursery maid.

And Annie Court had her own secret life.

Whenever the opportunity occurred she would creep upstairs, loosen her stays and lie down on her bed. Within minutes she drifted into a blissful haze in which she forgot all about the upsetting things in her life: the loss of her dear little Walter, Mimi's scorn and Jack's frequent absences from the over-crowded house with its scratched paintwork and discoloured walls – the constant struggle to keep up appearances of respectability. Just for an hour or two Annie would drift away to the Hampshire country-side in which she had grown up and once again she would be Anna-Maria Chalcott, a little girl walking with her sweet mamma through the garden at Pinehurst and down the lane that led to the edge of the fields.

And sometimes she would let herself drift into another dream – another summer garden where she was Anna-Maria Drummond, playing on the lawn with her little daughter Mabel.

I'd have married you, Anna-Maria, and called the child mine.

Mabel Drummond, the eldest of a family of healthy, nicely dressed, well-behaved children.

Just for an hour or two ... Annie Court's world was bathed in a rosy glow.

And nobody, she thought, knew about the screw-topped jar hidden behind the curtain.

Chapter Three

Mabel looked guiltily towards the wall clock. Gone half past four. Time she were home. The floor had been swept, the crockery washed and put away; the stove was raked out and the battered enamelled potties hung in a row beside the sink and towel rails. Matron was ready to lock up, but a little brother and sister still remained uncollected from the Hallam Road Babies Mission. Their mother who worked at Price's candleworks had not turned up and Miss Carter, the Matron, frowned and shook her head. 'This is the second time it's happened in two weeks, Mabel,' she said. 'If she's not here by five I shall have to take them home myself – and give her a warning. If she can't come herself, she should ask somebody else to fetch them.'

Mabel shone a reassuring smile at the forlorn little pair, both under four years old. If only she could take them home with her and look after them! 'D'ye want me to wait, Matron?' she asked, feeling obliged to make the offer, while hoping it would not be accepted.

'No, Mabel, not this time. It's been a busy day for you without Miss Clay. You'd better be going now.'

'Thank yer very much, Matron.' With a last smile and a wave to the two small children Mabel hurried off. Miss Carter watched her from the window, almost running along Hallam Road towards Lavender Hill. She found Mabel Court a willing worker and so good with the young children who poured into the Mission each day from just before eight o'clock until half past four. Thirty-eight of them had been in today and as she'd had to send Miss Clay home with a sore throat, she and Mabel had worked non-stop, with scarcely time for a cup of tea and the sandwich they brought with them. As the day's work ended, Mabel's face began to show signs of tension and she always seemed in a hurry to get home. Almost as if she was afraid of what she might find when she got there, Miss Carter thought, although there was no doubt at all that Mabel loved her work.

The Mission had been started by a lady who had given up her suffragist activities in order to devote her energies to what she saw as a more pressing need; her generous subsidy kept the fee down to threepence per day per child, and that included milk and bread and butter at midday. Miss Carter, a trained nurse from the East London Hospital for Children, had been appointed as Matron with a local grocer's daughter, Ada Clay, as her assistant. School leaver Mabel Court had at first been considered too young at fourteen to be taken on as extra help with such responsible work, but thanks to her teachers' report and Dr Knowles's enthusiastic letter of recommendation she had been given the job at five shillings a week. Oh, the thrill of that moment when the letter came with the wonderful news! Mabel had literally danced for joy at this first step towards achieving her dream and had quickly become indispensable to Miss Carter. Although two years on she earned only seven shillings weekly, her true reward was the love and trust she saw in the faces of the little children who crowded round her at the Mission.

*

On reaching Sorrel Street she found that there had been no need to worry. Her mother was in the kitchen brewing a pot of tea and Mabel breathed a secret sigh of relief. Alice was sitting on the piano stool reading a twopenny romance she had got from a classmate and George was bringing in coal from the back, ready for the range oven tomorrow.

There was a sound of quick, eager footsteps as little Daisy rushed to greet her eldest sister. 'Mabel, Mabel, where have yer been?'

'Up to the palace, to visit the Queen!' cried Mabel gaily, picking up the dark-eyed girl who gleefully continued with the adapted rhyme.

'Mabel, oh, Mabel, what did yer there?'

'The King an' Queen told me to sit on a chair!' replied Mabel and George looked up with a grin.

'I told 'em I'd only come up for a dare!' he added and Daisy squealed with laughter.

'The Queen's got lots o' nits in her hair!' She giggled.

But Mabel pursed her lips on hearing this version. 'Now then, that's quite enough o' that, little Miss Cheeky,' she said, putting the six-year-old down with a warning shake of her head. Turning to her mother, she asked, 'What sort of a day have yer had, Mum?'

'Oh, not too bad, dear, I was all right once I got going.' Annie gave her a tired smile and they exchanged a kiss.

'Alice, come and put this ironing away,' called Mabel. 'Don't leave it all to yer mother. Any news o' Dad?' she asked Annie.

'Still at Newmarket and might stay there over the weekend. You know he lodges with that chap who married the publican's daughter there, they're as thick as thieves. He'll probably be back on Monday, who knows with your father?' She shrugged and sighed.

They were all glad when Mabel came home. She had become the central pivot of the family as her mother's health had gradually declined into a vague semi-invalidism. Now in her middle thirties, Annie was thin and careworn, her face as lined as a woman of fifty. Half her neighbours envied her for having such a dutiful, home-loving daughter as Mabel, while the other half thought her far too dependent on the good-natured girl who at sixteen seemed to have no life of her own.

'Shouldn't Albert be in by now?' Mabel asked. 'He's bringin' supper, isn't he?' It was Friday, and her mouth watered at the thought of fried fish and chips, her favourite dish.

'They might have put him on lates again, you know how they take advantage of the young boys,' said Annie with a worried look. There had been a fatal accident in a railway siding the previous month and Annie was constantly anxious for her son's safety.

'Oh, I shouldn't worry, Mum, Albert's got his head well screwed on,' said Mabel quickly. 'He'll be a driver before he's twenty, you'll see.' She had long decided that her brother Albert was a law unto himself; he had gone to work at the railway depot on leaving school and came home as black as any coal miner from his shifts. At fifteen he contributed more to the household than Mabel and affected a workmanlike air of toughness that annoyed Alice who looked down her dainty nose at his rough manners; he teased everybody except his mother and Mabel, the sister to whom he remained as close as ever.

'Well, I hope he hurries up, or we'll all be starving,' said Alice, turning down the corners of her mouth. She had one more year at school and then had her sights on the city and the opportunities it offered to bright, ambitious girls. Alice saw herself as one of the new young businesswomen with a career in the Post Office, perhaps in the big new telephone exchange at St Paul's Churchyard, earning thirty shillings a week. No more dirty-faced, sticky-pawed children, no more coarse ragging from Albert or bossing from Mabel: the very thought of it seemed like heaven to the pretty, discontented girl.

'It'll be all the better for waitin' for, I reckon,' said George, referring to their supper and Mabel shot him a grateful look. Though not yet eleven, George was a serious-minded boy, old for his years and so *nice*, always sensitive to the feelings of others. He was far more willing than Alice to help in the house, even to pushing the wet washing through the mangle and hanging it out on the line or spreading it over the wooden maidens that took up so much room on wet washdays. He could be relied on to take Daisy to and from school, turning his back on diversions like football and tip-cat, and he usually managed to steer clear of fights. He could defend himself when he had to and would go to the rescue of smaller boys who were being bullied, but he preferred a quiet life. With his wavy fair hair and blue eyes, he was the complete opposite of Albert, who called him his little sister, a taunt that rolled off George like water from the proverbial duck's back; for like Mabel, George knew that his brother's good points far outweighed the deliberately sardonic impression he liked to give.

Albert swaggered in to cheers at half past six, accompanied by two other young railwaymen, each carrying deliciously greasy packets wrapped in newspaper.

'Ooh, don't that smell a bit of all right!' said George, sniffing appreciatively.

'Put them on the table, the plates are all ready an' warm from the oven,' ordered Mabel, bustling around and putting out extra knives and forks for the visitors whom Albert now introduced with a flourish.

'Sam Mackintosh an' 'Arry Drover, founder members wiv yours truly o' the union against exploitation o' young workers!' he announced, waving his arm towards the pair. 'Sam an' 'Arry, meet me mum an' me lovely sister Mabel – the rest of 'em ain't worf a mention, except for me little darlin' – come 'ere, Daisy, an' give yer poor old 'ard-workin' bruvver a kiss!'

The little girl's dark eyes sparkled as he lifted her up and twirled her round above his head.

'Daisy, Daisy, gimme yer answer, *do*! I'm half crazy, all for the love o' *you*!' he sang, while Alice rolled up her eyes at such caperings and Mabel smiled fondly, until she remembered her manners and turned to greet their guests. Sam Mackintosh was eyeing her up and down in a boldly admiring manner, while the other young man stood back as if rather unsure of himself. He was of middle height, slightly built, a few years older than the other two and, while not obviously good-looking, Mabel immediately thought what a kind face he had. Like Sam, he too was looking at her, but far more respectfully. She wanted to put him at his ease, but was not sure what to say and felt herself blushing.

'Cor, I'm that parched!' groaned Albert. 'Put the kettle on, Mabel, for 'Oly 'Arry, 'cause 'e's signed the pledge. Sam, pick up a couple o' jugs an' go down to the public for beer for us ordin'ry men, will yer?'

At fifteen, Albert was a well-grown lad, as handsome as his father with the same dark eyes and hair, the same strong white teeth with the two prominent incisors that added to his attraction. The difference was that Albert cared nothing about his appearance; his cap was stuck on the back of his head, his jacket sleeves were frayed and the bottoms of his ragged trousers were tied with string. He despised Jack Court's insistence on well-pressed suits and polished boots, and seemed to take a perverse pride in looking as if he had just come from the railway depot. Which, of course, he had.

As they gathered round the table for their fried fish banquet, Harry Drover glanced apologetically at Mabel who seemed to be more in charge than Albert's mother. 'I hope it's all right, comin' in on yer like this, Miss Court. Yer brother's such a card, the rest of us never know when he's serious or pullin' our legs.'

His natural politeness had an immediate appeal for Mabel. 'Albert's a comic right enough, but he's a good sort at heart and any friend o' his is very welcome here – 'specially as ye've brought yer own supper,' she answered with a smile. 'D'ye want a cup o' tea? The kettle's just boiled.'

'That'd be very nice, er, Miss Court.'

'And you're – Mr Drover?'

'Call 'im 'Arry – ovverwise known as 'Oly 'Arry, 'cause 'e don't drink, don't swear and don't go wiv wimmin!' chortled Albert.

Harry looked embarrassed and Mabel quickly cut in. 'Take no notice o' my brother, ye'll only make him worse if yer do. Er, would yer like to sit down,

Mr Drover? Over there with my brother George – Alice, put out the salt an' vinegar, and fetch some glasses down for the other, er, boys.'

'Can I have beer an' all?' begged George.

'No, yer can't. Tea for you, Mother?'

Annie nodded and Harry, who was still standing, handed round the cups as Mabel poured them out.

'Is there any bread an' butter?' demanded Alice.

'Margarine, an' cut it yerself if yer want it. Now, has everybody got what they want? Good, so let's all sit down.' Mabel passed a hand across her forehead to push back a stray lock of hair and was again aware of Harry Drover's brown eyes upon her. He immediately looked away, and she noticed that as he sat at the table he briefly bowed his head and lowered his eyes. She remembered how her mother had said grace before meals when they had all been children, though the custom had lapsed in recent years. On an impulse she decided to revive it now. 'Would yer mind sayin' grace for us, Mr Drover?' she asked.

His face lit up with pleasure at the request, though Albert gave a splutter and Mabel quelled him with a glance, looking swiftly round the table with a wordless command for silence. They all folded their hands and bowed their heads. Harry Drover cleared his throat. 'Heavenly Father, we thank Thee for this food, an' commend ourselves to Thy service,' he recited quickly and they all responded with 'Amen'.

Albert winked at Sam but made no comment; Mabel seldom insisted on her authority, but when she did she had to be obeyed.

Over the meal the talk was about the problems of the unskilled younger men who like Albert had gone straight from school to work on the rapidly expanding railways which now criss-crossed the whole country.

'Nothin's gonna be done about poor Tom, the boy 'oo was killed when an engine backed into 'im, up against the buffers in that sidin',' said Albert grimly. ''Is mum ain't gettin' a penny off the company, they're tryin' to make out it was 'is own fault, an' 'im only just started, poor little blighter. Bloody murderers, that's what they are – sorry, Mum, but if I 'ad my way I'd string the buggers up first thing Monday mornin'.'

'Albert, your language is terrible,' said his mother, 'though of course I understand how you feel. Can't your unions do anything to help the poor woman?'

'What union?' muttered Albert angrily. 'No good lookin' to ASLEF to do anythin'.'

'The fact is, Mrs Court, unions can't do much for a young unskilled lad who isn't – er, wasn't – eligible to join,' Harry tried to explain, stumbling over the unfamiliar word.

'If yer ask me, the unions are bleedin' useless 'alf the time, they got no power, it's all talk,' growled Albert with a bitterness unusual in a fifteen-year-old and Mabel flashed him a half-smile. She knew how deeply the tragic death of a former classmate had affected her brother.

'Tha's right, Albert's just abaht 'it the nail on the 'ead,' agreed Sam Mackintosh with his mouth full. Taking a deep gulp from his glass, he went on, 'If the men was all to get togevver, shoulder to shoulder, like, they could bring the 'ole o' the railways to a standstill. Cor! That'd be sommat to see, eh?'

Mabel was shocked. 'Yer mean that the railwaymen should go on strike?' she asked. 'And what good would *that* do? Only make life harder for everybody who has to travel by train. And the company would sack the ringleaders, an' then they'd be out of a job an' not much chance o' getting another.'

'Do we have to listen to this kind o' stuff while we're eating?' asked Alice, wrinkling her nose as if at a bad smell. 'You'll end up in prison, Albert, the way you talk.'

Albert snorted. 'Yer don't know what ye're talkin' about, gal. It's like Sam says, if all the workers 'ad the guts to get togevver an' stand firm, they couldn't all be sacked, could they? You just wait an' see, milady Alice – one o' these days the workers o' this country'll see they got the power an' bloody well *use* it!'

'But not if they've got families to support, surely,' protested Mabel, who always thought of the women and children, their helplessness in a world governed by men.

Harry Drover sensed her unease with the way the discussion was going and now tried to steer it in another direction – and perhaps gain a little of her attention for himself and what was the most important thing in his life. 'Have yer ever been to an open-air Salvation Army meeting, Miss Court? Some of our corps meet on the edge o' Battersea Park, an' a lot o' the bystanders come just to listen to the band.'

'That's right, yer should 'ear 'im blowin' 'is trombone, Mabel, talk about a fanfare o' trumpets!' Albert raised an imaginary instrument to his mouth and gave a passable imitation: 'Ta-ra-ra! Ta-ra-ra! – diddle-ump, diddle-ump, diddle-ump!'

Mabel cut in sharply at this disrespect to their guest. 'Just shut *up*, will yer, Albert!' she ordered.

'No, Mr Drover, I haven't attended a meeting, but I've often heard the bands playing, and – well, I think it would be very, er, interesting.'

'Why don't yer just come along, then, Miss Court, to the Citadel, any time.' Harry blushed furiously, ignoring the grins that passed between his two younger workmates who had to take orders from him at the depot. 'General Booth – he's our founder, y'know – his idea is to bring the light o' the Gospel to *all*, y'see, not just the churchgoers an' the, er, respectable, like, but to the poor, the downtrodden, the drunkard an' the harlot.'

Albert choked on his beer. 'Thanks a *lot*, 'Arry, we really appreciate yer concern for us!'

Sam tut-tutted in mock disapproval. 'Yer'd better watch yer language, mate. Can't yer see there're ladies present?'

'Yeah, that's right,' Albert chipped in. ''Oo d'yer think yer callin' a—' He broke off, then put on a very indignant expression. ''Ere, I'll 'ave yer know my sister Mabel's a very respectable young lady!'

Poor Harry Drover was aghast. 'Oh, Miss Court, I'm so sorry – I never meant to say anything against ... oh, heavens, what a ... a misunderstanding, please accept my apologies—' His words tailed off as he saw tears of mirth streaming down Albert's face and realised that he was being teased unmercifully. He lowered his face and went quiet, feeling that he had made a fool of himself in front of the whole family.

Mabel felt his embarrassment and her heart went out to this honest, sincere young man. It was time to come to his rescue. She glared at the two reprobates. 'Ye'll have to excuse my brother, Harry, he missed a lot o' schoolin' and doesn't know any better. Let me pour yer another cup o' tea, and, er, next time I hear a Salvation Army band playin', I'll certainly stop an' listen.'

He could only respond with a shy glance in which there was something more than just gratitude. He did not trust himself to open his mouth again for fear of putting his foot in it, but he glowed within because this sweet girl had called him Harry. It made up for her brother's teasing.

Later that evening when the table was cleared and the visitors gone, Albert looked very knowing. 'Hey, Mabel, d'yer know what? I reckon 'e's sweet on you, ol' 'Arry. 'Is eyes went all moony after yer stuck up for 'im, an' 'e kept gawpin' at yer when yer wasn't lookin'.'

'Go along with yer, Albert, don't be daft. He's just one o' those chaps with good manners who's nice to everybody. Which is more than can be said for certain other people I could mention,' she added pointedly. But her eyes softened as she spoke and there was a tender curve to her mouth as she thought about the look in Harry's honest brown eyes. Some deep instinct within her knew that his was a face to trust.

Albert stopped his banter, caught unawares by a fact he'd never noticed before. Which was that his sister Mabel at sixteen was a very pretty girl . . .

'Come on, Mabel, it'll be a lark! We can go up on the train and have a good look round the big shops – an' go in one o' those new tea shops where all the office girls show themselves off. Yer never know, we might find a couple o' nice fellas to treat us!'

It was the August Bank holiday weekend and Ada

Clay was determined to have a bit of fun. She was trying to persuade Mabel to spend the Saturday in the West End with her and made it sound tempting. The trouble was that Mabel had never been used to indulging herself and felt that she could not afford such extravagance. After contributing all but two shillings of her wages to the housekeeping, she felt that she should now start saving for Christmas rather than splashing out on a day trip with carefree Ada who didn't have to count the pennies so carefully.

'Oh, come *on*, Mabel, I'll treat yer to tea and it don't cost much just to look in Selfridges windows! I reckon we've earned a day out after a week o' wipin' little mouths an' bottoms at the Mission. All work an' no play, yer know what they say!' She laughed and poked Mabel affectionately in the ribs.

Ada's father was the manager of one of Lipton's high-class grocery stores and she was generous with her ready cash. In the end Mabel compromised and agreed to go just for the afternoon. After all, her father was home this weekend, and had mentioned taking his wife and daughters out walking in Battersea Park; Albert was working and George out playing with mates from school. It wasn't as if she'd be missed and Mum wouldn't be left on her own . . .

Mabel could not remember a time when she had not felt a tugging sense of duty towards her family, especially her mother. And in recent years there had been times when she'd had to be extra watchful: there had been those rare occasions when Annie Court was found lying on the floor by the children coming in from school – unless Mabel had been able to get home first and save them from the shock. She'd hastily hauled her mother up and got her to bed, laying her on her side and drawing the curtains, saying that it was nothing to worry about, Mum had fainted because of her thin blood. She avoided sending for Dr Knowles, and made light of the matter to Alice, George and Daisy. 'Just a faint, no need to fuss – don't tell Mrs Bull or anybody – she'll be better in the mornin' after a good night's sleep.'

The next day Annie would avoid her eyes when Mabel took her a cup of tea – for these incidents never happened when Jack was at home – and say nothing about her blinding headache and nausea. Mother and daughter would both pretend that it had never happened, and any comments from Albert or questions from Alice and Daisy were quickly dismissed. It had not happened often, but the worry was always there at the back of Mabel's mind, like a shadow waiting to pounce.

Leicester Square was crowded with shoppers and strollers as the two young women gazed up at the Empire Palace of Varieties. Many of the great names of music hall were making the transition to the more respectable family-based entertainment with seats in rows and no drinking in the auditorium. 'Better 'n the old Grand on St John's Hill, eh, Mabel?' said Ada. 'I'd love to see one o' them shows, wouldn't you? Ol' Marie Lloyd an' George Robey doin' their stuff!'

Mabel smiled. She knew by heart many of the songs made popular by the music halls and sold as ballads with words and music, but she had never imagined herself sitting up there in a real theatre; Ada's enthusiasm touched a chord somewhere within her and it made her think that life could include fun as well as duty. 'Yes,' she breathed. 'P'raps one o' these days we will.'

And that was the moment when she heard the

voice from the past. 'Is it? Can it be? My Gawd, it bloomin' well *is*, me ol' pal Mabel Court! What're yer doin' up the West End, then, gal?'

Mabel spun round and stared into the merry face of a girl in a smart striped skirt and jacket, a flowery hat pinned over her curls. She was leaning on the arm of a grinning youth in a passable serge suit topped with a cloth cap that proclaimed his servant status. For a couple of seconds Mabel stared at them blankly.

'Blow me dahn, don't yer know me, Mabel? 'Ave yer forgot yer ol' friend Maudie?'

'*Maudie*! Maudie Ling!' Mabel almost shouted. 'Oh, how I've wondered about yer, how yer were gettin' on! All those years ago – oh, Maudie, is it really you?'

'Dunno 'oo else!' And the two girls flung their arms round each other in a reuniting embrace. There was so much to say, such a lot to catch up on.

'Yeah, I lef' the 'ome at Dulwich when I was sixteen an' went into service – an' I ain't 'alf got a top-drawer place now, Mabel, 'ousemaid in a mansion on Bryanston Square, Lady Stanley's place, she's lovely but 'e's old an' bald, talk abaht a bird in a gilded cage, eh, Charlie?' Maudie turned to her companion. 'Charlie's a footman at 'Er Ladyship's, and me an' 'im's walkin' aht. An' 'ow are yer, Mabel, after all this time? An' that poor little bruvver?'

There was so much to exchange and exclaim over that Charlie suggested they go to one of the new Joseph Lyons cafés; Maudie and Ada readily agreed, though Mabel worried about the cost. Ada reassured her in a whisper that she'd pay for them both and Charlie was obviously treating his sweetheart. Sitting at a table for four over tea and little iced sponge cakes, Mabel felt quite overwhelmed by her surroundings, the smart waitresses carrying trays with china cups and plates; to her the café seemed to be the height of luxury and elegance.

Maudie was telling her of the changes in her life that followed her arrest for thieving. 'Best fing that ever 'appened to me, that was, Mabel!' she said gaily. 'They was damned good to Teddy an' me at the Waifs an' Strays – 'e's still dahn there at Dulwich, ten 'e is now, cheeky little blighter an' all – I goes to see 'im on me afternoons off. 'Er Ladyship always sends 'im cake an' stuff to share out – ooh, Mabel, she's better 'n any queen or duchess!'

Maudie was sorry to hear about Walter's death – 'though I never fought 'e'd survive, to tell yer the trufe, Mabel' – and wanted to be told about the Hallam Road Babies Mission. 'Cor, I bet that suits yer dahn to the grahnd, Mabel – yer was always good wiv kids. Don't pay yer much, do they? I get ten bob a week an' all found, which means we live like lords, don't we, Charlie? Summat diff'rent to the ol' days, eh? Cor!'

'Did yer parents ever come an' see yer in the, er, home, Maudie?' ventured Mabel in a low voice, not wanting to revive painful memories.

'Nah. Gawd only knows what 'appened to 'em. 'E never was no good, an' gave 'er a rotten time, poor fing. It was 'im as drove 'er to drink, 'e did. Reckon they'll bofe be gorn.'

Maudie's face briefly clouded, then cleared as quickly. She had put the past firmly behind her and Mabel could not help but be struck by the change in their fortunes. For a half-starved child of the streets, burdened with a baby brother and reduced to stealing food to stay alive, Maud was now a handsome, confident girl of eighteen living in comfortable servants' quarters, with the advantage of an indulgent mistress and a young man to take her out and treat her. Beside her Mabel felt shabbily dressed and ashamed that she had to rely on a friend to pay for her tea.

As was her constant habit, she glanced at the clock, and Ada noticed. 'Trouble with you, Mabel, yer can't ever let yerself go an' enjoy yerself,' she scolded. 'It's Saturday, an' we're out on the town with friends, so just forget about Sorrel Street for a couple o' hours!'

She was right, thought Mabel, there was no need to rush home, just as she'd met up with her old friend again.

"Ave yer got a young man, Mabel?' asked Maud with a wink. 'Ye're pretty enough for 'alf a dozen!'

Mabel shook her head, though Harry Drover came to her mind as he often did these days. He was probably out with his parents who were full-time Salvationists. She had caught sight of him once, playing in the band at an open-air meeting, and he had returned her smile but could not leave his place, and she had not liked to linger until the meeting ended. He was clearly dedicated to the Salvation Army and she could not imagine him joining them on a tour of the West End's theatreland, which they then undertook with Maudie as guide.

'That's the Gaiety where Mr Edwardes puts on 'is musical shows wiv lots o' pretty girls – all the young toffs are after 'em, mus'n't it be a lark? And over there's 'Is Majesty's, where they crowd in every night to see Mr Tree doin' 'is stuff, all doom an' agony – an' at the Savoy there's them comic operas, Charlie likes 'em, all about pirates singin' their 'eads off. Gi' me the Palace o' Varieties any time!'

The teeming life of London surged around them, a far cry from Sorrel Street and the Babies Mission where she worked so hard for so little. Yet Maudie Ling had known a much harder life as a child and look at her now, parading on her young man's arm, not giving a thought to past suffering and social injustice.

'Right, it's 'alf past six, an' we better be gettin' back to Bryanston Square, Charlie-boy,' said Maud, just as if she were Lady Stanley herself instead of a housemaid. 'It's bin good to see yer, Mabel, we'll 'ave to do it agin – what abaht 'Ampstead 'Eaf one Sunday afternoon?'

But Mabel's attention had been caught by the sight of a laughing couple who were meeting outside the Empire and her heart raced as she watched them. They had clearly arranged the place and the time, for they rushed towards each other and exchanged a very public kiss in the middle of the pavement. The woman was about twenty-five, dressed in blue with a wide feathered hat, and her pretty face looked up into his, laughing and welcoming. He was smart, with dark good looks, a typical man about town, older than the girl; in fact, his age was exactly forty. Mabel knew that, because he was her father, Jack Court. She instinctively turned away so that he would not see her, though it was not likely; he only had eyes for the attractive woman he was meeting for the evening. And probably for the night.

'What's up, Mabel? Seen anybody yer know?' asked Ada.

Mabel shook her head, quite unnerved by the shock she had received. 'It's all right, Ada, I'm just a bit tired, that's all. Time to go home,' she muttered.

But her friend had seen her blinking away tears

and squeezed her hand as they journeyed home on the train. Poor Mabel, she thought, it couldn't be much of a life for her with that houseful at Sorrel Street, an ailing mother and the father away half the time.

Mabel's own thoughts, when she had recovered from the initial blow, were full of disgust and anger on her mother's behalf. How *could* her father go after another woman when his own wife loved and trusted him so faithfully? Poor Mum, what would she give for a night out, a meal and a treat like going to the music hall? And what on earth would she do if she ever found out? Mabel could have wept aloud but, as so often in her life, she had to conceal her feelings for the sake of others.

On reaching home she found her mother, Alice and Daisy chattering eagerly about their afternoon in the park, and how Daddy had bought them chocolate bars and iced lemonade.

'There were lots o' people ridin' on bicycles, Mabel, ladies an' all – and wearin' *trousers*!' cried Daisy. 'They didn't 'alf look funny!'

'Yes, I never thought I'd see women in knickerbockers,' said Annie Court, shaking her head. 'There was one old lady there who was scolding them – you should have heard her, Mabel. "Hussies!" she was saying. "Brazen hussies, no modesty at all – what's the world coming to?"'

'She was just a silly old biddy,' said Alice scornfully. 'Anyway, Dad laughed and said that if fine ladies can ride horses in Rotten Row, why shouldn't girls ride bicycles in Battersea Park? I wouldn't mind having a try on one.'

'Oh, Mabel, it was such a lovely afternoon and we all enjoyed ourselves so much.' Annie sighed with touching appreciation. 'Such a pity that Jack couldn't come back with us, but he's got to be at Goodwood first thing in the morning.'

Mabel's face was blank.

'And he bought us a pound and a half o' cooked ham,' continued Annie, smiling, 'so we'll have it tonight with piccalilli when the boys come in.'

It was a long time since Mabel had seen her mother looking so animated and her indignation burned all the more at the thought of her father's hypocrisy. Annie Court could be happy with so little, while all the time Jack had clearly been scheming to get away up to town and meet his young mistress. Oh, how unfair life was! And the worst of it was that she would have to carry the burden of his secret, almost like a personal shame. On no account must her mother know, and neither must the children. If Albert found out his temper might flare up into a confrontation that could tear the family apart and what would that do to her mother?

And, of course, she must keep her knowledge from her father, too, and smile and talk as if nothing were the matter. She shivered involuntarily. It was not in her nature to deceive.

Alice answered the knock on the door later that evening and came back with a significant look at her elder sister. 'Mr Drover for yer, Mabel – in his bandsman's outfit.'

Mabel's heart gave a thump as she rose and went to the door. Sure enough, there was Harry Drover in a high-buttoned navy tunic and a round cap bearing the Salvation Army crest over his light-brown hair. He was carrying a case of some sort under his arm. They stared, then both spoke together.

'Oh, hello, er, Mr Drover, did you want to see Alb—'

'Good evening, er, Miss Court, I just wondered if yer—'

They both stopped speaking and waited for the other to continue.

'Er, I'm sorry, Miss Court,' he apologised, 'only I'm on me way to the Citadel for a meetin' tonight – the one on the corner o' Clapham Park Road – and, er, I just wondered if ye'd like to come along.'

Mabel was cross with herself for feeling flustered, but her pleasure showed in her eyes. 'Oh – yes, that'd be very nice, Mr Drover, but I'll have to ask me mother first. Could yer just step inside for a minute?'

He entered the narrow hallway, and she asked him to follow her into the living room where Annie sat with the four brothers and sisters; they had just finished their supper of ham and piccalilli.

'Mr Drover's askin' if I'd like to go to a Salvation Army service, Mum,' she said, praying that Albert would keep his mouth shut.

Annie looked up without smiling. 'You've already been up to the West End today, Mabel. I don't think you should go out again.' The truth was that she did not like the idea of her daughter going out with a young man.

'My father an' mother'll be there, Mrs Court, an' I'll make sure Mabel gets home by ten – or earlier if yer want,' pleaded Harry.

Annie's mouth tightened. 'I'm sorry, Mr Drover, but my daughter's only sixteen and I don't think she should be gallivanting around of a night-time.'

Mabel gazed from her to the young bandsman in

dismay, not knowing what to say next, when suddenly Albert spoke up. 'Cor, stone the crows, muvver, it's only a bleedin' Salvation Army do! 'Ol 'Arry won't get up to nothin'! Let the poor gal go, for Gawd's sake!'

Mabel could have hugged him and even forgave Alice for giggling at Harry's painful embarrassment.

Annie had no choice but to be reasonable. 'Very well, then, only mind you're home by ten sharp. I'll be waiting up for you, Mabel.'

'Oh, *thanks*, Mum, I'll just go an' get me jacket.'

Within minutes she was walking side by side with Harry up towards Clapham. It was the first time she had ever walked out with a young man other than Albert. He did not take her arm or make any attempt to touch her and their talk centred on their families, mainly his.

He was nineteen and not very happy in his job on the railways, though not yet old enough to train as a Salvation Army officer. He lived with his parents at 8 Falcon Terrace; they were both Salvationists, as were his sister Ruby and her husband Herbert Swayne. 'He'll be there tonight, I dare say, but Ruby has to stay with the children,' he told her, adding that his nephews' names were Matthew and Mark. Perhaps Mabel would like to meet them one day, he suggested, having heard of her fondness for children.

At the Citadel Mabel sat at the end of a packed row while Harry took his place with the band. The hymns were sung with gusto and the prayers led with uninhibited sincerity, some of them by Major Drover, an upright middle-aged man with a strong London accent. One or two people went forward to kneel at the 'mercy seat' where hands were laid on their heads and prayers said over them. Mabel found the atmosphere rather overwhelming, compared with St Philip's in Queen's Road where she worshipped every Sunday with her mother, and she knew that some of the shabby, wretched-looking individuals here would hardly be welcomed at St Philip's. Several of the hymns were sung to popular tunes, which she found strange.

At one point near the end of the meeting Harry took her over to introduce her to his parents. His mother at once asked how old she was. 'Ye're very young, dear,' she said. 'Have yer been born again?'

'Er, I've been christened and confirmed in the Church of England,' said Mabel hopefully.

The Major nodded. 'That's good, but do yer know the Lord Jesus Christ as yer personal Saviour and Friend?' he asked.

Mabel floundered a little. 'I believe in the Bible an' prayer book,' she replied, somehow feeling that it was disrespectful to talk about Jesus in such familiar terms.

The couple looked at each other and nodded as if to acknowledge that this was a start, and said they would pray for her.

Harry intervened at this point and said they must leave now if she was to be home by ten, and as they hurried along in the late summer dusk he tentatively took her arm. 'It's been a wonderful evenin', Miss Court,' he said seriously and she nodded, conscious of his light touch upon her arm; and when he asked if he might call her Mabel, she smiled and said she'd like that. 'And will yer call me Harry?'

Of course she would, and thus began their long courtship; for Harry Drover had fallen in love at first sight.

That night, tired as she was, she lay awake beside

Alice for some time. It had been a very long day and she had run the gamut of emotions from fury against her father to a kind of tremulous joy in Harry's company. A thought suddenly struck her. What on earth would Harry Drover – not to mention his parents – say if they knew about her father's wicked behaviour? Would a Salvation Army man want anything to do with a girl from such a family? The thought hung like a shadow over her happiness.

Mabel sat drinking tea with Miss Carter beside the stove-pipe on a chilly autumn afternoon. The children were resting on fold-up canvas beds, two or three to each one with a blanket wrapped around them, after their midday repast, augmented with titbits from Miss Carter's own kitchen. There were no cooking facilities at the Mission, only two kettles, a small one for making tea and a large one for heating water for washing. Some of the children had to be bathed and changed into clean smocks on arrival, and Mabel's heart ached at the sight of the undernourished little bodies, sore bottoms, the usual signs of dirt and neglect. Washed napkins and threadbare clothes were hung over the fireguard to air during the rest hour; and Ada was reading her secret copy of Elinor Glyn's *Three Weeks*.

Miss Carter suddenly spoke to Mabel in a low voice so as not to disturb the little sleepers. 'You've got a natural love of children, Mabel, and a real flair for working with them,' she said. 'Have you ever thought of becoming a children's nurse?'

Mabel looked up at her open-mouthed. 'Oh, it's what I want to do more than anything else in the world, Miss Carter! Dr Knowles said—' She checked herself and lowered her eyes.

Miss Carter smiled, thinking again what a very nice girl Mabel was. 'The Children's Hospital at Shadwell where I trained would be an ideal place for you, only you'd need to do your general training first.'

'But hospitals charge for trainin', don't they, Matron?'

'Yes, the big voluntary hospitals take "lady probationers" who pay for their training and so do the children's hospitals,' agreed Miss Carter. 'But the Poor Law infirmaries give training for nothing and you'd stand a good chance of getting a place in one of them.'

'But aren't they workhouses?' asked Mabel doubtfully, remembering the horrific stories she'd heard of such places.

'No, some of them used to be – like the Stepney and Poplar or the Whitechapel – but now they've been taken over by the LCC, with proper medical superintendents and matrons. The patients tend to be underprivileged, the old and the chronic sick, but you'd get just as good a training – and if in a year or two you decide to apply, I'd certainly recommend you.'

Mabel was silent for a minute or two. Matron's words struck a chord in her heart, that dream of looking after children in need of love and care. With her sketchy education and Sorrel Street background, she knew that she could not aspire to one of the big training hospitals, but Matron's tactful mention of the Poor Law infirmaries had started a new train of thought.

But there were stumbling blocks in the way. 'I'd love to be a children's nurse one day, Matron, but it'd mean leavin' home, y'see.'

'And why couldn't you, Mabel? Both your parents are living, aren't they, and you have a sister in her last year at school. I fail to see why you should still be so tied to your home.'

'My mother isn't very well, Matron, she suffers with her nerves and her blood's very thin,' Mabel replied seriously. 'My father's away a lot and my sister Alice isn't as close to our mother as I am. Mum depends on me, ever since I can remember.'

'Has she any other family near enough to help out?' asked Miss Carter.

'No, her father an' mother both died, that's why she married an' came to live in London,' said Mabel, innocently repeating the scrappy information she had been told. 'There's my father's mother in Tooting, she's a private nurse and midwife – only she and my mother don't really get on, so we don't see that much o' her.'

'Well, perhaps one day *she'll* be able to help you to train as a nurse, as it's her profession.' Miss Carter smiled, though Mabel simply gave a slight shrug. 'Anyway, you're only sixteen and perhaps things will have changed in another two or three years. I hope so for your sake, Mabel, you have exactly the right qualities needed for a good children's nurse.'

This was encouragement indeed and Mabel felt again the call deep down in her heart. She wondered if it was like the call to full-time service in the Salvation Army, such as Harry had.

Ah, Harry Drover. He had taken her to more meetings at the Citadel, and told her how he heard the Lord's voice calling him away from the railway depot and into the ranks of God's Army. At present he was not quite old enough for training college, but there was little doubt where his future lay.

On her part, Mabel was not sure that she was destined to be a Salvation Army wife. Harry knew that her father was quite a heavy drinker who made his living by taking bets on horses, and that her mother was in poor health and needed her at home. But of course they were both still very young...

Nevertheless, Mabel knew that her heart beat faster whenever Harry appeared at Sorrel Street, which he seemed to do more and more often these days.

Chapter Four

When Mabel answered the timid knock at the front door she found Miss Lawton standing on the step, dressed in her usual black and looking flustered.

'Miss Lawton, what a nice surprise! Mother'll be so pleased to see yer. Come in.'

'Please excuse me, Mabel, I ... I have a letter for Mrs Court – I mean for your mother,' faltered the lady, clasping her gloved hands together nervously.

The piano lessons had ceased after Mabel left school and Alice had stopped after less than a year, having no ear for music. Daisy had half-heartedly begun, but had giggled over poor Miss Lawton's little mannerisms that Albert mimicked and Mabel had rebuked them both.

'Mother! Miss Lawton's here to see yer.'

Annie half rose from her chair beside the fire where she had been dozing over a book. Mabel led the visitor into the living room and then went to the kitchen to put the kettle on.

'Oh, please don't go to any trouble for me. It's just that I thought I'd better bring it over, this letter I mean, Mrs Court,' gabbled the visitor. 'It's been on the mantelpiece for several days, and as Mrs, er, Court has been very busy and ... and away from the house quite a lot lately, I was afraid it might get mislaid.' She opened her black handbag and took out an envelope. Annie stared in surprise as it was handed to her. 'It's addressed to Mrs Anna-Maria

Court, you see, so I thought I'd better bring it over to you. I hope I did right – oh, dear!'

For Annie's face had paled and she closed her eyes momentarily, sinking back into her chair. She made no attempt to take the envelope, which disconcerted Miss Lawton who after a moment's hesitation took it out to Mabel in the kitchen. 'This ... this came for your mother some days ago, Mabel. I hope I did right to bring it – I could see that it was addressed to her and not, er—' She gestured helplessly and Mabel took the letter from her, turning it over. The handwriting was unfamiliar and she felt a sudden shock, though without knowing why. Her mother's name, Anna-Maria, was seldom used except when Jack called her by it, usually in a jocular way. But who was this?

'She doesn't seem to want ... she won't accept it, Mabel, and I don't wish to upset her. Perhaps you can, er—'

'Thank yer, Miss Lawton, ye're most thoughtful,' said Mabel. 'Would yer be good enough to go and sit with her for a minute or two? I won't be long.'

When she returned to the living room with a tray of tea and biscuits, and the letter beside the teapot, Annie appeared to have changed her mind, for she held out her hand for it. 'Give it to me, Mabel, it's mine. Thank you, Miss Lawton. Now let me offer you some tea.' She pocketed the letter and did her duties as hostess, pouring out cups for the three of them while Mabel handed the biscuits and enquired about life at 23 Macaulay Road. Conversation with poor Miss Lawton had always been uphill work; she fluttered her hands and dropped her teaspoon, apologising profusely while she bunched her table napkin into a ball. She asked about the Babies Mission, but

102

before Mabel could reply said that she must be getting back to Tooting, leaving her cup half full and a biscuit half eaten.

'Poor thing, she's a bundle of nerves, isn't she?' remarked Mabel after seeing her out. 'It's as if she's afraid of becoming too friendly with us – or anybody.' Picking up the tea tray she nodded to her mother. 'You just sit there by the fire, Mum, and don't worry about a thing.' By which she meant that Annie could read her letter alone and undisturbed.

But Annie made no comment about it; that evening, as they all sat round the table, she was silent and preoccupied, and Mabel thought she saw a secret sadness in the tired blue eyes. Was it possible that the letter was from the sisters she never spoke of? Mabel longed to know, but dared not risk distressing her mother.

It was not until two days later, when mother and daughter were in the kitchen stirring the Christmas pudding mixture, that Annie offered a brief explanation of the letter. 'It was from an older sister of mine, Nell – she was the middle one,' she told Mabel who looked up quickly, eager to hear more. 'It seems she's been married for ten years and hasn't had any children – so she took it into her head to ask about mine, though she's never shown any interest before.' She spoke in a dull, unemotional tone, adding, 'She even said that we might meet again.'

'Why, Mum, that's wonderful!' Mabel exclaimed. 'Your sister – my aunt – oh, how I'd *love* to have a real live aunt! And didn't yer say there was another sister? Does she – do they – still live down in Hampshire in that fine big house?'

But Annie's face was white and unsmiling. 'It's been too long, Mabel. Neither Kate nor Nell wanted to have anything more to do with me when I married your father. Everything in my life changed then, for ever. There's no going back. I don't want to rake up the past. Not now.'

'But Mum, she's *written* to yer, she wants to see yer!' cried Mabel. 'She wants to meet *us*, yer children – it doesn't matter how long ago it was, she's yer *sister*, with no children of her own, poor thing. Shouldn't we always be ready to forgive others, as we say every Sunday in church? Oh, Mum, it's nearly Christmas, the season o' goodwill, peace on earth – it's *never* too late to forgive an' be friends again.'

But Annie shook her head and set her mouth in a hard, straight line. 'No, Mabel, I've been dead to them all this time and I can't go back now, it's too late. Seventeen years too late.'

Mabel was unable to hide her disappointment. 'But it's yer *duty* to answer her letter, Mum.'

Annie turned on her with untypical vehemence. '*No!* I couldn't bear it and you've no right to ask me to, Mabel – you don't understand. They threw me out o' the family and I couldn't bear for Nell to see what I've come to now – I simply couldn't *bear* it!' And she covered her face with her hands and sobbed aloud.

Mabel was at once filled with remorse. 'Oh, Mum, I'm sorry – all right, all right, I won't say another word, only don't cry, please,' she said, enfolding her mother in her arms. 'I'm sorry, Mum, I'm sorry.' For in Annie's distress Mabel caught a glimpse of a deep and bitter hurt that had burdened her mother for a very long time: for the whole of Mabel's life.

So the matter was not mentioned again, though Mabel privately wondered about that unknown aunt who had no children of her own. It seemed such a pity if she was destined to have no nieces or nephews either.

The last weeks of 1910 sped by, bringing Christmas round again with all its excitement and nostalgia, the yearly expectations and inevitable anticlimaxes. Annie shivered as the days dwindled and dusk fell soon after three in the afternoon, but Mabel loved the glowing shopfronts and the crowds around the costermongers' stalls in Northcote Road, where she searched for Christmas bargains. On 5 December the whole family went to see the reopening of the Arding & Hobbs department store in St John's Road, gutted by a disastrous fire in the previous December but now by a stupendous effort rebuilt and ready to rise phoenix-like from the ashes in time for Christmas shopping. Much as Mabel enjoyed looking in its windows, the prices were mostly too high for her, though she bought one present there: a glass necklace for Daisy that cost a whole shilling, an extravagance that would have horrified her mother. Her main purchasing was done at places like David Thomas's in Falcon Road, who had a range of dolls and toys, haberdashery and all kinds of bits and pieces at affordable prices; and there was the parade of popular shops in Battersea Rise, which supplied something for everybody.

Hand in hand Mabel and Daisy went out to spend precious pennies on sheets of coloured paper to wrap presents and also to cut up into strips to make paper chains – or fold into 'pokes' to fill with boiled sweets. At 12 Sorrel Street there was a lot of whispering and secret wrapping and tying-up of oddly shaped packets that had to be hidden away from prying eyes.

Daisy's face lit up when Mabel quietly showed her the sock she had knitted for a certain young gentleman. 'Ooh, aren't yer clever, Mabel! Is it for Albert? Are yer goin' to make another?'

''Course I am, only goodness knows when I'll find the time – only eleven more days to go! An' remember that's a secret, Daisy – don't go telling Albert or anybody, will yer?'

When Jack came home with a Christmas tree to put in the front window, Mabel and Daisy happily set about decorating it with paper chains and George mysteriously produced a little fairy doll to stand on the top of it. Mabel promised to light candles on each side of the tree on Christmas Eve and draw back the curtains so that passers-by could admire it.

'I always like it when Christmas Day falls on a Sunday,' said Annie with a wistful smile. 'Wouldn't it be nice to go to St Philip's in the morning, all of us together, just as we used to do?'

Mabel at once agreed. 'Yes, we'll do that, Mum. We'll put the joint in the oven to roast with the potatoes before we go, an' leave the pudding simmerin' on top,' she said. 'Then, when we come back, it'll all be done and we'll only have to put the sprouts on an' make the gravy – oh, an' the apple sauce as well, if we're having pork!' She spoke with childlike eagerness, winking at Daisy as she made these mental preparations days in advance.

'Your father might even be back in time to come to church with us.' Annie's eyes brightened as she spoke, but Mabel made no comment.

After tea on Christmas Eve Mabel put all the presents around the base of the tree, assisted by

Alice, George and Daisy. There was a great deal of speculation as to what each intriguing parcel contained. Some were wrapped in coloured crêpe paper, others in plain brown, tied with lengths of ribbon or string. And all were labelled.

To Mabel, wishing you a happy Christmas, from Mother and Father.

For my little sister Daisy from Alice.

To Gorge many hapy returns Daisy.

And so on. George's December birthday meant that he often had to make do with one gift for both celebrations, but Mabel always gave him two.

Daisy had made cards and calendars at school, and Alice had embroidered handkerchiefs in Standard VI needlework class. There was an envelope from Mimi Court to each of her grandchildren, with a pound note inside; she had sent nothing for Annie, who had flatly refused Mimi's invitation to Christmas dinner at 23 Macaulay Road, and none of them knew what she had given Jack, though he seemed to have plenty of ready cash to spend.

'This one's for me, and it's big and soft – d'ye think it could be a pair o' gloves?' asked Alice.

'An' this one's for you, George, and it rattles – listen!' said Daisy excitedly.

'Bet it's a jigsaw!'

'These little boxes are ever so small,' remarked Daisy, shaking each one in turn. 'It sounds as if there's beads inside.'

'Now, no more feeling an' shaking, miss!' Mabel laughed. 'It's time to light the candles.'

'Well, don't go burnin' the blinkin' 'ouse down,'

warned Albert, coming in from the back at that moment. 'An' ye'd better save the paper orf them presents to put out in Biarritz, 'cos there ain't none left out there.'

'Oh, Albert, use what brain ye've got – there's more cut up ready in the cupboard under the sink.' Mabel rolled up her eyes at the uselessness of males, though she smiled at her swarthy brother who was so like his father in looks and so different in character. He had called the outside lavatory Biarritz ever since he'd heard that the late King Edward VII liked to go on holiday there and the name had stuck.

George grinned. 'In days of old, when knights was bold, before paper was invented,' he began.

But Mabel cut him short. 'We don't want any o' Albert's vulgar rhymes in front o' Daisy, thank yer, George.'

But naughty Daisy giggled as she completed the doggerel. 'Folks wiped their *arm* on a tuft o' *grarm*, an' walked away contented!'

Albert exploded with laughter and it took Mabel all her time to keep a straight face as she reprimanded them. 'Don't yer ever dare to come out with that in front o' visitors,' she warned. 'There'll be real trouble if yer do.'

'Why, was yer expectin' 'Arry to call an' wish us 'appy Chris'muss?' asked Albert innocently.

Mabel disdained to reply, though she had in fact been wondering all day if Harry Drover would call. His socks were finished and wrapped ready for him in the chest of drawers in the room she shared with Alice and Daisy, but of course she would not produce her gift unless he had one for her, otherwise it would be too embarrassing for words.

The candles were duly lit, the curtains pulled back

and the gaslight turned off. The little tree and Daisy's bright face glowed out for all to see, and smiling faces could be seen passing by in the soft light that streamed from the window.

Out of the dark street a familiar face looked in: a face that brought Mabel eagerly hurrying to open the front door. And there he was, looking up at her as if at a vision. 'Harry! I thought ye'd be out with the Army tonight.'

'No, I'm on me way home from work, Mabel. Father's helpin' at the Blackfriars Shelter, an' I'm goin' there tomorrow night, but, er, we're havin' an hour with the band in the mornin', in the park, playin' carols. Will yer like to join us, Mabel?'

'Oh, yes, Harry, I would,' she said, unable to deny it. 'Only – what time will that be?'

'I could call here for yer about half past ten and we'd join the band for eleven.'

Mabel's face fell. She was committed to going to church with her mother and the others, but oh, she *couldn't* turn down an invitation to spend an hour with Harry on Christmas morning!

Alice stood behind her and had heard what was said. She knew how disappointed Mabel would be to have to refuse this nice young man whom they all liked. 'You go with Harry, Mabel, and I'll take Mum and the kids to St Philip's,' she now offered with a thoughtfulness unusual in her.

Mabel was touched and grateful, though she hesitated. 'That's good o' yer, Alice, but I did promise Mum I'd go to church—'

'But the Salvation Army's the same thing, isn't it? Oh, go on, Mabel!' urged Alice while Harry stood waiting with bated breath.

Mabel succumbed. 'Thank yer, Harry, that'd be lovely. An' thanks, Alice, it's good o' yer.'

Harry beamed. 'Yes, thank yer, Alice. Oh, and Mabel, I got a little present for yer.' He put his hand in his pocket and drew out a small box.

So he *had* brought her a present!

'Just a minute, I got one for you as well.' And off she flew upstairs to fetch the pair of socks she had knitted and wrapped in red paper.

Daisy came running to the door, followed by George. 'Ooh, i'n't it cold out here? D'ye think the pond in the park'll be froze over tomorrow, so's we can skate?' Daisy jumped up and down as she spoke, while George, who had become interested in astronomy, looked up at the twinkling stars and offered to show Harry the Plough.

Mabel returned with her gift, flushed and self-conscious. 'I made 'em meself,' she said shyly. 'I hope they fit all right.'

'Oh, Mabel.' Words failed him as he turned the wrapped packet over in his hands and gazed up with frankly adoring eyes at the most beautiful girl in the world. Dumbly he handed over his own gift.

'Shut that door!' cried Annie sharply from inside the house. 'You're letting in all the cold air.'

So regretfully Mabel had to close the door on her young man and brace herself to tell her mother of the change of plan.

Annie was so disappointed that Mabel felt she had been very selfish, but could not deny herself the joy of going to the park with Harry. In the end it was arranged that Annie and Mabel would attend the Holy Communion service at eight o'clock, then Annie would stay at home to cook the dinner while Alice took George and Daisy to church. Albert would be working until one and Jack said he was visiting his mother overnight but would join them for dinner.

Mabel always blamed herself for what happened.

Christmas morning was cold and frosty, and Daisy was awake when Annie and Mabel slipped out to the early service, having first lit the fire in the range oven.

'Go back to bed, dear, and we'll have breakfast together when Mummy and I get back,' Mabel told the excited little girl. Albert had already left for work on the early shift.

'Merry Christmas, Mummy! Merry Christmas, Mabel!' Daisy's shouts greeted them on their return. 'Can I make toast in front o' the range?' she begged, wielding the three-pronged fork.

Annie was still shivering after the coldness of the church, and she and Mabel kept their coats on until the kitchen had warmed, by which time Alice and George had joined them for breakfast.

Daisy was clamouring to open some presents.

'We're not supposed to have them until after dinner,' Mabel told her. 'But all right, then, just one each.'

Mabel had already opened her gift from Harry and drew in a breath of sheer surprise when she saw the little silver cross on a chain. She had kissed it and held it to her heart. And to think she had only given him a pair of socks! How she wished that she had bought the book she'd seen, a collection of spiritual addresses to young men, published by the London Tract Society.

Daisy picked out a present for each of them from the pile around the tree and watched eagerly as each one was opened. Alice was delighted with the woolly hat, scarf and gloves she got from her parents, and so was George with his book from Mabel, *The Night Sky Illustrated*. Annie had a cameo brooch from Mabel and Daisy got a set of dainty handkerchiefs from Alice with a 'D' embroidered in the corner of each. Mabel could not resist opening her present from Albert and gave a cry of delight at finding a bottle of eau-de-Cologne. She passed it round for all of them to have a sniff and dabbed a little behind her ears to smell nice for Harry. Reproaching herself for opening it while Albert was at work, she rewrapped it so as to be surprised all over again when he came home. Daisy promised not to say anything if she could open just one more present and was allowed to unwrap the glass necklace that Mabel had chosen for her. The beads sparkled with the colours of the rainbow and Daisy's delight was more than enough reward for the shilling it had cost her sister.

'No more now,' said Mabel firmly, getting up to clear the table. 'Mummy and I must get the dinner ready and *you* must all get ready for church – come on, Alice, get moving!'

As she prepared the vegetables she smiled to herself in delicious anticipation of Harry's knock at the door, and could hardly wait to thank him for his present and hear what he thought about hers. By the time he called the leg of pork was in the oven, and Alice was ready to leave with George and Daisy.

'Oh, Mabel, those beautiful socks,' murmured Harry in a low voice. 'I'll always treasure 'em because *you* made 'em for me.' He had slept with them under his pillow and clearly had no intention of doing anything so gross as putting them on his feet.

For answer Mabel pointed to the cross and chain she was wearing, and they briefly clasped hands in wordless joy.

But no sooner were the children out of doors in their mufflers and mittens than they begged to go to the park instead of church. Alice wanted to show off her new tam-o'-shanter and scarf, and so they trailed along close behind the young couple, eagerly chattering about the dinner they would have and the games they would play afterwards. Once at the park they all dispersed, and Harry had to go to take up his place in the band. There were a fair number of people strolling around and some came to join in the singing of 'O Come All Ye Faithful' and 'Christians Awake'.

Soon after midday Mabel rounded them all up. 'Come on, everybody, we'll be late for dinner,' she said, becoming uneasy at the thought of her mother finding out that the children had not been to church as arranged.

Harry walked back with them to Sorrel Street, happy just to be at Mabel's side.

As soon as Mabel walked through the front door she knew there was something wrong. Very wrong. A smell of roast pork filled the house; she ran straight to the kitchen.

No saucepans on the range. No pudding simmering.

Annie lay stretched out on the floor, her eyes closed, her mouth open.

'Oh, my God.' Mabel knelt down beside her mother, smelt her breath. Saw the empty jam jar and quickly pushed it behind the bread bin, out of sight. Oh, no, not today of all days. 'George, get Daisy out o' the way, take her out again. Alice, give me a hand to get Mum up on her feet. Wake up, Mum, come on, get yerself up off the floor, for pity's sake.'

Her voice was unusually sharp as she pulled Annie up into a sitting position while Alice stared in horror. 'Harry's still at the door, Mabel,' she said. 'He's asking if there's anything he can do.'

'*No!*' Mabel almost shouted. 'No, no, tell him to go, Alice, get rid o' him – send him away, for God's sake, and then come and help me.'

Annie gave a groan. 'Sorry, Mabel – sorry, Alice, please, I'm sorry, little girls,' she muttered thickly.

'Thank heaven, she's coming round,' panted Mabel. 'Come on, let's get her on her feet and sit her at the table.'

Somehow the two girls managed to heave Annie up on to a chair, where she sat with drooping head. 'Sorry, little girls, sorry, little girls,' she repeated stupidly, though with an underlying anguish that cut Mabel to the heart.

'Is it serious? Ought I to go for the doctor?' faltered Alice.

'No, no, make a pot o' tea for her, and make it strong,' Mabel ordered. 'I'll get the sprouts on, but there's no time to boil the pudding. Oh, Mum, I shouldn't've left yer to do it all on yer own!'

'She's not ill, she's *drunk*, isn't she?' gasped Alice.

'Hush, Alice, she didn't mean to be,' muttered Mabel with a note of pleading. 'Come on, talk to her, help her, this is my fault, not hers – let's hope Dad'll be late.'

But he wasn't, not on that occasion. He arrived a few minutes afterwards, shortly before Albert and unsteady on his feet, having taken on board enough brandy to put him in a good humour for dinner with his family on Christmas Day. Until he saw his wife slumped in a chair with her head on the table between her knife and fork. Her face was flushed and her hair dishevelled, and she was moaning something about being sorry. Jack swayed slightly as he surveyed the scene. 'What the devil's goin' on 'ere? Christ! This is a fine sight f'r a man to come 'ome to!'

'She fainted, Dad, and it's all my fault,' pleaded Mabel. 'I left her all on her own to do the dinner, an' we came in an' found her – give me half an hour an' I'll have dinner on the table an' we can all sit down to eat it,' she gabbled, breathless in her agitation.

But Jack had decided that he was hard done by. 'Christ Almighty!' He brought his fist down on the table with a force that set the knives and forks dancing, and caused Annie to lift her head painfully.

She turned unfocused eyes on Jack. 'Sorry, Jack. Sorry, Mabel, sorry little—'

'Shut up!' Jack roared at her. 'Shut up, yer silly, stupid woman! I work me bloody balls off to keep this lot goin', an' what do I find when—' He lurched towards her.

In an instant Mabel lunged forward, throwing herself between them. 'Don't yer touch 'er! Don't yer *dare*!' she cried, lifting her hands to fend off any blow that might be about to descend.

The next thing that she and Alice knew was that Albert charged in like an enraged bull, still in his dirty working clothes, and grabbed his father by his coat collar. 'Bastard.' The single word was accompanied by a punch between Jack's eyes that sent him reeling across the table. He pulled on the cloth as he fell to the floor in a clatter of cutlery and Annie was dragged sideways as the cloth slid from under her head.

In the hallway Daisy screamed in terror and George tried to drag her outside. Alice burst into tears.

'Stop it – stop it *at once*,' ordered Mabel. 'Don't yer dare fight in front o' the children, I won't have it, d'ye hear?'

'I was only stoppin' 'im from lammin' into you an' Mum, Mabel,' Albert protested, but she rounded on him and told him to help her get their mother upstairs. 'An' stop blubberin', Alice, and make yerself useful. Get the dustpan and brush and a cloth, and start clearin' up this mess.' The authority in her voice reassured them that their world had not entirely fallen apart and they obeyed her immediately. Apart from Daisy's sobs there was no more noise or violence.

Jack got himself up and sat on a chair, his nose bleeding and his head reeling, though he mumbled under his breath that he had never once hit his wife or any of his children.

Nobody paid him any attention. Mabel and Albert half dragged, half carried their mother upstairs and laid her on her bed.

'She can sleep it off this afternoon,' said Mabel, 'but you an' me've got to save somethin' o' Christmas for the children, Albert – for George an' little Daisy.'

Breathing heavily from the exertion, the boy muttered, 'Whatever yer say,' adding something less polite under his breath as they went downstairs.

Slices of overdone pork were set out on plates, with potatoes roasted to rock hardness, plus quickly cooked sprouts and freshly made gravy.

'There's fruit in the bowl an' we've got a cake with icing on,' said Mabel. 'I can cut it now if yer like, an'

116

have it for pudding – or we can keep it for teatime. We'll have a proper dinner tomorrow with Christmas pudding, that's a promise.'

To everyone's relief Jack did not join them at the table, but got himself out of the house with tears of self-pity at the treatment he had received. 'Never laid me 'ands on any of 'em in me life – an' me own son raises 'is 'and against me.' Only after his departure did Albert sit down at the table with his brother and sisters.

After the meal Mabel told Albert and Alice to clear away and wash up while she played ludo and snakes and ladders with George and Daisy, though she had to blink away tears at intervals. She kept thinking of her mother sleeping upstairs in the cold, darkening room and the impact of Albert's fist in his father's face. Could that ever be forgotten, let alone forgiven? From the past she heard again Maudie Ling's words as a child, saying that she was glad when Christmas was over, because both her parents got drunk, mother as well as father . . . And she hardly dared think of how poor Harry must be feeling, sent away without a word: she could only hope that he hadn't heard any of the uproar. What a disastrous Christmas, after all their happy expectations . . .

But as always, she had to hide her own wretchedness and put on a brave face for the others. 'Ooh, look, Daisy, yer counter's home – ye've won again!' she exclaimed, forcing herself to smile. 'Let's have a nice cup o' tea – and then we've got more presents to open, haven't we?'

Daisy looked up at her with mournful eyes. 'Yes, but Mummy's ill, an' Daddy's not here, an' it's not like Christmas any more,' she said tremulously.

Mabel enfolded her in a warm hug. 'Oh, Daisy, my

117

little darling, Mummy'll be better tomorrow, an' Daddy'll be back again soon – sooner or later – and ye've got Albert an' George an' Alice an' me, haven't yer?' And she clasped her little sister tightly against her, while smiling at the others over Daisy's dark head, willing them to respond. Albert and George exchanged a look and did their best; only Alice's face remained hard and unforgiving.

Harry Drover, helping to serve soup and bread to the remnants of humanity at the Salvation Army homeless shelter, also had to force a smile to hide a heavy heart. The Christmas message of peace and goodwill sounded hollow in the grim reality of a fallen world. All his thoughts were with Mabel Court who had not wanted his help. *Get rid o' him, Alice, send him away, for God's sake.* That was what she said. He had heard her with his own ears: wounding words from the girl he had loved at first sight.

Yet that same love gave Harry an insight that another young admirer might not have had. He knew from Mabel's softly shining eyes that she cared for him and had knitted him the socks that he kept under his pillow after kneeling beside the bed to pray for the sweet girl whose nimble fingers had fashioned them, just for him. If she had wanted him out of the way, he reasoned that it must have been because of something she did not want him to see: perhaps something she was ashamed for him to know about. Was it her father? Not on this occasion, because he had seen Jack Court coming home, somewhat mellowed by drink but not in a belligerent mood. Mabel! She would always be the best and dearest of girls in his eyes, whatever trouble her family was in. Harry's heart ached at the thought of her being unhappy and he vowed that he would wait patiently, not intruding if she did not wish to share her secret burden with him. At nineteen, Harry Drover had had little experience of the opposite sex, but he loved Mabel Court with all his heart. For her he would do anything – and his dearest wish was that one day she would be his wife.

Chapter Five

Sitting on the side of the bed she shared with Alice, Mabel carefully pinned up her newly washed hair, squinting into a small, spotted mirror propped up on the top of the chest of drawers. When all her hair was up she placed the wide, navy-blue hat on her head and surveyed the effect. Ada Clay had given it to her almost new, saying that dark colours didn't suit her complexion, and Mabel had sewn a few pink silk roses to the crown; she now wished they were white, to match the high-necked, pin-tucked blouse she wore with a navy skirt.

'Ooh, yer don't 'alf look nice, Mabel,' remarked Daisy admiringly, kneeling on her own small bed and watching as her sister dressed to go out.

Mabel removed the hat and tugged at her pinned-up hair so that it puffed out more around her head; a few loose tendrils curled prettily at the nape of her neck. On went the hat again. 'That's better,' she said and proceeded to secure it with a long pin through the back. Daisy was right, she *did* look nice! And of course Harry would think so, too, he always did.

'I wish *I* was going up to London,' sighed Daisy, turning round and clasping her knees.

'I'll take yer one day soon, dear,' promised Mabel. 'Only today Harry and I are meeting my friend Maudie and her young man, and Ada Clay and Arthur Hodges – he's *her* young man.'

'An' Harry's *your* young man!' Daisy smiled,

bringing a blushing acknowledgement to Mabel's cheek.

For it was true. At this very moment Harry would be getting himself ready to go out, just as she was, at his home in Falcon Terrace. How wonderful it would be to walk out and meet her friends with Harry at her side, taking in the sights of London on a fine spring day! This was a treat planned by Maud and Ada for her seventeenth birthday two days ago; a date marked not only by her family and friends but touchingly at the Babies Mission, where Miss Carter had produced an iced cake and made a little speech.

'You've been a constantly reliable assistant ever since we began our work here, Mabel, nearly three years ago,' she said. 'I don't know how I'd have managed without you. And what's most important of all, the children love you because they know that you really care about them. One day I'm sure you'll be a first-rate children's nurse, so don't let anything stand in your way!'

Mabel had glowed with pride and resolved that she would live up to Matron's expectations of her. Afterwards Ada had told her of the treat planned for Saturday – today, the first of April. They were to meet Maudie Ling in Piccadilly Circus at two o'clock and all three girls would bring their sweethearts; in Mabel's case that meant a shy invitation to Harry Drover, which he had immediately accepted.

And there would be no need to worry about her mother. The shameful fiasco of Christmas had proved to be a turning point for Annie, who vowed that nothing like it would ever happen again. The treacherous consolation of the screw-topped jar was completely given up, and although an occasional tension showed in her eyes and the set of her jaw, she had kept faithfully to her resolve, and Mabel breathed freely again. Jack Court, too, seemed to have learned a lesson, and when he was at home played the indulgent husband and father with an easygoing bonhomie that relaxed the atmosphere. Albert continued to glower when his father was around, but the rest of them were willing to pretend that the disaster had never happened.

Mabel had no idea that Harry Drover had heard her frantically telling Alice to send him away from Sorrel Street on Christmas Day, for his manner towards her remained the same, perhaps a little more protective than before, and never asking questions about her parents, to whom he was always friendly and polite for her sake.

'Cor, Mabel, there's a proper toff come to call!' roared Albert from below. 'Better not keep 'im waitin'!'

Mabel rose and hurried downstairs to find Harry dressed in his fairly new brown serge suit and chuckling at Albert's banter. He would always be indebted to the young rapscallion for the sake of his sister, though he worried about the boy's involvement with the militants among the railway workers. Mabel and her mother hoped that Harry would have a restraining effect on their young hothead.

So there was a sparkle in Mabel's grey-blue eyes and a spring in her step when she and her young man set out for the West End. Plans were going ahead for the coronation of the new King George V in June, and London wore an air of expectancy as the couple walked down Shaftesbury Avenue to meet the others by the statue of Eros in Piccadilly Circus. Leaning upon Harry's strong arm, Mabel could gaze up at the huge new Bovril and Schweppes signs without being jostled by the Saturday crowds, and when they crossed from one pavement to another he guided her through the thronging traffic that seemed to be going in all directions. Open-topped horse-buses were giving way to their motor-driven counterparts and the hansom cab to the taxicab, though there was a new competitor, the electric tram with lines running out into the suburbs.

Mabel revelled in his attentiveness, his constant care for her, she who was so used to caring for others; and as for Harry, he thought every man must envy him the lovely girl whose arm rested lightly in the crook of his elbow.

'Over 'ere, Mabel!' called a familiar voice and there was Maudie, waving from the steps where the fountain played below the winged archer. At the same time Ada and her companion emerged from the Underground station, having come up the escalator from the Piccadilly Tube.

The girls greeted each other with hugs and kisses, and Charlie planted an uninvited kiss on Mabel's cheek, which made her blush and caused Harry to give him a very stern look. He did not offer his hand to Charlie, nor did he smile at Arthur who sported a smart suit and a bowler hat as befitted a junior cashier at one of Sir Thomas Lipton's chain of high-class grocery stores.

Mabel remarked on Maudie's eye-catching outfit, a velvet jacket in cherry red over a well-cut skirt in fashionable tartan, with a jaunty green feathered hat.

'Yer like me new get-up, then, Mabel?' Maud grinned, twirling round on the pavement to show a froth of lace petticoat and laughing at Mabel's round eyes. As they walked down Piccadilly, Maud pulled her friend close to her and began a whispered conversation. Harry stayed close to Mabel and Ada followed between the other two young men, chattering gaily.

'Yeah, well, me an' 'Er Ladyship's like *this*, see?' And Maudie linked the first and second fingers of each hand together in a symbolic grip. 'She's made me 'er own personal maid, which don't go dahn too well wiv some o' the toffee-noses above stairs, I can tell yer!' She chuckled. 'Knows I can be trusted to keep me mouf shut, see? Cor, she's a reg'lar little goer, is our Lady Stanley!'

'What about her husband?' asked Mabel, not quite sure what her friend meant and hoping that Harry could not overhear.

'What, that bald ol' coot? Aw, 'e's past 'is prime, 'e is, old enough to be 'er farver. Leaves 'er alone to go to 'is borin' ol' club, so wot's 'e expect 'er to do? Oho! Me lady 'as visitors of 'er own – 'specially one 'oo's right up 'er street, know wot I mean?' She giggled and tapped the side of her nose. 'She knows she can tip me the wink, an' I'll turn a blind eye, see? *And* I gets double money, straight from 'er 'and into mine. Ooh, yes, there's more new clo'es where these came from, Mabel!'

Mabel hardly knew what to say. Of course she was glad that Maudie enjoyed her life as a favoured maid to a generous mistress, but it sounded risky and Mabel hoped that her friend knew what she was doing. This Lady Stanley sounded no better than she should be.

'Now, wot're we goin' to do?' demanded Maud. 'Show oursel's orf in the park? 'Ave a look in Madame Tussaud's? Go to the zoo an' gawp at the lions? C'mon, Mabel, it's yer birfday treat, so wot's it to be, eh?'

Maudie was happily set to spend the extra bounty bestowed by Her Ladyship and Mabel looked to Harry, thinking that he would prefer a leisurely walk in Hyde Park beside the Serpentine, rather than Maudie's list of attractions.

While she hesitated Ada spoke up. 'Shall we go an' see one o' these – what do they call them, Arthur? Cine-ma-to-graphy, where yer can sit an' watch these moving photographs, like at the Electric Picture Palace out at Clapham.'

The idea met with general approval and Harry seemed as interested as Mabel to try the new entertainment. Sitting along a row of seats in a stuffy darkness pungent with the smell of oranges, the six young people gazed at a flickering rectangle of light that magically appeared on the wall before them. It was like a huge black-and-white photograph that moved as in real life: the London streets were reproduced on it, with traffic and pedestrians moving jerkily along. Trains sped silently forward on their tracks and then the scene suddenly changed to a racecourse where horses galloped towards the winning post while excited crowds cheered noiselessly and threw their hats up in the air. A piano played by a young lady tinkled or rumbled, according to what was being shown, and the main feature of the hour-long show was a touchingly sentimental story about a brave dog who finds and saves a lost baby, to the joy of the frantic parents. *Rescued by Rover* brought tears to the eyes of the girls.

'Wasn't it marvellous?' Ada sniffed as they emerged from the darkness into the light of day, to be taken to a tea shop for refreshment and to discuss the wonders of cinema photography.

'What did *you* think of it, Harry?' asked Arthur with a sideways glance at Charlie.

Harry cleared his throat. 'It got me wond'rin' how many thousands o' separate photographs they must've taken,' he said seriously. 'An' if ye're goin' to go to that sort o' trouble, yer might as well film somethin' worthwhile, I mean, like, er—' His voice trailed off as he searched for the right words.

'Like *what*, Harry?' asked Arthur as they waited for him to explain, the two young fellows grinning broadly while Mabel shared her young man's embarrassment.

'Well, like on the railways an' down in the coal mines where men work for starvation wages in fear o' bein' laid off,' Harry managed to reply, reddening with self-consciousness but looking Arthur straight in the eye. 'They could take pictures o' the way their families 'ave to live, an' show 'em to Members o' Parliament an' that. A lot o' them got no idea 'ow the other 'alf lives.'

Mabel put down her teacup and concentrated on every stumbling word forced out of Harry by his convictions. Lacking Albert's forcefulness and restrained by a humility ingrained by a strict Salvationist upbringing, he found himself at a disadvantage in the present company and on the face of it cut a poor figure beside the other two. A fierce protectiveness surged within Mabel and she now spoke up in words learned from Albert. 'That's it, Harry, ye've just about hit the nail on the head!' she cried. 'It was downright wicked to set the troops on them poor Welsh miners last year, an' somebody should've used the cinemato – camera, whatever it's called, to show everybody what was goin' on.' She paused.

Harry gave her a look of heartfelt gratitude and

Maudie picked up the teapot. 'That's right, Mabel, ye'll be givin' out like one o' them suffragettes before yer done. Now, wot abaht annuver cup all round?'

Charlie and Arthur noted the warning glint in her eye, but Ada was not so overawed. 'Aw, come off it, we're out to have a bit o' fun, not listen to speeches!' she protested. 'We get all that sort o' thing in the newspapers, we don't want it on moving pictures as well. Come on, let's go – nothin' like a London street for seein' somethin' goin' on all the time!'

'Depends what part o' London ye're in,' muttered Harry under his breath, but nobody heard him except Mabel who silently squeezed his hand.

Outside on the pavement again, she took his arm and gave him her undivided attention. It was easy for the others to smirk and dismiss him as a killjoy: in her eyes he was worth ten Charlies and twenty Arthurs.

Warmed by her support he felt able to speak more freely to her, hardly aware of the two couples sauntering along behind them. 'Yer see, Mabel, the streets o' London may seem to be full o' the sort o' vain attractions yer friend Ada talks about, but in the Salvation Army we see the dangers – the temptations below the surface,' he said earnestly. 'See them two poor women over there, look, on the other side o' the road, all dressed up in their finery an' lookin' for men who'll pay 'em—' He hesitated and glanced at Mabel's eager face before going on, 'Pay 'em for the use o' their bodies, if ye'll excuse me sayin' so, Mabel. London's full o' them, once fine girls who took a false step an' landed where those two are now, on a path to ruin, poor lost souls.'

Mabel gasped in genuine horror. 'Are yer *sure*, Harry? In broad daylight? I know there are women

127

who walk the streets at night, but not on a Saturday afternoon, surely?'

She looked towards the two women standing on the opposite pavement. One was older and tougher than the other, used to her way of life, with hard eyes and unhealthy skin beneath her painted face. Her companion looked more vulnerable and licked her lips nervously as she put on a smile for a man who passed them by without a second glance.

'Some o' these girls've had babies out o' wedlock, an' lost their jobs – an' this is the only way they can earn enough to support 'emselves an' the child,' Harry continued grimly. 'The child often gets put out to a babyminder who 'as to be paid, an' a lot o' them die from neglect. The Army tries to rescue as many street women as'll come to the way o' salvation, but most o' them are set on a path o' sin an'' – he lowered his voice to add – 'an' some o' them get horrible diseases that can't be cured, an' that kills 'em in the end. My sister Ruby's seen some awful cases at the Salvation Army's women's refuge in Pentonville.'

Mabel was shocked and saddened. 'Oh, Harry, how dreadful – and the poor little babies!' As always, her tender heart went out to the suffering of innocent children.

Harry at once regretted his frankness of speech. 'Oh, Mabel, I'm sorry – sometimes I let me tongue run away with me, I know.'

'Don't mind me, Harry, I'd much rather yer said what yer really think. It's one o' the things I like about yer,' she added shyly, which brought a tender smile to his lips.

As they walked on in silence, Mabel's sharp ears caught a stifled laugh behind them.

'Brother, are yer *saved*?' asked Charlie in doom-laden tones, mocking Harry's solemnity.

'Not yet, brother, I got a couple o' naughty girls to rescue first,' replied Arthur with a high-pitched snigger.

There was a yelp as if he had been dug in the ribs and Ada giggled. Mabel's face flamed with indignation and she turned her head round to glare at the scoffers. A glare that was not lost on Maudie who spoke up sharply. ''Ere, you two, jus' stow it, will yer? The Sally Army knows a bloody sight more o' what goes on in the world than a pair o' silly apes like you!'

The ensuing silence lasted until they reached Hyde Park, though Mabel shot her friend a grateful glance for her loyalty, even to rebuking her own sweetheart.

At the sight of the fresh greenness of the grass and the burgeoning trees glimmering in a mist of tender new foliage, Mabel's spirits lifted as if the early April sunshine had evaporated all else away but the glory of springtime. The three couples now had space to move apart and Harry led her down a verdant slope towards the glittering Serpentine, surely the loveliest lake imaginable, even better than the one in Battersea Park. Little boats bobbed on its surface and families sat or strolled at the water's edge.

'Listen to the birds singing in the trees, Harry!' exclaimed Mabel, enraptured. 'Isn't it all so *beautiful*? Ye'd never know yer were right in the middle o' London, would yer? It's like bein' out in the country. Can we walk across that bridge over the water?'

Harry was more than happy to indulge her every whim and they walked hand in hand through the park until they came to the bridge on which they stood together, watching the swans gliding gracefully beneath. When they passed over into Kensington Gardens he led her to a bench near to the Long Water.

And as they sat side by side, he turned to her and hesitantly put his arm round her shoulders. She caught her breath, thinking that her heart must have missed a beat, and made no attempt to move away; in fact, she sat as still as one of the marble statues they had passed.

'Dearest Mabel.' The soft whisper close to her ear sent a thrill coursing through every part of her body. She literally held her breath while she waited for what he would say next.

'Dearest Mabel, ye're the sweetest girl in all the world.'

Still she could say nothing, though she felt that he must surely hear her heart pounding. Past and future were forgotten in this precious moment, and Mabel wished that time could stand still, so that she could live it over and over again.

She had no words to offer in exchange and fearing that to speak might break the spell anyway, she let herself lean against Harry's best brown serge jacket, enveloped in the circle of his arm, simply sharing with him in the joy of first love, without so much as a kiss, for Harry had not yet kissed a girl and Mabel had never been kissed by a young man. Besides, they were in a public place.

In the days that followed Mabel lived in a dream world. She seemed to float through each day without touching the ground, hugging her secret to herself: she was young, she was in love, and it was springtime. In time to come she would look back on her eighteenth year as the last of her girlhood, but for the happy present there were no shadows of forthcoming events to darken her path. Not an hour of any day went by without Harry coming to her mind: she saw his face smiling in the sunrise over Nine Elms, in the noon-day dazzle on the lake in the park, and in the sunset over the Thames from Battersea Bridge. Never had the world around her appeared so beautiful, so magical, as seen through the eyes of love.

But there must come a time to return to earth and Mabel discovered that the world did not want to know about her happiness. Apart from a little good-natured teasing from friends like Ada and some curiosity on the part of Alice, she got scant response from her family. Her mother was particularly discouraging and frowned when Mabel rhapsodised over Hyde Park and Kensington Gardens in the spring. 'Weren't you supposed to be with Ada Clay and that Ling girl?' she asked suspiciously.

'Yes, there were the three of us – well, the six of us, Mother, I told yer – Charlie, he's Maud's young man, and Ada's been walking out with Arthur Hodges for a while, and yer know Harry.'

'I know that you're only seventeen, Mabel, and I don't like all this gallivanting around the streets with young chaps you hardly know.'

'Mother! How can yer say that? We *all* know Harry Drover, he's Albert's friend and he's called here lots o' times,' protested Mabel indignantly. 'And we weren't *gallivanting*, as yer call it – it was only a quiet stroll beside the lake and we sat on a ... a park bench.'

Poor Mabel stumbled a little over this account of

the brief, innocent idyll, and Annie noticed the hesitation. 'I hope you didn't canoodle in public.'

'That's not fair, Mum, an' yer know it. Of *course* we didn't, Harry's not that sort at all, yer know perfectly well what a good Christian man he is.'

Hurt and bewildered by her mother's lack of sympathy, Mabel had no idea of Annie Court's terror of losing her. So great was her dependence upon her eldest daughter, that she could not bear to think of Mabel growing up, leaving home and getting married. The very thought of it filled her with dread, remembering her own experience when only a year older: to think of Mabel tied to a husband and having babies every year, getting tired, growing old before her time – it was not to be imagined! Yet when Mabel made up her mind not to confide in her mother any more, it brought the inevitable accusation that she was being secretive.

Albert's reaction was also disappointing. All his time was taken up with the industrial unrest among the railway workers, and he became increasingly brusque as the mood on railways and riverside became more mutinous. There were ugly scenes at open-air meetings when union leaders such as Albert's hero Ben Tillett shook a threatening fist in the air and warned of impending disaster if dockers were not granted a minimum of eight pence an hour for a working shift of ten hours. 'It's like 'e says, we all gotta stick togevver,' Albert declared, banging his fist on the table. 'Railmen, dockers, miners, stevedores, a united front o' the workers!'

'All right, no need to knock the dinner flying,' said his sister Alice coldly, while Annie looked anxious and Jack annoyed.

Mabel sympathised with her brother up to a point,

but she preferred Harry's more cautious wait-and-see approach, though Albert was impatient with it and incurred Mabel's wrath by telling Harry not to be an old woman. He now spent more time with Sam Mackintosh and a group of other young firebrands, adding to Annie's apprehension. 'You're far too young to get yourself involved in disputes like this, Albert,' she remonstrated. 'Why can't you leave it to the unions?'

'The unions are too bloody slow,' he replied darkly. 'But jus' you wait, the workers'll 'ave the bosses by the froat 'fore this lot's over – we're gonna show the blighters!'

Annie shuddered. She knew very little about the causes of industrial unrest but enough about her son's hotheadedness to fear for his personal safety in the event of a strike.

It was Miss Carter at the Hallam Road Babies Mission who caused Mabel to consider some aspects of her future and unwittingly pointed to a possible source of conflict ahead. 'The time has come for you to move on from the Mission, Mabel,' she said seriously. 'You need to broaden your experience and I think you should apply to the Anti-Vivisection Hospital as a ward maid. It's not a large place, but Lady Headley takes a personal interest in the standard of nursing care and it's nearer to your home than the Bolingbroke Hospital. How do you feel about that?'

'Oh, Matron, I—' Mabel hesitated, somewhat taken aback at the idea of working in the rather ornate building on Prince of Wales Road, founded by the anti-vivisectionist Elizabeth Headley. At the same time she felt a thrill of excitement. 'D'ye think they'd have me?'

'Of course they would! And I'll recommend you. They'd soon appreciate your worth and I'm sure you'd quickly be promoted to assisting with care of the patients. Two years of experience at Lady Elizabeth's hospital will bring you to nineteen and you'll have a head start when you go to train at a Poor Law infirmary to become a real nurse.' Miss Carter smiled. 'It's your *future* we're looking at, Mabel!'

It was an attractive prospect indeed, and another step on the road to achieving her dream of being a children's nurse. Mabel should have been thrilled and excited, and so she was, but—

But. Something had happened since her last conversation with Miss Carter on this subject. When she looked into the future now, she also saw her young man, Harry Drover. He was in love with her and she with him. Which meant that one day they would be married. And he was talking of becoming a full-time serving officer in the Salvation Army, which meant that she would be expected to become a Salvation Army wife, wearing a uniform with a bonnet and working with street women, as Harry's sister Ruby Swayne did, going into places where only the dedicated Salvation Army brothers and sisters went . . .

So now there were two roads ahead of her – would she have to choose between them? And in any case the only really certain thing in her life at present was her mother's continued need of her at home, not to mention her father's philandering and Albert's dangerous involvement with the militants. Without her support her mother might be tempted to resort to the gin bottle again, which didn't bear thinking about. She simply could not be spared, and felt a need for some understanding friend with whom she could discuss the turmoil in her heart, the conflict between her love for Harry and her long-held conviction that one day she would care for children in need.

It was Harry – dear, honest, open-hearted Harry himself – who proved to be that friend. He called that same evening, looking worried and saying that he had to talk to her. 'Can yer come out for half an hour after supper, Mabel?' he begged and, promising her mother that she would be back by half past nine, she put on her hat and left the house. It was a very warm evening and there were a number of people out taking the air beside the river.

Walking arm in arm along the Albert Embankment he tried to explain his situation to her, following a very forthright discussion he had had with his parents. 'Dearest Mabel, yer must know how I feel about yer,' he began in a low, urgent tone. 'There'll never be another girl for me, I know, and one day I hope—' He broke off and swallowed, clearly agitated by what he felt he had to say.

'Go on, Harry, yer can tell me, whatever it is,' Mabel urged him, bracing herself.

'The fact is, y'see, Mabel, I can't make yer an offer, not yet, not for some time. I got no right to hold yer to a promise, not for three years at least.' And with an earnestness which endeared him to her all the more, he mapped out his circumstances to her. 'I'm twenty this year, Mabel, and I think the Lord's callin' me to full-time service – in fact, I know He is. That'll mean two years' trainin' at Clapton College before I'll have any money o' me own. Me parents say we're both much too young to be thinkin' that far ahead

135

an' it's true ye're only seventeen, though so wise an' sensible – but yer see, Mabel dear, I'm not in a position to make an offer o' marriage, not until I'm twenty-three – that'll be 1914, an' we'll both be that much older an' maybe earnin' enough to start thinkin' o' findin' a little place of our own.' He stopped to draw breath, then went on, 'So I've no right to hold yer to anythin', Mabel.'

The words had poured out in a rush and she realised that he too had been in a state of turmoil. She squeezed his arm to show that she understood.

In actual fact Harry had not told his sweetheart half of what had passed between him and his parents. They had been horrified at the mere suggestion of an engagement to a girl of seventeen whose only connection with the Salvation Army was her attendance at a number of meetings, but no real commitment.

'Ye're much too young to think o' marryin',' his father had said sternly. 'What *you* need, son, is to get down on yer knees an' seek the Lord's will for yer life.'

His mother had been even more direct. 'Yer need to get yer trainin' done at Clapton College first, like yer sister,' she told him. 'Yer need to conquer the worldly side o' yer nature, Harry. No doubt the Lord's got plans for yer to marry in due time, but He'll show yer the right one that *He*'s chosen for yer, as Rebecca was chosen for Isaac.'

In vain had Harry extolled Mabel's virtues, her dutifulness as a daughter, her housewifely arts, her fondness for children.

'That's as may be,' Mrs Drover had said, 'but her father's a gambler an' her brother's a blasphemer, inciting discontent among the young railwaymen.'

Of course, Harry did not repeat anything of this to his dear, sweet Mabel; it was quite bad enough telling her of his lack of prospects.

Had he only known, she experienced a certain relief in knowing that she was under no immediate pressure to make a choice. 'Don't worry about it, Harry,' she told him, looking up into his troubled brown eyes. 'It's the same with me, really, I couldn't possibly leave home while me mother needs me and besides, Matron at the Mission says I should apply as a domestic at the Anti-Viv for a couple o' years. I'll be paid more an' it'll be good experience. So there yer are, Harry, there's no hurry – an' we *are* young yet, aren't we?'

'Dearest Mabel, ye're so sweet an' understandin',' he said gratefully, glad at having got it off his chest and for being so well received. 'If the Lord wants us to be together to share our lot in life, He'll make the way plain for us in His good time. Only I feel I don't deserve yer.'

'Oh, Harry, don't be daft!' Impulsively she put her forefinger firmly on his mouth to stop him saying more. And felt that she had never loved him so much as now.

Following on from this thought, Mabel reflected that as Harry had been perfectly honest with her, it was surely up to her to treat him with equal honestly. Didn't she owe it to him? Up until now she had never seriously confided in him about her dream of becoming a children's nurse, perhaps because she feared he might be less than encouraging; but this had put a new aspect upon their immediate future. With at least three years to spare before marriage was even a possibility, she could look ahead towards her other important goal in life and she should tell him about it. Taking his hand in hers, she drew a deep breath. 'Harry, dear, ye've been frank with me and there's somethin' I ought to talk over with *you*.'

'Anythin' ye want to tell me, Mabel, jus' go ahead – it'll go no further,' he said eagerly, thinking that perhaps she was about to confide something to do with her family, remembering what had happened at Christmas.

'Yer know I love children and I've always wanted to look after 'em, as far back as I can remember,' she began.

'Yes, I've realised that, Mabel. I've heard they think the world o' yer at that Babies Mission.'

'Well, Miss Carter – she's the Matron – she thinks I ought to train to be a nurse and says that I could do general trainin' at a Poor Law infirmary where they don't charge for it.'

Harry looked doubtful. 'They were workhouses not so long ago, Mabel, and the work'd be ever so hard – and ye'd have to live in for three years.'

'But I'd be a trained nurse at the end of it, Harry.'

'Yes – and ye'd be welcomed with open arms in the Salvation Army,' he went on slowly, following a train of thought. 'We need nurses for the homes an' the children's refuges—'

'*Harry*! Yer mean I could join the Army as a nurse an' look after children? Them with nobody to look after 'em an' care for 'em?' She could hardly keep the excitement out of her voice.

He turned to her with a smile that reflected her own. 'Mabel, I've never really mentioned this before, but the reason I've held back from decidin' definitely about trainin' is because I could only marry another Salvation Army officer and I haven't been sure that ye wanted to join. If we was both to devote our lives to God's service, yer could be my wife *and* do yer wonderful work that ye've been called to do.'

'Oh, Harry, that'd be *both* me dreams comin' true!' And even though they were in a public place, she threw her arms round his neck and kissed him. It seemed the answer to all her uncertainties about the future.

But it meant that they would have to wait for a very long time.

Chapter Six

Fears of a city paralysed by strikes seemed to be unfounded when 23 June dawned fine and clear for the coronation of George V and Queen Mary. Tens of thousands of loyal subjects waited outside Westminster Abbey to see Their Majesties come out into the sunshine after the long ceremony and all over the country there were celebrations in honour of the new monarch, though Albert Court jeered at what he saw as a senseless extravagance when workers' families were living in want.

'Oh, take no notice o' him, Mum, he's like a bear with a sore head these days!' said Mabel, ignoring her brother's scowls. 'George, are yer comin' up to the park with us? There's goin' to be music an' dancin' tonight, and the world an' his wife'll be there!'

Annie put on her best jacket and hat, and hurried with Mabel, Alice and George to a transformed Battersea Park. Coloured electric lights gleamed in the trees and a military band played patriotic tunes like 'Rule, Britannia' and 'Hearts of Oak'. These later gave place to songs from the Gilbert and Sullivan operettas and later still to favourite music-hall songs. Ada Clay turned up all smiles, leaning on the arm of her newly engaged fiancé Arthur. Mabel was happy for her friend, but felt just a tiny bit envious when the young couple linked arms with a row of laughing revellers and cavorted gaily across the grass, zigzagging in ever wider circles while the indefatigable musicians played Albert Chevalier's most popular Cockney ditty.

> Wot-cher! all the neighbours cried—
> Who're yer goin' to meet, Bill?
> 'Ave yer bought the street, Bill?

To Mabel's amazement her mother was pulled from her side by a smiling Mrs Bull and led away to dance arm in arm with a whole row of other neighbours from Sorrel Street; it gave her a strange feeling to see Annie Court enjoying herself like a young girl. She imagined a laughing, golden-haired Anna-Maria who had grown up with her sisters in that big house somewhere in Hampshire, and longed to know more of her mother's history and the aunts she had never met.

She turned to ask her sisters if they wanted to dance, but Alice had already joined a giggling group of school friends and Daisy had run off into the crowd with George. Standing alone and watching them all having fun, Mabel could not help feeling a little wistful. Harry Drover would be out somewhere with the Army, she thought, more interested in doing good work than in having a good time. Should she join her mother with the other local women? She might as well . . .

That was when she felt an arm gently winding round her waist. She jumped back hastily, turning round to see who was taking liberties. Her face lit up in a radiant smile of joyous surprise. For there was her very own young man, bareheaded and with jacket unbuttoned, looking really handsome. 'Harry!'

'Shall we join in with 'em, Mabel? I'm not much of a dancer, but everybody else is doin' it, so why not us too?'

She needed no second invitation. Threading her right arm through his and with her left hand on her hip, Mabel stepped lightly back and forth and from side to side; the steps were a simple 'grapevine', backwards and forwards in time to the music, and Harry soon managed to follow quite well, without having to keep looking down at his feet.

'I'm gettin' the idea, Mabel!'

'Yes, ye're comin' on a treat!' she assured him, kicking up her heels and showing her ankles with the rest as she joined in the singing.

> Wot-cher! all the neighbours cried—
> Who're yer goin' to meet, Bill?
> 'Ave yer bought the street, Bill?

They repeated it over and over, Mabel lost count of the number of times, and only lived for the sensation of Harry's arm around her, his closeness, his living, breathing self, moving beside her, laughing over the words of the song.

> Laugh? Cor! – thought I should 'a' died—
> Knocked 'em in the Old Kent Road!

Dancing, singing and laughing, she thought they must surely be the happiest couple in the park. Nine o'clock, ten o'clock, eleven: the sunset faded and the stars came out above them. The air was still very warm and filled with a heady country smell of trampled grass. The crowd began to thin out as families with children made for home, but Mabel and

Harry still stood together in a moving sea of humanity, only half aware of the sights and sounds of the midsummer night, so lost were they in each other.

The band struck up again with a song from a dozen years back, when men went off to fight in the Boer War.

'Oh, listen, Harry, they're playing "Goodbye, Dolly Gray" – it's ever so sad.'

'D'ye know the words to it, Mabel? Can yer sing it for me? Go on, please do!'

Mabel's clear voice rose obediently above the shouts and jostlings of the crowd, a little uncertainly at first but gaining confidence as she went on:

'Goodbye, Dolly, I must leave you,
Though it breaks my heart to go;
Something tells me I am needed
At the front to face the foe—'

Other voices around them began to join in as she came to the end of the refrain:

'See, the soldier boys are marching,
And I can no longer stay;
Hark! I hear the bugle calling—'

A solitary *ta-ra-ra-ra-ra* was heard from the band-stand, an oddly melancholy sound, as if from a long way off, and Mabel paused before the final 'Good-bye, Dolly Gray!'.

There was an enthusiastic burst of applause and cries of 'More! More! Sing it again, Miss.'

Flushed and elated, she looked to Harry who was

gazing at her enraptured. 'Oh, Mabel, I could listen to yer all night long.'

When the song at last came to an end and the other voices died away, Mabel was conscious of a tiny shiver running down her spine and could not think why, perhaps because the air had chilled, though she still felt full of life. The rest of her family were nowhere to be seen. 'It's getting late, Harry. I suppose we ought to go.' She sighed and wished that the night could go on for ever. She felt she wanted to cling to him and never let him go.

So there they stood beneath the trees and his arm was again round her waist; it seemed to her as if the night was holding its breath. His head bent over hers and when she lowered her face she felt his forefinger under her chin, gently raising her head until she could no longer avoid his eyes.

'Dearest Mabel, I shall remember this moment for ever.'

'Oh, Harry, so will I – always.'

His lips were upon her cheek and then pressed to her forehead; she felt his warm breath on her face. Her hand was caught and clasped in his.

Then his mouth was upon hers and, light though it was, it took her breath away. She swayed and closed her eyes.

'I can't help bein' in love with yer, Mabel.'

Beyond them the band was still playing 'Goodbye, Dolly Gray'.

'I'll wait three years, Harry,' she told him quietly. 'Or four or five or six. I'll wait as long as we have to. And I'll work hard and save all I can.'

The kiss that sealed her promise held all the hopefulness, all the faith in the future that only the young possess.

'Why, *there* you are, Mabel! Where on earth did you get to? We've been looking everywhere – it's too bad of you!' Relief and anger blended in her mother's reproaches, while Daisy ran forward to fling her arms round her eldest sister.

'I'm all right, Mother, there's no need to fuss, I'm perfectly safe with Harry.' Mabel spoke firmly and Annie bit her lip in annoyance.

'Well, come home with us now – it's very late, and time Daisy and George were in bed.'

'You go on ahead, Mother, and we'll follow,' said Mabel firmly.

'I want to walk with Mabel and Harry,' announced Daisy.

'So do I,' added George.

In spite of the lateness of the hour, Annie made no objection to this arrangement.

The weekend newspapers were full of stories and pictures about the coronation, and Ada Clay came up with a specially juicy titbit. 'Look at this in the *Daily Mail*, Mabel. Here, halfway down the page – and a photograph!'

Mabel took the paper from her, following her pointing finger. She began to read aloud: 'Lady Cecilia Stanley attracted much admiration when she appeared at a state banquet at the Mansion House, wearing a gown of white silk trimmed with Honiton lace and a tiara of graded pearls. She and Sir Percy Stanley, Bart, reside in Bryanston Square and Farleigh Hall in Hertfordshire. Pictured here escorted by Viscount Eastcote, Lady Cecilia has captured the attention of London society during this coronation year, and is much sought after by hostesses for her beauty and wit.'

There was a good deal more in the same strain.

'That's *her*, isn't it, Mabel?' said Ada. 'The one your friend Maudie works for and makes out they're as thick as thieves!'

'Er, yes, I suppose she must be.' Mabel stared hard at the picture of a dark-haired, smiling young woman who lived in such a completely different world from their own. She remembered Maudie's boast: 'Me an' 'Er Ladyship are like *this*, see?' Was it possible that this society beauty, married to a rich man, even if he was old and bald, could have such a close understanding with a poor child of the streets? And if what Maudie said was true, the lady actually depended upon her maid's discretion in order to plan clandestine meetings behind old Sir Percy's back.

Reg'lar little goer, she is, Maudie had said admiringly. Was this good-looking viscount a lover – a paramour of hers? Mabel did not know what to think, but in the glow of Harry's love she would not have changed places with Lady Stanley, for all her beauty, riches and position.

Ada showed the paper to Miss Carter and their new assistant at the Mission, and it got passed around in the Clay household to the accompaniment of much oohing and ahing. Mabel kept quiet about it at Sorrel Street, knowing how Albert in his present mood would scoff at such goings-on among a lot of toffs who never had to go short of anything.

Jack turned up in an uncommonly cheerful mood and said how sorry he was not to have been home for the coronation. Mabel turned away in disgust, though she said nothing. 'Never mind, Annie ol' girl, I'll take yer to the Grand next week,' he promised. 'Harry Tate's on, and there's that family o' trapeze

146

artists we read about, remember? Go on, we'll have supper at the Plough an' make a night of it, what d'ye say?'

'An' abaht time, too,' growled Albert, though Annie's face lit up with a brilliant smile that took ten years off her and touched Mabel's heart. For the hundredth time she wished that their father could always be like this, and she compared him unfavourably with honest Harry Drover. All right, so Harry's earnest manner might amuse the likes of her friends' young men, but how much preferable he was to one of her father's kind, full of easy charm but not to be trusted once out of sight. She wondered if Jack was still meeting the girl in blue – and were there other women in the various racecourse towns that he visited around the country? Mabel had lost respect for her father ever since that time in Leicester Square when she had seen him meeting his ... she shied away from the word 'mistress', but there were worse words. And she knew that Albert had never forgiven him for what had happened at Christmas. The atmosphere between father and son was tense, though they saw little of each other now that Albert was often away at secret meetings of railway workers. Whenever she or Annie questioned him, he would adopt a surly expression and mutter that the country was about to be brought to a standstill, just see if it wasn't. As the thermometer in the backyard rose higher and higher, so did the tempers of the transport workers and stories of a blockade began to be circulated.

While Mabel bade a loving farewell to the Babies Mission, Alice's school-leaving day found her unexpectedly tearful as she closed her desk at Hallam

Road school for the last time. One day she was a reluctant pupil living for the day when she would earn her living in the grown-up world, the next she was a hesitant fourteen-year-old looking for a job. With the general atmosphere of unrest almost palpable in the heatwave, Annie Court would not hear of Alice going further than walking distance to work, so she had to be content to assist at the sub-post office in Queen's Road. Here she was not even allowed to touch the stamps, but only to serve sweets and newspapers under the eagle eye of Miss Chatt the sub-postmistress.

'The silly old bag thinks the place would fall down if she wasn't watching everybody through her pince-nez,' Alice told her mother and sisters. 'She's taken a dislike to me already because Mr Munday smiles at me and says I look nice and cool in all this heat. It's 'cause I wear short sleeves, like any sensible person.'

'Well, don't encourage the man, whatever you do.' Annie was immediately on the alert. 'Ought to be ashamed o' himself, a married man making personal remarks to a girl no more than a child.'

'Oh, he doesn't mean anything by it, Mum. It's just his way o' making me feel at home in his poky little shop – and maybe to annoy Miss Chatt as well,' answered Alice in a bored tone. 'You should see the way she goes all coy and giggly when he comes out o' his office. "Would you like a nice cup o' tea, Mr Munday?" Never offers *me* one.'

'I'm surprised she doesn't expect yer to brew up for them both,' said Mabel, a little amused.

'Oh, no! No hand but hers must touch the special teapot she keeps for Mr Munday! She has a little kettle and a spirit lamp in a cubbyhole at the back, with a tin of McVitie's biscuits, just for him an' her.'

Annie clucked her tongue in disapproval, though whether at Miss Chatt's foolish behaviour or Alice's bold comments on it was not clear. Mabel knew that her young sister was already disillusioned with her job, though she earned eight shillings a week, as much as Mabel had been getting after three years of carefully attending to the young children at the Mission.

'D'yer realise that the miners are askin' for five miserable pence a shift?' Albert demanded in disgust. 'Men wiv families to feed, scared o' seein' 'em out on the streets to starve – an' *she* gets eight bob for standing be'ind a counter all day. It's a bleedin' scandal!'

As usual it was left to Mabel to keep the peace as best she could.

Meanwhile she had begun a new phase in her own life and although she'd felt nervous on her first day at the Anti-Viv, as the hospital was locally known, she very quickly settled in and showed herself to be the willing worker that Miss Carter had recommended. She was not at first allowed on the wards, but swept and dusted the doctors' quarters, scoured pots and pans in the kitchen and sorted the laundry, some of which was foully stained and had to be sluiced by hand under cold running water. Knowing herself to be on trial, she tackled all these tasks with a will and earned the housekeeper's approving nods; but she also got surly looks and sarcastic mutters from a certain Dot Watson, the girl who shared her shift and was supposed to show her the methods of working, where things were kept and so on. Mabel got given the worst jobs and set about them without complaining, which infuriated Dot all the more. She was one of those unfortunate young women with plain looks and a grudge against the world; she had a natural suspicion of anyone who worked with cheerful good humour. It made her feel somehow inferior and she disliked Mabel so much so that she looked out for an opportunity to get her into some sort of trouble.

Still the heatwave persisted, with record high temperatures. Children died of dehydration, and men and women collapsed in the streets with heat exhaustion. All the windows of the Anti-Viv were opened to their fullest extent to let in a breath of air.

It was in this situation, one week into August, that Albert's dire warnings of a workers' revolt exploded into reality. The country woke up to find that a national strike of transport workers had brought London and other major industrial centres like Manchester, Liverpool and Birmingham to a standstill. Public incredulity and indignation were soon followed by widespread panic as the consequences became apparent. The city markets stood idle while on the wharves tons of accumulated fruit and vegetables rotted in the sweltering heat. The great railway terminals were eerily silent as passengers waited on platforms for trains that had ceased to run. Mailbags piled up, full of undelivered letters; food stocks began to run out in shops and the streets emptied as motor-buses and private vehicles felt the shortage of fuel.

Albert was jubilant. 'They asked for it an' by Gawd they bloody well got it, a complete stoppage!' His dark eyes flashed in triumph. 'We got 'em where we want 'em at last!' He was out of the house from dawn till dusk, cheering Ben Tillett who publicly addressed the strikers at Tower Hill, exhorting them to stand firm. And when the Home Secretary Mr Churchill cancelled police leave and called out armed troops to deal with public assemblies of strikers Albert was scornful. ''E'll 'ave to fink again when 'e finds 'alf the military on our side! The territorials won't touch us, they're all in sympafy wiv our ideals!'

Late that night, tired of the tension within the family and irritated by the inconvenience caused by the strike, Jack Court rounded angrily on his son. 'Ye'll bring us all to disgrace, Albert, to say nothin' o' worryin' yer mother to death.'

'Oho, look 'oo's talkin',' sneered Albert. 'A model 'usband an' farver 'oo never caused me muvver any trouble. Not much!'

Jack evaded the mocking black eyes so like his own and attempted a more conciliatory approach, glancing sideways at Mabel in an effort to enlist her support. 'Look, Albert, it isn't that I disagree with the principles o' the Labour movement; in fact, I go along with a lot o' what they stand for. It's just that I wish ye'd remember for yer mother's sake if for nobody else's that this is a respectable household, and—'

Albert's raucous yelp cut him short. 'Is *that* wot it is? Well, blow me dahn, and there was me finkin' it was a bookmaker's 'ideout! Remember 'ow yer used to send me and the lads out runnin' for yer? 'Ow we gave the coppers the slip, comin' rahnd the back-yards wiv the bets?'

Jack flushed. 'Oh, for God's sake, Albert, what do I have to say to show I *care* about yer?'

'Save yer breaf,' came the bitter reply. 'Save yer sweet talk, Jack Court, for yer fancy women!'

'*Albert!*' gasped Mabel, instinctively putting a

finger to her lips, though Annie had gone to bed. Caught off guard, Jack stared blankly and had no reply to make. Something unsayable had been said out loud and Mabel felt bound to rebuke her brother. 'Don't yer ever *dare* let Mum hear yer say anythin' like that, Albert. Not ever, d'ye hear?'

Albert glared and seemed about to speak again but glanced at Mabel and for her sake turned on his heel and clumped off upstairs to bed. Jack gave his daughter a brief, conspiratorial nod, which she did not acknowledge, nor did she say another word, but followed Albert upstairs.

It had been a very long, very hot day and Mabel felt as if she were sitting on a box of tinder that only needed one match to send it up in flames. And she blamed her father for it, far more than she blamed her hot-tempered brother.

The government itself was divided over the crisis. While Churchill condemned the strikers for endangering the nation's industries and bringing the population to the verge of famine, as he said, the Labour MP Keir Hardie spoke up for them to mixed cheers and boos. When he joined a strike meeting alongside Ben Tillett at Tower Hill, the angry altercations with the forces of law and order turned to fisticuffs and fights escalated into riots. The police used truncheons, resulting in some broken skulls, and a number of arrests were made.

Harry Drover, unable to work, spent his time helping at an emergency Salvation Army shelter for strikers' families, while keeping out of the political arguments. Late in the evening of the day of the Tower Hill riots he called at Sorrel Street to enquire about

Albert, but also to satisfy his longing for a sight of the girl he loved. He always said later that the Lord had directed him, because he landed in the middle of a family crisis. Albert had not come home from Tower Hill and Annie was frantic with worry.

'I can just picture him lying injured somewhere, trampled underfoot, bleeding to death under a railway arch,' she sobbed, while Jack tried to reassure her, thinking it more likely that Albert would be cooling his heels in a police cell.

Mabel raised weary eyes to Harry, melting his heart. 'I'll have to go and make some enquiries, Harry. None of us'll get any sleep tonight else.' She had worked all day and looked worn out, but anxiety for her brother overrode everything.

'Then I'll come with yer,' he replied at once.

'Oh, *will* yer, Harry? God bless yer!' she said thankfully and when Jack made a token offer to accompany them it was quickly declined by Harry, who said that Mr Court would be better staying at home to comfort his wife.

'My uniform'll take me where others might not be allowed,' he reminded them, thankful that he was wearing his bandsman's jacket and cap with the letters SA prominently displayed.

'For God's sake be careful, Mabel,' begged her mother, though with Harry's arm through hers, Mabel had no fears for her safety.

On foot – for there were no buses – Mabel and Harry set out on the long walk into the city, over the river and eastwards to Tower Hill. They found it practically deserted after the violent scenes that had taken place only a few hours earlier.

A solitary policeman told Harry where casualties of the riot might be found. 'There's a lot of 'em in custody for the night,' he said, adding that some half-dozen young fellows, hardly more than boys, had been taken to St Katharine's Infirmary, a one-time notorious workhouse on the edge of the docks. 'Some of 'em got knocked about when the troops charged, but they'd no business bein' there. Anyway, yer could ask, though if they're under guard yer won't get to see 'em.'

By now it was midnight and Mabel felt ready to drop, but she begged Harry to take her to the Infirmary. 'If he's in a police cell, he'll at least be safe, but if he's injured I *must* see him, Harry.'

'Whatever yer say, Mabel, but if he's not there I'm takin' yer home. There're still a few hansoms around.'

Holding his arm and half leaning her head on his shoulder, she let him lead her towards the grim old building that stood overlooking the disreputable Highway.

'We can't take no more in, we're overfull already,' said the hump-backed night porter who answered Harry's ringing of the bell pull.

On hearing that they were not seeking admission but looking for the young lady's brother, he grudgingly let them into the dimly lit entrance hall and fetched a sharp-faced woman in grey, who eyed them up and down and asked what they wanted. With an impatient clucking of her tongue she opened the Admissions Book and there, halfway down the list for the day, was the name of Albert Edward Court.

Mabel closed her eyes and put her hands together in thankfulness. 'Oh, thank God! Let me see him, let me see him, please!' she begged. 'I must know how badly he's hurt.'

"'E's under guard, along o' some other young ruffians, so it'll be up to the doctor whether yer see 'im or no,' said the woman ungraciously, adding to the porter, 'Ye'd better take 'em down.'

He led them along an echoing corridor to a ramshackle emergency ward where about fifteen injured men lay on pallets in the clothes they had worn on admission. Some were sleeping, some groaned as they lay, there were no nurses about and an aproned doctor was bandaging the leg of one of them, speaking quietly as he worked. Mabel caught her breath at the smell of blood, the sounds of pain – as always, she was moved by the sight of suffering.

The tired-looking doctor glanced up as they entered. 'Yes? Who let you in?'

'She sent 'em dahn from the front,' wheezed the porter.

Harry approached the doctor. 'My name's Drover and this lady is Miss Court who's lookin' for her brother Albert Court,' he explained civilly. 'We've been told that he's in here.'

The doctor noted his brass-buttoned jacket and the SA badge on his cap, and answered in a sympathetic manner. 'From Tower Hill? That's him over there. I must tell you that these men are all in police custody and I'm on duty as guard as well as doctor.' He gave a wry smile. 'Not much comfort here, I'm afraid, it's a converted storeroom, but—'

Mabel, however, had found her brother and was kneeling on the bare stone floor beside him. 'Albert! Oh, Albert, it's Mabel. What on earth've they done to yer?'

He turned his head quickly at the sound of her voice and winced involuntarily. His face was bruised and swollen, his left eye closed. His clothes were filthy and streaked with blood and he had not even got a pillow. 'Mabel—' The swagger had completely left Albert, and he began to whimper like a lost and frightened child. 'They walloped me round the 'ead, Mabel, and knocked poor ol' Sam Mackintosh unconscious, I fought 'e was dead – some of 'em ran away, but I stayed wiv Sam an' got beaten. I don't know where 'e is – oh, Mabel, take me 'ome – take me 'ome!'

She gently took his bloodied, bandaged head on to her lap. 'There, my poor boy, don't cry, Mabel's here,' she murmured, though her own tears were flowing. 'It's all right now, Albert, dear, we've come to take yer home.'

Harry came over and also got down on his knees beside the boy. 'How's it goin', ol' chap?'

'Is that 'Arry? 'Ave yer come to take me 'ome an' all?'

'Yes, we're both here, don't worry,' said Mabel soothingly.

The doctor was now standing above them. 'As I said, these men are in police custody and due to appear before the magistrates in the morning, if they're able,' he said. 'Your brother has a possible fractured skull, Miss Court, and extensive bruising. He needs to be kept under observation.'

'Oh, but we can look after him much better at home,' insisted Mabel, whose one idea now was to get her brother out of this place. 'We've got a very good family doctor – oh, please let us take him home, please!'

The doctor reluctantly shook his head. He was a young man, not yet thirty, and there was something oddly familiar about him, though Mabel could not recall ever having met him before. 'Look, Miss Court,

I was asked to come over from the London Hospital to take charge here for the night and if I were to let this young man go without proper authority—'

'He's only a lad o' sixteen, doctor,' pleaded Harry. 'I know him and his family well. He shouldn't be here.'

The doctor seemed half persuaded. 'That may well be true, Drover, but if the boy's condition became worse and possibly—'

'Me mother an' I'll take good care o' him – an' we'll send for our panel doctor first thing in the morning,' said Mabel, her tired grey-blue eyes imploring. 'Oh, believe me, Albert'll be far better off in his own bed, doctor!'

'Well—'

The brief hesitation was enough for Harry who went straight out to look for a hansom cab while the doctor gave Mabel some instructions. 'Give him drinks but no solid food for twenty-four hours. Keep him in bed and if he starts being sick or loses consciousness let your doctor know at once, Miss Court. And you'd better keep very quiet about this; don't go talking to people. I hope your doctor's discreet.'

'Dr Knowles will understand, I know,' Mabel assured him. 'He's a family friend.'

He raised his eyebrows. 'Not Henry Knowles of Hillier Road, Battersea, by any chance?'

'Yes, that's the one. Why, do yer know him?'

'I should do, he's my father!'

He smiled and she realised why his face seemed familiar. 'Then you must be Stephen! I've heard about yer.'

'What a happy coincidence, Miss Court. I'll be able to speak to him myself about Albert.'

Harry came back to say that he had found a cab drawn by a poor old stumbling horse that had been working since dawn the previous day. Dr Knowles lifted Albert's shoulders while Mabel supported his head and Harry held his legs; this way they carried him out to the corridor and along to a side door, avoiding the front entrance.

'Now are you sure you'll be all right, Miss Court?' asked the doctor and even in her preoccupation with Albert Mabel thought how nice he was, a true son of his father.

'Yes, with Mr Drover to look after us.' She smiled as he saw them into the cab, Albert lying across the seat with his head cradled in Mabel's lap. 'Thank yer, Dr Stephen!'

Annie wept for joy at seeing them return with Albert and shed even more tears at the state he was in. She thanked Harry for all he had done and Jack dug into his pocket to reimburse the cab fare. 'Sorry ye've had all this hassle, Drover – he'll be the ruin o' this family one o' these days,' he grumbled. 'Getting arrested won't help his job prospects; they'll never have him back on the railway. End up in prison, I shouldn't wonder. Thanks, anyway.'

Mabel was at last able to show her own gratitude with a loving kiss as they parted on the doorstep. 'I can't ever thank yer enough, Harry – I'd never've found him without yer an' I just couldn't bear to think o' him bein' stuck in that dreadful place all night. Oh, Harry, ye're so good to us!'

At which Harry Drover considered himself more than rewarded.

Tired as she was, Mabel's sleep was troubled, and she woke in terror from a dream about policemen wielding truncheons and bodies falling to the ground. At six she woke again: the daylight was pouring through the thin curtains and her mother was calling to her urgently: 'Mabel! He's been sick and his poor eyes are so swollen he can't open them – oh, Mabel, he's in a bad way!'

Jack was pulling his clothes on. 'I'd better get Dr Knowles out, or we'll have no peace,' he growled. 'That boy'll be the ruin o' this family, nothing's more sure.'

Annie was terrified and seemed quite unable to cope, so Mabel had to stay at home to care for Albert and comfort her mother; George was despatched to the Anti-Viv with a hastily scribbled note about sickness in the house.

When Dr Knowles arrived he was eager to hear about his son's encounter with Albert and his sister. He examined the patient's eyes and ears, and tested his reflexes; he looked at the bruises and gently felt the bumps on the boy's head, changing the bandage and pronouncing him to be suffering from the after-effects of concussion. 'The contusions will take a while to disperse, but there are no broken bones. I agree with Stephen – keep him on fluids and avoid upsetting him with news reports, and he should be all right. It'll keep the young firebrand out of trouble for the time being, at least.' He sighed and shook his head as Mabel saw him out. 'I don't think the strikers are going to win, poor devils. Anyway, I'll call back tomorrow – and you can go to work, Mabel,' he added, once again irritated by Annie Court's helpless dependence upon her eldest daughter.

Mabel immediately set out for the Anti-Viv, where she reported that her mother who had been poorly was now much better – which was true in a way, because Annie's state of mind had calmed as Albert's condition improved. The housekeeper nodded and told her that she could go to one of the women's wards to help with the afternoon teas that were served from a trolley. This was an unexpected promotion and Mabel was thrilled to be assisting the nurses in such a direct way. She was asked to help an old lady drink tea from a feeding cup and while not allowed to give out bedpans, could certainly empty them and clean them. Now she really felt on her way to being a proper nurse like the ones on the ward, so smart in their striped uniforms with starched aprons, caps and cuffs: she admired them from afar as she flitted up and down the ward, smiling at the women in the beds as she collected the teacups and plates.

But Dot Watson was filled with resentment.

The next morning Albert was obviously much improved and Dr Knowles said it would only be a matter of time before he was able to work again. But what work? He had no chance at all of going back to his job at the railway depot and Mabel wondered if he could try his luck at one of the many factories along the river – the biscuit and jam factories, the pottery, candleworks and tannery; but for the time being he seemed unusually pensive and sat out in the backyard in the sun as his bruises healed.

Then came an official brown envelope with GR prominently displayed on the headed paper inside: a summons to Albert Edward Court to attend at the South-Western Magistrates' Court on Lavender Hill the following Monday, to answer a charge of disturbing the king's peace and obstructing the police in the course of their duty etc., etc. Annie protested that he was not fit to attend, but Albert said that it had got to be faced sooner or later and he might as well go while he still had bruises from the police truncheon. He refused to allow Jack to accompany him and Annie would be too upset by it, he said. Mabel would have gone, except that she was working at the Anti-Viv and Albert would not let her lose any more time on his account.

The local juvenile strikers who had been arrested at Tower Hill were seen together in one morning session and on the whole they got off lightly. As the magistrate remarked, they had lost their jobs and learned a hard lesson. He lectured them on the importance of abiding by the laws of the land and bound them over to keep the peace. They were fined ten shillings each and Annie almost fainted with relief at Albert's narrow escape from being labelled a criminal. Mabel, too, threw her arms around his neck and Harry congratulated him. It had been an unpleasant episode, but it was all over now.

Until the following day, when the names of Albert Court, Samuel Mackintosh and the other young offenders were published in the *Evening Standard* as an example for all to see.

'Oh, how cruel! How unfair! Now he'll never be able to get a job,' cried Annie in dismay. 'Can't you do anything about it, Jack?'

'What can I do? He's brought it all on himself,' replied Jack impatiently.

'Never mind, Albert, it'll be a nine-day wonder and then there'll be somethin' else to keep 'em gossipin',' said Mabel comfortingly.

''S all right, Mabel, ol' gal, I'm gettin' aht of 'ere, anyway,' said Albert grimly. 'I couldn't go back to the railways in any case, not after the way we was treated – not wiv the bosses laughin' at us for riskin'

161

our lives and then not gettin' anywhere. It's the navy for me, soon's I'm back on me feet.'

Her heart sank, but she knew it was no use to argue with him in this mood. Besides, she was due back to duty at the Anti-Viv. 'Just don't say anything to Mum about it, Albert, not yet,' she warned as she left the house.

But when she reported for work she was directed to the Hospital Secretary's office and handed an envelope. She tore it open and found a brief letter of dismissal: '. . . due to certain circumstances in connection with the recent disturbance of the king's peace, we regret that your employment as a domestic assistant is terminated forthwith.'

'But I don't understand!' Mabel cried, brandishing the letter in the corridor outside the Secretary's office. 'I missed half a day's work 'cause of illness at home, all right, so I lose half a day's pay – but I've never disturbed the king's peace or anybody else's!'

A black-suited man came to the office door. 'Stop that, or I'll have you removed,' he said coldly. 'We want no agitators here, no strikers, nor any of their sympathisers or collaborators. You're to leave the premises at once, or the police will be called.'

'But—' Suddenly Mabel realised that this was all due to Albert's appearance in court and his name among the others in the evening newspaper. But how on earth had his name been connected to hers? She had never mentioned the matter at the hospital or anywhere else, remembering the warnings given by both the doctors.

'Are you leaving or have you to be forcibly removed?' asked the hospital official.

Which meant that Mabel had no choice. Sick at heart, she turned away and stumbled towards the hospital gates. Whatever would she do? How could she tell her family – and Miss Carter – that she had got the *sack*? And how had the hospital board found out about Albert?

Dot Watson's small eyes glinted with satisfaction as she watched the striken figure retreating from the Anti-Viv. Nice work – she was rid of that one!

Chapter Seven

At first Mabel felt that she simply could not go home and face the family, not straight away. Devastated by the blow that had fallen upon her and unable to control her tears, she walked blindly away from the Anti-Viv and up Albert Bridge Road, not sure of which direction to take, wanting only to be alone. To her right the cool greenness of Battersea Park beckoned and she turned aside to wander among the trees, a solitary figure with bowed head, clasping and unclasping her hands. Avoiding the other strollers and surrounded by the scenes of that glorious night of the coronation when she had danced so happily with Harry, she now gave way to her shock and grief at this turn of events.

Everything had been going so well at the hospital, she had quickly been promoted to working on the wards and had got on so well with everybody – well, all except that poor Watson girl who grumbled all the time and for whom Mabel had felt sorry. Apart from her there had been nothing but friendliness and encouragement. And now, like a bolt from the blue, it was all over, and so humiliatingly; she was shamed by association with a disturber of the peace. It would almost be comical if it were not so bitterly unfair. Poor Albert, she thought, and her tears flowed afresh at the realisation that they were both now out of a job. Had he really meant what he'd said about going into the navy? If so, how would she manage at home without his warmth and support, his quick and often caustic wit, his impetuosity, his fierce loyalty to herself and her mother? Without his protective presence she would feel bereft. Whatever happened, Albert had always been able to coax a laugh from her. Until now . . .

And what would Harry think about his *dear girl* in this kind of trouble? She hoped he wouldn't blame Albert, not that Harry would ever say anything unkind to his friend, but . . . she gasped as another thought struck her: would Harry be in trouble as well, if it were known that he had helped her find Albert and bring him home after his arrest? It was all too awful to contemplate.

By midday Mabel decided that she could not put off the evil moment any longer and made her reluctant way towards Sorrel Street.

Ill news travels fast. Mrs Finch had called at number 12 to say that another neighbour had seen Mabel Court walking up Albert Bridge Road in the middle of the morning, clearly very upset. 'Breakin' 'er 'eart, she was, so Elsie Tonks said. Is summat up wiv the poor gal?' she asked curiously. With a brute of a husband and a growing family to bring up on too little money, Lily Finch found her only comfort in the misfortunes of her more outwardly respectable neighbours.

Annie had said that it couldn't possibly have been Mabel, she'd gone to the Anti-Viv that morning as usual, but the seed of doubt had been sown and when Mabel walked in the door at half past twelve with a stony but determinedly composed expression Annie at once demanded to know what had happened. Albert came in from the yard, sensing bad news.

'I've lost me job, that's all, don't worry, I can get another,' said poor Mabel, putting her bag down and throwing her hat on a chair. 'I'll put the kettle on, Mum, I'm just dying for a cup o' tea – d'ye want one?'

But of course Annie and Albert bombarded her with questions, and there was no way of answering them without bringing in her brother's part in her dismissal. She showed them the letter, now creased and crumpled.

'I knew there'd be trouble when they printed those names in the paper!' wailed Annie.

'Bloody 'ell, Mabel, 'ow the devil did them buggers know yer was me sister?' asked Albert, scratching his head in genuine puzzlement. 'Yer ain't talked abaht me, 'ave yer?'

"Course not, I never once mentioned yer – I said Mum had been poorly in all this heat.' Mabel sighed, wearily getting up to put the kettle on, as neither of the others had.

'Then some sneak at that place must've got it in for yer, Mabel, that's all I can say,' said Albert with conviction. 'Wish I could ger me 'ands on the bastard. Was there anybody 'oo talked a lot abaht the strike?'

'Oh, *everybody* talked about it, Albert, it was headline news, remember?' replied Mabel a little irritably. 'How could they not notice? But nobody knew my brother was in it.'

'Whar abaht Dr Knowles? Does '*e* go in the Anti-Viv? Could've let it slip—'

'*No*! O' course not! Dr Knowles warned me several times not to say a word about yer outside, so did his son Stephen. Oh, don't keep on about it, Albert, it's bad enough to think we've both lost our jobs. And

166

for God's sake don't row with Dad about it when he comes home.'

Jack was out, but expected home that evening; Alice was at the post office and George and Daisy were at school, so Mabel had a few hours in which to ponder her jobless state and rack her brains as to where she might find work, any work, just so long as it brought in a little cash.

'Can't you go back to the Babies Mission, Mabel, just until things have died down a bit and you can look for something else?' asked Annie.

'Not really, Mum. Miss Carter's already got a girl to replace me and I'd feel such a failure,' replied Mabel sadly. In her heart she saw a return to the Mission as a backward step.

'Can't you try the Bolingbroke Hospital?'

'Not just yet, Mum, the word might've got around.' Mabel pictured herself as being on some kind of blacklist and tears welled up in her eyes again; but she told herself she must be brave, it would not do for Daisy to come home from school and find her crying.

The worst moment was when Jack Court came home. Annie took him aside to tell him what had happened and he turned on Albert, almost spitting with fury. 'I've said all along ye'll be the ruin an' the downfall o' the 'ole bloody family and so yer will!' he thundered. 'Losin' yer job for nothin', drivin' yer mother mad with worry, layin' around 'ere bein' waited on, stuffin' yerself with food I've 'ad to sweat for, an' now gettin' yer sister a bad name an' losin' 'er job – ye're nothin' but a bloody useless, good-for nothin', er, er—'

'Son of a bastard, that's right – yeah, yeah, I'm the Antichrist an' gonna rot in hell,' growled Albert, getting up and confronting his father eye to eye. 'Don't worry, I'm gettin' aht – goin' rahnd to Sam's an' from there to the navy. Anythin' to get aht o' this hell-hole.'

Annie and Daisy both began to cry as he slammed out of the front door, hatless and jacketless, for the air was still very warm.

Mabel rose to follow him. 'Albert! Albert, wait! Yer can't go round to the Mackintoshes, they got trouble enough o' their own. *Albert*! Wait for me!'

He walked on, hands in empty pockets, paying no attention. Mabel picked up her skirt and ran until she caught him up. She still had to hurry to keep up with his furious strides towards the river and the Embankment, where at last he slackened his steps. 'Gawd, I'm sorry, Mabel, I wouldn't've done this to yer for the world.' He choked on the last word and she put a hand on his shoulder.

'All right, Albert, I know it wasn't yer fault. And I'm ever so sorry that the strike ended without gettin' justice for the workers,' she sympathised, knowing how much it had meant to him. There was in fact a great deal of public bitterness and loud condemnation of the use of troops to bring the strikers to heel. 'Couldn't yer get some other kind o' work for a year or two, Albert? In a factory or on a buildin' site?' she pleaded. 'Give yerself a chance to think things over before signing up for the navy. Ye're much too young yet to go off on a ship.'

''Course I'm not, they take younger 'n me on them trainin' ships, an' the sooner I'm gone the better. I'll be orf up to Bishopsgate to apply termorrer.' He stopped and stared down the river where ships were once again being unloaded.

Mabel stood beside him, her heart aching for this

boy – for he was only sixteen – who had always been especially close to her. 'I can't bear to think o' home without yer, Albert,' she told him simply. 'We need yer – Mum, George, Daisy and me.'

'No, Mabel gal, yer don't need me – look 'ow I've buggered things up for yer. Tain't only the strike, neiver. I got to get away from the ol' man, or there'll be a right bust-up.'

'But he's still yer father—'

''E's no farver to me, not since I seen 'im makin' up to bits o' common fluff in pubs an' that. No wonder poor ol' Mum's let 'erself go.'

'But Albert, she doesn't know, an' she mustn't *ever* find out!' insisted Mabel urgently.

'Yeah, well, she's bahnd to know sooner or later, ain't she? I just can't stand arahnd an' see 'er bein' let dahn by 'im, Mabel, an' that's a fact. I'd fergit meself an' up an' slosh 'im one.' He put an arm around her waist and kissed her cheek with surprising gentleness after the harsh words he had been speaking. 'Nah, Mabel, this is the best way. I'll miss yer, o' course, an' Mum, an' dear little Daisy.'

His voice shook and they stood a while in silence, hands touching.

'Well, Albert, if ye're really goin' to join the navy tomorrow, come back home with me tonight, I dare say Dad'll've gone out again.'

She was right. Jack was not at home, but Harry was there, waiting for her with loving looks and words, ready to comfort her and hold out hope. 'The Lord'll bring good out o' this, Mabel, just yer wait an' see – put yer trust in Him an' wait on His own good time,' he whispered, enfolded her in his arms during a brief moment alone with her in the hallway. He never at any time uttered a word of reproach to

Albert, knowing that the boy was suffering enough regret on Mabel's behalf; nor did he attempt to dissuade his friend from his chosen course.

Resisting Annie's tearful pleadings, Albert took himself off to Clarke Place in Bishopsgate the very next day to offer himself for the merchant service. Mabel bowed to the inevitable and when he was accepted within a week for training on the *Warspite* in dock at Greenhithe, to commence in ten days' time, she comforted their mother and Daisy as best she could. An uneasy truce existed between him and Jack, both knowing that it would not be for much longer.

Miss Carter wrote indignantly to Lady Headley when she heard of Mabel's dismissal and received a somewhat lukewarm apology. If Mabel had been a nurse instead of a mere domestic, Miss Carter felt that she might have been reinstated, but a suggestion was made that she could try for a cleaning job at the Battersea Polytechnic on Northside, overlooking Clapham Common.

'I don't care to think o' you as a charwoman, Mabel,' said Annie in a deprecating tone, but Mabel said that it would do well enough for the time being; beggars couldn't be choosers.

But then came another offer. An afternoon visitor called. 'Mabel! You'd better come down,' called her mother up the stairs. 'Your grandmother's here and wants to speak to you.'

'Yeah, the Duchess o' Tootin' in person, in 'er own 'ansom cab,' added Albert in an undertone. 'Even the bleedin' 'orse is lookin' dahn its nose at its surroundin's.'

Mabel hurried down to find Mrs Mimi Court waiting, resplendent in a wine-coloured silk gown with a rustling taffeta underskirt and black lace-edged jacket. Her lightened brown hair was dressed in the style of Queen Mary and she was at her most gracious. Questioning Albert about the strike and how he had got injured, she heard of his intention to go to sea. When she asked to speak to Mabel alone, Annie frostily showed her into the front room. 'Well, Mabel, here's a fine how-d'ye-do!' she said in an amused but not unkindly manner, carefully sounding all her hs and gs. 'Sacked from the Anti-Viv, eh? Yer was only a servant girl there, no great harm done, surely?'

'I loved it there, Grandmother, and it was good experience for when I start proper nursing training,' replied Mabel seriously. 'And I got paid more than at the Mission.'

Mimi raised her black eyebrows. 'Oho? Yer could earn even more if yer cared to move into 23 Macaulay Road and assist me with my local maternity cases in Tooting. *Very* good experience, Mabel, and by the time ye're twenty-one yer could register with the Central Midwives Board. Ye'd be better off than at that silly Headley woman's hospital.'

Mabel stared at her, hardly able to take in what was being said.

'Matter o' fact, I had it in mind to suggest this anyway in another year's time, but seeing ye've had this bit o' bad luck on account of that reckless fool of a brother, I'll take yer this year. A pound a week and all found – *and* a first-class training. Well, what d'ye say, Mabel?'

What indeed could Mabel say? A whole pound a week to learn how to be a midwife, *before* embarking on general nursing training. Fifty-two pounds a year – think of what she'd be able to save! And to look after newborn babies, how wonderful! It was an amazingly generous offer and Mabel's thoughts whirled round in her head like a swarm of bees, refusing to settle. Part of her longed to accept thankfully, but there were obstacles in the way and the more she thought about them the more insurmountable they appeared.

The answer, when it came, sounded timid – feeble – even to Mabel's own ears: 'It's ever so good o' yer, Grandmother, but I can't.'

'Can't? Why ever not?'

'I can't leave Mother on her own – I mean with Albert going away, and ... Dad's away a lot—'

'Why can't yer mother look after herself, for heaven's sake?'

'She ... she's not well, her blood's thin and she relies on me so much. Oh, Grandmother, I'm sorry, but I can't take up yer offer, I tell yer, I *can't*!'

Her voice rose in her agitation, and Mimi looked at her questioningly. 'I hear ye've got a young man, Mabel. Jack tells me he's in the Salvation Army. Are yer plannin' to join up as well? Ye'll have to if yer marry him.'

'Yes, I know, Grandmother, and I *shall* join, but not for a long time yet. I'm going to train to be a nurse at a Poor Law infirmary in a few years' time, an' Har— Mr Drover's got to train at the staff college. Meanwhile I've *got* to stay at home and keep an eye on Mum – my mother.'

Mimi Court looked more amused than annoyed. 'So what will yer do now, Mabel?'

'There's a ... a cleanin' job at the Battersea Polytechnic.' Mabel felt herself blush and half expected a sarcastic rejoinder.

But Mimi just shrugged and got up to leave. 'Ye're

very young, Mabel, there's time enough yet. And yes, I think yer *could* make a good nurse one o' these days, that's if yer can ever get away from here. No, don't bother to see me out, I've nothin' to say to yer mother, nor she to me.'

As soon as she had gone, Annie tackled her daughter. 'What did she want to see you about?' she asked sharply. 'What did she say?'

'Oh, nothing much, Mum. She asked me if I . . . if I'd like to train to be a midwife.'

'*What*? Oh, my God, you mean with *her*?' Annie almost shouted. 'Oh, Mabel, you wouldn't, you couldn't – oh, *no*!'

'Sh, Mum, don't get into such a state. I told her I couldn't leave home, especially now, and I thanked her for her offer. She said she'd pay me a pound a week to help with her maternity cases and she'd train me at the same time, but I told her I couldn't and that was that,' said Mabel with an air of finality. 'Though I don't know why ye're so upset.'

'Thank God! Oh, Mabel, you don't know what she's like – what she does. She's a bad woman, Mabel, and I couldn't bear to think o' you living in that house. Are you sure you made it clear to her? You won't leave me and go to live at Macaulay Road?'

Mabel turned and looked her mother full in the face. 'I don't know what all this fuss is about, Mum, but I'm *not* going to Tooting, is that clear enough? Instead, I'll start work tomorrow morning at six o'clock, cleaning the Polytechnic till half past eight, and then I'll go to clean the hostel where the women students board, while they're at their lectures. Any more questions?'

Annie turned away, biting her lip at this untypical

display of impatience from her indulgent, good-natured eldest daughter, describing what her job would be like as a *charwoman*.

The work proved to be just as hard and dreary as Mabel had expected; she was the youngest of a team of three morning cleaners, the others being middle-aged women who needed the extra money for a variety of reasons. At first they were suspicious of her, but when they discovered that she had a sympathetic ear, she found herself endlessly regaled with stories about their marriages, their grandchildren, their ailments and daily concerns.

The women's hostel, also on Northside, was hardly more stimulating. Mabel was at the bottom of a domestic heirarchy of kitchen and domestic staff, and was firmly told not to talk to the students when she met them on stairways and corridors, though the young women often sent her off on errands, posting letters or buying buns to take to their rooms. It was their attitude that she found patronising – 'Oh, tell the maid to do it, it's what she's paid for,' or 'Sh, don't speak in front of the maidservant, wait till she's out of earshot.' As if I was deaf and daft, thought Mabel, tempted to retort that she had not the slightest interest in their silly gossip.

When the time came for Albert to take his leave of Sorrel Street, striding away with his rolled-up canvas bag over his shoulder, Annie wept dolefully. It was a Saturday, and Mabel and the children were at home. 'How could he treat me like this, Mabel? Did you notice, he didn't give us one backward glance!' She sobbed on Mabel's shoulder, which started Daisy off.

Mabel had to swallow her own heartache and be

strong for them all. 'I expect it was 'cause he couldn't bear to look back at us in case he cried, too,' she said, forcing a smile while Daisy sobbed and George bit his lip to stop it trembling. His struggle was not lost on Mabel and she raised her voice as she went on reassuring their mother. 'We've still got George, Mum, and he'll take care o' yer, just as Albert always did,' she said, holding out her hand to draw her younger brother close to them. He would be twelve at the end of the year and remained a shy, gentle boy, sensitive to his sisters' feelings and always ready to ease his mother's burdens in any way he could. 'Ye'll have to be our mainstay now, George, while I'm at the technical college,' Mabel told him. 'Keep an eye on Daisy and make sure Alice does her share o' the housework. At least *she* won't be sparring with Albert any longer, which'll be a relief!' she added wryly.

But no sooner was Alice released from the daily irritation of Albert's jeering and mimicking of what he called her fancy ways, than an unpleasant incident occurred with Miss Chatt.

The first Mabel knew that something was wrong was when Alice rushed in from work, brushed past her mother and flew straight upstairs to the room she shared with Mabel.

'What's up with *her*?' asked George, but Mabel decided to leave her sister undisturbed for a while, until she was ready to face them all. The two sisters had never been particularly close and Mabel hesitated to intrude on the fourteen-year-old girl whose dreams of a business career were not likely to materialise for some time.

'We're nearly ready to dish up, Mabel,' said Annie

with a worried look. 'I don't know if yer father's in tonight, but one of us ought to go up and have a word with her. I don't like her being upset – d'you think it's something to do with that Mr Munday? I'm not sure that I trust him.'

'I'll take her up a cup of tea and see if she's ready for some supper,' said Mabel, wiping her hands on her apron. 'Tea's always a good idea.'

With cup and saucer in hand she knocked softly at the bedroom door. A muffled sound was heard and the bed creaked. 'Alice? I've got a cuppa here for yer. Can I come in?'

'I don't want anything,' came the mumbled reply. 'Just want to be left alone.'

'It's my room, too, dear,' said Mabel gently. 'Let me come in, there's a good girl.'

There was no lock on the door and Mabel entered, setting down the cup on the chest of drawers and closing the door behind her.

Alice was lying on the bed and had obviously been crying. She sat up and dabbed her face with a handkerchief, avoiding Mabel's eyes.

'Come on, Alice, what's the matter? Yer can tell yer big sister.' Mabel sat down on the side of their shared bed and took the girl's hand in hers. 'Which one's upset yer, Miss Chatt or Mr Munday? Or was it a customer?'

Alice sniffed. 'It certainly wasn't a customer. *She* says they complain about my attitude, but they don't. Most of them like me, an' stop to pass the time o' day if they're not in a hurry.'

'Ah! And maybe Miss Chatt thinks they should stop and talk to her instead,' said Mabel with a teasing smile.

'She told me I was *pert*,' said Alice, 'and when I

asked her to name just one customer who'd said so, she lost her temper and went for me like a wildcat, claws out—'

'Did yer pull her tail?' asked Mabel.

'It wasn't funny!' retorted Alice. 'That was when she started saying the most awful, *wicked* things – oh, Mabel—'

'What sort o' things, dear? What did she say?' Mabel began to feel apprehensive.

'They were things about . . . about Dad.'

Mabel's smile disappeared in an instant. 'Oh, my poor Alice. What did she say about him? Tell me, dear, yer mustn't keep it to yerself.'

'She said everybody knows how he carries on, sittin' in the Falcon of an evenin', makin' up to . . . to hussies young enough to be his daughters—'

'Oh, Alice. Oh, yer poor little dear. I understand now.' Mabel frowned and shook her head, knowing that of all the Court children it was Alice who had always been closest to her father.

'And she said he visits a woman in Landseer Road who everybody knows has a reputation, and in broad daylight, as bold as brass, a cryin' scandal,' sobbed Alice. 'And she said to me, "Don't come here with yer cheeky tongue, little Miss Know-all, 'cause I won't have it, not from a flibbertigibbety somethin' or other from a family like that!" Oh, Mabel, I hate her, I do!'

'Sh, sh, Alice, Mabel's here, don't cry,' said her sister, stroking the dark hair that hung down over Alice's eyes. She felt deeply concerned for her sister, indignant with Miss Chatt and even more so with their father. What she had heard was no real surprise, but what should she tell Alice? How should the girl react to such taunts? At this moment Mabel was at a loss. 'And where was Mr Munday when all this was going on?' she asked at length.

'That was just it, he came out of his little office all of a sudden – I didn't know he was there and neither did she – but he must have heard it all, 'cause he was really angry an' told her off, even though there were customers in and they heard him – oh, Mabel!'

'Serve her right. What did he say?'

'That was the trouble, he said it wasn't my fault and she'd no right to take it out on me just 'cause o' my father,' said Alice with another burst of tears. 'He called me Miss Court and said I was a good little worker, and he wouldn't have me upset by spiteful talk.'

'Good for him – and what did she say to that?'

'She started snivelling behind her post office counter, and never said another word. But don't yer *see*, Mabel, he made it worse,' said poor Alice, lifting up her red and swollen eyes. 'He was nice to me, but he didn't deny the awful things she said – he didn't say it wasn't true, he only said I wasn't to blame for what my father did. Everybody's talkin' about us, Mabel, and we've never known about it!'

'And our mum must *never* know, Alice, whatever happens,' said Mabel solemnly. 'I'm very sorry ye've been so upset, but I doubt it'll happen again, after what Mr Munday said to the woman – but when yer hear anythin' like this, Alice, yer best way is to say nothin' at all. Be *dignified*, d'ye understand that, dear? Don't let people see that they've hurt yer and then they'll shut up. D'ye know what I mean?'

Alice sat up and brushed her hair back from her face with her hand. 'Yer mean ye've *known* about this, Mabel?' she asked incredulously.

'Yes, dear, for some time. So did Albert and it

made him very angry, so it's just as well he's not here. The one person who *doesn't* know is our poor mum – and the children, o' course – and yer must *never* say anything about this in front o' her or them. I'll tell her that yer got ticked off by silly old Miss Chatt and that Mr Munday stood up for yer. That's all she needs to know.'

Alice stared dolefully out of the window. 'But everybody else knows, don't they, Mabel? So why do *we* have to pretend?'

Mabel considered for a moment. It was not possible to explain the importance of preserving the illusion of respectability that meant so much to poor, tired, anaemic Annie Court after eighteen years of being married to Jack. 'Sometimes it's best to look the other way and not to say anything, dear, not when it'll cause trouble to somebody we love very much – like Mum.'

But Alice looked doubtful and Mabel realised that the girl was deeply disillusioned. And with both parents.

September gave way to October and the hot summer of 1911 passed into the records. Albert sent a postcard from the *Warspite* saying that he was doing well as a sea cadet and Mabel showed it to Harry. She was becoming increasingly bored and unsatisfied with life as a domestic at everybody's beck and call, but her meetings with Harry were a great consolation. He always gave her new hope and warmed her heart with his unfailing devotion. On Saturday evenings they went to the Citadel and for a walk in one or other of the London parks in midweek, though the evenings were rapidly drawing in and Annie objected to Mabel being out after dark; in any case she had to be up early to get to the Polytechnic for six.

'I wouldn't mind how early I had to get up, Harry, if only I was going to look after somebody who really needed me!' she said, knowing that with his own call to service he understood exactly what she meant; he had gone back to the railways after the strike and found the work more irksome than formerly, with a great deal of bad feeling among the men.

'I keep prayin' about both of us, dearest Mabel, and I know that it's all goin' to work out for the best in the end. We just got to be patient, my love.'

She would not have dreamed of arguing with him, but sometimes she felt a chill of doubt. All her hopes and plans to be a children's nurse seemed to have come to a standstill.

Then one day, as suddenly and unexpectedly as her dismissal from the Anti-Viv, came one of those chance occurrences that can change the course of a life. It was a Friday and Mabel had a half-day from the Polytechnic; she was on her way home at half past one, approaching the network of residential streets in her own part of north Battersea. Turning a corner, her sombre thoughts were interrupted by the sound of a woman screaming. It came from the upper window of the end terrace where their neighbours the Cluttons lived. 'Mabel! Mabel! Come to me mum, she's hollerin' summat terrible, and Mrs Lowe ain't nowhere to be found!'

Twelve-year-old Essie Clutton was clearly scared out of her wits, not being the brightest of girls, and two younger children were crying when Mabel hurried through the front door, not knowing what she would find but unable to pass by a cry for help. All other matters were forgotten as she rushed up the stairs and entered the front bedroom.

Mrs Clutton was writhing on the bed, clutching at her belly. 'Mabel Court – oh, fank Gawd, a gal wiv a bit o' sense! Me waters broke in the kitchen, don't know 'ow I got up the stairs, but me baby box is under the bed – aaah! Oh, me Gawd, it's comin', I reckon – 'elp me, gal, 'elp me—'

She gave a shriek of pain and fear, and Mabel knew that she must keep a cool head whatever happened. 'All right, Mrs Clutton, all right, sh, sh – let's get these off, shall we?' she said, her natural instinct prompting her to pull the woman's drawers down her legs. 'That's the way – now we can see what we're doin' – have yer got any newspapers? Whoops!'

And it was all over within the next half-minute. Between the woman's spread thighs lay a red-faced, squalling infant, still attached to the mother by the umbilical cord.

'Oh, Mrs Clutton, ye've got a little girl!' marvelled Mabel, putting her hands protectively round the slippery little body and wiping it dry with a fold of the sheet.

'Omigawd, annuver gal – 'e won't 'alf carry on – is it all right, Mabel?'

Mabel had to raise her voice to be heard above the baby's piercing, non-stop yells. 'Yes, she's fine, Mrs Clutton, just listen to her! Have yer got a towel or somethin' handy? Somethin' to wrap her in?'

'The baby box is under the bed, gal, everythin's in it, towels, clean sheets, ball o' string – the scissors are in the drawer, get Essie to find 'em for yer – napkins an' tie-up gowns, they're all in the box.'

Two neighbours drawn by the noise now rushed in through the back door and up the stairs. They stood open-mouthed at the scene before them. Mrs Clutton lay in a pool of blood and water, the smell reminding Mabel of the emergency room at St Katharine's Infirmary.

'But yer wasn't due till December, Mary! Is it a little 'un?' asked one of them.

'It's a gal, not all that little, is she, Mabel? Mabel Court's 'ad to do everythin' for me.'

'Nuffin' wrong wiv 'er lungs, anyway. 'Ere, give 'er to me, Mabel,' said the other neighbour, wielding the scissors and string. 'Let's get this tied orf – any sign o' the afterbirf?'

'I'll go down an' put the kettle on,' said the first woman. 'See what them kids are up to, an' all. Essie! Essie, where are yer?'

In another minute Mrs Lowe hurtled in through the open front door and shot up the stairs, hatless and out of breath. 'Is it born? Oh, well done, a fine little girl. And who was here for her? What about the afterbirth, is it still in? Right, soon have it out now, dear.'

'It's young Mabel Court she's got to thank. Where was *you*?' demanded the woman attending to the baby's cord.

'Up at the Institute off Lavender Hill – you know, the Women's Rescue,' explained the midwife, putting down her bag and feeling Mary Clutton's abdomen. 'D'ye feel yer could give another little push, dear? Did yer know that one o' those poor young creatures died last week? There's a midwife been dismissed over it because no doctor was called. That's right, dear, give another little push, that's right, good girl – an' one o' the domestics has been bringing drink into the place – I ask you, that's not right, is it? Oh, well done, Mrs Clutton, here it comes, nice and easy – yes, that's the afterbirth – is there a bucket handy? Oh, thanks, Mabel. Anyway, as I was saying, what that place needs is a decent, reliable body to help out, somebody with a bit o' common sense an' the right attitude t'wards those poor unfortunates, kind but not too easygoing, if yer see what I mean, an' a cool head on her shoulders. Can *you* think of anybody, Mabel?'

Mabel's eyes lit up with joy: she most certainly could!

'*What*? I can't believe I'm hearing you right, Mabel. You, a respectable girl, only seventeen and no experience of . . . of that side of life, are you seriously suggesting that you go and work in a home for fallen women?' Annie Court was horrified.

'I'd be a nursery maid, Mum, and help look after the little babies – oh, I'd be so happy to give 'em a little bit o' love, the poor mites! An' Miss Carter thinks it's a good idea as well, and says she'll give me a recommendation again – oh, Mum, I must do it, can't yer see? No more sweeping and dusting up at the Technical College, I'll be doing something really useful – and necessary!'

Annie Court could not argue, so certain was Mabel that this work was meant for her. And to Annie's surprise Dr Knowles thought so too. 'She's just the right sort of person for that place, Mrs Court,' he said seriously. 'There's been a new Matron appointed and she needs new, trustworthy staff. Your Mabel would be ideal as a nursery assistant.' And she'd have a genuinely compassionate attitude towards those poor young mothers, he added to himself.

Nobody could now remember the founder of the Agnes Nuttall Institute for the Rescue of Women, locally known as the Rescue. Mrs Nuttall had been a clergyman's widow who had bequeathed her solidly built mansion as a refuge for unmarried mothers and their babies. For years Mabel had passed it on her way to and from school and the Babies Mission, never dreaming that one day she would be on its staff.

Recent untoward events at the Rescue had led to reforms, and as a result of an inquiry there had been staff changes and a general review of rules and procedures. Mabel was duly recommended and interviewed by Mrs James, the new Matron, for the post of nursery maid, and could have danced for joy when she was accepted; her prospects were bright again and although the wages were about the same as for cleaning the Polytechnic, the work was indescribably more rewarding. 'Dearest Harry, yer said it'd all turn out for the best and so it has!' she cried, throwing her arms round his neck and kissing him with an enthusiasm which took him quite by surprise – and a very pleasant surprise at that.

'Yer look so beautiful when ye're happy like this, Mabel,' he told her, marvelling all over again that this lovely girl was in love with him and had promised to marry him one day, however long they had to wait. And he believed it would happen, in spite of the doubts and fears that sometimes plagued him, a sense of foreboding that all was not well in Mabel's home; he longed to protect her from the lurking shadows.

But for now she was jubilant at beginning her new job, and even her mother had to admit that Mabel was happier than she'd been for months.

At least she would still be living at home and not going to that woman at Tooting . . .

Chapter Eight

Happy and excited as she was to take up her new appointment, Mabel did not take long to discover that the Rescue was a place of sorrow. And that she would have to share in it.

On her first day she was taken into the nursery by Mrs James herself and the strict routine was explained to her. The fifteen babies who lay in their canvas cots had to be taken every four hours to be fed by their mothers. 'You have to change the ones whose mothers are still in the lying-in ward and carry them out in your arms,' said Mrs James. 'The other mothers have to come to the Agnes Nuttall room where they must change their own babies before and after feeding them. On no account are they to enter the nursery. That is the rule and must be kept.'

Mabel realised that Mrs James was a conscientious woman who did not intend to be unkind: her first thought was for the safety of the babies. They were fed at six, ten, two, six and ten o'clock on the dot, and whether Mabel was on the early or late shift this was her prime responsibility. All babies were breastfed; the boat-shaped glass bottles with their thick rubber teats were only used after the mothers had been discharged, when the infants were transferred to the babies' home at Merton. Those who cried between feeds were sometimes offered sweetened water on a teaspoon and at night were taken to their mothers at the discretion of the staff on duty. From her first day the sound of a crying baby touched Mabel's tender heart and she could never ignore it; she would lift the child out of its cot and either cuddle it on her lap or walk the bare boards of the nursery with the helpless little creature held against her shoulder. 'Sh, sh, little love, Mabel's here, never fear,' she would croon, stroking and kissing the downy head. 'Sh-sh-sh.'

At feeding times the girls – for they were mostly young – would reach out eagerly to take their babies from her arms. Sister Barratt who was in charge of the lying-in ward gave advice and assistance with breastfeeding, and Mabel soon picked up the essential points to remember: a comfortable position with the baby's head supported, its body firmly wrapped in a cot sheet, its mouth in contact with the nipple. She marvelled at this beautiful, natural bond between mother and child, the flowing out of love and nourishment in one mysterious stream. It was a new experience for each of these women and girls, and one they would always remember, thought Mabel pityingly, no matter what else happened to them later in life. For how could a mother forget her sucking child?

As time went by her thoughts often followed the babies to Merton, where arrangements were made for adoptions where possible; those with any kind of physical defect would go to children's homes. Mabel's distant dream sprang to life again, getting nearer, taking shape and substance: she saw herself, the future Mrs Drover, trained and experienced in nursing, pouring out love and care upon unwanted, unloved children in a Salvation Army refuge. This sad situation at the Rescue was another step on the journey towards her goal – and there was such a lot for her to learn.

The two-o'clock feeds were finished and the babies back in the nursery when Sister Lilley, the midwife, put her head round the door to ask if Miss Court could come and sit with Kathy Bagshaw again for half an hour.

'Not just at this minute, Sister Lilley,' Mabel apologised. 'There are a couple o' girls bein' discharged this afternoon and they . . . they're coming to see their babies for the last time.'

'Well, ask them to come to the Agnes Nuttall room *now* and get it over with. It's not a good idea to linger over the goodbyes, it only upsets them,' replied the midwife. 'I'll ask Sister Barratt to send them out directly.'

The two young women stood waiting with Mrs James when Mabel carried their babies, first one and then the other, to the room where they had been fed and loved. As nursery maid it was Mabel's duty to assist Mrs James in supervising this moment of farewell and she found it almost unbearable. One of the girls wept uncontrollably, her sobs echoing down the cream and brown painted walls of the first-floor corridor connecting the nursery with the Agnes Nuttall room and lying-in ward. Mabel put her arm around the girl's shaking shoulders, but felt that she had no words of comfort to offer. She could only think of the story in St Matthew's gospel, where the women of Israel wept for their lost children, and thought it the most heart-rending sound she had ever heard.

Mrs James nodded to Mabel to return the baby to the nursery and led the girl away, leaving Mabel with the other one who neither spoke nor wept, but just gazed upon her little son, the child she had borne and breastfed and come to love more than anything else in the world. She turned wide, despairing eyes to Mabel. 'Will there be somebody to love him, Miss Court?' she whispered.

'Yes, dear, he's such a beautiful baby, somebody's sure to want to give him a good home,' Mabel managed to say, though her voice faltered. 'Yer must go now, dear. Give him a kiss and then go without lookin' back.'

After that last kiss the girl had silently walked away, a blurred figure like an old woman with bent shoulders and a hand out to grasp the banister when she reached the stairs. As Mabel stood watching her go, her heart breaking with pity, Sister Lilley called out urgently from the birthing room. 'I need you in here at once, Miss Court! Hurry up, she's nearly ready to deliver.'

Kathy Bagshaw had been getting pains for more than two days; the last ten hours had been a terrible ordeal for her. Sister Lilley had asked Mabel to sit with Kathy when the nursery was quiet, to hold her hand, rub her back and generally encourage her while the midwife was otherwise engaged, and Mabel found it a harrowing experience, unable as she was to lessen Kathy's pain.

But now the birth was imminent and the exhausted girl had to make the final effort that pushed her baby's head out through the narrow passage. Sister Lilley turned her over on to her left side for the actual delivery, and Mabel had to hold up the right leg as the child's head emerged and the midwife received the limp body into her hands. Several vital moments passed before the child took a first gasping breath; its bluish-white face made Mabel think of her lost brother Walter, and she stared with a silent prayer on her lips as Sister Lilley held it up by the heels, blew upon the body and slapped its bottom and soles.

'Oh, the poor little thing—' Mabel almost groaned aloud at what seemed very rough treatment of the tender newborn baby after such a long and difficult journey.

But within a minute it gasped, breathed and cried weakly. Sister Lilley cleaned its nose and mouth, and said, 'It's a girl.' She handed it to Mabel while she attended to the mother, expelling the afterbirth and removing the blood-soaked mat of cotton wool and brown paper beneath her.

Mabel knew how to tie clean white string round the umbilical cord two inches from the child's body, and to powder the cut stump and apply a cotton bandage round the belly. After wiping the baby dry she dressed it in a plain tie-up gown and napkin secured with a safety pin; then she wrapped it in a small square blanket. Kathy Bagshaw's delivery was the fourth that she had seen, and the hardest and longest to date.

'Can I see 'er, Sister? Can I 'old 'er?' asked the mother.

The midwife handed the baby into her arms. 'The sooner you give the first feed, the better, Katherine,' she said. 'Undo your nightgown and make a start. All right, Miss Court, you can go now.'

'Fanks for all yer done, Mabel,' added Kathy weakly. A shaft of golden autumnal sunlight fell across the pea-green walls of the room, illuminating her drawn features as she hugged her baby close, and Mabel forced a smile at the sight of another girl becoming a mother, learning to breastfeed her child for six weeks and then . . .

Removing her white cap and rolling up her soiled apron, Mabel put on her hat and coat and went downstairs to the staff door at the side of the solid brick Victorian building. Out in the fading light of a late October evening she made her way down Lavender Hill, realising how tired she felt. It was not that the work itself was hard, on the contrary, the mothers themselves did most of the domestic work at the Rescue, both before and after delivery. They assisted in the kitchen, sewing room and laundry, and were responsible for cleaning their dormitories and living quarters. The only cleaning Mabel had to do was in the nursery and delivery room, so compared with the endless sweeping, dusting, brushing and sluicing at the Anti-Viv it was money for old rope, as Albert would say.

No, it was not the work that was hard. It was the situation of the relinquished babies that put an almost intolerable strain on Mabel. She yearned over the new lives in her care, each in his or her tie-up cotton gown and napkin, lying quietly asleep or awake and crying in the cots, peeping out at a world that was to take away a mother's love even before it could be comprehended. And there was nothing that Mabel could do: she felt emotionally drained dry, as if the last ounce of pity had been wrung from her heart – and what use was pity? She anguished for the baby who would never again be held in a mother's loving arms, or suck warm milk from her breast; from now on it would be held by a stranger and given a glass bottle with a hard rubber teat and a different kind of milk, sometimes too hot or too cold, not so satisfying, maybe causing the tender little stomach to reject it, to suffer pain and discomfort, diarrhoea, soreness – and to be all alone in the world. Hurrying down towards the maze of side streets between Queenstown and the Wandsworth Road, Mabel knew she would never get used to the sorrows of the Rescue.

And there was no comfort to be had at home. Annie would not allow her to talk in front of Alice and Daisy about what happened behind the high red-brick walls of the Agnes Nuttall Institute and discreetly lowered her own voice when referring to Mabel's place of work.

So where could she turn for counsel? Who would listen to the sad stories that haunted her? Who else but her best and dearest friend, her young man and future husband, Harry Drover. For him no subject was unmentionable, not if it concerned his dearest Mabel and he would listen endlessly on their walks while she poured out her thoughts and feelings about life at the Rescue. Looking down on her eager, upturned face, he realised how deeply she felt about the plight of the babies left motherless.

'There's this poor young girl we've got in at present, Harry, only fifteen, hardly older than Alice and so dazed by what's happened to her. Her father's a farmer in Surrey, honest country people – they must've been so shocked when they found she was . . . y'know, carryin' a child.'

'Who'd taken advantage of her, Mabel? Was she forced?' he asked, frowning.

'No, it seems she used to cross the fields to go to school with a boy o' the same age from a family livin' near. She told Mrs James they thought they were only playin'—' She broke off abruptly, lowering her eyes, conscious that her mother would have a fit, as the saying was, if she knew half of what Mabel confided in Harry Drover, things Annie Court would not have mentioned, let alone discussed.

But Harry's association with the Salvation Army had taught him a great deal about the darker side of life and he was not hampered by any such false delicacy. On the contrary, he was quick to reassure her that he understood. 'Ruby comes across cases like that, Mabel, and it's wrong to label that poor girl as a fallen woman,' he said in his thoughtful way. 'Though it's all too often the first step down the path to ... to prostitution. There's nothin' sadder 'n a good girl ruined.'

'It's just as sad for the baby,' rejoined Mabel quickly. 'Yer never saw such a poor little wizened-looking mite, scarce five pounds. She just sits an' stares at him when I put him in her arms. He'll go to the babies' home at Merton and she'll go back to her parents as if nothing had ever happened. But Harry, that poor little boy, I'm sure he'll die with nobody to love him.'

Tears welled up in her soft grey-blue eyes and Harry put his arm around her, ignoring the disapproving looks from a family group walking along the same path on the Common. 'Dearest Mabel, yer do wonderful work among them poor women and girls. Ye're an angel o' light at that Rescue and I'm that proud o' yer – and I believe the Lord'll show yer a way to help that girl an' her baby if that's what He wants.'

'Ye're a tower o' strength to me, Harry,' she murmured, nestling close to his shoulder. For it was true: his positive, understanding attitude never failed to raise her spirits and in a way he took the place of Albert, for in spite of the outward differences between the two they shared the same goodness of heart.

She told him that she was not really looking forward to Christmas at the Rescue. She could only see it as a difficult time for the young mothers waiting to give birth or contemplating the approaching separation from the new lives they had borne in pain. The Christmas story could hardly bring them comfort, she thought, for the Child born in a lowly stable had a loving young mother who kept Him and cared for Him throughout His childhood and young manhood; *and* she had the protection of a good husband to watch over her and the Child.

And what a pity that the arrival of a new baby should ever be cause of shame and disgrace. When she thought of her own mother's views about the girls at the Rescue, she found herself quite shocked by it, far more than by the fact of their unmarried state. Her discussions with Harry on the subject were a much-needed outlet for her feelings and brought the pair into a closer intimacy. On his part he was touched that she felt able to share these confidences with him and privately regarded them as being like talks between a married couple, which of course they would one day be – though he did sometimes wonder if he should gently warn her against expressing such charitable sentiments to anybody else but himself. She was so innocent in many ways, he thought tenderly.

The case of the fifteen-year-old mother was to have a happy ending, thanks to Mabel's intervention. She had quietly asked the girl where she lived and had written a letter to the parents at a place called Martyr's Green, begging the mother to visit her

194

daughter and the tiny baby son who, Mabel wrote, was not likely to survive if sent to the babies' home. The result had been beyond her best hopes, for not only the girl's mother but her father and two older sisters had all arrived at the Rescue and after one look at the baby had decided to acknowledge him as their own, whatever was said in the village. And home they all went, a triumph of love over social convention. Mabel was jubilant: it seemed that Harry's words had come true and she joyfully shared the happy news with him. He tried to advise her to be careful, but she could not resist quietly encouraging other girls with families to write their own letters home and tell their parents about their babies. 'Tell yer mother how beautiful he is and how much yer love him,' she would advise, or, 'Say she's the image o' her grandmother, an' got the family nose.' She helped them with the spelling, bought stamps and posted the letters off. Her satisfaction with the successes was only lessened by the failures, when the pleading letters had not brought about a change of heart.

'Hey, Mabel, yer grandmother's askin' to see yer, so ye'd better get over to Tooting before Christmas – don't keep her waitin' if she's feelin' generous!'

Mabel looked up at her father with a question in her eyes. 'I don't get that much free time, Dad, and when I do—'

She hesitated and Court correctly interpreted her shy little smile. 'Yeah, there's yer young man, I know. Well, get him to take yer over there – Mimi could give yer a helping hand if yer play yer cards right, girl.' He gave her a knowing wink. 'She wants to hear about this job o' yours at the Institute – it's in her line o' business, i'n't it?' He laughed good-humouredly. 'She'll probably tease yer about young Drover, but she could be a big help to both o' yer, Mabel.'

As always, Mabel consulted Harry who felt that she should go, especially as he was to accompany her, and they walked over to Tooting on the Sunday afternoon preceding Christmas. Mimi Court received them graciously and a smartly dressed maid brought in the silver tea service on a trolley. Mabel and Harry sat together on a settee opposite her and she eyed them with a general air of approval. Yet Mabel felt the familiar sense of unease that always came over her in this house, even with Harry at her side.

'So, Mabel, I hear ye're learnin' to be a midwife in a home for fallen women. Whoever would've thought it?'

'I only assist the midwife sometimes, Grand-mother, it's not a proper trainin',' said Mabel hastily, accepting tea and cake. 'I'm a nursery maid, but I get called to help in the delivery room an' lying-in ward.'

'Hm. They must think ye've got a good head on yer shoulders, then. And all the women are first-timers, which makes for long labours and more trouble all round. So yer get yer share o' hand-holdin' and back-rubbin' while the midwives are at their tea and gossip, eh?'

Mabel could think of no reply to this, but Harry answered promptly. 'They think the world o' her at that Institute, Mrs Court.'

Mimi nodded to him, a gleam of amusement in her dark eyes, and turned again to Mabel. 'But how d'ye like the work? Would ye care to take it up as I've done and have yer own practice one day?'

Mabel looked at Harry and answered firmly, 'I told yer before, Grandmother, I've always wanted to look after children and I'm going to train as a nurse when I'm old enough, at a Poor Law infirmary.'

'And what about Mr Drover here? Doesn't he come into these plans somewhere?'

Mabel blushed deeply and again Harry answered for her. 'One day when we're both older, Mrs Court, when I've trained as a Salvation Army officer and Mabel's a qualified nurse, we hope to serve the Lord together as a married couple in the Army. Mabel will be a great asset at one of the children's homes or refuges, and . . . and I shall be at her side,' he added with a loving glance at the girl of his dreams.

Mimi nodded again. 'Yer got a long time to go before then. Tell me more about the Institute, Mabel. Yer still haven't told me yet if yer like it. Do yer?'

Mabel hesitated. 'I feel I'm doing useful work there, but it's very upsettin', those long labours, so painful. But it's the agony o' parting with their babies that's the worst and breaks my heart.'

'What happens to them? The babies, I mean?'

'They go to a babies' home at Merton, an' some o' them get adopted from there.'

'But not all?'

'Some go to children's homes if they've got somethin' wrong with 'em – like we had one with a harelip that went to a hospital for an operation.'

'And the mothers go back to their homes as if nothin' had happened?'

'If they got homes, yes – only some go back into service if that's where they came from.'

'And everybody pretends there's never been a baby at all, eh?' Mimi's eyes darkened with a look of contempt. 'Hah! They make me laugh, these families who think they can shrug orf their daughters' little bastards, forget 'em, hide 'em away in homes – council homes, private homes, orphanages, Dr Barnardo's, Waifs an' Strays, homes for cripples, homes for imbeciles, Sunshine Homes for babies blinded by the clap – ugh, they make me sick!'

Her voice had become harsh, and Mabel looked at her in surprise, putting down her cup and glancing at Harry. 'One or two o' the girls *do* keep their babies, Grandmother, and get work as wet-nurses or find some woman who'll look after the child while they go out to work.'

This innocent remark seemed to infuriate Mimi all the more. 'Oh, yes? An' what sort o' work do they get, other than sucklin' another woman's child while their own goes short? There's no respectable work, no decent place for a girl lumbered with a baby, believe me! An' childminders more often than not take her hard-earned money an' let the child starve or die o' neglect. Oh, no, don't give me sentimental claptrap about keepin' their dear little babies, only to end up sellin' 'emselves on the street – 'cause that's what 'appens in the end, Mabel, yer can take it from me. An' what've *you* got to say, Mr Drover?'

Harry stared down at his hands for a few minutes, then replied in a low tone, 'Ye're only too right, Mrs Court, in a large number o' these sad cases. My sister Mrs Swayne, she's a servin' officer in the Salvation Army and, er, she sees—' He left the rest of his remark unsaid, but the drift was clear enough.

Mimi rose from her seat and went to the window, her plump shoulders tensed in unusual agitation. As always in times of emotion of any kind, her would-be genteel accent deserted her. ''Ave yer ever asked yerself 'ow your girls at the Rescue came to need rescuin', Mabel? Babies don't just turn up from nowhere, they 'ave to be planted. Do these girls ever tell yer 'oo the fathers were?'

'Not as a rule. Matron knows but she doesn't like it talked about,' said Mabel, thinking of the morning and evening prayers led by Mrs James, the exhortation to the mothers to lead pure and blameless lives in the future, resisting all temptations to sin.

'Well, I'll tell yer, Mabel – and Mr Drover too if 'e doesn't know already. 'Alf the fathers o' the bastards delivered at that Rescue o' yours are the 'usbands an' sons o' the families the poor girls work for, though there's precious few admit as much.' Mimi's voice fairly shook with rage. 'When it's one o' the men-servants 'oo's done the deed, a groom or a footman or some such, they don't get orf so easy – they may 'ave to marry the girl if they want to keep their place. But when it's young master, or old master, oh, dear me, no, the girl gets thrown out on 'er ear, an' if she's lucky she lands on the doorstep o' the Rescue, poor little fool.' She turned from the window and paced up and down the room, almost spitting out her words. 'It's the woman 'oo 'as to pay for the carelessness o' the man, Mabel, every bloody time!'

Harry rose to his feet. 'Ye're not well, Mrs Court, an' yer need to rest. I'll take Mabel home—'

This seemed to bring Mimi back to a recollection of her duty as gracious hostess. She shook her head, frowned and waved a bejewelled hand to indicate that there was no need for them to leave. She took a couple of breaths to compose herself and rang the bell for the maid. Harry resumed his seat, looking anxiously at Mabel who sat with downcast eyes; she had never before seen her domineering grandmother in such a state of turmoil.

The maid appeared and Mimi demanded more hot water. When the girl had bobbed a curtsey and gone, she looked hard at Mabel. 'Listen to me, my girl. I'd like to see yer make a good life for yerself. Ye've got Jack's brains but more common sense. Albert's a hothead and'll end up gettin' 'imself hanged, and I doubt George has got much upstairs, he's 'is mother's son. Alice is a pretty little thing who'll find 'erself an 'usband 'oo can keep her decently, an' Daisy's only a child as yet. But *you're* worth a helpin' hand, Mabel. My offer to take yer on as my assistant at a pound a week and all found still stands, so if yer want to save some money while ye're waitin' to start yer trainin' at nineteen or twenty, I'll make a midwife o' yer. But if ye'd rather stay at the Rescue for the pittance they pay, that's up to you. What d'ye say?'

She looked hard at Mabel and Drover was conscious of a feeling of revulsion towards this woman. Every instinct warned him that his Mabel would be making a great mistake by putting herself under obligation to her. Mabel looked at him for guidance and he frowned. 'It'd have to be your decision, Mabel.'

She nodded imperceptibly and turned to Mrs Court with her answer. 'Well, er – thank yer, Grandmother, it's good o' yer,' she said politely, 'but I'd rather live at home and go to the Rescue.'

Mimi shrugged and curled her lip. 'Suit yerself. Ye're still only seventeen, plenty o' time for yer to see sense an' change yer mind. Let me know when yer do.' Dismissing the subject, she turned to Harry. 'And what d'yer parents think o' yer young lady, Mr Drover?'

He coloured and hesitated. 'They, er, think we're

very young, but I shall never want any other girl but Mabel,' he answered, using the very words he had used to them.

'Hm. They sound as if they got a bit o' sense, then – for Salvationists.'

Mabel looked pointedly at the ormolu clock on the mantelpiece and drew on her gloves. 'We'd better be goin' now, Grandmother. Harry's got a meetin' and Mother expects me home for tea. It's been good o' yer to have us, an' thank yer for yer offer.'

'Ye're a fool not to accept,' said Mimi, getting up. 'An' before ye go, take this an' get yerself some decent new clothes – yer look a proper frump in that old-fashioned coat an' skirt.' She pushed an envelope into Mabel's hand. It turned out to contain ten pounds, nearly six months' wages at the Rescue.

On their way to the front door Miss Lawton came softly down the stairs. She stopped when she saw them and Mabel smiled up at her from the hall. 'Good afternoon, Miss Lawton.'

'Er, oh, yes, thank you – good afternoon, M-Mabel and Mr er—' stammered the pale, black-clad lady, turning to go back up the stairs.

'Oh, come on down for Gawd's sake if ye're comin',' snapped Mimi irritably, adding under her breath as Miss Lawton sidled past them, 'Give me strength! People'll be thinkin' this is some sort o' private asylum on account o' that one. Goin' the same way as . . . as the old lady. She'll end up talkin' to the fairies, I shouldn't wonder, an' I'll 'ave to pay nursin' 'ome fees.'

Mabel did not answer. She had always felt sorry for Miss Lawton who seemed to lead a very lonely life, yet she gave the house a certain air of respectability which Mimi lacked, for all her ostentation.

Was this why Mimi tolerated her, Mabel wondered: eccentric though she was, Miss Lawton was at least a *lady* and never uttered an unkind word about anybody.

They caught the tram back to Battersea and there was not much opportunity for them to discuss the visit. Harry did not speak of his instinctive dislike of Mrs Court, though he told Mabel that he would far rather she continued working at the Rescue than move to 23 Macaulay Road, no matter how generous her grandmother's offer.

'I'm glad yer think so, Harry. I know me mother wouldn't like it,' she answered wryly.

He said goodbye to Mabel when they reached Sorrel Street, as he was due to play in the band that evening, and she went in to find the family seated round the fire. Annie was smiling trustfully at Jack who seemed to be in a better frame of mind lately, though he could suddenly swing round to bursts of ill temper for no obvious reason.

As soon as she and Annie were alone in the kitchen Mabel knew that her mother would demand to know what had passed between her daughter and mother-in-law. 'Out with it, Mabel, what did she have to say this time?'

Mabel felt a little irritated by this interrogation. 'She asked me about the Rescue and if I enjoyed workin' there – how much I was paid—'

'Cheek! Go on. What else did she want to know? Come on, there was more to it than that.'

'Well, Mum, at least she showed some interest in my work, and asked about the mothers an' babies, which is more 'n you do,' Mabel pointed out.

Annie flushed. 'I don't like that sort o' talk in front o' your sisters and George. So did she want to know every unpleasant intimate detail? And in front o' Harry Drover?'

Mabel rolled up her eyes in exasperation. 'No, Mum, she offered to take me on at a pound a week an' all found, to be her assistant. That's what she said in front o' Harry, if yer must know. She said I could take me time and think about it. And there's nothin' else to tell, so there's no need for yer to be so funny about it.'

But Annie's eyes were blazing. 'I won't have you under any such obligation, d'you hear me? Not to *her*, I won't!'

'But Mum, she only made an offer to help me on in my career—'

'But don't you know what she *does*, Mabel? Good grief, you must know something o' the ways o' the world, working at that place!' Annie cried. 'Don't you know what she *is*?'

'She's a *midwife*, Mum! She delivers babies, mostly to women who can pay her well,' protested Mabel, completely bewildered.

'Ah, but what else? Not all o' her patients have babies, Mabel. Can't you see, don't you *know*? She gets *rid* o' babies, too!'

Just for a moment Mabel thought that her mother meant that Mimi arranged for adoptions. But then some words of her grandmother's came back to her and she remembered overhearing whispered stories between girls at the Rescue, about extreme measures taken by other girls they had known . . .

Mabel gasped as the truth gradually dawned on her. Of course. Mimi put an end to unwanted pregnancies in exchange for money. In a strange way she felt as if she had stumbled on something dark and dangerous that had been there for years, hidden from her knowledge but waiting to be revealed one day. Today. 'But that's murder – it's against the law and it's wicked,' she breathed, leaning against the draining board beside the sink.

'Of course it is and she could go to prison for a criminal offence – many times over, only she keeps it very dark. *Now* d'you see what I mean, Mabel? She's a bad woman and I don't want you to be beholden to her in any way!'

'How long have yer known, Mum? How did yer ... find out?' asked Mabel, her head reeling.

'It took me a long time, Mabel – I was very innocent, as you are, when I first met her and lived at that house before Jack and I were married and for six months after – until you were born, Mabel. She used to have girls coming to stay, to be delivered quietly or ... or to have it done away with. And she still does.'

'Oh, how *awful*, Mum, yer must've been so upset. Whatever did yer do when yer realised?'

Annie gave a brief, mirthless laugh. 'Oh, I was so green then, Mabel, I only gradually came to understand the kind o' woman she was, a thoroughly bad character. Why, she'd have got rid o' *you*, Mabel, if Jack hadn't been sure that he wanted to marry me and told her so in no uncertain terms! *Oh*! Oh, my God!' She suddenly clapped a hand to her mouth and stood staring at Mabel, her eyes dark in a sheet-white face. 'Oh, my God,' she repeated.

Mabel slowly took in the import of the words she had just heard and for a moment stood stock-still, returning her mother's anguished look. 'Yer mean yer were expectin' me before – oh, Mum!' And she burst into tears, overcome by the two shocks, one after the other: two revelations of human frailty beneath the surface respectability of their lives.

'Please try to forget you ever heard me say that, Mabel,' whispered Annie, shrinking back as if from a blow. 'Please, Mabel.'

As always, Mabel had to disregard her own feelings when faced with the sufferings of another, in this case her own mother, the woman who had borne her and now depended upon her – the mother she loved. She reached out to gather the trembling frame in her arms. 'Oh, Mum, don't worry about it – what difference does it make now, anyway? Oh, my poor mum, I'll never tell a soul, I promise. We'll never mention it again, ever.'

They stood there in the kitchen, their arms clasped around each other, and Annie's colour returned. 'I've loved you so much, Mabel – I've loved you all,' she said brokenly. 'And I loved your father. We were going to be married anyway, before we knew about – I mean there was never any question o' not going through with it. But the shock killed my poor father and my sisters never wanted to see me again.'

'Oh, Mum, yer poor dear – so *that* was why – oh, I see now,' said Mabel, nodding as she held Annie close and rocked her gently.

'Yes, you see now, don't you, Mabel.'

Yes, she understood a lot of things now. And then the thought came into her head: *Harry*. What on earth would he say if he knew about Mimi Court? Her own grandmother that she had taken him to see – an abortionist. She shrank from the very thought of the horrible word. He must never know, she decided quickly. In fact, the less said to anybody, the better. 'Come on, Mum, we'd better tidy ourselves up or they'll be wonderin' what's going on out here.'

Mabel forced a smile as she withdrew her arms. 'Let's put the kettle on for another cup o' tea all round!'

At that moment Jack came into the kitchen, followed by a trail of cigar smoke. 'Hey, what're you two up to, women's secrets? What's for supper? I'm famished, so are the others!'

He kissed Annie and winked at Mabel, clearly in a genial mood, and the two women busied themselves preparing the evening meal; Mabel did her best to help her mother behave as if nothing untoward had happened, but poor Annie burned with shame, not least because of her prudish attitude towards the women at the Rescue.

As for Jack Court, the truth was that he had received a humiliating rejection from a woman with whom he had been spending time, and at forty-two was feeling distinctly older and tireder. Maybe the time had come to put that sort of thing behind him and take on the role of the respected paterfamilias, to escort his family to St Philip's every Sunday and be looked upon as an upholder of Christian family values. And without Albert around with his accusing eyes, it was that much easier.

Or so he thought, before his world tragically fell apart and he lost everything.

Chapter Nine

Christmas Eve at the Rescue brought two happy outcomes within twenty-four hours of each other. Two young mothers who had written letters home received visits from relatives – the parents of one and the grandparents of the other – who tearfully took the babies into their arms and their hearts. Home they all went and Mabel was jubilant at what she had set in motion.

But Mrs James was not so pleased and looked hard at Mabel. 'It isn't always a good thing for a girl to keep a child born out of wedlock, Miss Court,' she said, frowning. 'There's been too many of them sending letters home lately and I think somebody may be putting them up to it. It's not something to be encouraged and the girls may live to regret it later in life. Others have no right to interfere in these matters.'

The meaningful look in her eyes as she said this made Mabel feel awkward and she suddenly remembered that she was needed elsewhere. Nevertheless, she could not regret what she had begun – how could she?

She often thought of her own mother and tried to imagine Annie's feelings when she'd discovered that she was carrying Jack's child while she was still Anna-Maria Chalcott – and how the shock of her hasty marriage had killed her father and alienated her sisters. Oh, poor Mum, what shame she must have endured and what sorrow! Mabel had promised never to mention it again, but she could not dispel the thought that her mother *might* have had to go to somewhere like the Rescue to have her baby; and that baby would have been herself, Mabel, given up to be adopted by some stranger or sent to a children's home. Or, if Mimi had had her way ... Mabel shuddered.

And she still thought her mother mistaken in not replying to Nell's letter. It would be so good for the sisters to be reconciled after all this time and how wonderful to have an aunt, perhaps two; to have *any* relations other than Grandmother Court!

On Christmas Day Mabel was on duty until five o'clock, and much of the morning was taken up with sitting beside a girl having a long and difficult labour. The local doctor on call for the Rescue was Dr Knowles and he was sent for to advise on Mary Cross's lack of progress after twenty-four hours of relentless painful contractions. Gravely he pronounced that the baby was lying in a transverse position and could not be delivered in the normal way, only by a Caesarean operation, a dangerous procedure that meant the patient had to be put to sleep. It could not be done at the Rescue. 'We'll have to send her to the General Lying-In at Lambeth,' Mabel heard Knowles say. 'And she'll need to go in an ambulance. I'm afraid they won't be very happy having to turn out on Christmas Day. Especially for one of these poor girls,' he added with a sigh.

Mabel helped to get the girl ready for her journey, putting a wool dressing gown over her nightdress, and socks and shoes on her feet. Mary was now too tired to groan; there was an acidic smell on her breath and she gasped as Mabel gave her a drop of water, which was all she could keep down.

Dr Knowles offered himself as escort in the ambulance and helped to carry Mary down the stairs, assisted by the cook, a burly woman whose services were called upon for heavy lifting.

Mabel followed them out to the waiting white van with its red cross painted on the side. 'Goodbye, Mary. God bless yer an' good luck,' she whispered. Mary's eyes were glazed and unfocused, but her hand clung to Mabel's until the door was shut with a bang and the van moved off.

A local butcher had donated a large turkey for Christmas dinner at the Rescue, and various churches and organisations had sent gifts of money and provisions to show their charity towards the fallen. Mrs James held an informal service of worship, as she did every Sunday in the Agnes Nuttall room, and Mabel was called upon to play the piano because the woman who usually played was away for Christmas. In spite of being out of practice, Mabel found to her surprise and relief that she had not lost the skill imparted by Miss Lawton, and was able to accompany them well enough. 'Away in a Manger' and 'Once in Royal David's City' were accomplished with only a few wrong notes in the bass, hardly noticed by the singers who had Mrs James's rich contralto to lead them.

After dinner had been cleared away there were the two-o'clock feeds to be given and by half past three, when the dull December dusk began to fall, an air of listlessness and anticlimax set in. There seemed nothing left to look forward to and they talked in low voices about poor Mary Cross, wondering if she was delivered yet.

Mabel's eyes turned towards the piano again. 'Come on, girls, what about a sing-song?'

They clustered round her eagerly, and old music books and sheet ballads were pulled out of the piano stool, a varied selection ranging from English folk songs to rousing patriotic ditties like 'Drake's Drum' and 'The British Grenadier'. Mabel racked her memory for favourite music-hall songs, but half of them were too romantic for the present company of deserted women and the other half too vulgar. So she began with carols, 'Good King Wenceslas' and 'The Holly and the Ivy', after which Mrs James chose 'Come into the Garden, Maud' which she sang as a solo to Mabel's careful accompaniment. The girls began to make requests and where there was no music Mabel played passably by ear.

An hour passed quickly by and it was time for tea, but eyes had brightened and hearts were lighter for the impromptu entertainment. A few tears were shed over memories the music conjured up for some of the young women, but they all agreed that it had been a happy hour.

'You've given us a lot of pleasure today, Miss Court,' said Mrs James. 'Go home now to your family and take tomorrow as a holiday – you've earned it!'

Mabel fairly skipped her way down Lavender Hill towards Queenstown and home to Mum and Dad, Alice, George and Daisy . . . and *Albert*, also home on a surprise visit and waiting for her at the door! Another Christmas present and what better?

'I was just abaht to come to that blinkin' Rescue an' kidnap yer,' he grumbled, but his dark eyes lit up at the sight of her and she could hardly speak as they embraced.

'He's learnin' to be a drummer, Mabel!' squeaked Daisy.

'You in a band? Never! Ye're tone deaf, ye're pullin' our legs!' Mabel laughed as he lifted her up off her feet and twirled her round like a ballet dancer.

'Thank Gawd yer got that job up the 'ill,' he muttered in her ear. She thought he looked older, and he kept them entertained with plenty of amusing and sometimes hair-raising tales about life on HMS *Warspite*. ''Ow's old 'Arry these days?' he asked. 'Still blowin' 'ell out o' that trombone an' trailin' after Mabel like a faithful 'ound?'

'Yer'd better watch what yer say, Albert, it was Harry who brought yer back from that awful infirmary, remember?'

'You an' 'im bofe, Mabel. Yeah, an' if 'e bags my favourite sister, well, I s'pose yer could do worse.' He grinned, dodging the back of Mabel's hand as it advanced towards his ear.

He had brought presents for them all: brooches for Annie, Mabel and Alice, a penknife for George, crayons for Daisy and even Jack got a tie. He seemed to have plenty of ready cash and was eager to throw it around. 'Got three days' leave, so we'll go up the Grand an' book a row o' seats in the name o' Court – might as well do the big while I'm 'ere, what d'yer say, Mum?'

Annie beamed happily from her elder son to her husband and back again, but her reply was interrupted by a knock at the door.

When Mabel saw Harry Drover on the step her heart leapt and she joyfully invited him to join them.

'Come in, come in, Harry, Albert's here,' she said, all smiles and blushes.

'Fancy an evenin' at the Grand tomorrer, 'Arry?'

'That's good o' yer, Albert, but I'm due to play in the band at the Citadel, y'see—'

'An' much as we'd all love to come along an' listen to yer trombone, 'Arry ol' son, we must admit we'd raver go for a little o' what we fancy at the Grand.'

'Don't be so rude, Albert!' cried Mabel, though she then turned shyly to Harry and put her head on one side in a prettily pleading gesture. 'Any chance o' gettin' out of it, Harry?'

How could he resist her? 'Well, er, p'raps I might be able to get a replacement.'

'Hooray!' shouted George and Daisy in unison, and Albert muttered, 'I 'ope yer realise what a favour I done yer, 'Arry, when I brought yer 'ere. 'Ooever gets Mabel'll be a lucky sod.'

'Oh, yes, I know I am, Albert,' replied Harry with such solemnity that even Albert hadn't the heart to tease him further, but clapped him on the shoulder and elbowed him in the ribs to show his approval. Harry winced, but flushed with pleasure.

Jack got up to open a bottle of wine. 'Get some glasses, Mabel, and we'll drink a toast. Welcome home, Albert, and Merry Christmas all!' He pulled the cork to echoes of 'Merry Christmas!' all round. Mabel caught Harry's eyes upon her and thought it the best Christmas ever.

Boxing Day brought another visitor to the door: two visitors, in fact. ''Appy Chris'muss, Mabel! A' right if we come in for a bit?'

'Maudie! What a lovely surprise – and this must be Teddy – my, hasn't he grown! But why aren't yer at

Lady Stanley's?' As soon as her old friend crossed the threshold Mabel sensed that all was not well.

'Yeah, well, she's bin dragged orf to 'Ertfordshire by ol' Bald-'ead, an' 'e reckons she don't need me there,' said Maudie, shivering a little. 'Cor, got a cup o' tea goin', Mabel? It's perishin' aht there and we jus' come all the way from Dulwich, Ted an' me.'

It seemed that Sir Percy Stanley had taken his young wife to their country estate for the festive season, away from her London friends and very much against her wishes.

'Fact is, the ol' man's bin gettin' suspicious,' confided Maudie as soon as she and Mabel managed to grab a moment alone. 'Sent for me an' asked no end o' questions, 'e did. Freatened me wiv the sack an' the police an' all sorts if I was shieldin' 'er. 'Course, I tol' the ol' fool she was as true as ever a wife could be, never looked at anuvver bloke, never even—'

'But did he believe you, Maudie?' asked Mabel.

'I dunno, Mabel, I jus' dunno.' Maudie shook her head dolefully. ''Course, I was lyin' in me teeth – I 'ad to keep lookout for 'er nearly an hour while she was closeted up wiv 'er special gen'leman friend – I fought they mus' be gettin' up to summat, but then I 'eard 'er cryin' 'er eyes out, poor fing – I s'pose she must've bin tellin' 'im 'ow she'd got to go away for Chris'muss.'

'D'ye mean that Viscount Eastcote?' asked Mabel abruptly.

''Ow did yer know that?' asked Maudie in alarm.

'Ada Clay saw a bit about her in the *Daily Mail* just after the coronation and it mentioned him. There was a picture o' them together.'

'Oh, my Gawd, I'd forgotten about that – might've

213

bin when the ol' man first started smellin' a rat. Ugh, gives me the creeps, 'e does.'

'I'd've thought they'd've taken yer with 'em to Hertfordshire,' said Mabel.

'Nah, 'e wouldn't let 'er, I *told* yer, 'e said I was to stay at Bryanston Square. Charlie's gone an' all the men, the place is like a morgue. It's no fun wiv'out 'Er Ladyship, there's only the ol' 'ousekeeper an' a couple o' catty maids 'oo've bin givin' me 'ell 'cause she ain't there to stop 'em. I was really lookin' forward to Chris'muss, an 'avin' Teddy to stay – I went down to Dulwich to take 'im out for the day – only we ain't got nowhere to go. Oh, Mabel!'

Mabel had never before seen her self-assured friend Maud Ling in tears. 'Oh, Maudie, dear, don't cry. Lady Stanley might be a bit more careful when she comes back, an' everything'll be as it was before,' she said, trying to sound hopeful, though in fact that situation between Lady Stanley and her husband and lover sounded distinctly tricky.

Maudie dried her eyes and finished her tea. 'Fanks, Mabel, ye're a pal. It's just that I really love 'er, yer see, she's been that good to me an' Teddy – said she'd take 'im on as a manservant soon's 'e leaves the Waifs an' Strays at Dulwich. But fings ain't goin' to be so easy now, an' I'll 'ave to keep in wiv ol' Bald-'ead if I wants to stay in me job!'

The brother and sister remained at Sorrel Street for the day, and Albert walked up to the Grand to see if there were any cancellations; there were two, but not near the row booked for the Courts. Albert cheerfully bought them, and presented them to Jack and Annie; the rest of them occupied the row, Mabel between Harry and Albert, then Maudie, Teddy, George, Daisy and Alice.

'Wasn't it a scream, Mabel? Cor, we'll never forget tonight, will we, Ted? Fanks a million times, Albert, ye're a good 'un!' exclaimed Maudie when they saw the Lings on to the train at Clapham Junction, just across the road from the Grand.

'Cheerio, Maudie,' said Mabel, kissing her. 'An' let me know how it goes.'

She was not at all happy about her old friend, but did not think it would be right to discuss her confidences with Harry, who now took her arm as they walked back to Sorrel Street. Instead, she remarked on her father's good humour over the festive season and how much it meant to her mother.

Of course Harry said he was pleased to hear this, but for himself he was not so sure. There had been a feverish gaiety, an exaggerated bonhomie on Jack's part, it was true, but Harry had looked at the man's eyes when he was not aware of being watched and thought he saw something like despair in their depths.

When Mabel returned to the Rescue the following day, it was to hear that Mary Cross had lost her baby and was still at the General Lying-In Hospital because she had developed an infection following delivery. Mabel heard the horrific details from Sister Lilley. It had been decided not to do a Caesarean operation as no heartbeat could be heard, and a 'destructive operation' had been done. A skull perforator and a decapitation hook had been passed up into the womb and the dead child removed piecemeal. Sister Lilley shrugged at Mabel's horror. 'What *should* they have done, then, leave her to die with it inside her? In her circumstances it's probably all for the best.'

Mary Cross was transferred back to the Rescue on New Year's Day, anaemic and hollow-eyed, vowing that she would never again conceive a child, in or out of wedlock.

It was Ada Clay, soon to be Mrs Arthur Hodges, who showed Mabel the brief notice in the *Daily Mail*'s Court Circular column.

> Sir Percival Stanley and Lady Cecilia returned to their town residence in Bryanston Square on Friday, 5 January, after spending Christmas at their country estate. Lady Stanley will be hostess at a charity ball to be held at Apsley House on Friday, 19 January, in aid of the Waifs and Strays Society, a cause known to be very dear to Her Ladyship's heart.

Mabel gave a sigh of relief and let Ada chatter happily on about the carefree lives of the rich. She would not talk of this to Harry, she decided. It was all very well to tell him stories about the girls at the Rescue, but Lady Cecilia's goings-on were best kept quiet. His time, like hers, remained fully occupied with his work at the railway depot and his voluntary activities with the Salvation Army. It was now 1912 and their dream of the future seemed to be forever receding, or so it appeared to Harry.

'I've been thinkin', Mabel, and I've got to talk to you,' he said one evening in early spring. They were standing in the narrow hallway of 12 Sorrel Street, taking the opportunity to exchange a goodnight kiss. During his brief visit there had been no opportunity to speak with her alone, and he had been rather unpleasantly conscious of Jack Court's glowering presence and Annie's nervousness. There had been a distinctly uncomfortable atmosphere and Mabel had seemed awkward, as she always was when her parents were with them. 'Mabel, dear, if I was to get me trainin' done, I'd be an officer by 1914,' he said earnestly, gazing into her eyes to note her response to each word. 'It'd mean givin' up what I earn from the railway, an' I won't be able to save while I'm at college, but I'm young, we both are, an' I feel I ought not to deny the Lord's clear call to me any longer.'

Mabel followed his reasoning and hastened to tell him so. 'Dearest Harry, yer must do exactly what yer think's right. Go an' do yer training and I'll carry on at the Rescue for another couple o' years.'

'We won't be able to see much of each other while I'm at Clapton,' he reminded her.

'But we don't have that much time together now, Harry, do we?' She sighed. 'And me thoughts'll be with yer every day, just the same as now!'

'Bless you, Mabel,' he whispered as she hid her face against his shoulder. 'Can I ask yer somethin', dear? D'ye feel the Lord's voice callin' yer to service in the Army?'

She looked up in some surprise. 'Why, yes, Harry, I want to be in it with you when I'm a trained nurse and we're married, just as we've always said.'

'It's just that it seems such a long way off, Mabel, an'—' He hesitated, seeing the troubled look in her soft grey-blue eyes; his heart yearned over her, but there was something that he felt he must say. 'The fact is, yer seem to be so tied to yer home, to yer mother – an' sometimes I wonder if there'll ever be a time when ye'll be free.'

She lifted her head and looked at him straight in

the eyes. 'I don't know, Harry. I'm needed here and that's the truth – for the time bein', I mean.'

There seemed to be nothing more he could say and he bent his head to kiss her. 'I'll pray for yer, Mabel, every night an' mornin' – my own dear girl,' he murmured, his lips touching her hair almost reverently. His arms were round the slender waist, feeling the youthful curves of her body beneath the white pin-tucked blouse. For him she was the most beautiful thing imaginable, a vision of all that young womanhood should be.

The sweet, shared moment was brought to a sudden shattering end as Jack Court flew out of the front room where he had been sitting with Annie and hurled himself bodily at Harry. 'What the bloody 'ell d'ye think ye're up to, Drover? Take yer slimy 'ands orf my daughter an' get out o' my 'ouse, yer cantin', preachin', Bible-thumpin' 'Oly Joe!'

'*Dad*!' screamed Mabel, struggling to pull her father away from Harry who was making attempts to evade Court's wildly flailing fists, but did not actively retaliate.

Annie appeared at the door of the front room, her pallid face aghast. '*Jack*!' she shrieked. 'Leave him, he's a good boy, he loves Mab—'

'Loves 'er enough to bugger up 'er life, stop 'er from betterin' 'erself. I know 'is sort, the crafty bastard. Salvation bloody Army – I'll *kill* 'im!'

Harry wrenched himself free and opened the door, panting heavily. 'Come with me, Mabel, don't stay 'ere – come 'ome with me, *please*!'

'I *can't*, Harry, I can't leave Mum an' the children,' she cried frantically. 'Go on, go on, I'll see yer when I can, only just *go* – get *away*!'

Looking back later, Mabel saw this incident as the

218

beginning of the trouble that was to befall them all, though Jack's rage evaporated as quickly as it had flared up and he seemed scarcely to remember it.

Annie tried to defend him to Mabel, though she admitted that his behaviour had been strange at times, alternating between loving moods and sudden abrupt rejections. 'Don't be too hard on him, Mabel, it's only that he doesn't think young Drover's good enough for you. Just leave him to settle down again – you can always meet Harry at the Citadel.'

'That's all very well, Mum, but he can't treat people like that – he'll get himself arrested if he does!' Mabel was extremely indignant. 'He'd never have *dared* to go for Harry like that if Albert had been at home!'

'Oh, don't make things worse, Mabel, your father's usually so kind and thoughtful, especially when I haven't been feeling up to the mark – you know, this heavy flooding, it leaves me so tired.'

Mabel knew only too well. The folded linen rags that her mother wore appeared in a bucket under the sink every three weeks, heavily bloodstained and with sickeningly large clots. When she had urged Annie to consult Dr Knowles, her mother shuddered at the very thought. 'It's a woman's lot, Mabel. Most o' the women I know have the same trouble after having a family and none of us want ... an operation.' She lowered her voice as she uttered the dreaded word. 'Anyway, it's not the sort o' thing a woman can talk about to a man.'

'But he's a *doctor*, Mum, and you've known him for years,' pleaded Mabel in exasperation. 'He might send you to a specialist at the Bolingbroke Hospital or the Anti-Viv and yer never know, there might be something they can do.'

It was of no avail. Annie was resigned to 'women's trouble' and trusted that the 'change of life' in a few years' time would release her from the regular ordeal. She was thirty-seven.

The next day after Jack's outburst Harry waylaid Mabel as she was returning from the late shift at the Rescue in the evening. He had been waiting for her to appear, having not had a minute's peace of mind since the violent scene of their parting. 'Oh, Mabel, there you are, thank God! How're things at home? Are yer all right?'

'Yes, yes, he settled down in an hour and behaved as usual, as if nothing had happened.'

'But he's *mad*, Mabel, dangerous – I worry all the time about yer. Let me take yer away from Sorrel Street, I know a Salvation Army couple yer can lodge with—'

'How could I, with me mother not well an' the children needing me?' she asked helplessly. 'It'd be best if yer got on with yer trainin', Harry, because I can't leave Sorrel Street, so don't ask me to.' She spoke with a finality that he knew it would be useless to oppose.

They were standing on the corner of Clapham Park Road, with people passing them by; it was not a time for embracing, but Harry took hold of her hand. 'I can't help worryin' about yer, Mabel, thinkin' o' yer under the same roof with that man.'

'I've *told* yer, I can't leave the others. Ye'll just have to pray for us all, Harry – and me dad.'

For once Harry Drover felt a lack of charity and his usually kind mouth hardened, aware of his own powerlessness in this frightening situation. 'Oh, Mabel, my love – yer know I'm always here, waitin' for yer. I'd wait for ever.'

'I know, Harry,' she answered. 'I know.'

Worried as she was about her mother, Mabel now began to be seriously concerned about her father's unpredictable behaviour. She could only speculate about what kind of pressure he might be under, but warned by Annie, she did not try to approach him in order to talk about it. There seemed to be a conspiracy of silence in the home and she did not question the children, which was something she later regretted.

Working long and often irregular hours at the Rescue, sometimes on the evening shift, it was some time before Mabel realised that George and Daisy were coming home later and later from school. They would glance warily at each other over supper and were oddly silent in their father's presence. This seemed to irritate Jack all the more and he constantly nagged at George, forever telling him to sit up straight, speak clearly and use what brains he had.

To celebrate her eighteenth birthday Mabel planned to bring home a fried fish supper for them all, and told Annie to have the table laid and hot plates ready. As she turned the corner of Sorrel Street with the newly wrapped supper in her leather shopping bag, she saw a knot of women standing muttering to each other near to her own front door, and at the same time she heard furious shouts and screaming from inside the house. Shoving her bag with the packets of fish and chips under her arm, she charged through the door and came upon Jack attacking George, punching him viciously round the head while the boy cringed and held his arms across his face to fend off the blows. 'You stupid, bloody idiot – you brainless little numbskull!' Jack was shouting, apparently beside himself with rage. Daisy was screaming in terror and Annie clung helplessly to an open-mouthed Alice.

Flinging her bag aside, Mabel flew straight at her father, a ball of fury, clouting his head with her bunched fists and shrieking at the top of her voice. 'Just like a little wildcat,' the neighbours told each other later. 'Stop it, *stop it*, leave him alone, don't yer *dare*! Shame on yer, Father, *shame* on yer!'

Jack Court whirled round and stared at her like the madman Harry said he was. She gave an involuntary gasp at the utter misery on his face. His eyes burned in their sockets and his mouth gaped open, a drooping cavity like the tragic mask depicted on the curtain of the Grand.

Two of the neighbours now ventured in, emboldened by the sound of Mabel's furious defence of her brother, and she heard a horrifying tale from them. 'Them poor little kids 'ave been afraid to come 'ome when that brute's there, Mabel – 'fraid to come 'ome, they been!'

George was giving little whimpering sobs and Daisy was still screaming, but once again Mabel knew that she had to compose herself and take charge. 'Hush, Daisy, quiet, I'm here now, it's all right. Mum, you see to George and Alice, you put the kettle on for tea. Mrs Bull – Mrs Clutton – will yer just stay with my mother an' Daisy for a couple o' minutes? Thank yer.' Then, trembling from head to foot, she turned to face her father, beckoning him out into the backyard. He followed her dazedly. 'Ye'd better make yerself scarce and be quick about it,' she told him with cold emphasis. 'Somebody'll've sent for the police or the cruelty people, an' they could be here any minute.'

He seemed to have lost all strength and leaned his head against the wall. 'Let 'em come, Mabel, I wish they'd come an' have done with it. I'm done for.'

She did not know what to think. Was he ill? Was he going mad? 'For God's sake, Dad, what's wrong with yer?' she cried. 'First yer attack Harry for no reason at all and now this. How *could* yer treat George like that? And *why*? He's always been a good boy, a son to be proud of – he's never deserved this.'

The only answer was a groan that seemed wrenched from his very guts. He was clearly suffering agony – was it remorse? – and when he finally managed to speak, his voice was hoarse and desperate. 'I've got to go away, Mabel. Ye'll have to look after yer mother and the kids.'

'Just tell me what's the matter, that's all I want to know. Are yer ill? Why don't yer see Dr Knowles?'

'Nothin' he can do, not for this,' he muttered.

'Then what is it, Dad?' she persisted. 'Tell me! I shan't breathe a word to a soul.'

'Oh, Mabel, Mabel, if only I could,' he groaned, putting his hand to his face as tears filled his eyes. 'God forgive me, girl, if only – if only—'

And in spite of having just seen him brutally attacking his twelve-year-old son for no reason, Mabel could feel pity for the man. She took a breath. 'Tell me, Dad, is it money?'

'No, Mabel. There's never been enough money in this house, but Mimi's helped out with the rent and we've managed. It isn't that.'

So she asked the other question, clearly and directly: 'Is it some woman, Dad? Some woman who . . . who's maybe expecting a child?'

He turned sharply away from her. 'No, Mabel, no.

Not a child. Don't ask me, Mabel, just pray for me, girl, that's all. An' take care o' poor Anna-Maria.'

He choked on a sob and she instinctively held out a hand to him. 'I'll do my best for her, Dad. And I'll pray for yer both. So will Harry Drover,' she could not resist adding.

'Forgive me, Mabel. I never deserved yer – or her.'

There seemed nothing more she could say. A terrible sense of foreboding gripped her as he let go of her hand and averted his face. 'I must go. God help me, I must go. Goodbye, Mabel.'

And he was gone.

George had to stay off school because of his swollen black eye and bruised lip. His condition could not be kept from the neighbours who denounced Court in no uncertain terms: 'Ought to be up before the magistrates, the drunken brute.'

But Court had not been drunk and Mabel had seen a soul in torment looking out of his eyes.

Chapter Ten

Jack Court had often been away from home; in fact, it was frequently remarked that he spent more time at racecourses (and heaven knew where else) than at Sorrel Street. But when two weeks had passed with no word at all, Mabel begun to wonder if she should make some enquiries at Lavender Hill police station and local public houses. Yet Jack had told her that he had to 'go away', which surely meant that he was some distance from Battersea and she had no wish to walk into the public bar of the Falcon or the Plough in search of his associates, arousing speculation and rumours.

She knew, of course, that she should first check with her grandmother, to find out if Jack had appeared at Macaulay Road. There had been little communication between the two households since Mabel had turned down Mimi's offer and Annie's subsequent revelations had distanced her still further in Mabel's mind. Besides, she was reluctant to face the scornful looks she knew she would get if she went looking for her father there and in the end she asked Alice to go over to Tooting. 'Just say casually that Dad's been away since the end o' March, an' ask if he's happened to call there,' Mabel told her sister.

Alice returned with no news, though she said that their grandmother had seemed irritable and out of sorts. 'She seemed bothered about something, Mabel, but she didn't let on about it.'

'Did yer tell her about him having these fits o' temper?'

'I said he'd disappeared after going for George on your birthday and she gave me a funny look, but didn't say anything – except that she was busy, so I took the hint.' Alice shrugged.

'And was that all? No message?'

'No, she was quite offhand, didn't ask how George was, or any of us. But she was worried and I'm pretty sure she knows somethin' more than she says.'

It was not that any of them – except Annie – actually missed Jack and wanted to see him again; life was far easier without his unpredictable moods. Not that they were without problems: Annie seemed to sink into a resigned hopelessness – and helplessness, too, Mabel thought, afraid that her mother might become semi-bedridden, growing progressively weaker as the regular heavy blood loss took its toll. Then she developed more alarming symptoms, sweating and shivering by turns, with a persistent headache and sore throat.

'Yer must've caught a chill, Mum,' said Mabel, bringing in the morning cup of tea. She plumped up the bolster on the old wooden bedstead with its sagging horsehair mattress, and put her own pillow under her mother's; she had taken to sleeping with her since Jack had left. 'Stay in bed today, Mum, and I'll try to get home around midday to see how yer are – and if yer won't take a little beef broth and milk pudding I'll ask Dr Knowles to call, whatever yer say.' Mabel blamed her mother's poor appetite for her low resistance to every passing germ.

Annie frowned and shook her head. 'There's really no need to have the doctor round. I'll be all right again in a few days, when I've finished with the –

226

you know, the other.' She could never bring herself to utter words like 'period' or anything appertaining to the reproductory system. 'Besides, he'd have to be paid.'

'We can pay him his five pence a week, we're on his panel,' Mabel answered firmly. 'Yer health's more important than new shoes, Mum.'

Yet money *was* a problem, there was no denying it. With nothing from Jack she could not support the five of them on what she earned from the Rescue, let alone pay the rent. Alice resented being asked to contribute all but two shillings of her weekly wages, but George had taken on an early newspaper round and willingly gave all his meagre pay to the housekeeping.

Had Mabel known it, her mother was not only concerned about paying the doctor, she was afraid of what he might find. If he asked to examine her woman's parts he would discover that hard, painless, nasty-looking place on her tender flesh. Was it the beginning of a growth of some kind? Annie had heard horrid stories of unfortunate women who developed huge cauliflower-like warts in that area, that spread and bled...

When the news of the sinking of the great passenger liner *Titanic* broke upon a stunned nation with reverberations that echoed around the world, it seemed to Mabel to be one more disaster in a year that had brought nothing but trouble so far. They had no personal connection with the tragedy, but the newspaper accounts and comments brought home in vivid detail the rapid destruction of the mighty vessel, broken up by an iceberg on her maiden voyage, as if to point up man's insignificance when pitted against the forces of nature. Mabel could hardly envisage fifteen hundred lives lost, and tried not to dwell upon the terrible scene; but Annie became almost obsessed by it, lying awake at night beside Mabel, picturing the last desperate struggles of the men, women and children drowning in the icy water. She saw their frantically waving arms, growing weaker as the cold penetrated their bodies, sapping their strength, dulling their minds. She heard their last cries stifled as their faces fell beneath the surface, becoming blank and still, water filling their lungs, stopping their heartbeats.

Her moans woke Mabel who reared up in alarm. 'What is it, Mum? Is it yer head again? Yer throat?'

'It's all right, Mabel, just a dream. I'm sorry – go back to sleep, dear.'

But more often than not Mabel would reach for her dressing gown and go downstairs to light the gas ring and brew a pot of tea for them both.

When Annie developed a reddish-brown rash on her trunk, Mabel hesitated no longer. 'I'll leave a message at Hillier Road for Dr Knowles to call today,' she said.

Annie's heart sank, but she knew that Mabel's mind was made up. She hoped that the doctor would be content with looking down her throat, and listening to her chest and back with that thing he stuck in his ears.

She was alone in the house when Knowles called at two o'clock on the fatal afternoon of Tuesday, 30 April and went upstairs to where she lay waiting in dread. As soon as he saw the rash he assumed a bland, professional manner to hide his shock and dismay. 'Right, Mrs Court, I'll take your temperature and pulse. Then I'll have to make a thorough general examination.'

When he asked her to open her mouth wide while he shone his electric torch into her throat, he saw the ulcers with the characteristic 'snail-trails'. 'Mm-mm. Now I'd like to feel your neck and armpits, Mrs Court. Sit up nice and straight for me, that's right. Let me see if you have any swollen glands. Ah, yes . . .' There were indeed hard, knotty little lumps on both sides of her neck and under her arms. And in her groins. 'Come on now, my dear, pull up your nightgown and let me examine you down here – don't worry, I shan't need to feel internally, just to look. Can you part your thighs just a little more?'

And he saw the primary chancre. My God, he thought, that this should happen to this woman of all people. How could he tell her? He couldn't. 'All right, Mrs Court, that will do. You can cover up again now. Let me ask you a few questions, if I may. I believe your husband's away at present?'

'Yes, Dr Knowles, and I don't have any idea when he'll be back. He's been gone four weeks now and we've heard nothing.'

'I believe his work has often taken him away over the years, hasn't it?'

'Yes, but not usually as long as this without even a postcard. I just can't think why he hasn't been in touch.' She sighed.

'Has his health been good on the whole?'

'Yes, but something's been troubling him lately, Dr Knowles – before he went away, I mean. Jack's always been a bit . . . unpredictable, you know, but he had two really bad brainstorms before he left and I know he was just as upset about it as the rest of us.'

'Mm-mm. Now, Mrs Court, I wonder if you can

229

remember when you and Mr Court last had conjugal union?'

The question, casually asked, seemed strange to Annie, even uncalled-for. She hesitated. 'Not for some time. I've had this heavy bleeding, you see. But we had been – we *seemed* to be – much more, er, settled. Christmas was such a happy time for us.' Her mouth curved in a little secret smile at the memory.

Knowles averted his eyes. 'But what about the last time, my dear, when would that have been?' he persisted gently.

'Well, January and Feb—yes, we had a time in February,' she recalled, 'just before I started my ... yes, that was it, about halfway through February, not since then.'

He nodded slowly. Not good.

'Why d'you ask, Dr Knowles? I know I've got the usual women's trouble, but d'you think there may be something else? Anything like a ... a growth?'

Knowles hesitated very briefly, entwining his fingers together as he replied, sitting on the side of the bed. 'Not exactly a growth, my dear, but it could be troublesome if it's not treated.' He cleared his throat. 'And I'm afraid the treatment could be quite long and difficult, involving regular injections of, er, fairly strong substances like mercury and ... another preparation. You'll need to have a blood test and attend at a special hospital, the Lock Hospital for Women.'

And then he noticed it, the other nightgown showing underneath the bolster. The sight of it was like a chill hand clutching at his heart.

Annie saw him raise his eyebrows and answered the question he was about to ask. 'Mabel's been sleeping with me since Jack went,' she explained.

'She's such a good girl, I just don't know how I'd manage without her.'

Oh, no. Knowles needed all his professional self-control as a doctor to hide his fears for Mabel. 'Ah. Now, I don't think that's advisable, Mrs Court. You need to avoid any spread of infection such as shared bed linen, towels, cups – contact such as kissing—'

'Why, it's not catching, is it, Dr Knowles?'

He cleared his throat again. 'Not in the usual sense, no, but it's best not to take any risks, my dear,' he said, thinking of Mabel working at the Rescue and handling the babies – and of what he would be obliged to do without delay, the further blow he must deliver to that unsuspecting girl. Oh, God, where was mercy? And justice? *She* would need to have a blood test, too, but he did not mention this to her mother. 'And you'd better keep to your room and have your own crockery and so on.'

'What shall I say to Mabel then, doctor?' Annie looked worried.

'For the time being you can say I'm arranging for you to see a specialist and ask her to come to my surgery when convenient. She can ask me any questions she might have then.' Though God alone knows how I shall answer the poor girl, he silently added to himself, overwhelmed with pity for mother and daughter. He took a small blue phial from his bag. 'Take five drops of this at night, Mrs Court, to help you to sleep and to settle you generally. It's only a solution of laudanum, nothing very strong. I'll call again tomorrow to let you know what I've arranged and also to take the blood sample.'

Having taken his leave of her, Knowles went downstairs and washed his hands thoroughly under the single cold tap at the kitchen sink. He wondered if Jack Court was aware of his wife's infection – and his own. It probably explained the man's absence, he surmised.

But never mind about Court, the longer he stayed away the better. It was Mabel's misfortune that now weighed upon Knowles's heart, for he must go straight up to the Rescue to tell her – and the Matron – that she must be suspended from her duties until the results of a blood test certified her to be free of infection.

Cycling up Lavender Hill with his direful message, he suddenly found himself caught up in the immediate aftermath of an accident. An omnibus had been in collision with a pair of young men on bicycles, and there was a great deal of shouting and accusation between the bus driver and one of the cyclists who was calling upon the witnesses to confirm the driver's disregard for safety. It was the condition of the other youth that concerned Knowles; he lay writhing in the middle of the road, unable to raise himself, and the doctor suspected a spinal injury. Two police constables arrived from the nearby station, and Knowles asked if one of them could go back and telephone for an ambulance. 'Better get him to the Bolingbroke as soon as possible,' he said, kneeling beside the man and asking him questions about where he felt pain, and quickly checking reflexes as well as he was able. Passengers on the bus were demanding treatment for the shock they had received, mothers were trying to calm squalling children, and an old lady said she had been hurled forward against the seat in front and 'broken her nose'.

By the time an ambulance had arrived to convey the injured man to hospital with his friend, and

Knowles had offered reassurance and advice to the shaken passengers, he had been delayed for over an hour; and when he at last reached the Agnes Nuttall Institute it was to be told that Miss Court had already left, having been allowed to go early because of her anxiety over her mother.

'But I have something that I must tell you, Mrs James.' And in the privacy of Matron's office the doctor explained to her that Mrs Court *might* have a serious contagious infection and that it just *might* have been passed on to her daughter, though he emphasised that this was very unlikely. However, in order to be absolutely certain, a test must be carried out on a blood sample and Miss Court would have to await the results of it before resuming her duties as nursery maid.

'Can you tell me what kind of infection this is, Dr Knowles?'

He managed to give an explanation that sounded scientifically convincing without actually naming his suspicions.

Which increased Mrs James's suspicions all the more. They'd had a couple of admissions to the Rescue who'd needed blood tests and one had been quickly transferred elsewhere . . .

Annie Court was left to ponder on what the family doctor had said and her thoughts at first made little sense, like the pieces of a jigsaw puzzle thrown on to a table, a jumble of unrelated shapes. Slowly they began to piece together into some sort of order; she closed her eyes and heard the doctor's words again, and saw the gravity on his face.

The Lock Hospital – where had she heard it mentioned before?

Mercury and ... some other strong substance. It sounded drastic and everybody knew that mercury was a deadly poison.

'Contact such as kissing' – and that intimate question about conjugal union and Jack's state of health ...

All at once the jigsaw pieces fell into place and Annie understood the truth with dreadful clarity. It was the streetwalker's disease. She had syphilis – the *pox*!

She cried out loud, a howl of utter despair, and writhed in the bed, her hands over her face. The *pox*, the 'hidden horror' spoken of only in whispers, that attacked every part of the body, causing blindness, madness and paralysis at the end. The awful punishment of fornicators and lechers, visited on the innocent as well as the guilty, even upon the children.

Oh, Jack, Jack, what have you done to us both? You've gone away to die because of this.

And almost immediately she saw what had to follow: *and so must I.*

For of course she could not live with it. Life held nothing more for her, with this hideous thing in her flesh, the result of Jack's infidelity – for she now squarely faced the truth that she had known for years, the women he had been with away from home, to which she'd turned a determinedly blind eye. She could not possibly face Mabel (imagine!) and her other dear children, knowing what was destroying her body. There was only one thing left for poor Annie Court to do now. And not much time to do it.

She got out of bed and dressed as quickly as she could. Downstairs she found a few sheets of writing paper in a drawer of the sideboard, which also yielded a school pen and a bottle with just enough ink in it. Annie sat down at the table and put a newspaper on it to protect the dark-red chenille cloth. She rubbed her hands together to stop them trembling and with difficulty penned a letter to Mabel. Being out of practice with writing, she had to cross out words and replace them with others; she would have liked to begin again, but time was pressing, and when she put it in an envelope and sealed it, she felt that it contained what she most wanted to tell her eldest daughter.

Where should she leave it? It must not be found too soon, or she might be pursued. She slid it under the chenille tablecloth, changed every four or five weeks; meals were laid on a white cloth spread over it.

She pinned up her hair and pulled on her brown velour hat, laced up her shoes and put on her seldom worn three-quarter-length coat over her plain brown skirt. She took her purse from the kitchen drawer and placed it in her straw shopping bag, along with an old handleless cup used for breaking eggs in and the little blue phial that Dr Knowles had given her.

It was time to say goodbye to 12 Sorrel Street. She picked up her bag and let herself out of the front door, she who had become almost a recluse, and looked up at the house that had been her home for eighteen years of marriage and family life. There had been a few good times, and in spite of much worry and disillusionment she had managed to maintain the image of a respectable suburban housewife. Locking the door, she pushed the key back through the letter box. It was nearly half past three and there was no more time to lose. And no going back now.

She wondered if she should go to St Philip's church on Queen's Road and kneel in a pew there for the last time; but she might meet somebody she knew, or worse still, Alice might see her from the doorway of the post office. No, she must board an omnibus to take her away over Battersea Bridge into the city where nobody knew her.

On the bus she kept her face lowered to avoid any neighbours who might see and try to speak to her, but it seemed there had been a serious accident on Lavender Hill and everybody was talking about it, so no one noticed the drab little woman clutching her shopping bag.

Getting off at Westminster, she looked up at the great Abbey and felt drawn to enter it for a last prayer. Wandering up the echoing vastness of the nave, surrounded by its soaring columns, Annie found a shadowy corner and knelt down on the bare stone paving to ask forgiveness for all her sins and especially for the one she was about to commit. She believed that God would be good to her and trusted that He would judge her mercifully because of the impossible burden she carried. How could He not? She was doing this for the sake of her dear children whom she loved with all her heart; she was taking herself away like an unclean leper of old, away from decent people and into the merciful arms of Him who healed the lepers. There she would be clean again.

Nobody approached her as she knelt and after concluding with the Lord's Prayer she rose and left the Abbey, feeling a sense of lightness, strengthened to carry out her resolve.

Then began a long, long walk towards Tower Bridge, keeping as close to the river as she was able.

Passing the Tower itself she continued on towards the docks, the wharves and warehouses of the Pool of London where a couple of great seagoing vessels stood at quaysides and a swarm of lighters and barges moved swiftly from one landing stage to another. Gangs of men hauled on ropes to shouted orders from above and below as they landed huge wooden crates of tea and hogsheads of sugar.

Annie Court continued walking, only half aware of her surroundings but intent on her purpose. When the sun began to sink her footsteps slowed; she had had nothing to eat all day and felt chilled and empty, though with no desire to rest, not until the time came for it. Weak as she was, she was impelled onwards by her intention, which now appeared to her as both duty and destiny.

As riverside activity lessened, dubious characters of both sexes began to appear on shore, lingering on the notorious Highway as they had done from time immemorial. A couple of drunken men lurched towards Annie with lewd compliments, asking if she was looking for company.

Little do they know, she thought: a poor, anaemic creature old before her time and *riddled with the pox*! Yet she boldly stepped towards one of the gin shops on the landward side and emerged with a bottle in her shopping bag.

The light was fading and it was time to get down to the water. A twisted iron railing separated her from a row of gloomy buildings going down to crumbling wharves and she noticed a narrow alley-way descending to the river, a dangerous place where heaven only knew what evil deeds had been done. Annie had no fear – why should she? – and ducked under the rusty rail to make her way down between the damp-smelling walls. Halfway down, the path gave way to a flight of steep, worn stone steps once used for passengers boarding ferries in the days when there was only the one Old London Bridge and watermen provided the quickest means of transport.

Putting her hands out to steady herself on either side, Annie descended to a narrow ledge with a single iron mooring ring. It was very close to the water, being nearly high tide, and the stone was damp, but she sat down thankfully at one end of the small perch, pulling her coat around her. As long as she was not seen – or roused no curiosity if she was – this place would do. She got out the bottle and poured a generous measure into the old cup, as daintily as if she were serving tea into bone china. She added the contents of the phial and, taking a breath, raised it to her lips.

Aaah! The rough, fiery liquid burned her throat as it went down, and she gasped and coughed; Annie Court had never liked the taste of strong drink. She did not have to wait long before a glowing warmth began to spread over her, wrapping every part of her body in its rosy haze, infinitely comforting. Leaning her head against the cold stone, she took another mouthful and felt even better.

What was happening now at Sorrel Street? Were they out looking for her? But no, she would not think about that, it was all past, over and done with. She no longer belonged there.

The sun was now sinking low in the west and it was getting chillier; a stiff breeze was blowing upriver. There were few craft on the water now, though as she watched, a masted pleasure boat went by, its lights beaming out across the water. Nobody saw her in her dark little corner. A few seagulls wheeled above in the evening air, calling to each other in that melancholy way they have and, far above her inland, she could just hear the distant strains of music and raucous laughter.

The bottle was nearly empty, and Annie's eyes were drooping and unfocused. A sense of unreality wrapped round her like a cloak, she looked down at the flowing water.

'Sweet Thames, run softly till I end my song.' The words of the long-dead poet come back to Anna-Maria from the schoolroom at Belhampton and she smiles as she recognises them. Sweet Thames! Soon she will be done with the troubles of this world – and such a beautiful world, too – just look at that sky above Tower Bridge! Dusk is falling and deepens into darkness. Anna-Maria wakes up with a start, realising that she has been asleep.

But now she is awake and it is time.

She crawls towards the edge of the green-slimed stone where the muddied water has lapped it for centuries. Her hands slide, her knees follow and there she goes, slipping into the water with scarcely a splash. Cold greenness swirls round her as she sinks below the surface: the gin has done its work well. Above her in the pale sky a single star looks down.

Anna-Maria can no longer remember why she embarked on this journey, nor does she know how she has come to this place, this haven of love and light and peace. For look, there is her dear papa smiling at her and beside him her sweet mamma, Mabel, is holding out her arms.

Anna-Maria has come home.

Chapter Eleven

Mabel could hardly wait to get home to find out what Dr Knowles had said and when Mrs James allowed her to leave early she practically ran most of the way to Sorrel Street, where she found George and Daisy hanging around at Mrs Bull's house, unable to get into their own.

'We ain't 'ad sight nor sound o' yer muvver, Mabel,' said Mary Clutton and several other women stood waiting to see whether Annie Court was at home, asleep perhaps, or . . .

Mabel swallowed. More trouble – and she had to keep her head for the children's sake. She straightened her shoulders and marched into the house. Annie's key was on the doormat. 'Hallo, Mum, we're home! Mum?'

The house was silent.

'You wait down here,' she said to the children, 'and I'll go upstairs.'

She hesitated at the door of Annie's room, then took a breath and went in. Nobody. The bed was neatly arranged, the counterpane pulled up to the bedhead. Mabel opened the wardrobe and saw at once that her mother's best hat and jacket were not there. A sudden icy fear gripped her heart, but she went downstairs, as always hiding her own anxiety behind what she hoped was a reassuring manner. 'Mum's gone out,' she told the bewildered children, 'and I'll have to go out, too.'

'Where to?' asked Daisy in alarm.

'The doctor's. I asked him to call and see Mum today, so he'll probably know where she is. Now, George, ye'll have to mind yer sister till I get back. Alice should be in soon, anyway.'

Daisy began to wail, 'Where's Mummy gone?' It was a question that was to be repeated many times in the Sorrel Street home before they learned the answer.

With growing apprehension Mabel half walked, half ran towards the better residential area between the two commons. She knocked loudly on the door of the Knowles's house in Hillier Road, to be answered by a young maid. 'Is the doctor at home?' she panted. 'He called on my mother today and now she's – I must see him, it's very important!' Her voice rose as she spoke.

'Who is it, Susan?' asked a man's voice from within the house.

'A young woman lookin' for yer father, Dr Knowles. She seems in a bad way.'

'All right, I'll attend to her.' And Stephen Knowles appeared, smiling down at Mabel. 'Would you like to step inside? My father's out on his rounds at present, but perhaps I can help you.'

Mabel followed him into a small study, puffing after her exertion. 'It's about my mother, Dr Stephen.'

On hearing his Christian name he turned and looked at her. 'Now where have we met before? Yes! Your brother was injured in the Tower Hill riots last August and you came to look for him. Let me see – Miss Court, am I right? Mabel? You had a young man with you; he had a Salvation Army uniform –

oh, yes, I remember you, Miss Court! So what's the trouble now?'

She was amazed at his memory, though in fact Stephen Knowles had heard the Court family history in some detail from his father, and Mabel would have been both surprised and embarrassed by his knowledge of them if she had not been so concerned about her mother.

'Take a seat, Miss Court, and get your breath back. Shall I ring for Susan to bring us tea?'

'No, thank yer, I can't stay, I'm needed at home. The fact is, I asked Dr Knowles – yer father, I mean – to call on my mother today and now she's gone. She's not at home, though she hardly ever goes out. She's not well and he might've said somethin' that upset her. Oh, I'm so worried!'

He nodded, frowning slightly. 'I can understand how you must feel, Miss Court, though there's probably a simple explanation. My father isn't likely to be back until—' He glanced at the clock on the mantelpiece. 'But the sooner he knows the better. Look, I've got my motorcar outside, so I could go in search of him and send him straight round to your house.'

'Oh, that's really good o' yer, Dr Stephen. I'll go straight home, then.' She rose with a grateful look.

He too got up from his chair. 'Let me take you in the car.'

'No, no, I'd rather yer went to find Dr Knowles,' she answered, following him to the front door where he held out his hand.

'You never know, Miss Court, by the time you get home, she may be waiting for you.'

'If only that'd be true, doctor!' she said fervently, shaking his hand.

'If not, Miss Court, I think you should let the police know. Anyway, I'll send my father straight round to Sorrel Street.'

He watched her slender figure hurrying along the tree-lined avenue, then put on his jacket and peaked cap, and got into his car. Such a pleasant girl, he thought, and really very pretty; what a shame that she had to carry so much responsibility on her young shoulders.

No news awaited Mabel at home, though Alice had arrived and the house seemed full of neighbours who had brought tea, milk, sugar and gloomy observations.

'First *'e* does a runner, an' now *'er*,' said Mrs Clutton significantly. 'Makes yer wonder, eh?'

'Shouldn't we let Grandmother know, Mabel?' asked Alice.

'Not yet, we don't want her puttin' her oar in,' Mabel replied somewhat irritably. 'If yer want to do somethin' useful, Alice, go up to the police station on Lavender Hill and tell them about Mum being missing. They'll send somebody round, I expect. And be quick about it!'

If only Harry were here! He was due to start training at Clapton College in September and Mabel was resigned to seeing even less of the man she loved; but at a time like this she simply longed for the sight of his face, his honest brown eyes. Just to hear his voice would give her courage, she thought, her mind reeling away from the nightmare possibilities. Oh, Mum, where are yer? If yer only knew the trouble ye're giving us all . . .

When Dr Knowles strode in she jumped up and faced him almost accusingly. 'What happened when

yer called today, doctor? What did yer say to her?'
she demanded, frightened by his worried expression.

'My dear Mabel, I'm very sorry to hear this,' he
said. 'Did she leave any word, was there a note in the
house – under her pillow, under the clock on the
mantelpiece?'

'No, no, there's nothing,' replied Mabel impatiently. 'For heaven's sake, Dr Knowles, what did yer
say to my poor mother? Did yer tell her what yer
thought was wrong with her? She's not well, I know
that, and she wouldn't have been able to go very far,
but—'

'But she could've got on a bus,' put in Mrs Bull.

Knowles firmly took Mabel aside, out of earshot of
the others. 'I told her I thought she needed to see a
specialist, Mabel, and said I'd arrange it.'

Mabel nodded. 'Yes, I thought yer might send her
to see somebody who could do somethin' for wom-
en's trouble.'

'And I also suggested a blood test.'

'Yes, she's so anaemic, an' no wonder, poor Mum.'
Mabel sighed. 'But why would she just get up and go
away without tellin' anybody or leavin' a message?'

The doctor frowned and shook his head. 'I'd better
tell you, my dear, she may be – probably *is* –
suffering from a form of bacterial infection.'

'Is that what yer told her?' asked Mabel in new
alarm. 'Oh, poor Mum! She could be wanderin'
around somewhere, thinkin' she's got somethin' very
serious. Haven't yer got *any* idea where she might've
gone, Dr Knowles?'

Her distress was painful to witness and Knowles
decided not to talk of blood tests, nor of the Institute,
at least not until Annie Court was found. 'She's
probably not very far away,' he said carefully, not

wanting to reveal his own fears for Annie. 'Perhaps she feels that she needs to be alone for a while, just to think things over. We mustn't let our imaginations run away with us, my dear.' Even to his own ears he sounded unconvincing and no wonder, for Mabel had put his uneasy suspicions into words.

He left the house soon after, patting Mabel's shoulder and promising to keep in close touch.

Daisy began to cry again and Mabel's first concern was to comfort the unhappy little girl. But what could she say to her? She prayed inwardly for courage and common sense.

And it seemed that her prayers were answered when Harry Drover arrived almost immediately after Knowles's depature, thanks to a neighbour who had sent a message round to Falcon Terrace. Mabel practically threw herself into his arms and for the first time that day she wept.

Harry at once enfolded her and Daisy together in one loving embrace, proving himself once more to be a tower of strength. 'We'd better send for Albert, Mabel dear. I can get a message to the *Warspite* through the Army, an' maybe the commandant could get transport for him in a case like this. I'll see what I can do, anyway. Yer'll be glad to have 'im here until she's found.'

'Oh, Harry, Harry, God must've sent yer!' And she kissed him in front of everybody. His arrival was well timed in every way, for Alice returned accompanied by a police sergeant and his assistant who asked questions about Annie Court's recent movements and behaviour, her state of health and mind. It was a great support to have Harry at her side throughout this questioning, in which Mabel also spoke of her father's abrupt departure on 30 March, since when Annie had become more depressed. When asked about other family relatives Mabel mentioned her grandmother Court, but decided not to say anything about her mother's sisters whom she had never met.

'Right, we'll send somebody round to 23 Macaulay Road, Tooting,' said the sergeant. 'What's the situation between yer mother and her mother-in-law?'

Mabel replied that there was no love lost between the two women and that they seldom met.

On hearing about Dr Knowles's visit to Annie that day, he said that he would go and speak to the doctor, a key witness as the last person to see and talk with Mrs Court, though a woman from Darnell Street, hearing that Annie was missing, now came round to say that she had seen her getting on a city bus around mid-afternoon, shortly after the accident on Lavender Hill.

Henry Knowles prepared himself to respond with apparent willingness when questioned by the police, while not revealing anything of what he considered confidential information, guarded by medical ethics. As a trusted, well-known general practitioner, he knew how to conceal without actually telling a falsehood. 'Mrs Court has suffered for some years with the usual women's problems, the result of childbearing,' he told the sergeant. 'I said I would arrange for her to see a specialist.'

'Was her condition serious, Dr Knowles?'

'It might turn out to be so, which is why I wanted a specialist's opinion.'

'Did Mrs Court realise this? Did she understand that her condition might be serious?'

'I tried to reassure her, but I was not able to give her a definite answer one way or the other.'

'But in your opnion, doctor—?'

'It would need further investigation to make a definite diagnosis.'

In response to more questions he admitted that it was possible that Mrs Court might have wandered off in a state of anxiety, believing that she had a fatal illness.

The sergeant thanked him for his co-operation, but looked grave, adding that a detailed description of Mrs Court and the clothes she was wearing would be sent to other police stations in the area and hospital accident departments. 'And suchlike places, Dr Knowles. Let's hope that the poor woman's found soon – and alive,' he said as he took his leave.

Knowles shivered, silently praying to whatever deity there might be. If Annie Court had thought about what he had said and hit upon the truth he had concealed from her – or if she believed herself to be suffering from the dreaded 'growth' that so many women feared – he knew there was real danger that what the police officer had hinted at might turn out to be true.

At Sorrel Street another police officer called to say that a telephone communication had been received from the station at Amen Corner in Tooting. 'Mrs Court senior says she ain't seen yer mother, Miss Court,' he told Mabel. 'Our man who spoke to 'er says she can't get over to see yer today. She'll try an' get over tomorow if there's still no news.'

This was cold comfort and Mabel remembered that Alice had found Mimi strangely preoccupied and irritable when asked if she had seen Jack.

While Daisy cried for her mother and the rest of

them hung about talking and drinking tea, George sat silent and white-faced, overlooked in the comings and goings around him. Suddenly he got up and took his cap off its hook in the hallway. 'I'm goin' out to look for 'er,' he announced.

'Oh, George dear!' Mabel at once reproached herself for not paying more attention to the quiet boy who never put himself forward. 'It'll soon be dark, an' there are lots o' people lookin' for her, policemen and—'

'But I know the places in the park where she liked to walk on Sunday arf'noons an' when we 'ad the coronation an' that,' faltered the boy, rubbing his eyes.

Harry caught Mabel's eye and shot her a meaningful look. 'George wants to do somethin' an' I reckon he's right, Mabel,' he said, getting to his feet. 'Tell yer what, George – you an' me'll go to the park together an' yer can show me the places where yer mother might've gone.' Turning to Mabel, he added, 'Don't worry, Mabel, it'll be best for him to be doin' somethin'. I'll take good care o' him.'

'Thanks, Harry, I know yer will.' His quick sensitivity was what she most loved about him, though at the mention of Battersea Park she immediately pictured the boating lake.

Somehow the day got through to its end. Harry and George returned from the park after an hour, and George and Daisy were persuaded to go to bed. Mabel advised Alice to get some rest, while she and Harry sat up with Mrs Bull to await any news. She was thankful when the other neighbours drifted away to their homes and, after what seemed like the hundredth cup of tea, silence fell upon the trio as midnight approached.

A loud knocking at the door caused all three of them to leap up from their chairs and upstairs Daisy called out, 'Mummy!'

Mabel wrenched the door open and saw Albert on the step. She burst into tears.

'Blimey, Mabel, this ain't much of a welcome for yer poor bruvver,' he said, reaching out to hold her. 'An' 'ere's me come all the way from Green'ive, fanks to the Sally Army. Hey! Don't ever remember seein' me big sister pipin' 'er eye before.'

He enfolded her in a bear-hug and she quickly wiped her eyes. 'I'm sorry, Albert, only—'

Only her tears were for disappointment at not seeing her mother and yet there was thankfulness too that it was not a bringer of bad news. And there was relief at having Albert home to share the burden with her, thanks to Harry's foresight.

Of course Alice, George and Daisy came down to greet their big brother, and when they were sent back to bed Albert suggested that Harry should go home and rest. 'Yer got work termorrer, 'Arry, so you get some shut-eye an' I'll sit up wiv Mabel, poor gal. An' yer can send 'er 'ome, an' all,' he added under his breath, nodding towards Mrs Bull.

Mabel gave a watery smile as she dismissed the chaperone, but Harry refused to leave her, so while she settled down on the sofa, he and Albert stretched out on the floor with cushions under their heads. They dozed fitfully, aroused by the slightest sound that broke the troubled night, clinging to the flickering hope that Annie Court would return to her home in the morning.

The first day of May dawned clear and bright. Mabel had fallen into a doze when Alice came down, pale and puffy-eyed, to start making tea again and cutting bread for breakfast.

They were all seated at the table – Mabel, Albert, Alice, George, Daisy and Harry – when the knock sounded at the door just before eight.

'It'll be Dr Knowles,' said Mabel quickly, though she had no real reason to believe so.

Albert told her to stay where she was while he answered the door. It was indeed the doctor, accompanied by one of the police officers they had seen before.

'Ye'd better come in,' they heard him say and Mabel rose, instinctively gesturing to Alice to take the children out to the kitchen.

Dr Knowles put his arm round her shoulder as the officer informed her and Albert that the body of a woman resembling the description of Anna-Maria Court had been taken from the Thames at low tide, near to Greenwich Pier. Her age, colouring and clothing corresponded to the details on the police file, but positive identification was needed.

Oh, no, no, no, no, no. Mabel heard a low moaning sound and found that it was coming from herself, her own mouth. Harry's hands were holding hers as she lurched against the doctor.

The policeman was saying that the body was lying in the public morgue attached to St Katharine's Infirmary near Tower Hill.

'That was where they held *you*, Albert,' Mabel murmured inconsequentially.

And it was to that chilly, white-tiled place that Mabel was obliged to go as next of kin in the absence of her father, accompanied by her doctor and her dearest friend, Harry Drover. Albert insisted on coming with them, saying that he was the man of the house and had a right. They all stood with her, waiting with bated breath when the aproned attendant drew back the sheet.

What did they see? Mabel never forgot that last sight of her mother's face, mottled blue and grey, the mouth agape with sagging purple lips. Drowned eyes, half open, held no sense of repose, no peace, only the blankness of death; but beyond doubt this was the body of Anna-Maria Court, so the last faint hope was gone.

Mabel leapt backwards with a jerk as a terrible despair rose within her, bursting forth in a great shriek. Dr Knowles, used to witnessing death and grief, tightened his hold upon her and Harry spoke her name, 'Mabel – Mabel, I'm here, my love.'

But Albert felt his blood run cold – for a split second he thought the cry came from the corpse. 'Christ,' he muttered, and for a moment he could not draw breath and swayed on his feet.

Within seconds Mabel regained control of herself, but felt faint and nauseated. With shaking limbs she let Knowles and Harry support her on either side and lead her out of that death-cold place.

There were formalities to be gone through and forms to be signed by Mabel and the doctor, confirming identification of the body. When they were free to go, Albert suddenly turned to the doctor, grabbing his jacket lapels. 'Why'd she do it, tha's what I wanna know! What the bloody 'ell did yer tell 'er – that she 'ad cancer or summat?'

'Stop that, Albert, take yer hands off this minute,' ordered Harry, though the doctor did not attempt to resist the gripping hands.

'I couldn't lie to her, Albert,' he said heavily. 'I said

251

it *might* be serious, that's all. I'm so very sorry for you all, more than I can say.'

'Tha's all very well, but yer didn't 'ave to scare 'er to deaf! It was 'cause o' what yer told 'er she went an' drahned 'erself!' shouted Albert.

'Cut it out, Albert,' Harry said with quiet authority. 'Think o' yer sister Mabel an' all she's had to go through – just pull yerself together.'

Albert lapsed into gloomy silence as they returned to Sorrel Street, where the news had to be broken to Alice, George and Daisy that their mother had fallen into the Thames and drowned. Daisy and George began to cry bitterly, and Mrs Bull drew the curtains to signify a house in mourning. The news quickly spread all over their part of Battersea that the Court children no longer had a mother and everybody wondered what Mabel would do.

First she had to deal with the grief of them all, particularly the two youngest who could not take in that they would never see their mother again. She had to be there for them, answering their questions as best she could, with no opportunity to do her own grieving over Annie Court's tragically shortened life and whatever had driven her towards her death on that fatal afternoon. All Mabel's attention had to be centred on the bereaved children.

And here was Dr Knowles again, with something else to tell her. 'Mabel, my dear, you may remember me saying that I was going to arrange for a blood test for your mother.'

Mabel looked up at him wearily and shrugged. Why mention that now?

'And although I'm sorry to intrude on your sorrow, my dear, I must tell you that you need a similar test, as you were in close contact with her.'

'*What*?' Mabel could not believe her ears, for in her experience blood tests were only done on very ill people. 'D'ye mean I've got to go to hospital for it?'

'No, no, Mabel, there's no need for that, I can do it at my surgery tomorrow – we only need about a teaspoonful of clotted blood. And to be on the safe side, I think I should also take blood samples from Alice, George and Daisy.'

'But whatever *for*, Dr Knowles?'

'Your poor mother may have had a bacterial infection and we need to know if it was passed on to others living in the house, you see. I don't think we need bother to include Albert.'

Mabel stared in horror as a thought struck her. 'Oh, my God, yer mean TB!'

'No, my dear, not TB, but it carries a similar danger and the sooner we get the matter cleared up the better. Tomorrow, then, in my surgery, shall we say about three o'clock?'

It proved to be a wretched experience, as Daisy screamed at the very sight of the needle and George turned deathly white when the doctor failed to find a vein in his arm on the first attempt. Alice was also upset and so was Knowles himself, for the possibility of any of the younger ones being infected was almost nil. He was sorry to submit them to it, but wanted to avoid appearing to single out Mabel.

'How long will it take before we know if we've got it, Dr Knowles?' she asked.

'About a week – but I'm sure there's nothing to worry about, Mabel, it's just a precaution.'

He did not add that the four specimens would have to be sent to the Lock Hospital, nor that he was personally paying for the relatively new and expensive Wasserman test to be carried out on each of them. 'You won't be going to the Institute again until after the . . . the inquest and then the funeral, Mabel, so the result will be back before you resume work. I'll have a word with the Matron if there are any queries,' he told her, hoping against hope for a negative result.

Messages of sympathy began to pour in. From the Agnes Nuttall Institute came a formal, rather stilted letter of condolence from Mrs James, and notes written on scraps of paper by the mothers. Miss Carter wrote from the Hallam Road Babies Mission and a card arrived from Mr Munday at the Queen's Road post office, also signed by 'Beatrice Chatt'.

The vicar of St Philip's church called to express his shocked sympathy and proved to be genuinely kind. Arrangements for a quiet funeral at Wandsworth cemetery were tenatively discussed – 'and of *course* she'll be buried in consecrated ground, my dear.' His visit was followed by one from Ada Clay whose wedding was planned for June, though she hesitated even to mention this happy event when she came to offer her sympathy and Arthur's.

The police now began a search for Jack Court, making enquiries at various places he had been known to frequent. His one-time crony Dick Sammons, now a prosperous publican and respectable family man, said he had not seen poor old Jack for over a year and Bill from Macaulay Road firmly denied all knowledge of his former drinking companion of the turf.

On the Thursday Harry returned to the railway depot where he had another four months to work, though he found time to call at Sorrel Street every day. Albert had permission to stay until after the funeral and Alice was likewise allowed to stay off work. George and Daisy were excused school, though Mabel privately thought they would be better occupied there than in the mournful atmosphere of home. She therefore sent them out to the park with Alice, so only she and Albert were at home when Mimi Court arrived, pale and grim-faced.

'Well, here's a fine how-d'ye-do, Mabel, I never thought she'd do such a thing,' she began and Mabel was silenced by her haggard face. There was no doubt that she was truly shocked and she had an air of disillusionment about her, as if all she had striven for had come to nothing. Yet she had not lost her domineering manner. 'Here, Mabel—' She opened her black velvet purse-string reticule and took out an envelope. 'Ye'll find twenty-five pounds in banknotes there. Take it, ye'll need it.'

Mabel stared at the very thought of such an amount. 'Oh, I couldn't take that much, Grandmother.'

'Yer can't afford to turn down good money. Take it.' Mimi put the envelope on the table.

Albert whistled. 'Go on, Mabel, yer can do wiv it.'

'And ye're goin' to have to think about the future, Mabel – what ye're goin' to do,' Mimi went on. 'Yer can't make any decisions until the funeral's over – an' that'll have to be paid for – but yer might as well start thinkin' about placin' the children.'

'What d'ye mean, *placing* them, Grandmother?' asked Mabel, thinking of the babies at the Rescue. 'What about Dad, he'll have some say, won't he?'

Mimi's expression was bleak. 'He'll be away for some time. He's got troubles that've got to be seen to.'

'Yer bet yer bleedin' life 'e's got trouble!' Albert burst out. 'Our muvver's only gorn an' drahned 'erself on account o' trouble!'

Mimi eyed him with distaste. 'Ye'll have to leave yer father out o' yer calculations for the time bein'. And I'll tell yer now, ye'll have to get out o' this house.'

Since the horrors of the past day and night, Mabel had scarcely given a thought to their future. It occurred to her that the threat of poverty that had always lurked in the background of their lives might now have to be faced squarely. She glanced at Albert to command silence from him, then gave her full attention to their grandmother. 'I . . . we appreciate yer coming, Grandmother, and the money. Please go on and say what ye've come to say.'

'Thank yer, I'm sure,' said Mimi tartly. 'Well, to start with, you and yer sisters Alice and Daisy can come to live at Macaulay Road. I need an assistant to help with the midwifery, as yer know, and Alice can get work at the main post office in Tooting. Daisy can go to the church school in Church Lane, much better 'n that place in Hallam Road.'

Mabel's gasp of disbelief was followed by Albert's low mutter. 'That ain't a bad offer, Mabel, don't turn it dahn out o' hand.'

'And with Albert in the merchant service, p'raps George could join him on that, er, ship at Green-hithe.'

'But he's only twelve and still at school!' cried Mabel.

''Sides, 'e's much too soft for the navy,' Albert cut in. 'Be the butt o' every bully on board, they'd 'ave 'im for their breakfuss!'

'In that case there's an excellent Dr Barnardo home

for boys in Clapham,' said Mimi, who had obviously been making her own contingency plans. 'It's run by a Mr Maillard who trains the boys for—'

'*What*? George in a *home*?' Mabel was by now unable to believe her ears.

'Well, yes, why not? I can take you three girls, but there's no room for a boy, an' besides, George'd be better orf with other boys.'

This was too much for Mabel. 'I beg yer pardon, Grandmother, but until I hear somethin' from me father, we shall all stay together *here*!'

'Oh, yes, madam? I'll be interested to know what ye'll use for money, then. Who d'yer think's paid the rent for this place, more often than not? As I said, ye'll 'ave to get out of it.'

Mabel felt that it was time to speak plainly and ask what Mimi Court knew. 'That'll depend on what Dad says when he turns up again. Yer seem to know somethin' about him that we don't, Grandmother – can't yer tell us where he is?'

'Yeah, is there goin' to be anuvver body dredged up out o' the river?' demanded Albert.

There was a long pause. A look of blank desolation passed over Mimi's face, but she answered without faltering. 'I haven't come over 'ere to be questioned about me son's business, an' yer can keep a civil tongue in yer 'ead, Albert. Yer may *look* like Jack, but yer was never 'is equal in manners.' She heaved herself up and smoothed her skirt with a black-gloved hand. 'I'll see meself out, don't trouble yerselves – an' yer can be thinkin' over what I've said, Mabel. Good mornin'.' And without further leave-taking, she took herself off, though without her usual aplomb; from the back she looked like an old woman and Mabel remembered that she was now over sixty.

'I'd dearly love to refuse her money,' she muttered, looking at the envelope on the table.

'Bloody 'ell, Mabel, beggars can't be choosers,' said Albert with a grimace. 'If the Duchess o' Tootin's willin' to 'elp us out, yer can't be too prahd, can yer?'

Mabel turned down the corners of her mouth at hearing him echo her own thoughts. She remembered that long-ago occasion when she and her mother had confronted Mimi with Jack's improvidence and they'd accepted her two ten shilling notes. Now she must accept twenty-five times that amount and be thankful.

'It might not be such a bad idea, yer know,' Albert went on. 'George an' Daisy got to 'ave a roof over their 'eads an' food in their bellies, an' money don't grow on trees. The girls'll do well enough at Macaulay Road—'

'I'd never let my sisters live under *her* roof!' Mabel broke in, knowing what her mother had said about Mimi's other source of income. 'And as for George goin' into a *home* – well, I'll never agree to it, *never*!'

Albert did not reply. He could not bring himself to point out that she might have no choice in the matter. And by her shadowed eyes and the grim set of her mouth there was no need. He stared moodily at the worn hearthrug and for once could think of nothing to say that would lighten his sister's heart.

When the police discovered that Jack Court was a patient undergoing treatment in the Lock Hospital at Hyde Park Corner, they went to interview him there and found that he already knew about his wife's death, having received a message from his mother.

He was in such a state of shock and grief that he was scarcely able to answer their questions about his marriage and his relationship with his children. The hospital authorities were able to confirm that he had been an in-patient since 11 April and would be unable to attend the inquest on his wife's death or the funeral. He pleaded that his family at Sorrel Street should not be informed of his present circumstances; only his mother knew where he was.

Nevertheless, a discerning police officer decided to pass this information on to Dr Knowles and let him decide how much or how little to reveal. Knowles listened, nodded and saw no reason to divulge his knowledge. Not at this juncture. The inquest loomed before him and he might have to use it then, though he was counting on his former acquaintance with the grey-haired coroner to keep the medical evidence to a minimum, particularly the post-mortem report.

The inquest on the death of Anna-Maria Court, formerly Chalcott, took place on the following Monday at Lavender Hill South-Western Magistrates' Court, in the small wood-panelled room adjacent to the main courtroom. Mabel attended, dressed in black, with Albert at her side. The coroner expressed his sympathy for the brother and sister, and the business was mercifully brief. When Dr Knowles was called upon to tell the hearing about his last visit to Anna-Maria Court on the afternoon of 30 April he stated that Mrs Court had expressed fears that she might have a 'growth', as she put it, and that he had neither confirmed nor denied the possibility.

'Did you detect any evidence of cancer, Dr Knowles?' asked the coroner.

'She was anaemic due to menorrhagia and I could not rule out malignancy.'

'Were there signs of any disease of a serious nature?'

The doctor spoke up clearly. 'I suspected a bacterial infection in addition to menorrhagia, but I could not be sure and intended to arrange for a blood test.'

'Which, of course, she never had?'

'No.'

The coroner handed the clerk a copy of the post-mortem report to pass on to Knowles who took it and glanced at the findings. Suffocation by drowning – a high alcohol level – skin lesions and enlarged glands consistent with primary infection by *spirochaeta pallida*, the causative organism. He nodded and handed it back to the clerk.

'Would you agree with this forensic report, Dr Knowles?'

'Yes, I would.'

'Thank you. And did you give any indication to the deceased of your suspicions?'

'I told her that she might have a serious condition, yes, and that I would arrange for her to see a specialist in women's diseases.'

'Nothing more than that?'

'No.'

The coroner seemed satisfied with these answers and, after considering that there was no conclusive evidence of suicide, he brought in a verdict of accidental death by drowning. Dr Knowles momentarily closed his eyes in thankfulness and Mabel whispered to Albert that she would be able to tell the children truthfully that it had been an accident.

'I'll tell them that Mummy slipped on the quayside

near to the Tower an' fell in the water. No need for them to go through life with the burden o'—' She broke off, leaving the sentence unfinished, and tightened her hold on her brother's arm while she struggled with tears and agonised silently about what their mother must have gone through in those last hours.

It seemed to Albert that something had been hushed up. That report had been handed round but not read out, and he had a jolly good mind to call at the court the next day and demand to see it. Then he decided that he'd better not; for one thing it would make no difference now and perhaps he didn't want to know anyway.

With the burial certificate duly signed, the only thing left now was the funeral, a very quiet graveside ceremony at Wandsworth Cemetery on the Thursday of that same week. Again Mabel was supported by her brother, leaving George and Daisy at home in the care of Alice.

Just as the vicar began to intone 'I am the Resurrection and the Life', Mabel saw Harry Drover slipping through the gate and hurrying over to join them in the corner of the burial ground where the plain coffin was about to be lowered. Comforted by his presence, she stole a glance at him as he stood bareheaded in the early May sunshine and felt the warmth of his loving thoughts directed towards her, though they did not get a chance to exchange more than the briefest of greetings. As soon as it was over he returned to the railway depot where the company made him forfeit a day's pay.

When they reached home, Mabel found a brief note from Dr Knowles to let her know that all four blood tests had proved negative and that there was no need for further action on that score. Pleased as she was with this assurance, she could not have imagined Henry Knowles's profound relief on her behalf.

The next day, Friday, Albert returned to the *Warspite* and the parting was painful. 'I 'ate leavin' yer wiv this lot, Mabel, gal, not knowin' where *'e* is, an' nobody to turn to bar that ol' crow at Tootin',' he said glumly. 'Take my advice an' don't get on the wrong side of 'er, yer never know when yer might need 'elpin' 'aht and she's all we got left. I ought to be due for leave again in anuvver free monfs, an' I'll send yer what I can—'

'Albert! As if I'd take money off yer, don't be daft,' she said quickly. 'Don't forget I've got Harry, not that I'd take cash off him either, but yer know what I mean, havin' him around makes all the difference. I've never forgotten it was you who brought him home with yer, Albert.'

'Yeah, 'e's a good bloke is ol' 'Arry,' he agreed, touched by the tender smile that lit her tired face. 'But 'e'll be off to this bleedin' college in a couple o' monfs, an' then yer won't see much—'

'*Albert*, your language! An' it's four months yet before he starts at Clapton. Don't forget I'll be back at the Rescue next Monday, so that'll be a bit o' reg'lar money comin' in. Oh, an' won't I be glad to see 'em all again! I've really missed the babies, I can tell yer.'

But another shock awaited poor Mabel. On the Saturday morning a note arrived from Mrs James telling her that her position as nursery maid was no longer available; it had been filled by an older girl. She thanked Miss Court for all the valuable work she had done at the Agnes Nuttall Institute and wished her success in finding new employment.

'But this can't be right – I don't believe it's true!' cried Mabel to Alice, waving the piece of paper in her face. 'She's always praised me – said they couldn't wish for a better nursery maid, an' even Sister Lilley told me I had the makin's of a good midwife – she *can't* treat me like this!' And putting on her hat, jacket and gloves, she made her way straight up to the Institute.

Mrs James was embarrassed by Mabel's direct demand for an explanation. She had been thoroughly unnerved by Dr Knowles's gravity when he'd spoken of the blood test, and having read of the bizarre circumstances of the unfortunate Annie Court's death in the local paper – which sounded like suicide, whatever the coroner said – even the doctor's message about a negative result could not persuade her to re-employ Mabel Court. After all, she had the safety of the babies to think about, didn't she?

Besides, there was something else. 'I've had a letter of complaint from a girl's father, Miss Court, a Mr Parsley of Benfleet, who says that you encouraged his daughter Ellen to write home and ask her parents to come and visit her and the baby – with a view to letting her take the child home and keep it.' Mrs James adjusted her pince-nez and looked hard at Mabel, who coloured and bit her lip. 'And seeing that the Parsleys went to a great deal of trouble and expense to keep Ellen's condition unknown to their acquaintances, this has caused them much distress. Mr Parsley says his wife hasn't had a night's sleep since receiving the letter and I feel that I have no course but to . . . to replace you, Miss Court. I'm very sorry about your mother, of course—'

'Please, Mrs James, *please*, let me come back an' I'll never tell another girl to write home!' implored Mabel, devastated by the prospect of losing her job at the Rescue, especially as it now meant more than ever to her as a source of income. 'I've always wanted to nurse children an' I've loved every minute I've spent with the babies – please don't sack me now – *please!*'

It was Mrs James's turn to look flustered. 'I'm sorry, Miss Court, I really am, but I've filled the position now and haven't another to offer you. This business over the Parsley girl has caused me a lot of trouble, and—'

'Beggin' yer pardon, Matron, it was nothin' like the sort o' trouble that was goin' on here just before I came,' interrupted Mabel with a flash of spirit. 'An' if Mr Parsley looks upon his dear little grandson as somethin' to be hushed up an' kept out o' sight, then it's *him* who ought to be ashamed of 'imself, the old humbug!'

'Mabel!' Mrs James was so taken aback that she used Mabel's Christian name and could not bring herself to utter a rebuke. The truth was that she found it difficult to meet the girl's clear grey-blue eyes. 'Mabel, I'm so sorry, you didn't deserve this – I'm sorry,' she repeated lamely. 'I'll pay you a month's wages in lieu of notice.'

And so once again Mabel Court, now the breadwinner for her family, could not afford to be proud. She took the money and left the Agnes Nuttall Institute for ever.

*

'What did she say, Mabel?'

Alice was alarmed by her sister's white face as she swept into the house. Her eyes burned with a bitter sense of injustice and she now turned them on Alice. 'Just take over for me, will yer, I got to think what to do. No, don't say anythin', Alice, just leave me to meself for a bit. Sort the jobs out between yer, an' get somethin' on the table for dinner. I shan't want anythin'.'

In their shared bedroom she threw off her hat, jacket and gloves, sank down on the bed and, for the first time since losing her mother, gave vent to her true feelings, sobbing into the pillow for sorrow and beating it with her bunched fists in helpless rage.

What could she do in the face of this latest blow? Where could she turn for help?

Mimi? No fear, *she* would put George in a Dr Barnardo home.

Harry? Dear, patient, loving Harry who had said he would wait for ever. How could she expect him to keep that promise now that she had full responsibility for the family? George was twelve and Daisy only eight – how many years before they'd be independent of her? And how would she pay the rent, feed and clothe them, keep them *respectable* as their mother had always insisted, with only Alice's wages coming in until she, Mabel, could find some wretched cleaning job or slave all day in one of the factories on the riverside, when the children needed her to be at home? She had eighteen pounds left of the money Mimi had given her, but when that was gone, what options were open to her?

To work at home would mean making matchboxes or brushes by the hundred, notoriously ill-paid employment and poor women slaved over it round the clock to make a bare living. She could hand-sew but had not got a sewing machine or the requisite skill to do dressmaking to order, or even alterations. To take in washing would turn every day into Monday, with other people's sheets and towels forever hanging across their living space and the ironing board always at the ready. 'Oh, Mum, why did yer – Mum, where are yer?' she groaned, remembering how Annie had looked when she had spoken of her lost life in Hampshire – and her shame when she had inadvertently let out to Mabel the circumstances of her hasty marriage.

Oh, poor Mum – was there anything Mabel could have done to save her that last dreadful act? Mabel could not believe that it had been an accident, but could never be sure.

'Mum, I loved yer so!' she sobbed afresh. She bit on the sheet to stifle her crying, in case the others heard. Poor little Daisy had already suffered enough without having to listen to Mabel giving way to despair.

Then she remembered Harry telling her that he prayed for them all every night and morning; if she was going to be a Salvation Army wife one day, shouldn't she do the same?

Kneeling down beside the bed, she tried to think of the right words. She began to say the Lord's Prayer, but stopped halfway through and simply prayed from her heart: 'O Lord, just give me the faith that Harry's got and listen to his prayers for us!'

Chapter Twelve

Henry Knowles could hardly conceal his anger and dismay when he called at Sorrel Street and found Mabel out of a job. He cursed himself for frightening Mrs James unnecessarily and felt directly responsible for this latest misfortune.

'I was well on me way to becomin' a nurse, Dr Knowles,' Mabel told him miserably. 'I'd been hopin' to go from there to start trainin' in a year or two, only . . . only—'

'Only now you've got to be mother and father to your brothers and sisters, you poor child,' he said heavily. 'All I can say is that you're young, Mabel, only eighteen, and there's plenty of time ahead of you to become a nurse, but – oh, dear, I'm so sorry.'

'And unless Dad turns up again pretty soon, I'll have to earn some money, Dr Knowles. If I go back to cleaning the Polytechnic' – she grimaced – 'I'll have to leave the house very early and Alice'll have to do a lot more to help.'

She spoke grimly and the doctor ached with pity for her, unable to think of anything useful to add, though privately he resolved to find some sort of suitable work to tide her over.

Then a knock on the door brought her to her feet with a sudden smile that lit up her face. She jumped up to let in Harry Drover and glanced shyly from him to the doctor. 'Dr Knowles is here, Harry. He's ever so sorry to hear about the Rescue.'

Harry smiled politely. "Aft'noon, doctor. Er, I been shoppin' at Lipton's, Mabel, an' brought yer some Lyons chocolate cake, an'" – he searched in his string bag – 'ah, here it is, some o' that Cheshire cheese yer like, about three-quarters of a pound.'

'Oh, Harry, ye're too good to us – yer shouldn't spend yer money like this; what would yer mother say? But thank yer, oh, thank yer, dear Harry!'

Knowles tactfully looked away as she threw her arms round her young man's neck. Heaven only knew what lay in store for these two, he thought, or how many years would have to pass before they could be together in a home of their own. Would Mabel ever realise her dream of caring for children in need? If there was any justice in life she should. Yet his expression softened at the sight of them: he felt privileged just to witness the love on their young faces. Meanwhile it was a matter of honour that he should find a way for Mabel to earn some money without tiring herself out, now that she had to be breadwinner for them all.

He lost no time on this resolve and surprised Mabel by returning that same evening. 'Mabel, my dear, I have this patient, an elderly lady who lives on Bromfelde Road with her daughter and sister,' he began, as if about to ask a favour of her. 'Mrs Goring is a doctor's widow and has sadly lost her memory, and Miss Goring teaches music at Carlyle College. They live in, er, reduced circumstances because of an unwise investment, and poor Miss Goring has to support both her mother and her aunt, Miss de Lisle, so life isn't easy for her.'

He paused and glanced at Mabel who sat waiting for him to come to the point, unable to see what this strange-sounding household had to do with her own problems. He cleared his throat. 'And Miss Goring is looking for a suitable person to go in each day to keep an eye on things while she's at college.'

Mabel suddenly understood and sat bolt upright on the sofa. 'D'ye mean *me*, Dr Knowles? What would I have to do?'

He explained that Mrs Goring needed a little assistance with washing and dressing, and Miss de Lisle's sight was poor, so she liked somebody to read aloud to her. 'And if you could prepare a light midday meal for them, Mabel, and keep the place reasonably tidy – it wouldn't be hard work, not like the Rescue, and the pay would be about the same. They'd need you from eight each morning till Miss Goring gets home at around five. What do you think?'

He smiled, but Mabel felt nervous and uncertain. Still reeling from the events of the past ten days, she was unable to see herself as a daily housekeeper, nurse and cook. Knowles saw the weariness in her eyes and the droop of her shoulders; what this poor girl needs is a holiday, he thought sadly, not another new job to worry about. 'If I couldn't get away before five, I wouldn't be at home when Daisy and George get in from school,' she murmured, thinking aloud. 'Though I s'pose I could ask a neighbour to take 'em in for an hour.'

'I'll have a word with Miss Goring and see if something can be worked out about that,' said the doctor. 'Shall I speak to her and arrange for you to meet?'

In other circumstances Mabel would have been highly diverted by the sight of Mrs Goring sitting majestically on the commode-chair, discussing the shortcomings of servants she no longer kept, and the reminiscences of Miss de Lisle who wore a feathered toque at all times and had been an intimate of Mrs Patrick Campbell. Mabel often thought wryly of how she would have amused her mother with her stories about the two old ladies, but in her present anxious state they sorely tried her patience. No sooner did she start preparing a meal or dusting a room than Mrs Goring would pull imperiously on the bell rope, or Miss de Lisle would ask her to read aloud from *The Times*. Mrs Goring had to be sat on the commode every couple of hours if accidents were to be avoided and neither sister had any sense of time. They lived in a past world and looked upon Mabel as a servant with no life of her own, while she fretted about Daisy and George, wondering how they were coping with school and longing to see their faces each evening.

Miss Goring, a pleasant but harassed woman of about forty, arranged for a nearby friend to go to the house on Bromfelde Road at four o'clock on most days, so that Mabel could hurry home in time for George's and Daisy's return from school.

Alice arrived about an hour later, usually complaining that she was tired out after a busy day at the post office, and grumbled when asked to help prepare supper or do the ironing. 'I'm on my feet all day and then come home to wait on ev'rybody,' she said crossly. 'And then yer ask me to give up all my wages – it's not fair!'

'Oh, shut up, Alice, and do yer share,' snapped Mabel whose head and feet were aching. 'What d'ye think I do with *my* wages? I don't spend a penny on meself.'

'What about that money Grandmother gave us?' demanded Alice. 'Ye've kept *that*, I notice.'

'That's put by for a rainy day,' answered Mabel. 'An' she said she wasn't goin' to pay any more rent for this house, so we may need it for *that* if we run short.'

Alice stuck out her lower lip and Daisy looked troubled at hearing this sharp exchange between her sisters. Mabel missed Albert's abrasive wit, for even her devoted Harry seemed unable to lighten the gloom of the motherless household.

However, with his usual perception he saw what was needed and called on Ada Clay to ask her to visit Mabel. 'She needs a woman friend to talk to, Miss Clay,' he said earnestly. 'So could yer go on yer own, like, without Arthur?'

Ada readily agreed and was received with joy one Saturday afternoon, demanding to hear about Mabel's elderly charges. The little house soon rang with her laughter.

'Each of 'em tells me stories about the other one, Ada. Miss de Lisle wears this peculiar thing on her head with a long feather that waves up and down as she walks – I think she must wear it in bed, 'cause I never see her without it – and she comes along shakin' her head and says Mrs Goring used to be completely under her husband's thumb and never had a thought of her own. "That's why her brain's failed now he's gone – *and* she's lost control o' her bladder!"'

'Is that what she says? Did yer ever!' Ada giggled.

'Yes, an' then Mrs Goring's sittin' there on the commode, shakin' *her* head an' whisperin' in me ear that Miss de Lisle was disappointed in love and has been jealous o' Mrs Goring all her life. "Ever since she was my bridesmaid, the poor woman's envied my status as a wife, you see!" I tell yer, Ada, I can hardly keep a straight face!'

The sight of Ada convulsed with mirth and holding a handkerchief to her streaming eyes was a much-needed tonic for Mabel, but the smiles disappeared when Daisy rushed in, flushed and triumphant, with Mabel's shopping bag which she put down on the table. 'There y'are, Mabel, sausages for tea an' a loaf o' Nevill's bread!'

'Daisy! Where'd yer get this?'

'Hemmings' bakers in Queen's Road and that smarmy ol' butcher – off o' his delivery van.' Daisy's dark eyes gleamed as she spoke.

'What d'ye mean? Where'd yer get the money for 'em?' demanded Mabel, at which the little girl faltered and glanced at George. 'George, did *you* give Daisy the money to buy these?'

George reddened and shook his head, and Daisy spoke up defiantly. 'Yer said yer hadn't got enough money, an' ... an' ... yer said yer had to pay the rent, an' yer never spent anythin' on yerself, Mabel. Don't be cross with me!'

Mabel could have wept as she led her little sister upstairs to talk with her alone. 'Daisy, dear, just tell me the truth an' I won't be cross, I promise. Did yer take the bread an' sausages without payin' for 'em?'

Daisy hung her head and her eyes filled with tears. 'Nobody saw me, Mabel, so don't say any more!' she pleaded.

'Yer *poor* little thing,' whispered Mabel, horrified and touched at the same time. 'But yer know that stealin's wrong, an' yer must never do it – yer do know that, don't yer, Daisy?'

'Oh, Mabel, I only did it for you!'

'I know, I know, dear, but it's still wrong. The

272

food'll have to be paid for and yer must say ye're sorry to Hemmings' and Mr Ashworth. I'll come with yer, an' we must go straight away.'

Mabel's heart sank at the thought of the shame they would both have to face, but it had to be done in order to teach poor Daisy a lesson for life.

But fate was kind on this occasion. At the very moment that the two sisters were setting out on their errand of humiliation, Harry Drover turned up in his bandsman's uniform on a quick visit. His eager smile faded at the sight of their faces, and Mabel's voice shook as she explained where they were going and why. 'Then I'm comin' with yer,' he stated firmly. 'Yes, Mabel, don't argue, I'm comin' and I'll listen while Daisy tells 'em she's sorry – they won't say too much to her with me standin' there in me uniform – and I'll pay for the stuff. *Yes*, Mabel, yer heard what I said, an' now let's get goin'!'

That evening, after George and Daisy were in bed and Alice out visiting an old school friend, Harry Drover called again. It was nearly ten o'clock, but the sky was still light after a warm, sunny day. She let him in and made room for him beside her on the worn sofa. 'I'll never be able to thank yer for what yer did for Daisy today, Harry – and for me.'

His eyes glowed in the fading light. 'Then give us a kiss, Mabel,' he said, unusually bold.

Her arms went round his neck and her lips pressed upon his for an exquisite moment. 'Ye're my tower o' strength, Harry,' she told him softly, and he kissed her again, more fervently, his mouth lingering on hers as if to draw the sweetness from her, like a bee hovering over a flower. As his arms tightened around her he gave a sigh that was almost a groan: he felt his body's instant response to her closeness.

Mabel also experienced a tremor of desire, a quickening of her heartbeat and breath. It was as if their bodies carried on their own unspoken exchange, quite independently of their minds, ignoring the restrictions of convention, the dictates of prudence. I want you, said his flesh to hers, and her body softened and relaxed in response.

But caution prevailed. Mabel drew apart from him and rose trembling from the sofa. 'I ... I think Alice'll be in soon,' she said shakily. 'Would yer like a cup o' tea, Harry?'

A cup of tea was the last thing young Drover wanted at that moment, but he sighed and nodded reluctantly. Then she turned back and leaned over him to kiss him again. And then once more, holding his face between her hands. It was a wordless exchange between lovers, full of promise for the future.

But it would be a very long time indeed before they were so close again.

The fatal day came without a hint of warning.

Mabel was hurrying down from the sedate residential avenues of north Clapham to the humbler area off the Wandsworth Road where Sorrel Street lay. As soon as she saw number 12 her heart seemed to miss a beat: the door was open and Daisy cowered outside, her face full of terror. A man's voice could be heard within, slurred and shouting incoherently.

'Mabel, Mabel! He's in there with George!'

'All right, Daisy, all right – listen, go to Mrs Bull's an' stay there, d'ye hear? Don't cry, just hurry off to her house – go on, be a good girl,' panted Mabel, already breathless from running most of the way home. Then she braced herself to enter the house.

Even on the threshold she picked up an ominous smell, a mixture of whisky and stale, unwashed clothing ... and fear. She heard another shout, a thud and then a sound of impact: a hard object meeting something that broke with a sickening crack.

At the door of the living room she stood and watched as her father's body fell, first across the table and then slithering off and hitting the floor, dragging the red chenille tablecloth down with him and lying quite still, with one leg awkwardly bent beneath the other. His face was towards her, his eyes open and staring without sight. A thin trickle of blood oozed from the corner of his mouth. Mabel knew instantly that he was dead.

Her brother George stood beside the table, still clutching the thick glass vase that had delivered the fatal blow. The marguerite daisies it had contained were strewn over the table top and floor, and water dripped off the side of the table on to the crumpled body on the hearthrug.

As when she had seen the body of her mother in the public mortuary, a wave of horror and nausea swept over Mabel, but this time she did not cry out as she looked up and met her young brother's stricken gaze. She realised that if ever she had to keep her head it was now, because George's whole future could depend on her reaction. She took a deep breath. 'Put that vase down on the table, Georgie,' she said, keeping her voice low. 'And tell me exactly what happened.'

The twelve-year-old boy shuddered violently and she reached out to enfold him in her arms. ''E was 'ere when we came 'ome – 'e was drunk an' ravin' about our mum, 'ow 'e never meant to 'urt 'er, never wanted 'er to die – all that sort o' rubbish.' His face crumpled and he began to sob.

'Sh, George, *sh*, there's no time for that. Did he hit yer?'

'No, 'e was talkin' all this stuff about Mum an' I couldn't stand it, Mabel, I couldn't *bear* it – so I picked up the vase o' flowers orf the table an' 'eld it upside down with both me 'ands, an' ... an' ... I brought it down on the back of 'is 'ead. There was a crack—'

'Yes, George, I heard it. Now listen to me, I'm goin' to send for Dr Knowles, 'cause if anybody can help us he can. I'm goin' to tell him that Dad fell downstairs.' Mabel tried not to pant as she spoke. 'Go up to yer room an' stay there. Whatever yer do, don't come down, d'ye hear me?'

She gently took his arm and led him out of the room; she helped him up the first few stairs, then left him to climb the rest. There was not a moment to lose, it was essential to act quickly and she closed her mind to everything other than what had to be done.

Oh, God, help me. Help me to save George, please.

She went to the front door, which was still ajar. A younger playmate of George's was idly kicking a ball around the street. 'Johnny!' she called. 'Johnny Tonks! Come here, I need yer to go for Dr Knowles in Hillier Road. D'ye know the way?'

"Course I do, Mabel. What's up?' he asked with interest.

'Go straight round to Hillier Road and ask the doctor to come at once, d'ye hear? Say my father's fallen downstairs and knocked himself unconscious. Hurry up, don't stop to talk to anybody, just fetch me the doctor and I'll give yer sixpence.'

Please, God, let Dr Knowles be in, please, Lord, please.

The boy whistled. 'Cor! I'm on me way.'

She was about to shut the door when Mrs Bull appeared, aproned and highly curious. 'What's up, Mabel? That brute back again, is 'e?'

'It's all right, Mrs Bull, just look after Daisy for me, please. I got the doctor comin' round.'

''E ain't gorn for poor little George again, 'as 'e?'

'No, George is all right, it's me father who's been taken bad. Just take care o' Daisy for me, Mrs Bull, an' I'll let yer know later. Thanks, goodbye.'

She shut the door on any further questions, went to the kitchen and put on the long hessian apron she wore for cleaning the stove and other dirty jobs. Back in the living room she seized hold of both Court's legs and straightened his body; then she pulled him round and dragged him by the legs out of the room and into the passage, to the foot of the stairs. There she took another deep breath, braced her muscles and heaved his legs up the first three stairs until his head was just at the foot of the bottom stair, his arms trailing on either side. He was not as heavy as she had expected and she noticed even in the present desperate moment that he had lost a lot of weight. She quickly arranged his legs so that one pointed straight up the stairs and the other was kinked at the knee. She spread one of his arms across his chest and saw the thinness of his grey face: his head seemed already a skull.

I'm sorry, Dad, I'm sorry. I'm doing this for George.

Next she went to the kitchen to fetch a floorcloth, a broom, dustpan and brush. She wiped the table top and took a clean cloth from a drawer to spread over it. She picked up the glass vase, re-filled it with water and rearranged the marguerite daisies in it. She picked up the damp red chenille tablecloth and drew in a sharp breath when she discovered a wet envelope marked *Mabel* in her mother's handwriting – so there *had* been a letter – no time to read it now. She thrust it into her pocket and took the cloth out to the kitchen, pushing it under the sink.

Then she tidied the room, rearranging the hearthrug. Off came the apron to go under the sink with the tablecloth and she wondered if there was time to check on George. There was not a sound from upstairs and she pictured him cowering in his room; should she go up past the sprawled body on the stairs to try to comfort her young brother? As she hesitated she heard Dr Knowles at the door and Johnny Tonks demanding his sixpence; while she went to the kitchen for her purse the doctor fished in his pocket and found a sixpenny piece. Then she opened the door, he entered the house and saw the body lying at the foot of the stairs.

He gave a groan, quickly stifled. 'Oh, Mabel, Mabel. Your father? Oh, my God.' He closed the door behind him. 'What happened?'

'I came home from Mrs Goring's and found him lyin' here, Dr Knowles,' she said, her voice sounding unnaturally high. 'George must've come in and gone out again, leavin' the door unlocked – he's out somewhere – and Dad must've come in and tried to get up the stairs, but he was drunk and fell. Then I came home and found him,' she repeated.

The doctor knelt down beside the body and put his hand inside Jack's clothes to feel his chest. He looked at the eyes, touched the nose and ear lobes. Smelt the whisky. Without looking up, he spoke very gently and kindly to Mabel: 'Did you do this, Mabel? You can tell me, my dear, and I'll do all in my power to get you off.'

She drew in a sharp breath and put a hand to her throat. 'What? No, I, er, he was drunk and sayin' things about our mother, how he never—' She stopped with a gasp, realising that she had just contradicted herself and not knowing how to go on.

But George shouted down from the landing above them, where he had been listening. 'No, *no*, she never done it, not Mabel! *I* done it, *I* 'it 'im over the 'ead – she wasn't even 'ere!'

'Oh, George,' moaned Mabel, covering her face with her hands as her brother came flying down the stairs, jumping over the body.

'*I* done it, I tell yer, doctor! – don't listen to 'er!'

'Be quiet, George, we don't want the whole street to hear,' said Knowles quickly. He was thinking fast, concentrating his mental powers on the situation before him. He knew he had to be bold and resolute to carry out the plan forming in his mind. First of all, he needed to get the body out of the house before the police were involved. 'Your father's deeply unconscious, but I think I can make out a heartbeat,' he said levelly. 'He must go to hospital immediately if he's to have a chance. The Bolingbroke's the best place, but there's no time to ask the police to send for an ambulance – Joe Cribb's wagon may be around – can you send that boy out again, Mabel?'

Johnny Tonks was asked to go and fetch old Joe Cribbs and the versatile horse-drawn vehicle he hired out to carry furniture, drums of paraffin, sacks of potatoes or whatever needed to be shifted. It had a rickety covered frame to conceal Joe's cargoes from prying eyes and was locally known as Joe's wagon.

While they waited for it, Knowles carefully examined the back of Court's head and found grim evidence of a violent blow that had shattered the occiput. 'Must have hit the edge of the bottom stair where the carpet's worn thin,' he murmured. 'Can you bring me a towel, Mabel? There's a fair-sized blood clot here.' While he wrapped the towel around the head and neck, he continued to talk to them both, keeping his voice low and matter-of-fact. 'He came in drunk and started attacking George who had just come home from school. George ran up the stairs to escape from him, and, er, Mr Court pursued him, but fell and hit his head on the bottom stair. Mabel came in from work and found him lying here. George was hiding in his room upstairs, not realising that Mr Court had fallen and knocked himself out. Do you both understand what I'm saying?'

Mabel and George looked at each other and then at Knowles.

Mabel steeled herself. 'Yes, Dr Knowles, we understand.' She nodded and managed an encouraging smile for her brother. 'We heard that, didn't we, George?'

The boy nodded dumbly. He looked terrified.

'And then Mabel sent young Johnny for me and I got here as quickly as I could,' went on Knowles. 'I found that there was a heartbeat, so got him away to hospital as soon as possible, so that he could have one of those X-ray photographs taken of his head. Ah, now I think I hear Joe at the door, so remember what I've said about what's happened. For your sister's sake, George, keep your mouth shut, there's a good lad.'

He went out to answer Joe's cheery 'Hello!' at the door, putting a finger to his lips. 'Sh-sh, Joe, we've got a chap unconscious here and he's pretty bad, I'm afraid. I'll need a hand to help get him into the wagon, only we'll have to be careful, he's got severe concussion.'

Joe turned down the corners of his mouth as they carried Court out of the house and into the wagon. 'Jack Court's a goner, ain't 'e, doctor?'

'No, I think there's a chance of saving him if you can get him to hospital. I'll get in at the back with him. Don't hang around, Joe, there are enough eyes watching us already.' He quickly turned to Mabel. 'I'll be back, my dear. Put the kettle on and make some hot sweet tea for George and yourself. You'll get neighbours coming round, so just tell them what we've agreed happened this afternoon. Don't let them question George, keep him quiet in his room and tell him I've got it all in hand. Oh, and Mabel – there's a small bloodstain on the living-room floor, near to the hearth. Get it wiped away, my dear.'

She nodded and even managed a half-smile. 'Yes, Dr Knowles, thank yer.'

'All right, Joe, get going,' he said and got in beside the corpse. Joe tightened the reins and the wagon rattled out of Sorrel Street.

Under Thursday, 13 June 1912, in the Admissions Book at the Bolingbroke Hospital, an entry was made concerning a John Court, forty-two, of 12 Sorrel Street, Battersea, London SW, who had arrived at 5.10 p.m. but had not been admitted, due to being certified as dead on arrival.

When Alice came home Mabel had to break the news to her of their father's fatal accident, and how badly it had affected George who was resting in bed and not to be disturbed. Before Alice could start asking questions Mabel told her to go to Mrs Bull's and bring Daisy home. From then onwards neighbours came and went, as they had done after Annie's disappearance, and the news spread like wildfire through Sorrel Street and beyond.

Dr Knowles was very much in evidence, assisting the police by his presence when they came to interview Mabel and George, so soon after the tragic loss of their mother. George simply nodded dumbly to the questions gently put to him and the brief statements bore out the story already on everybody's lips, interspersed with comments like 'Drunken brute, 'e got what 'e deserved' – though there were those who remembered how charming and open-handed Jack Court could be in the right mood. It was generally agreed that he had deteriorated in recent months. 'Why 'e even went for Mabel's young man, 'im in the Sally Army.'

Harry. Mabel's heart sank at the thought of that excellent young man who had supported her throughout her mother's disappearance and death, and since. How could she face him now, knowing what she knew, and having done what she had done? The deception that she and Dr Knowles were engaged upon was undoubtedly wrong, no matter how good their intentions; and for the sake of her fellow conspirator – and George – she could never tell another person the truth about how her father had met his death. Not even Harry. So either she must deceive the man she loved, or break with him and let him find a worthier wife. And how could she possibly do *that* when they loved each other so much and had promised to wait for years, if necessary, until they could be married?

Harry, of course, rushed to Sorrel Street as soon as the news reached him, intending to put his arms around Mabel and comfort her – and George and Daisy – as well as he could.

But Mabel drew back. 'No, Harry, George is in bed and mustn't be disturbed, and I'm too tired to think. Please, I can't talk to yer tonight. Thank yer for comin', but I need time—'

'*Harry*!' Daisy came hurtling down the stairs and ran straight into his arms. He rocked her backwards and forwards while he and Mabel looked helplessly at each other over the top of her head. There were so many things he wanted to say: that Jack Court had been a troubled soul but was now at rest, and God would be his judge – or, putting it another way, he would no longer be a menace to his family. Harry longed to sympathise and soothe, but for some reason words deserted him and, not being allowed to see George, he departed with a sense of loss that he could not understand.

A message arrived via police officers that Mr Court's mother had been informed and was in a state of shock, unable to visit or receive visitors. No condolences were exchanged between Macaulay Road and Sorrel Street, which was a small relief to Mabel who had no desire to see her grandmother. She felt as if she were in the grip of an evil dream from which there would be no awakening and which nobody could penetrate.

Except . . .

The door of number 12 was open when Albert Court walked in just before ten. Seeing him, Mabel swayed on her feet and almost fell into his outstretched arms. 'Bloody 'ell, ol' gal, sod this for a lark, eh?'

He was the most welcome sight in the world and they held each other close for a long moment without saying anything at all. A police message had arrived for him only hours before he was due to join a merchantman at Tilbury Docks, his training days being over. 'I got word from ol' 'Arry an' all, it's gettin' a bit of a reg'lar thing, i'n'it, 'im fetchin' me 'ome?'

How much should she tell her brother? Or rather, how could she conceal anything from Albert? As it turned out, there was no need to think about what she should say, because as soon as she took him to George's room the boy burst into floods of tears and she left them alone together. Albert slept with his young brother that night and Alice was asked to let Daisy take her place in Mabel's bed.

At midnight, when the house was silent, Mabel crept downstairs and turned on the gaslight. Sitting down at the table, she at last took out the envelope containing her mother's letter and spread the scrawled and blotted sheet before her.

My dear Mabel best of daughters, I have not much time to ask you to forgive me. I have an illness which will kill me and I cant face the pain and lingering as I seen other poor women go that way. Your father may not come home again and he also may not live long.

Now Mabel, you must write to Mrs Elinor Somerton who is my sister Nell and tell her that you are orphans. I shoud ansered her letter but now you will anser it and ask her to come to her neices and nepews to give help if she can.

She lives at Pear Tree Cottage, Beversley Lane, Belhampton, Hampshire.

I pray you will be happy with the Drover boy who is a good Christian as you were all broght up to be. Time is short and I leave you with a mothers love my own beatifull little Mabel.

Anna-Maria Chalcott Court.

Mabel seemed to hear her mother's voice speaking clearly to her as she read and could picture her face as vividly as if she stood before her in life. Although her tears flowed freely, she was consoled by the message that had waited six weeks to be found. It brought her a measure of reassurance, even though it confirmed that Annie Court had taken her own life. Mabel had never believed that her death had been accidental.

There and then she set about obeying the instructions it contained.

Dear Mrs Somerton,

I hope you will let me call you Aunt Nell, because I am your niece Mabel Court, and I have some very sad news to tell you . . .

The next day Mabel showed Albert their mother's letter and they agreed not to share its contents with the other three. His presence in the house greatly lightened the atmosphere and, while not pretending to mourn for Jack Court, he avoided harsh words and encouraged them all to behave as normally as possible. He continued to share his old bed with George and that Friday night Mabel heard the brothers' voices murmuring as she fell asleep. Albert never divulged what George had said, nor did he ask her questions about that fatal 13 June, but she felt sure that George had told him everything and was thankful beyond words for his solid support to them both.

'Albert, ye're a life-saver,' she told him, while faithful Harry Drover found himself relegated to taking Daisy out to the park accompanied by a white-faced, silent George. Alice resigned herself to helping in the house and Mabel avoided being alone with Harry. There was too much that had to be concealed and she was feeling increasingly unfit to be his life's partner. First a suicide in the family and now a . . . she could not even say the word to herself. Plus a grandmother who regularly carried out illegal operations for money. What kind of Salvation Army wife would have such a background?

The inquest on Court's death was fixed for the following Wednesday, 19 June, and the thought of it hung like a cloud over them, including Dr Knowles. As a trusted, respected general practitioner, the son of a doctor and father of another, he had made himself an accessory to a concealment of manslaughter and would have to give false evidence to the coroner. He would need to choose his words with great care and hope that Mabel's nerve held.

On the Monday as the courts had just finished a midday repast of soup and bread, there came a tentative knock at the door. Albert nodded to Alice who rose to answer it.

Two middle-aged women who somewhat resembled each other were standing outside, both soberly dressed in black; the older was the taller.

'Please excuse us, but is this the home of Miss Court? Miss Mabel Court?' asked the younger one nervously.

'Who is it, Alice?' Mabel called out.

'Two ladies asking to see yer.'

When Mabel hurried to the door the women stared at her as if transfixed. Then they both exclaimed together, 'Anna-Maria!'

Mabel knew at once who they were. Her face lit up and she held out her hands. 'Ye're her sisters – my aunts! Oh, ye're more 'n welcome! Oh, my aunts, my own *aunts*!'

For Elinor Somerton had put her arm round Mabel, and was laughing and crying. 'Yes, dear, I'm your Aunt Nell and this is your Aunt Kate – you're so like your mother, I'd have known you anywhere as her daughter – oh, Anna-Maria!'

The other lady stared a little uncomfortably at Alice who was completely mystified.

'This is my sister Alice, Aunt Kate,' said Mabel eagerly. 'An' I've got another called Daisy – oh, here she is, look! An' two brothers – but what're we doin' on the doorstep? Come in!'

The aunts were shown into the living room where Albert got awkwardly to his feet, nudging George to do the same. There was a moment of complete unreality as the women looked at the two boys, the elder one the image of *that man* – swarthy-complexioned with two strong front teeth – and the other fair like Mabel. Like Anna-Maria.

In a surprisingly short time the aunts felt that they knew their nieces and nephews, and the youngsters felt the same; the instinctive stirrings of blood relationship drew them together. The aunts explained that Mabel's letter, posted the day before, had arrived that morning and Elinor had rushed round to show it to Katherine who lived at Pinehurst, the family home in which they had all grown up. They had agreed at once to set out for London and from Waterloo Station they had taken a taxicab to the Battersea address that Mabel had given them.

'So here we are, but our poor, dear sister's gone for ever – oh, my God, what a dreadful thing to happen!' Mrs Somerton wept. 'I wonder if she ever got the letter I sent last year to that address in Tooting—'

'Yes, she did, Aunt Nell,' said Mabel mournfully. 'She just couldn't bring herself to answer it after all that time, though I told her she should. It was all so sad, the way her – your – father died, and I know it was like a shadow over her life, all that sadness in the past. She could've been reconciled with yer and we could've all met years ago.'

'All those years,' echoed Elinor, wiping her eyes. 'And it's been her death that's brought us together at last. Oh, Mabel, you're so like her, as pretty as a picture!'

And so they started to get to know each other in the course of that afternoon and evening. The girls were particularly fascinated by their aunts' descriptions of their mother, first as a little girl and then a young woman. Mabel and Daisy warmed to Nell, while Alice found it easier to talk to the less emotional Kate. The two brothers sat as if hypnotised by this sudden revelation of a whole new family and two aunts they'd never known they had. It was unbelievable!

Arrangements were made for the aunts to stay overnight, and Mabel and Alice made up the double bed with clean sheets. The experience of sharing it gave Kate and Nell some insight into the cramped conditions in which their sister had brought up a family of five – Mabel had told them of the loss of little Walter. The constant struggle to make ends meet was visible in every crack and stain, the thin curtains, the chipped ewer on the washstand. Compared with Pinehurst and Pear Tree Cottage, 12 Sorrel Street was a poor place in a poor area.

'But she was a mother, Kate, which is more than either of us has been.' Nell sighed as they got into their sister's matrimonial bed. 'And such nice children, too. That poor little Daisy looks so lost, I'd like to take her home with me – and Alice, too.'

'That Albert's a tough character, though, the father all over again,' said Kate. 'That awful London accent! I wouldn't care to take *him* on.'

'He's in the navy, anyway, so he's no problem,' replied her sister. 'I shall talk it over with Thomas and say I'd be happy to take the girls if they'd like to come to live with us, and George too – at least until they're able to support themselves. Oh, Kate, it's as if it was meant to be! Thomas and I have been so disappointed in having no family.'

'I'm thinking of offering a home to Mabel as a companion,' said Kate reflectively.

'Look, shall we suggest taking the younger children back to Belhampton with us tomorrow – or Monday?' said Nell eagerly. 'It would make life easier for Mabel with that dreadful inquest to face next week, and then there'll be the funeral. It would be better for her and the children, surely, to have them away from all that.'

Having made up her mind, Nell soon fell asleep beside her sister, but Kate stayed awake for several hours, staring up into the not-quite-darkness of the midsummer night, with its jarring noises from the street and more distantly from the river. For the rest of her life Kate Chalcott knew that she would regret the cruel letter she had written to Anna-Maria following her elopement with Court, and all the bitterness that had resulted from it, the harm that could now never be put right. The least she could do was to offer a home to her sister's daughter.

Lying beside Daisy in their bed on the other side of the wall, Mabel too stared up into the half-darkness, rejoicing at the arrival of their long-lost aunts. It was like a shaft of light piercing the gloom, and she felt as if the memory of her mother had become lightened in some way, easier to bear. For the past six weeks she had feared to dream of seeing again that pale, drowned face, but now when she closed her eyes she saw the young Anna-Maria, not in the cold blankness of death but alive and smiling, a bright-eyed girl looking down upon her first-born child who so closely resembled her.

Mabel and Albert talked over their aunts' offer and decided to accept it gratefully. Alice could hardly wait to see Belhampton, but Daisy was not happy about parting from Mabel and neither was George who frankly begged to be allowed to stay near her. In the end Mabel told Daisy to be a good girl and go with Alice to her aunt's, while George would stay at Sorrel Street.

She and Albert agreed that George was a worry. His eyes were haunted by what he knew and his sleep was disturbed by terrifying nightmares that woke Albert, and which could be disastrous if he were at Belhampton for what he might reveal. Dr Knowles prescribed a teaspoonful of syrup of choral each night to help him sleep and they could only hope that time would do its healing work.

So on Monday morning Mabel, Albert and George waved off their aunts and sisters on the train from Waterloo, while bracing themselves to face the next ordeal: the inquest.

Chapter Thirteen

The inquest into the death of John Masood Court was attended by his mother, Mrs Court, his eldest daughter Mabel and son Albert. It was mercifully brief as the facts were not in dispute and the coroner wanted to spare the relatives distress, so soon after the death of Court's wife. George was not required to attend in view of his age and the fact that he had already been through so much; his evidence was read out by the police officer who had questioned him at home on the day of the accident, and corresponded with Mabel's account and that of Dr Knowles.

Albert was allowed to stand beside his sister while she described how she had come home just after four o'clock to find her father lying unconscious at the foot of the stairs and George up in his room. She had sent for Dr Knowles who was once again the key witness. He told how he had discovered a weak heartbeat and made immediate arrangements to get Court to the Bolingbroke Hospital where they had arrived too late, Court having died on the way.

An autopsy had been performed on the body and the report showed a severe depressed fracture of the back of the skull with extensive intra-cranial haemorrhage, corresponding to a violent impact with the edge of the stair. There was a high alcohol level in the blood.

In addition, it was revealed that Court had

recently been treated at the Lock Hospital and that his condition was seriously advanced.

Albert gasped. 'Bloody 'ell,' he muttered under his breath.

Mabel looked at him in surprise. 'Sh!' she whispered, shaking her head. Mimi Court, seated alone on a bench behind them, momentarily closed her eyes.

The coroner did not hesitate to bring in a verdict of accidental death and extended his sympathy to the doubly bereaved family. He praised Dr Knowles for his prompt action in attempting to save Court's life.

The hearing was over. Knowles took a deep breath and assumed a deliberately bland expression to hide his profound relief as he joined the brother and sister, little suspecting that the worst was still to come. As they left the courtroom Mabel told Albert that she would have a word with their grandmother.

'What for? She ain't honoured us wiv a visit.'

'But she's lost her only son – her only child. It's worse for her than for us, isn't it? Come on.'

Out in the corridor they came face to face with Mimi. Dressed in black silk, her shoulders back and her eyes leaden, she spoke to Mabel with business-like directness. 'Yer won't be able to stay at Sorrel Street now – yer can't support that lot. The offer I made yer's still open, Mabel, and yer won't get a better. There's bed and board for you and yer sisters at Macaulay Road, and I'll pay yer a pound a week to assist me with local births. I don't want the boy, though – he can go to the Barnardo home in Clapham.'

Her mouth hardened as she mentioned George and it was this last remark that stung Mabel into a proud retort. 'My mother's sisters have taken Alice

293

and Daisy to live with them at Belhampton in Hampshire, so I don't need yer offer, thank yer. They'll get a good standard o' livin' there and Daisy'll go to a church school.'

'Better 'n what Tootin' can offer,' added Albert incautiously.

Mimi's jaw had dropped, but she quickly recovered herself. 'Oho, so *they've* turned up again, have they? My, oh my! Them Chalcotts must've made a tidy little fortune out o' their drapery an' furnishin' store, and I dare say they think 'emselves somebody when they're nobody but jumped-up tradespeople. Jack an' Annie never 'ad a penny orf 'em.'

'An' 'oo was Jack Court, then?' demanded Albert. 'Nuffin' but a waster an' a womaniser – couldn't even run a bleedin' book so's to make a profit.'

Mimi rounded on him, her eyes blazing. 'Guttersnipe! Jack's father was somethin' more than yer country tradesmen, he was a prince among men – a *prince*! And Jack could've done a lot better 'n he did, only he went an' made a foolish marriage to a woman who hadn't got the sense to – oh, get out o' my sight, the lot o' yer!'

She was about to walk away, but Albert would not swallow this insult to his mother. 'Oh, so it was our muvver 'oo gave 'im the pox, then, was it?'

There was a stunned silence and Dr Knowles put a hand on Mabel's arm.

Mimi visibly shrank back from the burning scorn in her grandson's eyes, so like Jack's. 'No need for that kind o' talk in front o'—' She nodded towards Mabel who stood rooted to the spot, her eyes wide and unbelieving.

'No, it was the ovver way rahnd, wa'n't it?' went on Albert, leaning forward with his face menacingly

294

close to Mimi's. ''E got it orf 'is fancy women, an' passed it on to 'er, don't yer reckon? I'd say it was 'er, poor woman, that made the foolish marriage – eh?'

'Be quiet, Albert, for heaven's sake,' hissed Knowles. 'Have some thought for Mabel!'

But Mabel had found a voice. 'Never mind me, Dr Knowles, I want to know what they're talkin' about. What *was* my father treated for in – what was the name o' that hospital?'

Knowles cursed silently under his breath. The inquest had gone off better than he had dared to hope, but now there was to be another kind of reckoning. He would have spared Mabel this.

'*Now* ye've set the cat among the pigeons, yer young fool,' Mimi told Albert, who had the grace to look shamefaced.

'Don't yer know what the Lock Hospital's for, Mabel?' he muttered.

That was when she understood. 'Oh, my God, that blood test, Dr Knowles – was it for that ... that horrible disease, *syphilis*?' She stared at the doctor who could not meet her eyes. 'Yes, that's what yer tested me for, wasn't it, an' the others, poor innocent children – the pox, the prostitutes' complaint. An' if *he* had it, then *she* ... that rash an' sore throat she had, was that it? Come on, tell me, nothin' can hurt her now, not any more!' Her voice rose and heads turned towards the scene in the airless corridor of the old Magistrates' Court.

Albert also turned to the doctor. 'I got it wrong, di'n't I? Yer tried to keep it quiet, an' I shouldn't've spoke the way I did. Sorry.'

Knowles tried to give them an answer. 'To the best of my knowledge your mother didn't suspect it. She had a much greater fear of cancer, which I don't think she had.'

'But did she 'ave – the ovver?' asked Albert.

'It seemed like the primary phase, yes. I was going to confirm it with a test, but—'

'But yer tested me instead, 'cause yer thought *I'd* got it.' Mabel felt that the world was crashing around her.

'I had to be absolutely sure, Mabel, because of the babies at the Institute—'

'So that was it, *that's* why I was sacked from there! Oh, now I see why Mrs James was so cagey with me!'

'Mabel, will you *listen*, for heaven's sake! The Wasserman test was *negative* for you and the others. You have *not* got it, it was only a precaution because you'd been sharing bed linen, teacups – there was skin contact and though it's very unlikely to be passed on this way I had to be sure. And you're absolutely *clear*, my dear.'

But Mabel was devastated by the fact that he had thought it necessary to check her for that shameful disease and she continued to stare at him, her eyes a dull and lifeless grey without a hint of blue, two pools of misery in a chalk-white face.

'Listen, Mabel, your poor mother's at rest now and you're a young, healthy woman with all your life before you. One day you'll be a wonderful children's nurse—'

But she scarcely heard him. She turned and leaned heavily on Albert's arm. 'Let's go home, Albert,' she said brokenly. 'George'll be waitin' for us.'

If Mabel's girlhood had ended, so had George's childhood. This much was evident when she and Albert got home to find their brother in a near-hysterical state. 'Where've yer been? It's been *hours*, I been lookin' out for yer – thought they must've found out what 'appened—'

'Oh, George, don't be silly, we haven't been that long. It's all over an' there's nothin' to worry about. Let's put the kettle on, I'm dyin' for a cup o' tea.'

George's need for comfort and reassurance had the effect of taking Mabel's mind off the shock she had received.

'Did they ask a lot o' questions?' he persisted.

'Come orf it, mate, they 'ad nuffin' but sympafy for yer,' said Albert. 'No need to worry abaht a fing, honest.'

Albert spoke lightly, but George's nerves were at breaking point and that night his fears surfaced in terrifying dreams from which he awoke with a loud shout that woke Albert.

'Bloody 'ell, George, pipe dahn or ye'll 'ave the 'ole street quakin' in their beds!'

Albert held his brother as he struggled with unseen assailants and Mabel left her bed to comfort George as she had done when he was a scared little toddler, turned out of his parents' room to make way for the new baby whose arrival had filled the night with frightening noises.

'I don't like leavin' yer wiv 'im in this state, Mabel,' said Albert who was due to return to the merchant service after the funeral. 'To be honest wiv yer, I don't fink 'e's goin' to get over it while 'e's in this 'ouse. 'E needs a complete change.'

Mabel sighed and shook her head. 'I know, I know, but where can he go? He says he doesn't want to be with the girls and to tell the truth I'd be afraid o' what he might come out with, especially when he gets these awful nightmares. I'd rather have him near me. They say that time heals everything and he's young. Poor Georgie!'

'It's early days yet.' Albert shrugged. 'The ol' man ain't even buried.'

It was George himself who made the suggestion that was to change the whole course of his life. The three of them were at breakfast the next day. 'D'ye know that Dr Barnardo's sends a lot o' boys over to Canada to make a new start, like?' he suddenly asked his brother and sister.

'Eh?' grunted Albert, munching bread and margarine.

But Mabel cried out in dismay, 'Barnardo's? Canada? Yer don't mean—'

'Yes, I do, Mabel. I'd like to go out there with 'em, get away from this place an ... an ... yer know, everythin'.'

'But yer couldn't, George, not all on yer own!'

'Wouldn't be on me own with all them other boys,' he mumbled.

'Come orf it, George, no need to go that far,' said Albert with a significant look at Mabel. 'Why don't yer go an' stay wiv yer aunts an' the girls at Bel'ampton?'

'Nah, that wouldn't do.' George shook his head emphatically. 'I'd rather be with a whole lot of orphan boys with no fam'lies, goin' out to make a new ... Canada's a big place.'

'But George, ye've got a family – ye've got us!' Mabel was both shocked and hurt by this insight into George's sense of isolation. And his desolation.

'This fam'ly's broke up,' he said dully. 'I can't go on dependin' on *you* for everythin', Mabel. I got to learn to shift for meself.'

'But ye're only *twelve*, Georgie!'

Albert was as much concerned by the pain and anxiety on his sister's face as by George's expressed wish to cross the Atlantic ocean. 'We know ye've 'ad a bad shock, mate, but it'd be better to go an' stay wiv the girls in the country.'

'*No*, Albert, I couldn't face 'em, not after what's 'appened.' And poor George began to cry, getting up from his place at the table.

'Sit dahn an' finish yer breakfus',' ordered Albert, motioning to Mabel not to speak again. 'Tell yer what – we'll go an' see Dr Knowles today when yer get 'ome from school, an' ask 'im what 'e finks abaht the idea. See if we can't sort summat aht. 'Ow's abaht that?'

George nodded, wiping his hand across his face, while Mabel looked helplessly from brother to brother, sharing their unspoken thought: that the doctor was the only other person who knew their dreadful secret. He alone could understand their situation and give them guidance. She therefore agreed and George finished his breakfast.

'I 'ope the doctor comes up wiv somefing, Mabel, else our little bruvver could land us all in Queer Street,' Albert said later when George had gone to school.

'Yer mean if he told his friends or teachers—'

'Or any bugger else 'oo 'appened to be passin' if 'e broke dahn an' let it all aht.'

'I don't like the thought o' going back to Brom-felde Road while he's in such a nervy state.' She sighed.

'Er, look, Mabel, I bin thinkin' abaht what 'e said – nah, don't shout at me, 'cause it might be the best way aht – an' the best fing for 'im, yer know.'

'What might?'

'Goin' orf in one o' these child emigration schemes, makin' a new start.'

'*What*? Albert Court, he's only a child – he's twelve years old!'

'Yeah, but 'e's not just any twelve-year-old, is 'e? In 'is case it might be a . . . a way aht for 'im, along o' them ovver poor little buggers wiv nuffin' to keep 'em 'ere. Remember, 'e was the one to say it first. Let's see what the doc says.'

In fact, Henry Knowles had been extremely worried about George and had already considered the possibility of a child emigration scheme as a solution to his need for a new beginning, an escape from the knowledge about which he could not talk. The problem lay in putting the idea before Mabel and, of course, to George himself. So when Albert and George marched into his consulting room and took the words right out of his mouth, so to speak, he was more than happy to consider what they said and offer all the help he could.

'Well, come on, tell me, how did yer get on?'

'What d'ye want first, Mabel, the good news or . . . or the ovver? Nah, come to fink of it, yer got to 'ave the good news first, 'cause the ovver follers on.'

'Don't play guessing games, tell me straight out,' said Mabel, trembling in her shoes.

Albert hesitated, but George spoke up, searching her face for her reaction. 'Dr Knowles agrees it'd be best for me to get right away, make a new start – an' 'e reckons I ought to go to the Barnardo's in Clapham – an' if yer like, 'e'll see about gettin' me in there straight away.'

Mabel's heart gave a lurch and she sat down. 'An'

yer call that the good news,' she said faintly. 'Go on, then, tell me the rest.'

'Which is—' began Albert, looking at George. 'Which is that there's a shipload o' boys sailin' from Soufampton a week termorrer, June the twenty-eighth, goin' to 'Alifax, Nova Scotia.'

'An' I want to be there with 'em,' added George.

Mabel felt the blood drain from her face. 'Oh, my God. Oh, no.' Visions of the *Titanic* passed before her mind's eye. 'No, no.'

George came and sat beside her. 'Don't worry about me, Mabel, it's what I *want*, can't yer see? This 'ouse ain't 'ome any more, not after what's 'appened. I'll be better away from 'ere, I can't wait!' He spoke with a certain animation and when she put out her hand to him he took it in both of his, the first positive gesture he had made.

'But Georgie, ye're all I've got left!' And her tears began to flow at the thought of the breaking up of the family, the bleak emptiness she would face when both her brothers had left the home they had known all their lives: the only home they had.

'Don't cry, Mabel, yer can't go on supportin' me. There's no money comin' in now and ye've got yerself to think about. Oh, Mabel, don't cry, don't worry about me!'

'Dear George, yer were always a good boy,' she said, wiping her eyes. 'But I'll have to see Dr Knowles meself and talk it all over with him.'

'He's comin' rahnd later this evenin',' said Albert. 'I fink 'e reckons George is right.'

And so in what seemed to be a very short time the arrangements were made. The doctor was willing to sponsor George Court as an emigrant on the SS *City of York* bound for Halifax on 28 June and sent in a medical report. He personally put up the thirty pounds' fare that would normally be paid by the charity fund of Dr Barnardo's homes. 'I've spoken to Mr Maillard and he'll take George into the Clapham home any day convenient to you, Mabel,' he said. 'It'll give him a chance to meet and get to know his fellow passengers before they sail.'

'It's all for the best, Mabel,' urged Albert who was worried about his sister being left alone at Sorrel Street. 'Can't yer get a livin'-in job like yer friend Maudie, jus' till ye're old enough to start yer trainin'? Get out o' this place, an' stop stewin' over the rent, eh?'

Mabel shook her head. 'I can't think about anything at all right now, Albert. We got the funeral to get through next.'

The truth was that she was feeling close to despair and too exhausted by shock and sorrow even to contemplate the future. As Albert had hinted, Mimi's money was rapidly diminishing and there was nothing coming in. The rent man called on Friday evenings and there must be no falling behind with it, because Mimi had said she would no longer step in and pay off the arrears as she had done when Jack was alive. But Mabel had neither the energy nor the inclination to start looking for work again.

Jack's funeral was a very quiet affair, held at nine o'clock in the morning of the following Monday. It was attended by Mabel and Albert, with Mimi Court standing on the other side of the opened grave, a grim-faced figure in black who laid a wreath of red carnations on the coffin. A little group of Sorrel Street neighbours followed the small cortège out of respect for Mabel or for curiosity's sake. None of Jack's former associates turned up.

The vicar of St Philip's read a short passage from St John's Gospel and said a prayer as the coffin was lowered to lie beside the one committed to earth barely seven weeks before. 'Enter not into judgement with thy servant, O Lord, for in thy sight shall no man be justified.'

The words seemed to Mabel exactly right for the occasion and she whispered 'Goodbye, Dad' as Jack's mortal remains disappeared from their sight.

Mimi turned away without a word to anybody and made her way to the south gate where a black hansom cab waited for her. Mabel and Albert walked home at a leisurely pace; George had been left with Mrs Bull who promised to have breakfast ready on their return.

'So George'll be orf to the 'ome termorrer, an' I'll stay for as long as yer want me,' said Albert. 'We can bofe go an' see 'im orf togevver.'

'My friend Ada Clay gets married the day after he sails,' remarked Mabel inconsequentially.

'Does she? Good, that'll be a nice little do for yer to go to an' enjoy yerself.'

'D'ye think I should?' asked Mabel without much interest.

''Course yer should, don't be daft. What's the sense in mopin'? Our poor muvver—' He suddenly faltered and Mabel took his hand. After a moment he continued, rather jerkily, 'We'll never know for sure 'ow much she knew, will we? Whether she fort it was cancer or . . . or the ovver. Ol' Knowles did 'is best, but she might've twigged what 'e was finkin', an' she'd never 'ave bin able to live with that. When I fink o' them last hours she went frough—'

Mabel took a handkerchief out of her pocket for him. 'She's done with trouble now, Albert dear. We mustn't dwell on it.'

He patted her arm and swallowed. After a while he turned to another matter that had been on his mind. Harry Drover. 'When 'e came rahnd the ovver night I tried to get George to come to the park, but yer wouldn't let us go, so poor ol' 'Arry was never on 'is own wiv yer. Why was that, Mabel? I 'ope ye're not goin' back on 'im 'cause of all this.'

She stopped in her tracks and faced him squarely. 'For goodness' sake, Albert, how could I possibly marry a man like Harry? Yer might as well ask why don't I join the Salvation Army? *Think* about it, both me parents had that . . . that disease, an' I had to be tested for it as well. An' my mother took her own life, and my father—'

"Ad a nasty accident, yeah, not a pretty story, but no reason for yer to go orf poor ol' 'Arry. It'd break 'is 'eart, Mabel, it really would. 'E worships the grahnd yer walk on.'

And how do you think I feel? What about my *heart?* thought Mabel silently. Aloud she said, 'I've made up my mind, Albert, I shan't marry anybody.'

'Go on wiv yer, ye'll change yer mind in anuvver year or two.'

'No, I won't. It's a funny thing, I once vowed when I was a little girl that I'd never get married. I couldn't understand why any woman 'ud want to.'

'Not surprisin', after what yer saw of our muvver's lot.'

'I remember when it was. I must've been about seven, 'cause Mum was nearly due to have Walter and it was near Christmas. Dad came home rollin' drunk an' singin' his head off, and she was tryin' to get him up the stairs. The noise woke me up, an' I went to help her. When we'd got him on the bed, she asked me to hold the pot while he pee'd into it – talk about the Victoria Falls! – and there he stood singin' "Lily of Laguna" at the top o' his voice, and she cried 'cause I'd seen an' heard it all. That's when I said I'd never get married. I didn't realise that there were men like . . . like Harry in the world.'

'Pig. Swine. Bastard.'

'Sh, Albert, he was yer father, an' we've just come from buryin' him. He wasn't a bad man so much as a weak one. And he must've gone through hell at the end, when he knew what he'd got – an' given to Mum. God help him, if ever a soul in torment looked out of a man's eyes, I saw one then.' She shivered at the memory. 'It's not for us to judge, Albert.'

Albert sighed deeply. 'D'ye ever wonder where 'e came from, Mabel? The ol' girl's never talked abaht 'is farver, 'as she?'

'Except to say he was a prince!'

'Oh-ah, must've bin ol' Edward the Seventh 'fore 'e was king, I dare say,' said Albert with the ghost of a grin. 'Touch o' the tarbrush, more like!'

'Albert! What a thing to say!'

'Didn't I ever tell yer they call me the Wog in the navy?'

'*Do* they? You an' Alice an' Daisy all got his dark looks – specially you.'

'As long as that's all I got off 'im.'

They walked in silence for a while and then he returned to the subject of Harry. 'Jus' give yerself time to get over all this, Mabel, find a cushy little job wiv some ol' girl wiv a bit o' money an' ye'll change yer mind about marryin', see if yer don't.'

'No, Albert. I shan't marry Harry – or anybody.'

She spoke with sorrowful conviction and her face warned Albert not to press the matter.

She knew that even he could not comprehend the turmoil in her heart and mind when she thought how much she must hurt the man she loved – and herself – for his own future good. Harry could never be told the truth: that George had killed his father and that she had conspired to conceal that fact, giving false evidence in a coroner's court. It was a burden she must carry all her life, like the shadow of syphilis that continued to haunt her. All she could hope for now was to pick up her dream of training to be a nurse and eventually to fulfil her lifelong hope of looking after children; but for the time being she felt utterly tired and dispirited, and soon she would be all alone in the world.

Events moved swiftly. Mabel persuaded Albert not to delay his return to sea any longer and so he took his leave of her two days after George moved into the home on Clapham High Street. Letters arrived from Belhampton asking her when she was coming to stay, but she wrote back delaying the visit, wanting to keep in touch with George and see him off on the day of his departure.

The brother and sister stood on Waterloo Station where a crowd of around forty boys were herded on to the platform awaiting the train to Southampton. Their ages ranged from about seven to sixteen, and all wore dark knickerbockers or trousers, with shirt collars turned back over their buttoned jackets and peaked caps. To Mabel they all looked alarmingly alike, and though there was excitement in the air, she saw some pale, scared little faces and most seemed to be without relatives. She desperately hoped and prayed that George would find friends among these boys whom nobody wanted.

All at once she caught sight of a tall, fair lad of about fourteen, square-jawed and blue-eyed. She had never seen him before and knew nothing about him, but something in his face attracted her, and on an impulse she marched up to him to introduce herself and George. 'Hello – er, good mornin'. I see ye're off to Canada with all these boys,' she said, forcing a smile. 'This is my brother George Court who's comin' with yer.'

'Oh, yeah?' The lad looked George up and down. 'Yeah, I seen 'im a couple o' times in the 'ome. Only come last week, di'n't 'e?'

'Yes, well, he's twelve and a half, and I ... I'm asking if ye'd keep an eye on him if yer wouldn't mind,' faltered Mabel. 'We've lost our parents this year and so he – that's why he's going to Canada with yer.'

The lad looked at her curiously for a moment. 'Yer want me to guard 'im, eh?'

Mabel nodded.

'Right.' He straightened himself up to full height. 'Davy 'Ook at yer service, gettin' chucked aht o' Barnardo's at last. It was eiver Canada or prison, so they tossed a shillin' an' it came dahn 'eads.' He raised his eyebrows in a question.

Mabel responded at once. 'I'm not askin' why ye're here, Davy, I just want yer to look after me brother. Soon as I saw yer face, I knew I could trust yer.'

He looked hard at her, then his face lit up in a broad grin. He gave a thumbs-up sign. 'It's as good as done, miss. Anybody lay a finger on 'im an' they'll

307

rue the day. Wotcher, George! Get in along o' me an' ye'll be all right.'

Mabel felt that she had passed some kind of test and smiled back at the boy. 'Thank yer, that's really good o' yer, er, Davy. George, yer heard what he said – stay with him, won't yer?'

George nodded and Davy gave him a wink. 'Don't 'ang abaht, miss, kiss yer bruvver goodbye an' 'op it,' he advised. 'George, yer stay close to me, savvy?'

Of course she could not leave until she'd seen George on to the train and somehow she managed to keep smiling as it drew out, taking her brother away for – how long? Heaven only knew. For years, perhaps for life.

'Goodbye, George! God bless yer – oh, Georgie—'

He was gone and only then could Mabel give way to the tears she had held in check until now; they poured down her cheeks as she left the station, praying that Davy Hook would be as good as his word, whether or not he was the young criminal he made himself out to be.

That was the moment when she saw a familiar figure hurrying towards her and in spite of all her resolutions her heart leapt for joy, followed at once by the anguish of knowing she must not give way to weakness. This must be another final goodbye.

Yet his dear face was here before her and she heard the sound of his voice reproaching her. '*Mabel*! Oh, Mabel, I got here as fast as I could, but – has he – have they gone?'

She turned away, walking quickly. He tried to keep up with her, but she did not stop. 'I never told yer it was today,' she muttered.

'No, but I asked at the boys' home, an' they said – Mabel, why didn't yer let me know? I'd've been here

308

for yer, my dearest girl. I didn't get a chance to say goodbye to 'im, nor give 'im the present I got – oh, Mabel, why won't yer let me help yer? Why've yer changed? Is it somethin' I've done? Only tell me, Mabel—'

She quickened her pace. 'We can't meet any more, Harry. I can't ever join the Army. I'm not . . . not the girl I was any more, not the girl yer think yer know – knew. Leave me, Harry, just let me go.'

'But Mabel, *why*? How can yer be so cruel?' He put a hand out to touch her, but she shrank away.

'Let me *go*, I said – let me *go*!' And knowing only that she must tear herself away, Mabel broke into a run, her skirt flying up around her legs, her hat askew, held on by a couple of pins. He started to pursue her, and bystanders watched in astonishment as she tripped and fell headlong. Just as he reached her she scrambled to her feet without his aid and went on running, gasping and sobbing as she ran, until he gave up the chase for the sake of propriety and followed at a distance, never taking his eyes from her.

Where could she go? Not to 12 Sorrel Street, empty and silent, and besides, he would follow and find her there. No, there was only one place left to her now. A place where she had been offered bed and board, and a chance to learn the art of midwifery while earning a pound a week.

Curious passers-by saw the wild-eyed girl jump on the electric tram that went down from Westminster to Tooting.

Chapter Fourteen

When Mabel arrived on the doorstep of 23 Macaulay
Road, hatless and half fainting, her grandmother
asked no questions but summoned Elsie to help get
the girl upstairs to a small bedroom where she drew
the curtains and assisted Mabel to undress. A
nightgown was found and Mabel was put to bed.
Mimi herself brought in a tray of tea and poured out
cups for them both, adding a generous top-up of
brandy and a spoonful of sugar to Mabel's. 'Ye'll stay
there till tomorrow mornin',' she said, eyeing Mabel
with a keen professional air. 'Yer look terrible, girl,
worn out an' thin as a rake. Come on, drink up, it'll
help yer to settle. Yer did well to come here,
anyway.'

Mabel finished the tea and lay back on the pillow,
closing her eyes. Two tears spilled from under her
swollen lids. The brandy began to blur the edges of
her consciousness and a great weariness spread over
her body.

She heard water being poured from a pitcher into
a bowl and felt a warm, wet facecloth being applied
to her face and neck, with a fragrance of carnation-
scented soap; her hands were washed and dried on a
soft towel, and a comb was run through her
unpinned hair.

'That'll do for now – yer can have a proper wash
later. Go to sleep. The chamber pot's under the bed if
yer need it.'

A summer breeze stirred the curtains and Mabel gave a long sigh as she drifted into sleep. She had completely forgotten that tomorrow would be Ada's wedding day.

Her granddaughter's precipitate arrival was by no means unwelcome to Mimi Court. She too had been feeling the desolation of bereavement, the loss of her son in such a shameful way, though she was not entirely convinced by the coroner's verdict. Incapable of truly unselfish affection, she nevertheless felt bereft of the family she had liked to rule; the money and possessions she had acquired over the years could no longer be used to bestow or withhold favours and the future looked bleak. Albert's bitter hostility had cut her deeply, in spite of her scorn of him: what a disappointment he had been! And the departure to Belhampton of Alice and Daisy with their newly found aunts had been an even more devastating rejection; she had assumed that Mabel – and presumably George – would follow them after the inquest, while for herself the threat of a lonely old age loomed.

And yet here was Mabel in a desperate state, clearly at the end of her tether, come to throw herself on Mimi's mercy, in spite of all the harsh things that had been said outside the coroner's court. Mabel had come *here*, rather than to Belhampton.

Yes. Mimi allowed herself a slow smile of satisfaction. This was one in the eye for those Chalcotts! Mabel would rest and revive in her care; she would be patient with her, biding her time until the girl was ready to talk. All at once the future appeared decidedly less bleak.

Over that weekend Mabel stayed in her room, waited on by her grandmother and Elsie. On the Sunday afternoon she put on a dressing gown and went downstairs to the parlour where over tea and seed-cake Miss Lawton timidly enquired if she felt better.

When that lady had gone to Evensong at St Nicholas's church, Mimi sat down in her place. 'Ye're lookin' better, apart from the circles under yer eyes,' she said. 'Have yer got any thoughts about Sorrel Street? Stuff yer want fetched from there? I shan't be payin' any more rent and the landlord'll want to let it to somebody else.'

'Yes – oh, yes, I've brought nothing except what I stood up in,' Mabel said helplessly.

'No matter, no matter, them clothes are threadbare anyway. We'll soon get yer some new things. I was thinkin' more about books an' stuff, yer little bits an' pieces. When yer feel like it we could go over there an' have a look. The furniture isn't up to much and might as well be sold to a dealer for what we can get.'

In fact, it was decided to let the neighbours in to take their pick of the furnishings, curtains, carpets and Jack's and Annie's clothes. Mimi turned her nose up at everything she saw, but Mabel retrieved her mother's Bible and prayer book, also a pathetic handful of cheap trinkets in a drawer, brooches that Jack and Albert had given her, a necklace of china beads that had been a present from Mabel and a few treasured birthday cards. Alice and Daisy had taken their favourite books, but Mabel reclaimed Elizabeth Wetherell's *The Wide, Wide World* and Charlotte Yonge's *The Daisy Chain*. On the doormat lay a couple of handbills and an envelope addressed to her in Harry Drover's handwriting; she quickly stuffed it into her pocket. It made her think of other letters that might arrive, particularly from Canada, and she asked Mimi to let her call at the main post office on Lavender Hill to request that letters be redirected to Macaulay Road. She had already written a brief note to Aunt Nell to say she was staying with her grandmother and giving her new address. 'It's most important that yer send on anything from Canada,' she told the postmaster anxiously and he promised it would be done.

Mimi had listened intently when Mabel told her about George's hasty departure to Canada with the Barnardo boys. She asked only one question. 'Yer say this Dr Knowles – the one who spoke at the inquest – yer say *he* arranged it?'

'Yes, he's always been our family doctor and he saw that George's nerves were in a shockin' state, so he spoke with Mr Maillard and got it all fixed up. George wanted to go, he needed to get right away – and there was this older boy, Davy Hook, on Waterloo Station. I asked him to look after poor Georgie, an' . . . an' . . . oh, it was terrible!' Mabel gave way to tears again at the memory of her last sight of her brother, and Mimi sat silently waiting for her to compose herself.

'And what about Mr Drover?' she asked at length. 'What's *he* say about all this?'

Mabel turned her face away. 'I'm not seein' Mr Drover any more, Grandmother,' she replied in a deliberately hard voice. 'I can't ever join the Salvation Army now and it means so much to him – it's his life. We've got to forget each other.'

'Hm. So that's the way of it, I thought as much.

Well, Mabel, I reckon ye've made the right decision. I never saw a future for yer there. Now listen to me. My offer still stands. Yer can help out with local confinements and learn midwifery from me. Not a bad class o' woman in Tooting. I don't take on the low sort, they book with that old gossip Taylor in Fishponds Road. But for the next couple o' weeks yer can rest and feed yerself up. Yer won't be sorry yer came here.'

'Thank yer, Grandmother.' Mabel tried to sound appreciative, but she was drained of energy and enthusiasm, and felt that her dreams had all collapsed around her. Her sisters were being well cared for at Belhampton and Albert seemed happy enough in the merchant service, but she was haunted by the thought of George somewhere out on the Atlantic and the words of Harry's impassioned letter were written on her brain:

Dearest Mabel,

Whatever your feelings to me may be changed yet you must know that your in my thoughts every day. I pray that you be happy again and in the Lord's care.

I believe that your suffering is because of the grate shock of your parents deaths and then to say goodby to poor George going so far away. I trust it was the right thing to do but it seems so hard when he has a kind Aunt to go to in the country and him so young only twelve.

Mabel I will not trouble you in your grief but I beg you to send me word of how you are. You must know that I will wait for as long as my love for you which is for the rest of my life until you feel better and able to see me again. I prommise not to follow you or trouble you but I pray for your Salvation and the Peace which passeth all understanding.

In September I shall start my training to be an officer in the Army. It is at Clapton, but you can write to meet at 8 Falcon Terrace at any time.

From your Friend as always,
    Harry W. Drover

Mabel had intended to throw the letter on the range fire, but could not bear to part with such a declaration of love. She thought of putting it in her mother's Bible, but in the end she hid it under the clothes in the bottom drawer of the little chest in her room at number 23. In time she trusted that he would forget her and find another girl to share his life . . .

But would she ever forget him? 'Oh, Harry, Harry, I'm doing this for your good,' she whispered into her pillow when she could not sleep and saw his pitying face in her mind's eye.

More letters followed as the July days passed. 'My dear Mabel,' wrote Aunt Nell.

Your Uncle Thomas and I thank you for your letter. We are very shocked to hear of poor little George's departure to Canada and sorry that we were given no opportunity to discuss the matter with you. We could have offered help, both practical and financial, and there is plenty of work for young boys on farms around Belhampton. We could hardly believe that he has gone so far away with those poor orphaned Barnardo boys, and only twelve years old.

I am sorry to say that Daisy has been badly affected by this news and we have been at our

wits' end to deal with her. She was sent home
from school for her behaviour and was very rude
to our rector when he came to talk with her. We
can only hope that the passing of time will have its
healing effect on her. I am thankful to say that
Alice has accepted the news and borne it well,
though she too was sorry and surprised to hear
about her brother . . .

Mabel laid the letter aside, longing to hold her poor
little sister in her arms. As it was, she could only
write to her, sending loving messages in which she
hoped that Daisy would be a good girl even though
she felt sad. She told her sisters about Davy, 'a very
strong and handsome boy' who had promised to
take care of George on the voyage. What more could
she say? Only to hope and pray that Davy would
honour the trust she had thrust upon him.

Then came a very surprising letter from her friend
Ada. 'Dear Mabel,' she wrote.

This has been a summer of sorrow and disappointment. My poor Arthur has been very ill, in
fact his life was feared of, and I have been sick
myself with worry for him. He started with a sore
throat and his glans swole up with the Mumps,
but the doctor said the rash was Scarlet Fever and
wanted to send him to Tooting Grove Fever
Hospittal, but his Mother said she would nurse
him at home and keep all visiters away, even me,
which you can gess nearly broke my heart and his
too.

Now thank God my dear future husband is
much improvd, but looks pale and has lost a lot of
wait. We hope to be joined together in Matrimony

on 17 September when I hope you can come. He
will be well recoverd by then I hope, for I woud
only wish for death if I was to loose my beloved
Arthur.

What is this about your brother George going
on a ship to Canada, I can not belive you would let
him do such a foolhardy thing, my father says,
and him only twelve, poor boy.

When I called at 12 Sorrel Street Mrs Bull told
me you live with your grandmother at Tooting, I
thoght you did not get on.

With love from your afectonate friend,
    Ada, sadly still Clay

Oh, poor Ada! Mabel had completely forgotten about
her wedding, but this postponement meant that she
could attend it after all, if Mimi had no objection. But
oh, the endlessly repeated expressions of surprise
and disapproval over George's emigration, every one
of which Mabel took as a personal reproach to
herself. Her aunts, her friend Ada, even Harry – and
poor little Daisy. Only her grandmother had not
offered a comment, and Mabel had the uneasy
feeling that Mimi suspected some kind of cover-up
and was glad to have George out of the way. At least
she did not add to the chorus of shocked dismay.

And neither did somebody else. 'Oh, er, excuse
me, Mabel, if you're feeling well enough, there's a
young lady to see you,' announced Miss Lawton one
afternoon when Mimi was away on one of her
private visits to a special client.

Mabel jumped up from the sofa. Who could this
be? When she saw the smiling, saucy face at the door
she literally wept with emotion, holding out her
arms.

"'Ere, that ain't no way to greet an ol' pal – hey, Mabel, what's all this abaht, eh?'

'Oh, Maudie, I never was so glad to see anybody in me life!' And Mabel frankly gave way to sobs while Miss Lawton fussed around them.

'W-would you like to sit in the garden where the maids can't, er, hear you, and I'll make some tea for you both,' she offered.

'Fanks, Miss, er, that sahnds like a good idea. 'Ere, come on, Mabel, wipe yer eyes an' tell me all abaht it. Ada Clay tol' me yer was 'ere, an' 'ow ye'd lorst bofe yer muvver an' farver. Gawd, I'm sorry, Mabel.'

On the wooden garden bench Mabel clung to her old friend and it was some time before she could bring herself to speak of her mother.

Maudie groaned. 'Christ, Mabel, yer poor muvver. Fought she 'ad a growf, did she? So many poor souls get pulled aht o'—' She checked herself from saying *the river* and simply shook her head, truly shocked at what she had heard.

Mabel then told her of Jack's death, the accepted version from the inquest, and how the aunts from Hampshire had turned up and taken Alice and Daisy, and of Albert's return to the merchant service after the funeral.

'Well, did yer ever? An what abaht young George? Nice little chap, couple o' years older 'n Teddy, ain't 'e? 'As 'e gorn wiv 'is sisters?'

Somehow it was harder to tell Maudie about George than it was about the deaths of her parents. Mabel prepared herself to hear the expected wail at the way he had been packed off to Canada with a shipload of Barnardo boys, straight after his father's funeral. 'He had to get away, y'see, Maudie, out o' that house after what he'd seen. I didn't want him to go, but I knew it was best for him – and there was this older boy who said he'd look after him. Oh, Maudie, I didn't send him away, though everybody thinks I shouldn't've let him go.'

Mabel wept afresh, and Maudie held her close as they sat in the sunshine. 'Don't mind what ovver people say, Mabel. Yer know fings abaht yer own bruvver that they don't. Same wiv me an' Teddy, after all what we've been frough. Only we don't look back, an' neiver must *you*, darlin'.'

She kissed her friend's cheek, and Mabel was overcome with sheer gratitude for her understanding. They sat in silence for several minutes while Maud considered what she had been told. She knew plenty about domestic violence and last straws, and she suspected that Mabel had not told her all. Poor Georgie, she thought, shouldn't wonder if he'd been sent off to get him out of the way and shut him up, poor little bugger. Mabel had been lucky with that old doctor, anyway, and Maud wondered which one of them had chucked the bastard downstairs. 'So what're yer doin' 'ere, then?' she asked, thinking a change of subject was called for. 'Never thought yer liked yer grandmuvver.'

'I didn't think I'd fit in at Belhampton, somehow, Maudie, and she's goin' to teach me to be a midwife while I'm waitin' to get into a Poor Law infirmary to train as a nurse – if they'll have me,' replied Mabel dully. 'There are plenty o' worse places than this.'

'That's what I fought – looks all right to me.' Maud looked round appraisingly. 'Where's Mrs Court now – out on a baby case, is she?'

'Er, yes, in a manner o' speakin'.' Mabel hesitated because Mimi was visiting a wealthy woman who required another service than midwifery. 'Oh, I'm that glad to see yer, Maudie! It's time yer told me somethin' about yerself now.'

For the rest of the visit they talked of Maud's life at Bryanston Square and Ada's postponed wedding to which they had both been invited. Maud longed to ask about Harry Drover, but sensed that the subject would be distressing to Mabel, and there had been sufficient tears for one afternoon. There would be time enough to talk at the wedding, which was something to look forward to, like a treat in store.

'Well, what d'ye think of it, Mabel?'

Mabel stared in wide-eyed wonder at the most expensive present she had ever been given: a brand-new bicycle from Jewell's cycle shop in Tooting High Street. 'Oh, Grandmother – I've always wanted to ride one.' She could not believe that this smart black-and-white machine was truly hers alone.

'Yes, well, ye'd better learn to ride it, then. I can't take yer to every case in a cab.'

Mimi spoke briskly, but was obviously pleased by Mabel's reaction; and within the next two days the bicycle was being successfully ridden by its first owner who pedalled vigorously up and down the asphalt surface of Macaulay Road and out into Church Lane, still an unmade-up dirt road where she promptly caught the front wheel in a rut, wobbled out of control and lost her balance: over went the cycle and down went Mabel with it.

Mimi tut-tutted when she saw the grazed knee and torn stocking. 'That'll teach yer to look where ye're going,' she observed, though Mabel was far more concerned about the machine. It was well supplied with accessories, including a wicker basket attached to the handlebars in front, and a toolbox behind the saddle. It also had a metal bracket at the back to which a small wooden box could be attached for carrying equipment.

For this bicycle was for work rather than pleasure, though Mabel loved the sense of freedom it gave her as she pedalled around the neighbourhood, pushing the machine up steep inclines and freewheeling down the other side. It was for visiting the homes of local women to attend them in labour under her grandmother's supervision. Mimi would go on the first visit when called out, travelling in the cab of a local driver she used, while Mabel followed on her bicycle. When the necessary preparations had been made and if labour was at an early stage, Mimi would return home, leaving Mabel with the woman. Hours of sitting with girls at the Rescue had given her good insight into the process and, when she judged the delivery to be near, she sent the husband or a neighbour to fetch Mrs Court whom she would then assist. Mimi's reasoning was that if labour was quick the delivery would be easy enough for Mabel to cope with on her own, and if it was longer and more difficult, there was time enough to send for herself and possibly a doctor if need be. Mimi was on familiar terms with the local general practitioners, private and panel, and whatever they thought of her, it did not take long for them all to appreciate Mabel; the women also liked her and trusted themselves to her care, even though she was not on the midwives' register.

'A couple o' years with me and ye'll go in front o' the board for registration, twice as good as them hospital know-alls,' said Mimi, well pleased with her assistant, though Mrs Taylor, another local midwife and deadly rival of Mrs Court, was loud in her condemnation of such use of a young unregistered girl.

'There'll be big trouble one o' these days,' she predicted grimly. 'Just you wait an' see!'

By the end of July Mabel was reasonably settled into the day-to-day life at 23 Macaulay Road with Mimi and Miss Lawton. There was also Elsie, now nearly forty and taciturn as ever, who occupied a special position in the household as Mimi's assistant with her *other work*, as Mabel mentally referred to it. When certain female clients arrived at the house, Elsie made up the bed in the small back room, usually only for a day, though they occasionally stayed overnight. Only Elsie waited upon them, taking up drinks and refreshments on a tray, and staying closeted with them after Mimi had carried out the treatment they had come to receive. Once Mabel met Elsie on the stairs carrying an enamel can with a red rubber tube attached to it which had a bulb on the end, like the 'soap syringe' used for giving enemas to women in early labour to empty the bowel. Elsie whipped the apparatus out of sight, but Mimi was heard berating her behind closed doors: 'Why the 'ell don't yer put a cloth over it, yer fool?'

Mabel glanced questioningly at Miss Lawton as they sat in the living room. As always, the lady was unwilling to comment, but Mabel felt sure that she must know what was going on.

'Th-they have these little upsets, Mabel, it's no business of ours. Don't take any notice.'

When Elsie was heard clattering down the stairs and Mabel rose to go and speak to her, Miss Lawton intervened with uncharacteristic firmness. 'No, Mabel, keep out of it – keep out of it, for God's sake –

oh, I, er, beg your pardon, but it's best to let Elsie get on with her, er, work.'

Mabel turned to face her and asked a direct question. 'Why d'ye stay here, Miss Lawton: Why d'ye let my grandmother treat yer the way she does?'

The lady looked terrified. 'Oh, I assure you, my – Mrs Court treats me very well, she's been most generous to me and . . . and poor mother w-when she was alive. I don't have anything to do with . . . with what she does and I . . . I hope you never do, Mabel. I . . . I'd better go to my room.'

'Please don't trouble yerself, Miss Lawton,' said Mabel gently. 'Sit down and wait till it's clear up there. I shan't ask yer any more questions, don't worry.'

Mabel soon found out that in addition to local confinements and the women who came to the house there was a third group of clients, like the one Mimi had been visiting on the day that Maudie called. These lived at some distance, often at prestigious addresses, never in Tooting, and although Mabel was told nothing about them, she gradually learned that this group accounted for the greater part of Mimi Court's income; in return for her services they paid for the daily running of the household, including the expense of keeping Miss Lawton and Mabel.

It was a tolerable life, and Mabel began to enjoy her work with the mothers and newborn babies; it was a long way from the hopes and dreams she had shared with Harry, but she believed that the Lord had given her useful work to occupy her hands and mind, and prevent her from dwelling on dreams that could now never be fulfilled.

But Mimi's secret activities troubled her; what she did was both wicked and criminal, and although

Mabel played no part in it, she was always aware of the shadow that hung over the house, darkening all their lives.

And then – oh, then, on the very last day of July came the message that Mabel had been waiting and hoping and praying for: a letter from George! It was short but she kissed it and wept over it in her room. 'Dear Mabel,' he had written.

> We docked at Halifax after two weeks on bord the city of *York*. And then it seemd like another week on a train but it must of been 3 or 4 days. We got to a place caled Calgary and a distribushon center. Was very hard for some yong boys but Davy Hoek says he wont go to Macbanes Farm if I dont go so the man took me on and we both go now. I hope you get this. God bless you Mabel and love from
>   your Brother George Court.
> I will write to you again from Farm. It is McBanes, Calgary, Alberta, Canada. Davy's father was dutch sailor but drownd at sea, name of Hoek.

Mabel knelt down by her bed to give thanks, tucking the precious envelope inside her liberty bodice, for she could not bear to be separated from it. Her heart overflowed with thankfulness, because he sounded happy enough, certainly not homesick. Though the whole world might disapprove of what she had agreed to, she now felt that she – and Albert and Dr Knowles – had been right. She must send the doctor a note. And she could write to George at this farm, and to Davy, whom she wanted to thank in person. In fact, she longed to share the news with the world.

On her way out of the house to visit a couple of delivered mothers she met Miss Lawton, also on her way out to play the piano for the old people at the Tooting home in Church Lane. She turned round in nervous haste when Mabel called after her with shining eyes. 'Oh, Miss Lawton! I've heard from my brother George, he's got safely to Canada and he's working on a farm with his friend Davy Hoek!'

'What? Oh, yes, of course, little Georgie – oh, I'm so happy for you, my dear! I . . . I've known how sad you've been about him – how anxious – yes, oh yes. Thank God, Mabel!'

And there at the gate they embraced in spontaneous joy at the news. Mabel caught the smell of lavender and camphor balls, and felt a wave of affection towards this lonely spinster. 'Thank yer, dear Miss Lawton, thank yer,' she whispered.

Neither of them noticed Mimi at the door, a look of scornful incredulity on her face. 'What in the name o' God's goin' on out here? Actin' like a couple o' maidservants 'oo've been at the gin – I'm surprised at yer, Mabel, and as for *you*, Ruth, yer might as well stay at the Tootin' home when ye've finished strummin' – ye're ready to join 'em!'

Mabel opened her mouth to protest at such unkindness, but Miss Lawton, blushing and stammering, answered for herself. 'Th-there are worse places I could go, M-Mrs Court. Mabel was only telling me about her brother George who . . . who's reached Canada—'

'All right, all right, spare me the details and get goin', both o' yer.'

Even her grandmother's venom could not touch Mabel today; she smiled at Miss Lawton and mounted her bicycle, touching her bodice where the letter reposed.

'There y'are, Mrs Hollis, she's all dressed up an' ready for her first breakfast!'

It was a happy morning at the Hollis household in Furzedown Road, and the August sunshine streamed in at the bedroom window as Mabel packed away her scissors, cotton wool, cord powder and methylated spirit. The delivery of the third Hollis baby could not have been smoother. Mabel had arrived just after four and the child had been born at half past six. The husband's mother had been an able assistant, keeping the fire burning and the kettle boiling; baby gowns and clean towels were warming on the fireguard, and a delicious aroma of frying bacon drifted up the stairs. The Hollises were full of praise for Mabel and she was included in the happy circle that surrounded the mother sitting up in bed with the new baby. Mr Hollis smiled down on them and the two little boys in their nightshirts sitting on the bed and gazing open-mouthed at the new arrival who was to be called Anna.

'And what about a second name?' asked the father. 'Something to go between Anna and Hollis. Has anybody got a suggestion?'

'What's *your* Christian name, Nurse Court?' asked Mrs Hollis.

'Mabel' met with general approval and so it was decided that the baby would be called Anna Mabel, and the young midwife was invited to come to the christening.

Mabel had to make an effort to blink away tears, even though she was glowing with pride at this joyful outcome of the mother's pain. Her pride in the chorus of praise gave her a feeling very close to happiness again, something she had not felt for so long. A sense of renewed vocation sprang up like a green leaf in a desert and she foresaw a time when she might practise as a midwife independently of her grandmother, away from the secret shadows of Macaulay Road. If only all newborn babies could be as lucky as little Anna Mabel Hollis, compared with the poor mites born at the Rescue! Once again Mabel's tender heart longed to care for all unwanted, unfortunate children, and her dream of running a refuge on behalf of the Salvation Army – but she must not think about that. Not any more.

Nevertheless her heart was light as she left the house and climbed on to the trusty bicycle. At the end of the avenue she turned left and cycled down to Mitcham Road where shops were already opening up and workers were queuing for the trams in both directions.

A woman suddenly called to her from outside a newsagent's. 'Nurse Court! 'Ave yer got a minute? Can I 'ave a word with yer, please?'

Mabel braked and put one foot to the ground.

The woman was nervous and apologetic. 'I think I might've fallen again, Nurse Court, it can't be more 'n a month, but I been sick twice an' the baby's only seven months,' she gabbled in an undertone. 'Is there anythin' ye can give me to take, like? I got five already, y'see, an' with 'im bein' laid orf from the brewery with 'is back, I don't know as I could manage with another so soon.' She licked her lips and lowered her voice to a whisper. 'I know Mrs Court 'elps women out if they're not too far gorn, but if there was somethin' I could take to bring the flow on again, like – oh, Nurse, what can I do?'

What, indeed, could she do and what could Mabel say? Tell her to consult Mrs Court? Tell her to take a large dose of castor oil followed by a hot bath (in a house that probably had no bath) and jump up and down a hundred times, with or without a skipping rope? Gin? Slippery elm bark? Mandrake root? Tell her that what she was suggesting was a criminal offence in which Mabel could play no part at all?

In the end Mabel told her to apply to Mrs Court for advice, but refused to act as go-between. Remounting her bicycle she pedalled away, but the woman's pale, anxious face floated before her mind's eye, dulling the happy satisfaction of the Hollis confinement. It bothered her.

'Good girl.' Mimi nodded on hearing about Mrs Hollis's baby. 'I'll visit there this mornin' and check on 'em. No need for yer to go back there today.'

It would be Mimi who presented the bill for attendance at delivery, but Mabel did not complain. The twenty shillings she received each week was entirely her own to spend as she chose: no rent to pay, no food to buy. She had never been so comfortably off.

A few days later Mimi called her into the parlour. 'What's this yer been sayin' to that poor creature May Shotter?'

Mabel was puzzled. '*Who* did yer say, Grand-mother?'

'May Shotter, lives in Mitcham Road, five brats under seven, baby not seven months an' a layabout husband. Remember now?'

Mabel blushed as if caught out in some misde-meanour. 'Oh, yes. The one who—'

'The one who asked yer if there was anythin' she

could take and yer kindly referred her to me. That's the one.' Mimi's eyes were hard as she looked straight at Mabel. 'Yer don't have anythin' to do with my other cases, so I don't expect yer to go around Tootin' recommendin' me to all an' sundry who wants helpin' out.'

'I didn't recommend yer, Grandmother, I only—' Mabel began in confusion.

'Yer told 'er to ask me, that's enough. Don't do it again, d'ye hear?'

'Yes – I mean no, Grandmother. I'm sorry.'

'I select my cases very carefully and none of 'em from around here. Too close to home for one thing and nothin' to pay me with. I 'ave to charge danger money for that sort o' thing. So if anybody else asks yer, the answer's no, I don't do it, see?'

'Yes. I'm sorry,' Mabel repeated, feeling thoroughly uneasy. Now that she knew Mrs Shotter had asked for advice and got nowhere, she felt that she had let the woman down. She stared with downcast eyes at the floor, wondering if she was dismissed.

Mimi cleared her throat and spoke a little less severely. 'As it 'appens, I sent her off to Dimmock, that old rogue of a chemist on the Broadway. He might sell 'er some o' this herbal extract, comes from a mould that grows on rye, 'e says, an' makes the womb go into spasm. I wouldn't want the responsibility meself, but it'll be up to 'im if 'e takes a chance on killin' the mother along o' the child. So there y'are, Mabel, no more sendin' 'em to me, d'ye understand?'

Thus cautioned, Mabel made her escape, unable to shake off a sense of guilt.

Two days later she was accosted by a chalk-faced but grateful Mrs Shotter. 'Thanks ever so much,

Nurse Court – nearly did me in, that stuff, but it did the trick!'

And Mabel was ashamed all over again, just for feeling thankful too. How long would it be before poor Mrs Shotter 'fell' again, she wondered; the incident had given her a disturbing insight into the lives of women living constantly in fear of further pregnancies. But remembering her mother's horror at Mimi's activities and her own instinctive recoil from the very thought of taking the life of an unborn child, even her sympathy for Mrs Shotter seemed wrong, an indication of falling standards.

As for what Harry Drover would say if he knew about this ... and the truth about Jack's death ... and why she'd had to leave the Rescue in a hurry, for fear that she might have had a shameful disease ... it did not bear thinking about. He would want nothing to do with her now.

At least there was Ada's wedding to look forward to and Mabel heard that it was to be a big do. Thomas Tilling and Sons were engaged to supply one of their horse-drawn wedding carriages to take the bride from her home to St Philip's church for three o'clock, and then the happy couple would drive to their reception at Woodlands, one of the fine old mansions on Clapham Common's Northside. The guest list included practically all the staff at the Lipton's store where Ada's father and future husband were manager and cashier, but Mabel looked forward above all to seeing Maudie there.

The great day dawned with an early mist over the city that rose and cleared to fine, unclouded September sunshine. Mimi had graciously given Mabel the whole day off and breakfast time brought her a wonderful surprise: another letter from George, with good news. 'Dear Mabel,' he had written. 'I send my love and hope your well. MacBanes is a big prairie farm with grainfields as far as you can look. The old man is a hard case but the wife not so bad. She has give me new sherts and pants are a bit big but Im growing quick. Davy is the best frend I ever had more like a brother and stands up to the old man. We work hard and get brown in the sun is very hot. I think of you Mabel and Albert and Daisy and Alice and Harry but I am better of here. With love and God bless you from your brother George Court.'

Mabel kissed the pencilled scrawl, an undoubtedly truthful reflection of George's new life. Whoever Davy Hoek was and whatever he had been, she blessed him from her heart. It was the best possible beginning to the day, as she confided to a sympathetic Miss Lawton.

At twenty to three the church was already filling up. Mabel knelt down beside Miss Carter from the Babies Mission and said a prayer for the health and happiness of Ada and Arthur, adding her thanks for George's letter. Maud Ling, fetchingly dressed in blue and white silk with a flowery hat and matching folded parasol, came in with Charlie and sat behind them. She caused quite a stir, especially when Ada entered on her father's arm, all in white with a gauzy veil over her head.

'Ooh, look at 'er, Charlie – ain't she a picture?'

Mabel caught Miss Carter's eye. Could this vision be the chatty, giggly girl who used to read racy novels during the children's rest hour?

Nobody noticed a slightly built young man with a Salvation Army cap who entered the church just after the ceremony began and quietly took a place at the back.

The bride and groom made their promises, and were duly pronounced man and wife. The organ pealed out the wedding march as they progressed down the aisle and out into the sunshine where a photographer waited to take a picture.

Maud rushed to Mabel's side. 'Don't she look a treat, eh? When're we goin' to do the same, Mabel? Hey, why ain't yer wiv yer young man?'

Mabel shook her head. 'He's not here, Maudie.'

''E jolly well is, y'know! Look be'ind yer, over there – must've been sittin' at the back. Look, 'e's as moonstruck as ever for yer!'

Mabel froze. Yes, Harry Drover stood just a few yards away, his brown eyes fixed on her. Whatever should she do?

'Wotcher, 'Arry!' Maud called out, running up to him and planting a smacking kiss on his cheek. 'Now go an' pass that on to Mabel. She's waitin' for yer to take 'er up to the big do!'

Red-faced with embarrassment but warmed by Maud's exuberance, Harry hesitantly walked over to where Mabel stood. 'Hello, Mabel,' he said shyly. 'It was nice o' them to invite me, an' I'm so glad to see yer.'

Mabel's heart was pounding as she lifted her eyes to his. How handsome his honest, open face appeared to her, more kind and sensitive by far than Arthur's or Charlie's. But he was not for her, not now that everything had changed. 'I thought ye'd be at Clapton College,' she muttered and the words sounded cold.

'Well, yes, I am, but I've come over for this,' he

332

said, smiling with careful politeness. 'How are yer, Mabel? I heard ye'd moved to Tooting.'

She swallowed. 'Yes, I, er, I live with my grand-mother.'

'Oh, yes, Mrs Court. Er, have yer heard anythin' o' George, Mabel?'

At the mention of her brother's name she immediately wanted to share the news she'd received that very day. 'Oh, yes, a letter came this mornin' – he sounds as if he's happy, workin' on a big farm in Alberta. An' he's got this good friend Davy Hoek, it's a Dutch name, an' George says—' She stopped, realising that she was gabbling.

Harry noticed how her eyes had brightened when she spoke of George. 'I'm very glad to hear that, Mabel,' he began and she dreaded that any minute now he'd start asking her why George had been sent so far away.

She abruptly turned to Maud, her eyes pleading to be rescued, and her friend laughingly obliged, taking her arm. 'C'mon, Mabel, let's walk up togevver an' let these two gents foller on. I got lots to tell yer!' she said gaily, though in fact she had just as much to ask.

The bride and groom having left in their carriage, followed by the more important guests in their conveyances, the less important now began walking up to Northside.

Maud bent her head close, so that their hats touched. 'Never a dull moment at Bryanston Square, Mabel. 'Er Ladyship's 'avin' the time of 'er life. I worry abaht 'er sometimes, to tell the trufe – she sails awful close to the wind, if yer get me meanin', and I 'ave me work cut aht coverin' up for 'er wiv ol' Bald-'ead. She couldn't do wivout me, an' that's a fact.'

Mabel had to smile at the idea of the brilliant

society hostess being dependent upon a doting cockney maidservant and Maudie's touching sense of responsibility towards her mistress.

'Honestly, Mabel, I wouldn't dare take the sort o' risks she does. Charlie knows just how far 'e can go wiv me, an' no farver. No sense in *arskin'* for trouble, is there?'

'Be careful, Maudie, ye'd be right up the creek if she got caught.' To Mabel Her Ladyship sounded both reckless and unprincipled, for all her beauty.

Maudie looked behind her. "Op it, bofe o' yer,' she ordered the two young men. 'Me an' Mabel wants a bit o' privacy. See yer at Woodlands, right?'

When they were a little apart from the other walkers, Maud whispered a question. 'What's up wiv poor ol' 'Arry? Summat's wrong, i'n'it? Go on, yer can tell yer auntie Maud. Is it 'cause o' the Sally Army?'

Mabel almost groaned out loud. To confide in her old friend would be such a relief. 'Ye've just said it, Maudie,' she answered, her voice shaking. 'I can't marry into the Salvation Army, not after what's happened – how could I?'

'Yer mean – yer muvver doin' 'erself in, an' yer farver takin' a header dahn the stairs, like?' Maud's tone was gentle but meaningful and Mabel nodded wretchedly.

'And . . . and they both had a . . . a horrible disease, Maudie, and the doctor thought I might've got it an' all, only he tested me blood and I hadn't, but—'

'Christ, Mabel, d'yer mean the pox? Oh, my Gawd, yer poor muvver, no wonder she – oh, Mabel, this is bad. An' poor little George, did 'e—?'

'I can't talk about it, Maudie, 'cause of our doctor

334

who helped us out an' saved George – oh, Maudie, everythin's *changed*, can't yer see?'

'Sh, Mabel don't get het up – as a matter o' fact I fought it might be summat like that,' said Maud quietly, tightening her hold on Mabel's arm. 'Listen, I jus' want to ask yer one more question, that's all. D'ye still love 'Arry?'

'How can yer ask me such a thing?' cried Mabel in rising agitation. 'What's it matter anyway? He couldn't stay in the Army if he married me, could he? And it's his *life*, Maudie, his father and mother and sister an' her husband, they're all in it. An' more 'n that, he says it's what the *Lord* wants him to do!'

She was on the verge of tears, and Maudie quickly cut in. 'A'right, Mabel, ye've answered me question. Don't upset yerself any more, let's just enjoy Ada's weddin'. Look, we're nearly there – cor! Nearly as posh as Bryanston Square! Nah then, no more sad talk, an' that's an order. C'mon, let's find the fellers – that's if they ain't fahnd anuvver couple o' gals while we bin jabberin'!'

Maud's determined gaiety concealed an aching pity for the friend whose outburst had so plainly proclaimed her continuing, despairing love for Harry Drover. And as for that shocking bit she'd let out about the pox, what a thing to happen to *her*, of all people. Poor, poor Mabel . . .

Through the arched gate of Woodlands the guests progressed into an imposing entrance hall and spacious reception room where the bridal pair were waiting to greet the foot soldiers, as Charlie called them.

'Thanks for coming, Mabel.' Ada smiled, enveloping her in a cloud of crumpled white muslin. 'It was

Arthur's idea to ask Harry, so's you an' him can get together again!'

And there he was, standing alone and looking towards her while guests mingled around them, chatting and sipping wine from trays handed round by waiters. He only had eyes for her and she stood rooted to the spot as he came to her side. 'I hope ye'll let me take yer in to tea or supper or whatever they call it, Mabel. The food's all laid out in the next room along,' he said pleasantly, clearly attempting to put her at her ease.

She looked up at him helplessly. Maud was nowhere in sight.

'I've missed yer so much, Mabel. Can yer give me any idea o' how long it'll be before yer feel able to – I mean, are yer feelin' any better yet from the trouble ye've been through?'

Still she could not speak, could not turn away from this dear friend, this young man who adored her as much as ever. They stood simply looking into each other's eyes and Harry saw the love in hers as plainly as if she had declared it. And yet her words were a denial. 'No. No. Please don't ask.'

At that moment there was a sudden commotion in the entrance hall and heads turned to look at a black-clad figure who had come in. With an unbecoming black hat perched on her head and glancing distract-edly round her, this strange-looking woman was clearly no wedding guest; on the contrary, supersti-tious onlookers might have thought her an ill omen, a messenger with bad news.

Good heavens, thought Mabel, it's Miss Lawton. She put a hand to her throat. What new trouble was this? Leaving Harry's side, she hurried towards the woman in black. 'What is it, Miss Lawton? Why're yer here?'

'I . . . I'm sorry, Mabel, just when you're, er, but Mrs Court says you're to come at once. I've got a c-cab outside,' faltered Miss Lawton, wringing her hands.

'But why? What's happened? For God's sake, tell me – out with it!'

Maudie had sidled up to Mabel, overcome with curiosity. 'What's up?'

'Sh, Maudie, let Miss Lawton speak.'

'I . . . I'm sorry, Mabel, but your little sister – little Daisy—'

'*Daisy*? Oh, my God, what's happened to her?' Mabel's eyes dilated with fear.

'It . . . it's all right, Mabel, she's at . . . at Mrs Court's house. She's run away.'

'Run away? From Belhampton, yer mean? All on her own?'

'Yes, sh-she caught a train to Waterloo Station and then got on a Battersea bus, but didn't have enough money – she went to the police station. She's very upset, and M-Mrs Court says you must come and . . . and deal with her.'

'Oh, my poor little Daisy!' Mabel put her hands to her head. 'I'll have to go, Maudie, *now*, this minute – did yer say ye'd got a cab, Miss Lawton?'

'Ye-es, Mabel, it's waiting. M-Mrs Court sent me in it. I'm so sorry.'

Harry appeared at Mabel's side. 'Let me come with yer, Mabel,' he begged. 'Daisy'll trust me, it'll be easier if I'm with yer.'

Mabel turned round and faced him squarely. Already overwrought by what had passed between her and Maud, her head was throbbing and she had

had nothing to eat since a light breakfast. This latest blow was too much to bear and her self-control gave way altogether. 'For Christ's sake leave me alone, will yer?' she shrieked. 'Go back to yer college and find a Salvation Army girl to marry! Can't yer see that everythin's *changed*?'

His face paled. '*I* haven't changed, Mabel, nor will I ever,' he said levelly. 'I shan't marry any girl but you.'

'Then ye'll stay single all yer life. Oh, *God*, Harry, can't yer see I'm savin' yer a life o' disgrace an' misery? Just go away, can't yer? *Go away*!'

Maudie, Charlie, Miss Carter, the bridal couple and other guests watched in horrified disbelief as Mabel grabbed Miss Lawton's arm and dragged her from the room, through the entrance hall and out to where the cab stood waiting on Northside.

Chapter Fifteen

'Mabel, Mabel! Let me stay with yer, Mabel, *please*!'

Daisy rushed at her sister with outstretched arms as she'd done as a toddler and at once Mabel knew that she had to make a supreme effort to pull herself together. 'Sh, Daisy, it's all right, Mabel's here,' she whispered, resolutely stifling her own emotional turmoil. Looking up over the child's dark head, she met her grandmother's sardonic gaze; and beside her stood a uniformed policeman.

'Well, here's a fine how-d'ye-do, I must say! And there was me thinkin' that Daisy was livin' in the lap o' luxury, with all the comforts that her Aunt Bountiful could provide – an' now she turns up on the doorstep sayin' she's run away. Dear me!'

'Don't send me back, Mabel!' cried Daisy.

Mabel hugged her closely. 'No, dear, I won't send yer back, sh, sh.'

'But what do we say to the constable who's had his valuable time taken up?' demanded Mimi. 'He's been tellin' me all about yer poor aunt an' uncle, nearly out o' their wits with worry.'

Mabel was annoyed by this heavy sarcasm directed at a frightened child. 'I'll take care o' her, constable,' she said promptly.

'That's up to you, miss, only I'll 'ave to telephone through to the Bel'ampton police to let 'em know she's turned up 'ere,' he replied, glancing down at his notebook.

'And I'll write to my Aunt Somerton as soon as I can,' said Mabel.

'Good. It's best to keep in touch with all yer family at a time like this.'

He looked at Mimi who gave him a smile and a gracious nod of dismissal. 'I'm very sorry ye've been troubled, officer, but I think we can sort this out ourselves now. Good day to yer.' After seeing him out, Mimi irritably asked Miss Lawton what she was gawping at and, seating herself in an armchair, turned her attention to the runaway. 'So what happened, Daisy? What went wrong?'

Daisy's eyes turned to Mabel who smiled back encouragingly. 'I just missed Mabel – and George,' she said in a small voice, overawed by her grandmother's stern presence.

'But yer had yer aunt and uncle – and Alice?'

Daisy hung her head in silence, fidgeting with her hair ribbon that had come adrift. Tears welled up in her eyes and Mabel decided to intervene. 'For goodness' sake, Grandmother, she's only eight and she's been through so much. Can't I take her up to my room and let her rest an' have somethin' to eat? She must be starving.'

As had happened in the past when faced with Mabel's defiance, Mimi Court capitulated. Her heavy features softened somewhat. 'Yer can share a room up on the second floor. I'll tell Elsie to make up the bed an' bring yer up some cold mutton and bread. I'll put the kettle on meself.' She got up from the armchair. 'An' I'm sorry I had to fetch yer back from the weddin', but with the copper standin' there takin' notes, I needed yer to show yer face an' calm the child down.'

'Thank yer, Grandmother,' replied Mabel, though

she perceived that Mimi Court was as pleased as Punch at this development. Another point scored over those jumped-up Chalcotts!

The sisters shared their supper picnic-style on the bed and Mabel felt it was time to ask some questions. 'Now, Daisy, tell me exactly why yer ran away from Aunt Nell and Uncle Thomas. Weren't they kind to yer?'

'Yes, they thought they were kind, but I missed yer so much, Mabel, and it made me naughty,' came the innocent reply. 'Alice doesn't care about Albert or George, she's so pleased to get away from that post office an' Miss Chatt, an' all she thinks about is nice clothes an' havin' her hair up, and Aunt Nell kept on sayin' how sensible she is an' why can't I be good as well – an' even *you* wrote an' told me to be good, and – oh, Mabel, I just want to be back like we were before!'

Mabel shook her head. 'Daisy, dear, nothing can ever be the same as before, because things change. *We* all change – I mean, for a start we have to grow up—'

'There're other people livin' in our home now, Mabel, did yer know?'

'Yes, dear, that's why I'm livin' here with Grandmother since George went to Canada,' replied Mabel, realising that Daisy had been given only sketchy information about recent events.

'Where's Canada, Mabel? When will he come back? Uncle Thomas said it was a long, *long* way across the sea, an' I told him yer wouldn't've sent George that far – would yer, Mabel?'

The same question again, with the same implied reproach. 'Daisy, dear, I can't explain everythin' now, but George really wanted to go, and he's workin' on a big farm and sends yer his love. He's got a good friend called Davy who looks after him.'

'The one yer told us about, the handsome boy with blue eyes?'

'That's the one. He's as good as another brother, George says. I'll show yer the letter I got from him this morning. Now, d'ye want a slice o' bread an' butter with yer meat an' pickle?'

'An' yer will let me stay here with yer, Mabel?' repeated Daisy, anxiously scanning her face.

'Yes, dear, yer can stay until—' Mabel was about to say *until ye're ready to go back to Aunt Nell*, but settled for 'as long as yer like'. She had not the heart to promise anything less and, while realising that Daisy needed more time to adjust to the enormous changes in her short life, Mabel did not foresee the extent to which she was compromising, even endangering, her own future prospects.

Going to church the next morning, Mabel took the opportunity to thank Miss Lawton for coming to fetch her from Woodlands on Saturday.

'Oh, I – it was no trouble, M-Mabel, Mrs Court asked me to—'

'I just want to thank you, Miss Lawton, that's all.' Mabel smiled.

'An' I'm goin' to stay an' live with Mabel an' Grandmother,' added Daisy, looking up brightly.

This produced a disappointing reaction from the lady who clutched her black prayer book convulsively and looked very doubtful. 'Er, I see. But Mabel, d'you think it might be better if – I mean such a . . . a young child, yet old enough to . . . to—' She glanced quickly at Daisy, then shook her head.

'Forgive me, I didn't intend to speak out of . . . out of turn.'

'What exactly d'ye mean, Miss Lawton?' asked Mabel, though by the sinking of her heart she already knew. Miss Lawton had touched upon a doubt in her own mind.

'It's nothing to do with me, M-Mabel. I do beg your pardon. Please excuse me.' And not another word did she utter on the subject.

The sisters were in their shared room upstairs when the knock came at the door on Monday, announcing the visitors that Mabel had been half expecting. She knew that Aunt Elinor and Uncle Thomas would not give up Daisy without a fight, and Aunt Kate was with them when they arrived on Mimi Court's doorstep.

The doorstep was as far as they got. 'I beg yer pardon, but little Daisy's restin',' Mabel heard Mimi say. 'She's worn out after makin' 'er escape from Bel'ampton.'

'Look here, Mrs Court, we demand to see my wife's niece,' said Thomas Somerton angrily.

'Oh, yer do, do yer? Well, excuse me, my good man, but yer can't demand anythin'. I'm 'er natural grandmother, closer in blood to my son's child than any o' you lot. An' after the way the poor little thing was treated, I wonder yer dare show yer faces 'ere.'

Up in her room Mabel winced at such incivility towards her mother's relations.

'We treated Daisy with all the kindness and patience due to our poor sister's daughter,' retorted Aunt Kate, for Aunt Nell was in tears. 'We had the doctor to see her and the rector. She's only suffering the effects of . . . of what's happened and her place is with us.'

'Pity yer never felt so kind and patient to 'er mother, then, 'stead o' turnin' yer backs on 'er. Yer never cared a brass farthin' for 'er children then,' sneered Mimi. 'And as I got work to do, I won't detain yer any longer. Good day to yer.'

'But Mrs Court—'

'Get orf my property, or I'll call a policeman to 'ave yer shifted. Go on, shove orf!'

This parting shot sent the Belhampton relations from the door, Somerton white with rage and his wife sobbing openly. Kate said nothing, but walked stony faced behind them, pondering the truth of what the woman had said: she would be haunted for the rest of her life by her cruel rejection of Anna-Maria.

When Mabel tried to write a letter of apology to the Somertons she found it very difficult. In the end she thanked them for all their kindness and said that perhaps it was better for Daisy to spend some time with herself after all the upheavals she had been through that year.

There was no early reply. Not until Christmas could Nell bring herself to write to that address.

Later that week Mrs Court took her youngest granddaughter to register as a pupil at the old parish school in Church Lane. It had all the advantages of the church school at Belhampton, with the added attraction that the children spoke like Londoners and Daisy felt accepted from her first day.

As soon as Ada and Arthur Hodges returned from their honeymoon at Clacton-on-Sea, they visited all their relatives and friends. When Mabel went into the parlour and found her grandmother chatting amiably with the couple she burned with shame. How on earth could she face them after her hysterical outburst at their wedding?

But Ada stepped forward to greet her friend with a smile and a kiss. 'Hello, Mabel, how are yer? Arthur and me – and I – we've been that worried about yer, and yer friend Maudie said it was all 'cause o' losin' yer parents an' George goin' to Canada, as if it was any business of anybody.'

The words poured out in a rush, for the new Mrs Hodges had been practising her speech. In fact, she had been quite angry and upset by Mabel's behaviour, and it had needed a talking-to from Maud Ling to make her understand the pressures that Mabel had been under. Maud had told her not to be a silly little goose but to be thankful for her own good luck; so with her new and attentive husband at her side, Ada was prepared to be forgiving.

She was rewarded by Mabel's tears of gratitude and Mrs Court's gracious reception. 'And, er, I've brought this for yer, too, Mabel,' she added, fishing in her handbag and taking out an envelope. 'It was dropped in at Lipton's and addressed to you.'

Mabel recognised the writing and thrust it deep into her pocket. What was there left for Harry Drover to say to her after the way she had treated him? As soon as she was alone she took out the brief note. 'If your ever in need of a Freind send to me by the S. Army and I will come to you. H.D.' She decided to tear it up and throw it on the fire. The trouble was that her hands refused to obey orders, and it joined the other two at the bottom of the drawer with the little silver cross and chain.

The girls settled down into everyday life at 23 Macaulay Road and Mabel so enjoyed having her little sister back in her life again that it took her some time to see that Daisy's arrival had trapped her in that house of secrets. The weeks went by and 1912 drew to a close.

'Ooh, Mabel, look, we've got presents from Auntie Nell and Auntie Kate, and picture cards with holly and snow on!'

Mabel was both touched and embarrassed when gifts arrived from Belhampton, and insisted that they must wait for Christmas morning before unwrapping them. She herself had been able to afford really good presents for her family this year, including her two brothers, both so far away. She bought shirts and socks for them, not forgetting Davy Hoek, wrapped them carefully, had them weighed, stamped and committed to the uncertainties of sea travel a good two months before Christmas. To her aunts she sent embossed leather purses and to Uncle Thomas gloves, while Alice got a petticoat with broderie anglaise edging. For Daisy she bought a pretty lavender-coloured frock and a pinafore to go over it, and for her grandmother she decided on a bottle of lily-of-the-valley scent.

Alice had written them a letter all about dancing lessons and how she was learning to ride at the Paddocks, an expensive school for young equestrians. She described her new silk dress, which she was planning to wear at a Christmas ball. It all sounded a very long way from life at Macaulay Road.

Daisy had a letter from her friend Lucy Drummond, the rector's daughter, who said that life at

Belhampton was very dull without Daisy Court and begged her to return.

'Can we go and visit 'em all in the new year, Mabel?'

'*No*, we certainly *can't*, not after yer ran away and gave Aunt Nell all that trouble in return for her kindness.' Mabel spoke quite sharply and Daisy looked downcast. 'It's very good o' the aunts to send us anythin' at all, Daisy, and yer must be sure to write and thank 'em.'

But Mabel's spirits rose on Christmas Eve when a short message arrived from George and Davy, saying that Mabel's gifts had safely reached McBane's farm. It proved to be the highlight of Christmas, which was otherwise rather disappointing. Several calls came in from women in labour, some brought on by overwork or over-indulgence, and Mabel was out for almost all of Christmas Day and Boxing Day.

Daisy was vexed at her absence and declared crossly that she didn't want to go to church with Miss Lawton. 'She fidgets all the time and drops her book,' she grumbled to Mabel who was just on her way out to a case. 'It makes me feel silly standin' there beside her.'

'Ye'll jolly well go to church with her, and what's more ye'll behave yerself an' be civil to the poor lady,' Mabel told her sternly. At breakfast she had given Miss Lawton a framed print of St Nicholas's church at the time of its dedication, when it had been surrounded by fields.

'Oh, yes, a . . . an excellent reproduction, just like a country church – thank you, Mabel, thank you – most kind.' And to Mabel's surprise there were tears in the sunken brown eyes.

When she came in late that night, tired and chilled,

she found Miss Lawton waiting up for her, fussing with a teapot and cups. 'I . . . I've got the kettle on, Mabel, and there's some Christmas cake if you, er—'

'Ooh, that's nice.' Mabel sighed, sinking wearily into a chair without removing her coat.

'And . . . and if you wouldn't mind, there's something here that belonged to my dear mother – see, I made it for her years ago, and now I . . . I'd like you to have it.' It was a bookmark embroidered in tiny cross-stitch on stiff linen, with the words, *Do not be afraid, the LORD is with thee* in blue lettering surrounded by white and yellow daisies in a green stem-stitched border.

Mabel pictured the young girl with her needle and silks, and was deeply touched. It was obviously of value to the lonely spinster. 'Are yer sure yer don't mind partin' with it, Miss Lawton – Ruth?'

'Yes – er, no, Mabel. I want you to have it, because . . . because it's good to have you here and makes me think of your dear mother when she . . . when she first came here and you were born. I . . . I was glad for her when she moved into her own home, but . . . but I missed her.'

'Thank yer, Ruth. I'll put it in her prayer book and never part with it. Thank yer.' And she kissed Miss Lawton who smiled and blushed as she poured out the tea. 'Tell me about that time, Ruth,' she said, also smiling. 'What was my mother like then?'

'Oh, no, it's very late and I mustn't keep you up, Mabel, you must be so tired, and I . . . I'd better go now. Goodnight, Mabel, and thank you.' And she fluttered away upstairs as if she were afraid of what might be said if she stayed.

On the 27th there was at last some time to spend

with Daisy and to examine their presents: the books from Belhampton about good children and noble deeds, the new shoes and dresses from their grandmother; but Mabel was tired and Daisy was bored with staying indoors.

Mimi snapped irritably at Miss Lawton as they sat in the living room, 'For God's sake stop fussin' an' shufflin' around, woman. Get yer crocheting out and fidget with that instead.'

Daisy rolled up her eyes at Mabel who suggested that they play ludo. At once the memories of that disastrous Christmas two years ago returned and Mabel reflected on what changes there had been since them. Both parents were gone, Albert and George immeasurably far away, Alice was living the life of a well-bred young lady, and only herself and Daisy were left, the eldest and youngest of Anna-Maria's children. Whatever would she think if she could see them living here at the house of the woman she had never liked?

And of course there were thoughts of Harry: where would he be spending Christmas? Very likely at some shelter for the down-and-out, giving up his time in the service of those society had no time for. Dear, faithful, loving Harry whom she had spurned so savagely, yet who still considered himself her friend.

Oh, Harry, Harry, I only did it for your good . . .

'Come on, Daisy, it's your turn to shake the dice – ooh, look, ye've thrown a six!'

With the beginning of another new year Mabel's doubts and dissatisfaction grew. Although she enjoyed the work with local mothers and babies, and had more money than she'd ever had before, she became increasingly uneasy about the other aspect of her grandmother's practice. True, she played no part in it, but the fact of living in a house where such things took place gave her a sense of being tainted, of associating with something dark and dangerous – and criminal. If Mimi were to be found out one day, who would believe that Mabel had nothing to do with it? With Harry gone from her life, her lifelong ambition to be a children's nurse was all that was left of her dreams, but how could she hope to pursue a respectable career with such a stain on her character? Whichever way she looked at it, she could not pretend that she did not know. How long could she go on turning a blind eye to something that offended against her deepest instincts? It would be better to get a low-paid job as a cleaner or a minder of old ladies, as she had done before.

But now there was Daisy. As Miss Lawton had hinted, Mimi Court's house was no place for a child, but where else could she go? And while she remained at 23 Macaulay Road, Mabel had to stay there too. Too late she realised her mistake in not being firmer with her sister and returning her to Belhampton straight away.

She was trapped and her worst dread was that sooner or later she would be drawn into her grandmother's grim speciality. Try as she might to keep out of it, she feared that one day it was bound to happen . . .

It happened at the end of February.

The uncommunicative Elsie suddenly collapsed on the stairs, a victim of a virulent strain of influenza. The bucket she was carrying tipped over, sending a stream of bloodstained water across the landing and pouring down the stairs.

Mimi swore, having just completed a procedure on a young woman in the back bedroom. The two maids were in the kitchen, knowing better than to show their faces when Mrs Court had a special client. In the living room Mabel and Miss Lawton heard the commotion.

'I'd better go and see what's up,' said Mabel, rising. She had been writing up her casebook for February.

'Oh, no, Mabel, stay here, do!' implored Miss Lawton.

But then Mimi called down, 'Are yer there, Mabel?' – and when Mabel went upstairs she found Elsie lying on the landing in a pool of dirty water.

'Me 'ead – me throat – oh, Gawd,' she moaned feebly.

'Get 'er into 'er room, will yer? An' then get a cloth an' a mop to clear up the mess,' ordered Mimi through the half-open door of the back bedroom.

Mabel dragged Elsie by the shoulders into her room and somehow or other got her to climb up on to the bed. Covering her with a blanket and faded eiderdown, she went to fetch a mop and bucket from a cupboard next to the back bedroom. Having cleared up the spillage and wiped down the area with carbolic, she went to attend to Elsie who was sweating and shivering with a high fever. She managed to take off her top clothes and pull on a thick woollen nightgown she found under the bolster; then brought a mug of water to moisten her dry lips. 'How long've yer been feelin' bad, Elsie?' she asked.

'Since yes'day evenin', only I didn't dare say

nothin',' muttered the woman. 'An' then I jus' couldn't stand up no more.'

For the rest of that day Mabel checked on her at intervals, giving her drinks and helping her to sit on the chamber pot. At ten o'clock she took her a cup of weak tea and two aspirin tablets to swallow. She wiped the burning forehead with a moist facecloth. 'Try to sleep, Elsie – ye'll feel better in the mornin',' she told her, fervently praying it would prove to be true.

Mabel had no idea of the time when Mimi called her in the night with a tap on the door. 'Come an' give me a hand, Mabel – I got a bit o' trouble 'ere.'

'What is it, Mabel?' asked Daisy, sitting up in bed.

'Sh, dear, it's nothin' – go back to sleep,' answered her sister, getting out of bed, and putting on her dressing gown and slippers. Closing the door behind her, she followed Mimi's broad figure into the back room where an ashen-faced girl of about twenty lay in the bed. A white enamel pail beside her was filled with bloodstained rags and there was blood splashed on the bed, on the floor, down the front of Mimi's apron and even streaked across her face.

What nightmare was this? Mabel shivered involuntarily as she met Mimi's eyes.

'Bleedin' like a stuck pig, an' I'll 'ave to pack 'er,' muttered Mimi, breathing heavily. 'We'll 'ave to raise the foot o' the bed – get it up on this chair.'

Mabel obeyed, and together they heaved and strained to lift the bottom of the bedstead until it rested on the seat of a wooden chair. The girl's head fell back on the single pillow, her eyes closed and her mouth slackly open. For one terrible moment Mabel thought she was dead.

'Fainted,' said Mimi. 'All to the good, 'cause 'er blood pressure'll drop. Let's 'ave another look.' There was a rolled-up huckaback towel between the girl's legs which Mimi removed; it was soaked through with blood. 'It seems to 'ave stopped, but I'll put a cold pack in. You keep yer 'and on 'er pulse while I get the doin's.'

Mimi began by passing a rubber tube into the girl's bladder to drain off the urine, not an easy matter in the circumstances, and her hands shook slightly as she located the orifice. Then, for what seemed an eternity, Mabel supported the girl's parted legs while her grandmother inserted a length of wet gauze into the vagina with a pair of forceps, inch by inch, foot by foot, yard by yard, until it was tightly packed. *This girl ought to be in the hospital round the corner*, said an insistent voice inside Mabel's head, though aloud she said nothing.

'Right, that's done,' panted Mimi at last. 'Now down with 'er legs an' keep 'em together – careful! – that's right. What's 'er pulse like? Ah, she's comin' round, that's good – all right, Rowena? Ye've 'ad a bit of a bleed, nothin' to worry about. I s'pect yer could do with a drink o' tea – no, better stick to water for now.'

The girl's eyelids fluttered. 'Drink,' she whispered through dry white lips.

'Give 'er a glass o' water, Mabel – make sure she drinks,' ordered Mimi. 'I'll go an' tidy up this lot. 'Er name's Rowena if she says anythin'.'

Mabel sat down beside the girl who appeared to be asleep, but suddenly opened her eyes. 'Where's Sister Mimi?' she asked in a weak but well-bred voice. 'I'm dying of thirst – and I've got the most fearful headache.'

'All right, Rowena,' replied Mabel. 'Here's a drink o' water for yer.'

'Thanks. Are you a maid or something?'

'No, I'm ... I'm Mrs Court's granddaughter,' said Mabel and immediately wished she had not admitted to the relationship.

She held the glass while the girl drank gratefully. 'Ah, that's better. What's your name?'

'Mabel.'

'Mabel, your grandmother's a saint. She has saved me and I'll always be grateful to her,' whispered Rowena, closing her eyes. Mabel realised that she was referring to the pregnancy that had been ended, not the haemorrhage that had followed. This girl clearly had no idea how close she had come to bleeding to death.

"Ow's she doin'?' Mimi had come back with tea on a tray. 'Hm.' She nodded approvingly. 'Feelin' better now, Rowena? Ready for a nice cup o' tea? There's one for yerself, Mabel, plus a drop o' the old oh-be-joyful.' She put down the cup and poured out a weaker one for Rowena, adding two teaspoons of sugar. Lowering her head close to Mabel's ear, she whispered, 'Close thing, but she'll be all right now. Thought we was goin' to end up in Tooting Bec,' she added, referring to the hospital facing Graveney Common. 'Which would've taken a bit of explainin'.'

Mabel made no reply. She was sickened by the way Mimi had put Rowena's life at risk and despised herself for not disputing the issue of sending the girl into hospital; but how could she have defied her grandmother? And how could she have refused to assist, thereby adding to the danger of a fatal haemorrhage?

She picked up the cup of tea, took a sip, tasted the

brandy and put it down again. 'D'ye need me any longer?'

Even Mimi must have heard the coldness in the question, for she raised her eyebrows slightly. 'No, go back to yer bed, I can manage, thank yer.'

In the morning Daisy asked innocently if a baby had been born in the night. 'I heard a lot o' talking and hurrying up and down, and yer weren't there with me, Mabel, so I thought maybe somebody was having a baby.'

'No, dear, not a baby – just a lady not very well, that's all.'

'D'ye mean Elsie?'

It seemed simpler just to nod and say that poor Elsie was feeling better this morning.

Rowena stayed another night and left after Mimi removed the pack. Elsie remained in bed for the rest of that week, gradually recovering from influenza and cared for by Mimi who summarily banished Mabel from the sickroom. 'You got yer own work to do on the district,' she said. 'I'll take over now.'

But this was not good enough for Mabel, who had thought long and deeply about Rowena and what had very nearly happened to her. And to them all. 'I've got somethin' to say to yer, Grandmother.'

'Oh, yes? Go on, then.'

'Don't ever ask me to assist yer again with somethin' like that, because I shall refuse.'

Mimi Court stared at her. 'Oho, Miss Prim 'n' Proper! Don't yer get on yer high horse with *me*, Mabel Court. Remember where yer liveli'ood comes from – yerself an' Daisy both!'

'Yer don't keep me for nothin', Grandmother,' retorted Mabel in a voice of cold anger. 'I'm yer assistant midwife, an' do more 'n half yer work out on the district. I may turn a blind eye to the rest, but don't ask me to help yer with it again.'

Mimi was about to reply angrily, but decided to use a different approach. 'Listen, Mabel, I saved that girl. She was desperate an' told me straight out that she'd do 'erself in if her parents found out she was expectin'. Now they never will. She'll be presented at Court an' do the season along of all the other young ladyships, an' all 'cause I helped her out. All right, so she 'ad complications, but I pulled her through. So yer can save yer breath. An' by the way, there's yer money for this week – five pounds.'

'I'll take one pound as usual, Grandmother, I don't want any more,' Mabel said, picking up one of the five one-pound notes.

'Call it for lookin' after Elsie.'

'No, thank yer.'

'I'll give it to the Salvation Army, then,' said Mimi with a knowing look.

'Give it to who yer please, *I'm* not takin' it.'

'Suit yerself.' Mimi looked as if she might say more, but seeing the unflinching blue-grey gaze confronting her without fear, she merely shrugged.

It was a small triumph for Mabel to refuse payment from Mimi and tell her that she would not assist her in that way, but the atmosphere remained charged and Mabel found it difficult to meet Miss Lawton's frightened eyes after the Rowena incident. There seemed no way out of the situation she had got into and as her nineteenth birthday approached she pictured herself pedalling around Tooting for years to come, doing more and more work for which Mimi got paid. And if another emergency arose such as had occurred with Rowena, how could she possibly refuse to help? Beliefs and principles were all very fine, but in matters of life and death Mabel was learning that they could become compromised.

What on earth would her aunts at Belhampton say if they knew of her dilemma? As for Harry – but she would not let her thoughts stray in that forbidden direction.

And still it went on. Since Rowena's near fatality Mabel noticed that fewer women came to the house, but Mimi Court still went on her visits to clients in their own homes, having usually been recommended by others she had saved from social disaster. She would set off in the morning, often returning the same day, sometimes the next, saying nothing of where she had been but looking quietly pleased with herself. Her absences were never remarked upon and sometimes it seemed to Mabel that the whole household took part in a conspiracy of silence.

How long would this state of affairs continue? However Mabel might twist and turn, she could see no way of escape from the house of secrets.

Chapter Sixteen

Spring returned and daffodils danced on the edge of the common where the horse-chestnuts were coming into bud along Dr Johnson's Walk; in April Mabel could hardly believe that a whole year had passed since her mother's death. At Macaulay Road life went on as usual, with no prospect of changing. Mabel cycled to the homes of mothers before and after the birth of their babies, Daisy attended school and Miss Lawton, who had given up teaching the piano, went twice weekly to the Tooting Home, an imposing building that had formerly been a college and was now endowed as a home for the aged poor. It was no workhouse but a genuine refuge for its elderly inmates who enjoyed Miss Lawton's musical afternoons.

'I love to see the pleasure on their faces, and I ... I feel that I can still be of service,' she told Mabel, tucking her music into a large tapestry bag.

'I bet they count the days to Tuesdays and Fridays, Ruth.' Mabel smiled, knowing how much these afternoons meant to the lonely spinster. She wished that they could have a closer relationship, but Miss Lawton always shied away from any attempt at intimacy; it was as if there was an invisible barrier around her that prevented it.

'That'll be the butcher's delivery, Mabel – just go and pay him, will yer? I've left the money out by the door,' called Mimi one afternoon following the mournful anniversary.

Mabel drew back a little when confronted not by the butcher's boy on the step but a tall, dark, foreign-looking man with rough black hair and a distinctly bristly chin. She stared at him. 'Heave to, lady, an' spare a copper for a seafarin' man in port!' He grinned, showing two prominent white incisors.

'Albert? It's *Albert!*' Mabel took a moment to recognise the boy who'd turned into a man. 'But ye're so tall and brown and—'

'An' good-lookin', yeah. Steady on, gal,' he added as she flung her arms round him on the doorstep.

'But it's been that long, Albert – there've been times when I'd've given anythin' to see yer – speak to yer – come in, come in, Daisy's at school, but she'll be that excited – oh, Albert!'

Mimi appeared in the passage, drawn by Mabel's excited welcome for her brother.

'Look who's come home from the sea, Grand-mother!'

Mimi offered a cool cheek for him to kiss, asking how long he was on leave and where he was staying.

'Docked this mornin', got ten days an' stowin' me kit wiv a pal up the Mile End Road.' Albert was quick to sense that he was not welcome to stay in this house. 'Left 'em unloadin' at Tobacco Ware'ouse – couldn't wait to see Mabel an' Daisy. 'Ere, let's 'ave a proper look at yer, Mabel. What're yer up to nah, then?'

Happy as she was to see her brother, Mabel felt constrained in Mimi's presence and was thankful there was no client in the house. 'I'll put the kettle on. Are yer hungry, Albert?' she asked.

'Wait a minute, gal, I got somefin' for yer.' And

from his rolled-up bag he produced a beautiful soft cashmere shawl in cream and brown. 'Soon's I spotted it I could jus' see it on yer,' he said admiringly, arranging it round her shoulders. 'I got a bunch o' them little coloured bangles for Daisy to put on 'er arms, an' bits o' jade an' stuff for the aunts at Bel'ampton. Cor, yer look a treat in that, Mabel – really suits yer!'

For his grandmother there was a black silk scarf.

'Yer must've spent a fortune, Albert,' said Mabel, blushing with pleasure at this luxurious gift.

'Get away wiv yer, I got me pay, ain't I? Rollin' in it, I am.'

When Daisy came in she was a little overawed at first by the laughing young sailor who picked her up bodily and kissed her. She had not remembered him having a bristly chin, nor that he was so dark, tanned by months in the tropics. Mabel saw their grandmother's sharp brown eyes appraising him with a strange expression, though she made no comment.

That evening the brother and sisters went walking on Graveney Common, Mabel wearing her shawl and Daisy her half-dozen bangles on each arm. When the little girl ran on ahead of them, Albert linked his arm affectionately in Mabel's. 'Come on, ol' gal, tell yer bruvver what's bin goin' on, an' no messin' abaht. What're you an' Daisy doin' stuck in that 'ole wiv the Duchess o' Tootin'? Didn't yer want to go in for nursin'?'

Mabel gave a long sigh. 'It's a job to know where to start, Albert. It was after George went to Canada, see – I'd lost me job at the Rescue an' had to get out o' Sorrel Street – an' there just wasn't anywhere else. She offered to teach me midwifery and give me a pound a week an' all found, and it seemed like a good idea while I waited until I was old enough to start me trainin' as a nurse at a Poor Law infirmary.'

He nodded. 'Yeah, but what abaht Daisy? She an' Alice went to Bel'ampton wiv the aunts.'

'Yes, she did, but—' She then told him the full story of Daisy's flight on the day of Ada's wedding.

'Little monkey! Seems all right nah, though, don't she?'

'Yes, she's much better, but—' She hesitated, unwilling to tell him the whole sordid story of 23 Macaulay Road. 'But it's no place for a child, y'know.'

''Ow d'yer mean?'

'D'ye know what our grandmother does for a living, Albert?'

'Summat that brings in a tidy whack, I can see. Blimey! It ain't a bleedin' 'ouse o' ill fame, is it?'

''Course not, don't be daft.'

He grinned. 'Yer never know, poor ol' Miss Lawton might 'ave 'idden talents.'

'Don't joke about Ruth Lawton, she may be a bit eccentric but she's all right at heart. Poor soul, I'm sure she knows what goes on, an' ... an' I can understand, 'cause I'm ashamed about it, too.' She trembled against his arm and he could see that she was truly upset.

'So, what goes on, then? The ol' girl's a midwife, ain't she? Delivers babies?'

'Yes, and I assist her with *that*, I go out on my bicycle – nice job, but—'

He picked up the implication in the word *that* and all at once he understood. 'Gawd Almighty, yer mean she gets rid of 'em an' all, is that it?'

'I couldn't've told yer, Albert, but yes, that's it –

she does abortions.' And in rising agitation she went on to explain that Mimi's special clients were mostly wealthy women who lived out of the district.

Albert whistled through his teeth. 'Hell, Mabel, see what yer mean. No place for Daisy, nor you neiver. Ye'll be tarred wiv the same brush if yer stay under 'er roof – not to mention endin' up in clink. Yer got to get out o' there, gal, or kiss yer nursin' plans goodbye.'

She heard the deadly seriousness in his voice. 'I know, I know – but what can I *do*? I shouldn't't've let Daisy stay, I see that now, but—'

'Take 'er back to Aunt Nell.'

'But how *can* I? I just can't go to the Somertons and say I've brought her back after all this time, not after the way grandmother insulted them – ye should've heard her, Albert, it was *awful*, I didn't dare show me face, I was that ashamed. If I took her back now, they'd have every right to send me packin'.'

'Yer ain't got no choice, Mabel. You an' Daisy got to get *aht* o' there. Look 'ere, I'll come wiv yer, an' 'ave a word wiv this Thomas Somerton. The aunts are decent sorts an' I reckon they'd do it for our muvver's sake. Fact is, Mabel, it's got to be sorted aht before I go back.'

Albert spoke with urgency and Mabel saw that he was very concerned. 'And yer really think Aunt Nell 'ud agree?'

'I'd lay even money on it.'

'Shall I write a letter to her? And to Aunt Kate?'

'Nah, let's use the element o' surprise, as we say in the navy. Go dahn there this weekend, all free of us, an' stay somewhere in Bel'ampton, an' send a message from there sayin' we'd like to see 'em, very sorry for what's 'appened, *you* can do that bit, and leave it to yer bruvver to do the rest!'

Persuaded by his determination, Mabel agreed. Mrs Court was politely but firmly told that they were taking Daisy on a visit to her Belhampton relations, and although she compressed her lips and said they were making a big mistake by unsettling Daisy all over again, she noted the gleam in Albert's eye and made no attempt to stop them. Daisy was cock-a-hoop with excitement and chattered happily about seeing her friend Lucy Drummond again.

On the train down to Belhampton that Saturday morning, Albert told Mabel that he was staying at the Seamen's Mission on Mercer Street in Shadwell. 'No need to tell the ol' girl; let 'er fink I'm puttin' up wiv a pal. If she can't even give me a bunk to kip dahn on—'

'Oh, what a shame, Albert, havin' to stay at a hostel on yer leave!'

'Nah, 's all right, clean, food not bad. No beer, an' a bit on the 'oly side, but decent an' cheap. Stops the young 'uns from bein' robbed by crimps an' 'ores. And talkin' o' missions an' stuff, 'ave yer seen anythin' of ol' 'Arry?' He asked the question quickly, catching her off guard.

Her mouth hardened and he saw that the subject was painful. 'No, I broke off completely and yer know why. Please don't speak of it, Albert.'

'Poor ol' 'Arry, worships the grahnd yer walk on, Mabel. Yer won't ever find a better.'

'I'm not lookin' for a better, Albert. I've told yer before, I shan't marry anybody.' Lowering her voice so that Daisy would not hear, she went on, 'As soon as she's back at Belhampton, if they'll take her back, I shall see about trainin' to be a nurse. I'll apply to the Booth Street Poor Law infirmary, over Lambeth way.'

'Yer mean the ol' sick asylum? Gawd, Mabel, it's a bleedin' work'ouse!'

'Not any more it isn't. It's been taken over by the LCC an' got proper wards and an operatin' theatre. One of the mothers was tellin' me her sister's trainin' there, and lives in the nurses' hostel. The work's hard, but I was never afraid o' that, and once I've done the three years an' got me certificate, I'll look for a job nursin' children.'

He saw her eyes soften at the prospect and said gently, 'That's what yer was plannin' to do one day in the Sally Army with 'Arry, wa'n't it?' She did not reply and he went on thoughtfully, 'My Gawd, Mabel, ye've 'ad a few setbacks, ain't yer? First yer lose yer job at the Anti-Viv 'cause o' me, then our muvver an' farver went the way they did, and there was all that scare over the p—er, that damned blood test, an' yer lost yer job at the Rescue an' fell into the clutches o' the Duchess o' Tootin' – bloody 'ell, Mabel, there's always been summat to knock yer backwards. Well, I ain't goin' back to sea until ye're free o' that miserable 'ole.'

His face was grimly set and only relaxed when Daisy looked up at him and smiled. 'D'ye think Auntie Nell might say I'm a good girl now, Albert?'

'Not 'alf!' He tapped the side of his nose and gave her a knowing wink.

From the train they watched the sprawl of London give way to leafy suburbs with gardens, parks and tennis courts; then came woodlands and stretches of common land with Surrey pines towering above sandy tracks. Even busy towns like Woking, Aldershot and Farnham were surrounded by green countryside, and when they reached the low, rounded Hampshire hills and pretty villages clustering around their church spires, Mabel wondered if her mother had missed the country when she found herself in Sorrel Street.

From Belhampton Station the little trio walked into the town and Albert led them into the biggest hotel he could see, the Wheatsheaf, where he booked a room for himself and a larger one for his sisters to share. They had a midday dinner at a table in the dining room, though Mabel was too nervous to eat much, and spent the time rewriting the note she had penned to her aunt and uncle Somerton. In it she told them that Albert was home on leave, and that she and Daisy had come down to Belhampton with him.

> We are staying at the Wheatsheaf Inn, and hope that you will allow us to call on you and Aunt Kate. We would like to see you again and Alice. May we visit tomorrow if convenent for you. We send our sinsere regards.
> Mabel, Albert and Daisy Court

She put the note in the addressed envelope she had brought with her and Albert gave sixpence to a messenger boy to deliver it to Pear Tree Cottage, a mile out of the town. 'Wait an' see if there's an answer,' Albert told the boy, and Mabel spent the next hour on tenterhooks, wondering if any answer would be forthcoming and what it would be.

Standing in the yard of the one-time coaching inn, she looked out at the busy little market town, the horse-drawn carts and wagons, the shoppers and strollers. There were very few motor-driven vehicles here as yet, though she saw an open-topped omnibus setting off for Winchester. 'I don't see any sign o' the boy, Albert,' she murmured. 'And it's been an hour since he left.' She spoke quietly so that Daisy would not hear.

But Daisy was not listening. She was jumping up and down at Mabel's side. 'There's Uncle Thomas's carriage, look! And there they are, Aunt Nell and Alice – and Aunt Kate, see, they've all come to meet us!' she cried, running out of the yard and waving.

And so they had. Daisy was joyfully reunited with Aunt Nell whose tearful smiles of welcome included all three of them. Mabel kissed her aunts and her sister Alice, now a very attractive girl of sixteen, and Thomas Somerton shook hands with Albert.

Mabel was so relieved and thankful for their forgiving attitude that she forgot all Albert's instructions and began speaking at once to her aunt and uncle Somerton about the true reason for their visit. 'Daisy's ready to come back to yer now if ye're willing to have her after all the trouble ye've been caused – the way my grandmother Court behaved to yer,' she said in a rush. 'It's been eight months and Daisy's much better now. Yer see, she needed time to recover from—'

Elinor and Thomas Somerton exchanged a nod of understanding.

'We have always been willing to have her back and in fact we have missed her very much, Mabel,' said Somerton gravely. 'But if we do take her back, it must be on our terms this time. We would have to adopt her and change her name to Somerton. And she must not ever enter the house of that Court woman again.'

Mabel looked at Albert, who stepped forward, beaming with approval. 'Exactly what I was goin' to suggest meself, Mr Somerton. Yer took the words right out o' me mouf!' he exclaimed, causing his sister Alice to grimace with embarrassment. 'Mabel meant well, but it's been a trouble to me, I can tell yer, knowin' they was livin' at that house with such a woman. Ye've taken a great weight orf me mind, sir.'

Which left Mabel with little to add except her grateful thanks, while tears of relief flowed. 'I just don't know what I'd've done if ye'd refused,' she admitted guilelessly and Aunt Kate put a comforting arm round her shoulders.

'How could they – how could we possibly refuse, Mabel? You're so like your mother – our sister Anna-Maria.'

And that, it seemed, was reason enough for their forbearance and forgiveness. There was no need for any of them to stay at the Wheatsheaf that night, for Daisy's room was waiting for her at Pear Tree Cottage, while Aunt Kate insisted that Mabel and Albert should stay with her at Pinehurst, the family home where their mother had grown up with her sisters.

Nothing had prepared the brother and sister for the spaciousness and many comforts of the house, the luxury of feather beds, an indoor water closet, gleaming polished furniture and a garden with green lawns and flower beds. Even Albert was overawed and Mabel knew that his thoughts, like hers, were of their mother and the life she had left behind for ever when she married Jack Court. When she *had* to marry him, thought Mabel, and all because of *me*. Had Anna-Maria wished that she had never indulged in that long-ago lovemaking? For the resulting changes and events had ruined her health and brought her down to the grave at thirty-seven. In the silence of the country night Mabel mourned afresh for her mother.

On the Sunday morning they all walked to the parish church where they occupied a whole pew four rows from the front. Again Mabel pictured her mother worshipping in this same church, following the same order of service and singing the familiar hymns. She watched the handsome middle-aged rector move towards the carved pulpit and ascend its curving steps to deliver his sermon. 'My text this morning is taken from the first epistle of St Peter, chapter 4, verse 12,' he began, his fine voice resounding through the nave. Then he stopped and gripped the side of the pulpit, his face drained of colour as he stared intently at one face among the many upturned before him: the girl in the pew with Miss Chalcott and the Somertons.

Mabel felt his gaze upon her and shifted uncomfortably. Murmurings began to be heard in the congregation, and Aunts Nell and Kate exchanged a significant glance. The rector's wife half rose from her place in the front pew where she sat with their five childen.

The rector must have made an effort to take command of himself, for he turned his eyes away from Mabel, took a deep breath and collected his thoughts sufficiently to continue with his sermon, though at times he hesitated, as if he had lost the thread of his subject.

As was customary at the end of the service, the rector greeted each member of the congregation as they left by the south door. As he held out his hand to Mabel, he once again seemed unable to say a word.

Miss Chalcott quickly interposed. 'This is our niece Mabel Court, Mr Drummond, and this is her brother Albert. They are in Belhampton on a visit, and little Daisy has come back to live with her aunt and uncle Somerton.'

'Oh – ah, I see,' he said quietly, managing a smile for the brother and sister. 'I hope you enjoy your visit, Miss Court – Mr Court.'

Mabel was swiftly moved on by her aunt, and when they were away from the crowd around the door, Albert turned round and asked, 'What d'yer reckon was up with '*im*? Looked as if 'e'd suddenly seen a ghost.'

'Ah, yes,' murmured Aunt Nell who was standing nearby, and Mabel saw that her eyes were full of tears. 'I'll have a quiet word with you later, Mabel.'

They all ate Sunday dinner together at Pear Tree Cottage, and when it was finished Nell drew Mabel aside and took her out into the garden. 'My dear Mabel, I feel that I should tell you something,' she began. 'As a young man our rector was in love with your mother; in fact, they were practically engaged. But then that man – your father – came on the scene. Father had engaged him to take our photographs, and as soon as Anna-Maria saw him she completely lost her head and never gave another thought to poor Mr Drummond. He was quite heartbroken and I'll never forget his face when – oh, Mabel, it was dreadful – such a scandal.'

Mabel looked wordlessly at her aunt on hearing this incredible tale, or so it seemed to her. It showed yet another aspect of her mother, a wilful, flirtatious girl who had let her heart rule her head, spurning the love of a worthy young man who adored her, in favour of the charming, improvident Jack Court. And to think how it had all ended . . .

'And as you're so like her as she was then, Mabel, Mr Drummond must have indeed thought he was seeing a . . . a ghost,' said Nell sadly. 'He was inconsolable at the time.'

'But he married somebody else, didn't he?' Mabel pointed out. 'The lady in the front pew.'

'Yes, happily he went into the Church and married Miss Perrott as soon as he was ordained. But Anna-Maria was his first love and he's never forgotten her, one could see that this morning.'

But now she's dead, thought Mabel, only a ghost from the past. And Mr Drummond has got a wife and family.

Just as Harry Drover will, one day . . .

Before Mabel and Albert left Belhampton, Aunt Kate made her eldest niece an offer of a permanent home as her companion. 'You'd be near to your sisters without having the responsibility for them, Mabel, and you'd benefit from a healthy country life. And I'd love to have you here at Pinehurst.'

There was a note of pleading in her words, and Mabel wondered if, like Mr Drummond, her aunt saw Anna-Maria in her niece and wanted to make amends for past unkindness. 'It's ever so kind o' yer, Aunt Kate, but I'm goin' to apply to train as a nurse, so I'd best go back to London, y'see.'

'But Elinor and I can't bear the thought of you going back to that dreadful woman at Tooting and staying in her house.'

'It won't be for much longer, Aunt, I can't wait to escape! But I want to be a nurse above all else and I

370

need to get me general training done.' She went on to explain that with Daisy back in Belhampton, she was now free to pursue her lifelong dream, and that her friend Miss Carter had advised applying to a Poor Law infirmary as the best option for a girl of her background, and that the training was free.

'My dear Mabel, if it was a question of paying for you to train at a good hospital—'

'No, Aunt Kate, you and Aunt Nell have done more 'n enough for us all,' said Mabel quickly. 'I'd rather go to Booth Street infirmary – I'd fit in better there, if yer see what I mean. But thank yer, Aunt Kate. I'll never forget how kind ye've been – you and Aunt Nell and Uncle Thomas.'

Without being asked, Daisy willingly promised to settle down with her Hampshire relations. 'I'll be good this time, Mabel – I really *will*,' she said and Mabel knew that at nine years old her sister had learned that there could be no going back to the old life. 'I like bein' here at Aunt Nell's house better than Grandmother's,' she confessed. 'Ye're not goin' to stay there for ever, are yer, Mabel?'

'No, dear, I'm going to be a nurse and look after ill people.'

There were hugs and kisses and promises to write when the brother and sister boarded the London train, and although the parting was painful Mabel's elation at the prospect of freedom from Macaulay Road buoyed her up; she was ready to face a furious outburst on her return without Daisy.

But Mimi was coldly dismissive, and hardly seemed surprised. 'Hm. I thought as much, yer had it all planned with that foul-mouthed brother o' yours, didn't yer? She'd better not decide to come back, 'cause I won't have her, the ungrateful little minx.'

Mabel did not answer. She had already composed her letter of application to the Matron of the Booth Street Poor Law infirmary and Albert had warned her not to breathe a word about it to anybody, though she wrote to Miss Carter and Mrs James to ask them for references. Both consented, Mrs James all the more readily because she had a conscience about Mabel's summary dismissal from the Institute at a difficult time in her life. Mabel was also asked to give the name of her general practitioner who unknown to her sent a highly commendatory letter.

On the day before Albert was due to return to sea, he had another serious talk with his sister. 'Good luck wiv yer interview, Mabel, an' remember, not a word to the Duchess until the day yer sling yer 'ook. I wouldn't put it past 'er to try an' scuttle yer chances. She's goin' to miss yer pedallin' all rahnd Tootin' doin' 'er work.'

'I can't ever thank yer enough for what ye've done, Albert,' she said seriously. 'It's made all the difference in the world, gettin' Daisy back to Belhampton.'

'Well, she couldn't've stayed 'ere, could she? An' the sooner *you* get out o' the damned place the better, an' all. I worry about yer, ol' gal.' He pinched her cheek as he spoke and she knew how much he meant what he said. Then he told her he had been to see Harry Drover at Clapton. 'Still pinin' for yer, Mabel, an' 'e ain't never goin' to alter.'

Her heart gave a lurch at the thought of the meeting between the two of them and what might have been said. 'Yer didn't say anythin' about me, did yer?' she asked anxiously.

He gave her a quizzical look. 'I did as much

listenin' as talkin'. Don't forget he's a Sally Army man, which means there ain't much 'e don't know abaht yooman failin's.'

'Oh, Albert, yer didn't talk about anythin' ... confidential, did yer?'

'Sometimes there ain't no need to discuss anyfin', Mabel. People ain't always as daft as yer fink. Anyway, toodle-oo, old gal, an' take care – I won't be 'appy until ye're shot o' the ol' witch.'

'Goodbye, Albert. And thanks for—' She hugged him close, unable to say another word.

'I must tell you, Miss Court, that a large number of young women have applied for nursing training at this hospital since it came under the jurisdiction of the Local Government Board and the appointment of a Medical Officer. Daughters of clergymen, schoolmasters, councillors – I've taken them on as probationers and you have to realise that with over seventy applicants for less than twenty appointments, I have to be very careful in selecting the right ones.'

Mabel's heart sank. The Matron of the Booth Street infirmary was a square-faced, broad-shouldered woman of about forty-five, with a starched and frilled white cap perched on her iron-grey hair. She sat opposite Mabel across a desk on which lay the application letters and details of the other young women being interviewed that day, and she prided herself on her intuitive judgement of character. 'I see that since leaving school you have worked at a nursery for pre-school children and a refuge for unmarried mothers. Miss Carter gives you a very good reference and Mrs James describes you as a willing worker.'

Mabel nodded nervously. 'Thank yer, Matron.'

'I also note that you lost both your parents last year, Miss Court, which must have been a sad and difficult time for you. What was your father's occupation?'

'He travelled around racecourses and did a bit o' – he was a bookmaker, Matron.'

'I see. And you now live with your grandmother?'

'That's right, Matron,' answered Mabel, who had said nothing about her work with Mimi's maternity cases, for fear of what might be asked.

'And your brothers and sisters, what has happened to them since losing your parents?'

Mabel gave a brief account of each one and the Matron nodded, studied her papers and then looked intently at this honest, likeable girl before her. 'I find you a suitable applicant, Miss Court, though you will have to be considered along with the others when the Board's committee meets to make the appointments. I like your general attitude and will personally support your application. You'll be notified within a week.'

'Er, I see, Matron. Thank yer.'

'So if you are accepted for training, Miss Court, would you be able to commence with the next new intake on Monday, September the first?'

Mabel's mouth dropped open and a look of incredulous joy lit up her grey-blue eyes. 'Would I, Matron – *would* I? Oh, yes, I most certainly would!'

'Very well.' The woman's stern face softened in a smile of appreciation – this girl she had liked at first sight. 'All new appointments are on a three-month trial, Miss Court, with an examination at the end. Right! I shall look forward to seeing you again.'

Mabel rose from her chair and took the offered hand. She very nearly kissed it.

Looking out for the postman the following week, Mabel feared that she might be out on a case when the letter of notification arrived. She therefore confided in Miss Lawton who promised to look out for it each morning when the post arrived. Exactly a week after the interview she slipped the all-important letter into Mabel's hand. 'I . . . I've got it, I picked it up off the mat before M-Mrs Court came down,' she whispered. 'Oh, what does it say? Open it, do, do!'

With trembling fingers Mabel tore open the envelope and read the brief typewritten letter: 'We are pleased to inform you that . . .' The two women hugged each other silently in the narrow hallway. Three months to go and then goodbye to Macaulay Road.

Meanwhile life went on in much the same way, with only one untoward incident in the midwifery practice. On being called out to a woman in labour with her fourth child, Mabel was not sure that the child's head was presenting, as had been assumed by the panel doctor. And if it was a breech presentation she was not competent to deal with it. She sent the woman's neighbour to fetch her grandmother, only to be told that Mrs Court was out visiting another patient. Mabel therefore had no choice but to send for Mimi's deadly rival. 'Yer need a qualified midwife, dear, so I'll ask Mrs Taylor to come and see what she thinks,' she told the woman and the neighbour was accordingly sent to Fishponds Road.

Mrs Taylor, who had been loudly complaining for some time that Mrs Court left half her cases in the charge of a young, unregistered girl, was highly delighted when that same young girl asked for her advice and opinion. The baby was indeed in the breech position and the doctor was called, but being a fourth child it slithered out with no difficulty and the story had a happy ending in that respect. The explosion came when Mimi heard of her detested rival's triumph, and she was absolutely furious with Mabel.

But her fury made no headway: Mabel remained calm because she was confident that she had done the right thing. 'Yer weren't there, Grandmother, and I wasn't goin' to risk a baby's life just 'cause yer don't like Mrs Taylor.'

'Like her? The woman's incompetent! She's envied my reputation as a midwife for years and now what's she goin' to say all round the district? Yer knew it was the woman's fourth baby and not likely to give any trouble, surely to God!'

'It was a breech, Grandmother.'

'An' she dropped it like shellin' a pea.'

'It was a *breech* and I might've run into trouble deliverin' the head.'

'Yer shouldn't've sent for that old fool.'

'And *you* shouldn't've been away from home.'

Mimi glared incredulously at such defiance. 'Ye'll be too bloody clever for yer own good one o' these days, my girl.'

She knows I'm not afraid of her, thought Mabel with grim satisfaction, counting the days to her liberation. She kept the letter of acceptance under her pillow.

The gentleman who called to see Mrs Court was tall

and aristocratic in appearance. He was also obviously very worried, and fidgeted with his hat and gloves as he talked with Mimi in the front parlour. From her window Mabel watched him bow and replace his hat as he rejoined his waiting cab and driver.

True to form, the next day Mimi set out dressed inconspicuously in black, saying that she might not be back that day, and giving instructions to the maids about meals and household duties to be done during her absence. 'And if Mrs Betts at the bakery goes into labour, Mabel, and yer run into trouble, don't send for that creature on Fishponds Road, get the panel doctor straight away.'

'Yes, Grandmother.'

Mimi did not return until the next day, but looked pleased with herself; the outcome of her visit had clearly been both satisfactory and lucrative. Nobody asked any questions, but Miss Lawton absented herself from the evening meal and stayed in her room.

'Good riddance to the old black crow,' muttered Mimi. 'Gettin' more an' more of a problem, she is. End up in a private asylum at this rate and I'll have to foot the bill.'

Mabel made no answer.

Two days later, a Sunday, Mabel and Miss Lawton had returned from the morning service and were about to sit down to Sunday dinner with Mimi when there was a loud knocking at the front door. 'It's a young woman for yer, madam,' said the maid and Mimi rose at once, wiping her mouth on her table napkin. A brief exchange took place on the doorstep and Mabel gasped on hearing a voice she thought she recognised, shrill with anxiety. 'Ye'll 'ave to come to 'er, missus, she's really bad!'

'All right, all right, I'll come, no need for all this to-do,' she heard Mimi say crossly. 'Wait there while I fetch me bag.' She puffed her way up the stairs and they heard her call, 'Elsie!'

Mabel simply had to see who was at the door, and while her grandmother was upstairs she got up from the table and peered into the hallway.

Maudie Ling stared back at her. '*Mabel*! What the bleedin' 'ell – oh, Gawd, fergit yer saw me – fergit yer saw me, Mabel, don't let on.'

Thoroughly shaken and with a dreadful suspicion dawning in her mind, Mabel returned to her seat just as Mimi came down the stairs with her black bag, Elsie following in a hastily donned hat and jacket. 'Be back tomorrow, most likely, Mabel – remember about Mrs Betts, get the doctor in if yer can't manage.' And they were gone.

Mabel hid her shock from Miss Lawton, though her mind was in turmoil. There could be no doubt as to who Mimi Court's latest client could be. Maudie had told Mabel enough about Her Ladyship's amorous exploits and the risks she took. Yet the *operation* had been on Thursday and this was Sunday – what had happened? What, thought Mabel fearfully, had gone wrong?

Mimi did not return that night, nor the following day. Another night passed and it was Tuesday morning. Miss Lawton's nerves seemed stretched to breaking point, though she said nothing about Mimi's absence; nor did Mabel want to speak of her own personal knowledge.

As breakfast finished a message was brought from

Betts's Bakeries in Upper Tooting Road. Mrs Betts's pains had started.

Thankful to have something to do to occupy her mind, Mabel fastened her box to the back of the bicycle and pedalled round to see what was happening. Mrs Betts was a chatty, plump woman of thirty who was expecting her first baby. She and her husband lived above the shop, and Mabel found her in her dressing gown, pacing between bedroom and living room. 'Ooh, there's another twinge – how long d'ye think it'll be, Nurse Court?'

Mabel smiled reassuringly. Mrs Betts was getting a few tightenings, but labour was by no means established and the delivery might be many hours away.

'My mother'll be comin' round soon, and I must say I'll be glad to see her, Nurse Court. Yer need yer mother with yer at a time like this, don't yer? Shall we have a cup o' tea an' look at the paper? We take the *Daily Mail* and it's just been delivered.'

The woman's voice faded to a background blur of chatter as Mabel's eyes fell upon the news item. It first impinged upon her consciousness as a row of black capitals; then, as she stared at them, they arranged themselves into a headline that struck her like a blow between the eyes:

TRAGIC DEATH OF LADY CECILIA STANLEY

Chapter Seventeen

Icy fingers clutched Mabel's heart; her mouth went dry as she stared at the headline.

Mrs Betts followed her gaze towards the front page. 'What is it, Nurse Court? *Whose* tragic death? Ooh, that's sad, i'n't it? Was this lady only young, then?'

She picked up the paper and held it so that she and Mabel could read the printed column together. 'All of London society will be shocked by the sudden announcement of the demise of one of its brightest stars,' they read. 'At twenty-three, Lady Cecilia's beauty and wit put her among the most sought-after hostesses of the season ... wife of Sir Percy Stanley of Bryanston Square and Farleigh Hall in Hertford-shire ... sudden death due to peritonitis ...'

'Peri-perimatitis, does it say? What's that, Nurse Court?'

In an instant Mabel remembered her duty towards her patient, and forced herself to think ahead and keep outwardly calm. Her grandmother had not come home and after this calamity would not be likely to reappear in the foreseeable future. Which meant that she, Mabel, must obtain a properly trained midwife to attend Mrs Betts in labour. 'I ... I'm sorry, Mrs Betts, but I think I'd better call Mrs Taylor to come and see yer,' she said.

The woman gave her a curious look. 'You all right, Nurse Court? Yer gorn ever so white.'

Mabel plunged on breathlessly, 'Well, I, er, the fact is, I don't think Mrs Court's goin' to be around today – y'see, she's got this other case that's takin' up her time. Look, Mrs Betts, I'll go round and see Mrs Taylor an' ask her to come to yer.'

At this point Mrs Betts's mother arrived, full of concern for her daughter and wanting to know why the midwife could not attend. 'My Susan's booked for Mrs Court, not Mrs Taylor,' she protested crossly. 'I s'pose *she's* cleared off to some woman with more money.'

'I'm sorry, but it'll have to be Mrs Taylor, unless yer got anybody else in mind,' faltered Mabel, her own mind full of unnamed dread. 'I'll go off on me bicycle now and let her know.' And without stopping to answer any more questions she left the bakery and headed for Fishponds Road.

'It's her first baby and she's only early yet, but she'll need yer when she's gettin' her pains reg'lar,' Mabel told the astonished Mrs Taylor on the doorstep of her home. 'Me grandmother's out on a ... a very important case, so she can't deliver Mrs Betts. Please, Mrs Taylor, ye'll have to come, there's nobody else near that I can call.'

Mrs Taylor swallowed a mouthful of buttered toast and wiped her lips on her apron. 'Well! I call it a damned cheek, I do! Here's me in the middle o' me breakfast and don't know the woman from Adam. Where's this very important case, then?'

'Oh, it's out o' the district, somewhere up the West End, I think, I ... I'm not sure,' replied Mabel, hoping that she did not sound as unconvincing as she felt.

'Oh, yeah? Yer ol' grandmother ain't got no right

to clear off kowtowin' to posh women when she's got bookin's 'ere in Tootin'. She got no business to leave yer on yer own, a young girl with no trainin'. I've said so all along, she'll end up with a death on 'er 'ands one o' these days.'

Mabel flinched at the grim aptness of the phrase and the midwife's eyes narrowed. Nevertheless, Mrs Taylor was clearly gratified at being called upon to take over her rival's case and she was not ill-disposed towards Mabel for putting her in a position to gloat. However, she was extremely curious as to Mimi's whereabouts, and would have asked a great many more questions if Mabel had not quickly got on her bicycle and pedalled away.

Where should she go? Back to Macaulay Road? She was oddly reluctant to return there. She needed to think, to go over the possibilities of what might have happened and sort out what she should do.

Lady Cecilia Stanley was dead. This was a tragedy in itself and Mabel could imagine Maudie Ling's grief – and almost certain involvement in the circumstances of her beloved mistress's death. But the implications for Mimi Court might be equally devastating and as for Mabel herself . . .

Her breath came in uneven gasps as she cycled towards Graveney Common where she dismounted and walked, pushing the bicycle across the grass. She now saw the situation in all its frightful clarity. Lady Cecilia must have been expecting a baby that was not her husband's but another man's, probably Viscount Eastcote's, and *he* must have been the gentleman who had come to see Mimi on her behalf. Faced with the awful prospect of public disgrace Lady Stanley had engaged the services of a woman recommended to her by some former client, possibly Rowena for all

Mabel knew, to perform an illegal operation. And it had gone hideously wrong: some perforation, some septic infection had occurred and rapidly led to her death.

Mabel's thoughts went out to poor Sir Percy, that 'bald-'eaded ol' coot' as Maudie had contemptuously referred to him. Had he guessed the reason for his wife's sudden fatal illness and had he made her confess to him? Or had she confessed of her own accord and asked for a doctor to be sent for? No, she had sent Maudie to recall Mimi Court two days ago and too late – not that anybody would have been able to save her once the womb had become septic and the infection spread to the abdomen and blood-stream.

And where on earth was Mimi now? And Elsie her assistant? And Maud the devoted maid?

Mabel shuddered involuntarily. Too late she remembered Albert's shocked reaction on hearing about their grandmother's illegal sideline and his urgent warning that she could get away from 23 Macaulay Road as soon as Daisy had been returned to Belhampton: *Ye'll find yerself tarred wiv the same brush – be the end o' yer nursin', Mabel.*

Mabel's knees went weak as she pictured a terrible scandal with headlines in all the newspapers reporting Mimi Court on trial for killing a society lady and being sent to prison.

And herself, known to be living in the same house as her grandmother's assistant on the district – what would happen to *her*?

She saw that it could mean the end of her only hope, the last remaining dream left to her after losing Harry Drover: her career as a children's nurse. Was it too late to get away? She thought of running off to

Belhampton, but dismissed the idea at once, for what sort of a story could she tell her aunts? And if there was a scandal the police might come after her, and bring her back to stand beside her grandmother in court. 'Oh, Lord, have mercy upon me!' she moaned aloud, then thanked heaven that at least Daisy was safely out of the way, because of Albert's insistence. He had been far more alert to the danger than she was and she had not paid him half enough attention. Now *this* had happened and suddenly it was too late . . .

The morning hours passed, and Mabel remembered a woman who was due to be confined any day now and should be advised to book with another midwife. She forced herself to call upon the woman to tell her that Mrs Court was unavailable. She wondered how Mrs Betts was progressing, but kept away from the bakery, unable to face Mrs Taylor's insistent questions.

There was now nothing for it but to return to Macaulay Road, dreading what she would find there. Would Miss Lawton have heard anything of Mimi? Or Elsie? And if she had, would she tell Mabel? The nervous lady had always been evasive on *that* subject.

The first thing she saw was a black bicycle propped up outside number 23. Attached to the front was a police badge, bearing the initials GR. So they were on to Mimi already . . .

As soon as she turned the key in the lock and stepped into the hallway the very air seemed charged with fear and tension. One of the two housemaids rushed out of the living room and started babbling at her. 'There's a policeman with an 'elmet in the parlour, an' Miss Lawton keeps tellin' 'im she don't know where Mrs Court is – do *you* know, Miss Court?'

Mabel forced a smile. The house without Mimi was like a ship with no captain on the bridge and there was only herself to take charge. With an awful sense of responsibility she made up her mind to answer all questions as truthfully as possible but not to volunteer any information not asked for.

The parlour door opened to reveal a distraught Miss Lawton, her face flushed and hair dishevelled. 'Thank heaven! Oh, thank God you're here, Mabel. I ... I keep telling this man I know n-nothing of M-Mrs Court's whereabouts, I'm only a lodger here, only a lodger—'

'All right, Miss Lawton, yer can go.' The constable sighed in some relief, rising as Mabel came in. 'Miss Court? Good afternoon.'

Mabel nodded as Miss Lawton made her escape, muttering that she knew nothing, it was nothing to do with her, nothing at all.

'Close the door and take a seat, Miss Court,' he said politely. 'I'm Police Constable Derrick and I'm making enquiries about a missing person who's wanted for questioning in connection with a criminal offence. A woman generally known as Mrs Mimi Court who normally resides at this address. I'd like to ask yer a few questions about her.'

He waited until she was seated before he sat down again and Mabel braced herself. 'Yes, constable.'

A barrage of questions followed: her name, age and occupation, her relationship to Mrs Court, the length of time she had lived with her and a brief family history. 'Can yer tell me the lady's full Christian name, Miss Court?'

Mabel could not. She had only ever heard her grandmother referred to as Mimi.

'Now, Miss Court, can yer tell me where Mrs Court is now?'

'No, constable.'

'No idea at all?'

'No.'

'What about the woman known as Elsie? D'ye know where she is?'

'No.'

'Now, Miss Court, was yer grandmother here last Thursday night, the tenth of July?'

'No, she was away that night.'

'D'ye know where she was?'

'I don't know – I think she said she was going to London.'

'D'ye know why?'

'No.'

'When did she return?'

'Friday.'

'The following day?'

'Yes.'

'And when did she go away again?'

'On Sunday, at midday.'

'The thirteenth?'

'Yes.'

'Why did she go?'

'Somebody came for her.'

'D'ye know who?'

'No.' It was a lie. (*Fergit yer saw me, fergit yer saw me Mabel*.)

'Was it a man or a woman, did yer notice?'

'I ... I was at Sunday dinner and didn't see.' Another lie.

'Who answered the door to this person?'

'One o' the maids. She came and told Grand-mother there was somebody askin' for her.'

'And Mrs Court left straight away, with the woman Elsie?'

'Yes.'

'And yer haven't seen her since?'

'No.'

He made a note to speak to the maids. 'Now, Miss Court, was yer grandmother in the habit o' going to see her patients and staying overnight?'

'Sometimes.'

'How often?'

'About once or twice in a month, not so much lately. And she didn't always stay overnight.'

'And were these patients, er, maternity cases o' hers?'

'I suppose so.'

'Yer say yer work as her assistant with her local cases?'

'Yes.'

'But not with these others that she goes further afield to see?'

'No, I don't have anything to do with those.'

'What's different about 'em, Miss Court?'

'Well, they ... they're better off than the locals, they pay her more, and she ... she gives 'em her personal attention.' Mabel was aware that she was breathing more quickly, her heart was racing and her forehead was moist with perspiration which she could also feel trickling down from her armpits. So far so good. She steeled herself to keep still and appear calm.

But the policeman looked searchingly into her face as he asked the next question. 'And did yer know nothing at all about who yer grandmother went to see last Thursday and again on Sunday, Miss Court? Think before yer answer.'

Mabel took a deep breath. She had to lie, which went against her nature, and she had to sound convincing. 'I had no idea at all where she was – not till I saw the newspaper report this morning.'

There was a long, dreadful silence. St Nicholas's church bell chimed the hour, sounding out the strokes like the knell of doom. The constable's hand hung poised in the air, holding a pencil. And she realised what she had just said.

'What did yer see in the paper this morning, Miss Court?'

Too late, Mabel struck her head with both fists. 'No, *no*, I didn't mean that. I just saw that . . . that somebody had died – nothin' to do with me grandmother – I didn't mean that!'

'Are yer talking about the case o' Lady Cecilia Stanley, Miss Court?'

Mabel burst into tears. What had she said? What had she done? The words had been spoken and could never be withdrawn. She'd let it out, given herself away!

'Miss Court, I'm afraid I'll have to take yer back to the station with me for further questioning. Get yer hat an' coat, and pick up yer handbag. I'll leave my bicycle here and we'll walk down together.'

'Oh, my God – my God!' she cried wildly, wringing her hands as her dire situation took shape in her head, with all its implications. Public shame and disgrace loomed much closer now that she had virtually admitted her grandmother's involvement in Lady Stanley's death.

'Ye must try to control yerself, Miss Court, or I'll

have to send for a conveyance. Come along now, the sooner we get to the bottom o' this, the better.'

Somehow or other she managed to take a hold on herself and asked if she might tell Miss Lawton where she was being taken. Unable to face that distracted lady, Mabel scribbled a note and pushed it under her bedroom door. Then, putting on her hat and jacket, she walked with PC Derrick down Rectory Lane to the junction with Mitcham Road known as Amen Corner.

How many times had Mabel cycled past the police station on that corner, wondering what it must be like to be taken through those gloomy portals and charged with an offence, perhaps to be taken down to a police cell overnight? Little had she thought it would ever happen to her, yet here she was at the front desk where Derrick waved her straight past and down the passage, his boots clumping on the stone floor. And now she was being shown into the custody office with barred windows, its dull grey walls bare of any decoration. A whiff of stale pipe smoke hung on the air.

Mabel was told to sit at a large desk opposite a florid-faced, balding police officer who regarded her severely. The single door was closed and locked, and a young constable sat at the side of the desk to record everything she said. It was like being in the grip of a nightmare from which there was no awakening.

Her interrogator introduced himself as Police Sergeant Whittaker. 'Ye're in big trouble, Court,' he told her. 'A very serious crime has been committed and a lady of quality is dead as a result. I'll tell yer now, Court, Sir Percy Stanley's determined that we find the woman responsible for his wife's death and have her committed to prison where she belongs. I shall require yer full co-operation and strongly advise yer to stick to the truth. It'll go against yer if yer try to obstruct the course o' justice. Now, then!'

He rolled out the stock phrases used by policemen, giving them full dramatic emphasis and bringing in the less formal language of a man who liked to see his victims squirm. The questioning now began in earnest, a grilling about Mimi Court's activities as a nurse, whether on the local district or further afield. Mabel was asked if any of her grandmother's patients had come to 23 Macaulay Road for their treatment.

'I believe some of 'em did, but I never had anything to do with those,' she said wretchedly.

'Where in the house did she treat these women?'

'In a back bedroom, but I never saw – it was nothing to do with me.'

'Did anybody assist Mrs Court?'

'There was a domestic, Elsie – I never knew what her surname was.'

'The same woman who accompanied Mrs Court to Bryanston Square?'

'Yes.'

The sergeant fixed her with an accusing eye. 'Let's not mince our words, Court. This grandmother o' yours performed abortions on these women, didn't she?'

Mabel made no reply.

'I require yer to answer me, Court.'

Still no reply. Mabel hung her head in abject misery.

'Did yer assist her in this criminal activity, Court?'

Here Mabel could truthfully protest her innocence. She looked up and met his gimlet eyes. 'No, I did not. Never.'

'So what *did* yer do in that house?'

'I assisted her – Mrs Court – with the maternity cases she had in Tooting. Yer can ask any o' the women I attended in their own homes, I was learnin' to be a midwife so's I could—'

'Just answer the questions, Court, don't try to foist me off with that sort o' stuff.'

At seven o'clock, when Mabel thought she could endure it no longer, the sergeant nodded to his assistant. 'That's as far as we can get with that one. I've got enough evidence to charge her as an accessory to crimes committed by the woman known as Mimi Court, present whereabouts unknown. With something as serious as this—' He glanced towards the defeated figure seated at the desk, head drooping, shoulders bowed. 'Better get the ol' girl over to take charge – the usual care o' females and then down to the cells – better go in number 5.' He looked up at the clock. 'Dunno about you but I reckon it's time for some supper.'

The young constable hesitated and spoke almost apologetically to Mabel. 'There'll be a woman comin' over, er, Miss Court, and she'll look after yer, get yer a cup o' tea and maybe a bite to eat. If yer change yer mind about anything ye've said so far, or want to add somethin', just say so and an officer'll come and take it down, no matter what the time is.' Mabel was silent and he cleared his throat. 'I'm sorry about all this, m'dear, but because o' the circumstances o' this case, the sergeant thinks 'e shouldn't let yer go.'

She turned haggard eyes upon him. 'What'll happen to me in the morning?'

'Ye'll be taken to the Magistrates' Court at Lavender Hill and it'll be up to them to decide.'

'And if my grandmother – if Mrs Court turns up, will I be allowed to go?'

'Ooh, that depends, miss. Yer could both be charged if ye're an accessory.'

A Mrs Cheale came bustling over from Stella Road, complaining that she had just been about to sit down to her supper. She was a big woman in navy-blue with a voluminous white apron and a small white cap, a sort of combined nurse and wardress, sent for to attend to females in custody. She glared at Mabel and was about to march her away when something struck a chord in her memory. She stared hard at her charge. '*What* did they say yer name was – Court? Tell yer what, gal, I knows yer! Yer was there when me friend's daughter 'ad 'er baby at Chris'muss, name o' Brewer, Sally Brewer, an' 'er little boy's doin' ever so well! Spoke very 'ighly o' yer, she did. 'Ooever'd a' thought ye'd land in 'ere? Jus' goes to show, yer never can tell wiv people, can yer? I'd never 'a' believed it if I 'adn't seen yer wiv me own two eyes, oh, my! What've they pulled yer in for, then?'

'I ... I'm supposed to be a ... an accessory,' croaked Mabel, hoping that the woman would not probe further.

'Well, I never did!' exclaimed Mrs Cheale, though her manner became noticeably warmer. ''Ere, come on, gal, I'll take yer dahn to 'ave a wee an' a wash first.'

Mabel's period had started and she needed clean linen strips. Mrs Cheale fussed over her in the lavatory and finally led her down to the cells. Number 5 was like the others, small and gloomy, with a low wooden bed covered with a straw-filled mattress, a small stool and a bucket.

'Take yer shoes off, gal, an' lay dahn in yer clo'es. I'll fetch yer a blanket,' said Mrs Cheale with a sympathetic shake of her head. 'At least it ain't winter – these cells can be perishin'.'

The stone walls still struck a chill into Mabel's heart, even on a July night, and being unventilated it was also stuffy, with smells lingering on the stale air.

'All right then, gal, I'll be in to see yer in the mornin'. Fings'll look a bit better then, I dare say. Night-night!'

Mrs Cheale left, closing the door with a clang and Mabel was alone in a police cell without a friend's voice or hand to comfort her. She sat down on the hard bed. Her brothers and sisters, aunts and uncle knew nothing of her plight, and for this she was thankful, though she would have welcomed the sight of Albert.

Tarred with the same brush.

'If yer could see yer sister now, Albert,' she whispered. How right he had been! Again and again she reproached herself for ever going to live at Macaulay Road. Her mother had never received good at the hands of Mimi Court, and now she herself had been brought down to shame and disgrace through association with dark, unlawful deeds.

These doleful thoughts were interrupted by a sudden commotion, a jangling of keys and the hoarse voices of two women brought in for disturbing the peace with a drunken quarrel. No Mrs Cheale for them: they were pushed unceremoniously into a cell by the night guard, and Mabel's ears were assailed by the sound of retching and coarse mutterings. After a while the noises faded, but the place was never quiet, for at intervals the guard would patrol the cells and peer into each one by the light of the flaring gaslights in the corridor; his heavy footsteps approached and receded, again and again. Mabel did not sleep a wink all night, though the hideous waking dream went on and on, and her thoughts led her down ever darker paths. Surely this could not be happening to her! But it *was*: she had reached her lowest ebb.

Lady Cecilia Stanley was dead. That fact went round and round in her head like a buzzing insect caught in a glass jar. And from there to the Magistrates' Court which she would have to face in the morning – 'up before the beak,' as Albert would have said. And from there to the very worst fate of all, the report of the court proceedings in the *Evening Standard*.

It had been the publishing of Albert's name in the newspaper as a railway striker that had lost her the job at the Anti-Vivisection Hospital. Now her *own* name would appear and in connection with a much more scandalous event. There it would be, in black and white for everybody to read and pass round. Her shame would be public property, known to the neighbours, shopkeepers, Dr Knowles, Mrs James and Miss Carter – and the Booth Street Poor Law infirmary. She pictured the Matron crossing her name off the list of new probationers due to start training on 1 September and she would never be allowed to work as a nurse again. That, surely, was the very worst aspect of this whole horrible business.

And there was somebody else who would be bound to see the newspaper report.

Harry Drover. Yes, he too – and his parents and sister – would read about the depths to which his one-time 'dearest Mabel' had sunk. She uttered a heartbroken low moan at the thought of his horror and disgust: at last he would be free of her and in his disillusionment able to forget her ... which was what she wanted, wasn't it? Oh, but at what a cost!

And yet the thought came to Mabel that if Harry were ever in such a situation as this, confined in a police cell for something he had not done – what would he do? Where would he turn for comfort and strength? She knew the answer: he would pray.

And so would she. Going down on her knees beside the rank-smelling mattress, Mabel could think of no words of her own, only the remembered cry of the Psalmist in his extremity: *Out of the depths have I cried unto thee, O Lord: Lord, hear my voice.*

Chapter Eighteen

The reverberations of Lady Stanley's death spread far and touched many lives, including some who had never even heard of her.

Ruth Lawton lay tossing and turning, her unquiet conscience giving her no rest. She had read the note pushed under her door and when Mabel did not return from the police station Ruth believed that she should go there too and tell what she knew – what she had known for years but had kept secret, held back by a promise extracted from her long ago. Getting out of bed, she paced up and down her small room through the hours of the night, wrestling with her fear and indecision until she truly thought she was losing her reason. And still her courage failed her. 'Coward! Coward!' she muttered in accusation against herself, seeing her whole life as an empty sham, her churchgoing and professed Christian beliefs meaningless; but to unburden herself of the weight of years would mean breaking her side of a bargain by which she and her mother had been saved from destitution. And she feared the woman known as Mimi Court.

So was she going to betray Mabel by keeping quiet and leaving the girl to her fate?

As the summer dawn began to pale the eastern sky, Ruth Lawton did as Mabel had done: she fell on her knees and prayed for deliverance from what she saw as her despicable cowardice. And as she prayed it seemed that her mother was at her side, alive and radiant, with all her faculties restored, sent to bring comfort and good counsel to her unhappy daughter.

Sir Percy Stanley's first reaction had been to bring down vengeance on everybody who had played a part in causing his wife's death. His poor Cecilia had confessed her sins and repented of them all before she died; he had held her lifeless body in his arms and cursed her murderers. He would see to it that Viscount Eastcote was publicly accused and shamed; he would have to leave the country, so great would be his disgrace. The woman Court would be tracked down and charged with manslaughter and the maidservant Ling arraigned as her accomplice. They would both be judged and sentenced to whatever punishment the law considered they deserved. So vowed the betrayed and bereaved husband, keeping vigil beside the body of his wife, still beautiful in the pallor of death.

Then, on the Tuesday evening, he discovered the maidservant Ling whom he had earlier ordered to be thrown out on the street, lying in an agony of grief outside the room in which the body lay; and instead of ordering her to be thrown out again he had found himself weeping beside her.

Whatever lack of principle the girl had shown, whatever foolishness in conniving with his wife to deceive him, her impertinence towards himself, the bare-faced lies she had told – no matter what she had done, there was no doubt of her bitter sorrow now. She was as inconsolable as if she had lost her mother, her sister and her dearest friend.

'Well, my girl, you've learned a terrible lesson and you must leave here tomorrow,' he told her heavily.

397

'There's no further need for a lady's maid in this house of sorrow.'

The maid did not raise her head, but went on crying as if her heart would break. Sir Percy put out a hand and touched her heaving shoulders. 'I can tell you that the police are on to that evil woman and it's only a matter of time before they catch her,' he said. 'They've already arrested an assistant of hers, another woman called Court, probably her daughter, and engaged in the same disgusting business.' He shuddered. 'Such women ought to be hanged.' He turned away and left her lying outside his wife's silent room. And it was at that moment that he changed his mind.

Nothing could bring his lovely Cecilia back again, and he now saw his prime duty as being to safeguard her good name and keep it untarnished by scandal. He would therefore drop the charges against the woman Court. The police now knew what her game was and would keep a watch on her in future; she would not be likely to practise her evil trade again. And as for Eastcote, let his conscience, if he had one, be his scourge and let the wretched maidservant Ling be discharged without a character, taking her misery with her.

Sir Percy went to his lonely room and the maid suddenly stopped crying as she realised what he had just said.

Maudie did not care what happened to her now that her beloved lady was gone. Charlie had been scared stiff by the catastrophe and had stayed well away from her: so much for men, she thought, at the first sign of trouble the bastards always took care of their own skins.

But Mabel, her old friend – that was a different

matter. If Mabel had landed in Queer Street because of this, something must be done to get her out of it. But what? In the circumstances Maudie wanted to keep away from the police and police stations, and to reveal their friendship would do Mabel no favours, quite the opposite. She thought hard. Whom did she know among her acquaintance who would go to Mabel's aid if asked? Somebody who loved her and would do anything for her? Somebody thoroughly trustworthy . . .

Maud Ling got to her feet, and put on her cloak and hat. It was almost ten o'clock and darkness was falling over the city.

After a slow start Mrs Betts's labour progressed painfully but steadily and a baby boy was delivered soon after midnight, to the relief of his parents and grandmother, not to mention the midwife. Mr Betts opened a bottle of home-made parsley wine and Mrs Taylor downed two glasses before she realised how potent it was. Worn out after her exertions, the midwife decided not to go home but to spend the night in an armchair in the Bettses' living room, to be on hand in case of problems, she said. 'She might 'ave a bleed in the night, or the baby might choke,' she told an alarmed Mr Betts. 'I'd rather stay 'ere in case I'm needed, y'see, I'm not a one to take chances, not like some I could mention.' Saying which she fell deeply asleep in the chair and snored loudly until morning, when the neighbours came in to offer their congratulations and to share the incredible news that was on everybody's lips.

"Ave yer 'eard the latest, Mrs Taylor? About them Courts?'

'No, what?' The midwife shook her head to clear

it, her ears immediately alert. "As that ol' toe-rag turned up at last?'

'No, an' she ain't likely to, neither. There's a big scandal on, summat really *bad*, yer know' – the speaker tapped the side of her nose – 'up the West End. The ol' girl's done a runner!'

Mrs Taylor's puffy eyes popped. 'No! Yer mean – ooh! I've always known she was up to no good, the way she visited women out o' the district. So sommat's gorn wrong, 'as it?'

'Not 'alf – the woman's dead, an' she was a ladyship an' all.'

'*Never*!' Mrs Taylor goggled.

'Yeah, she went Sunday night, it's in the papers.'

'An' what d'ye think,' added another woman, 'that poor Nurse Court, the granddaughter, she's bin taken down to the police station and locked up!'

Mrs Taylor's jaw dropped. 'Good Gawd! When?'

'Been in the nick all night, she 'as.'

Mrs Taylor was already putting on her hat and the navy coat she wore summer and winter for going out on her rounds. 'Down the station, eh? D'yer mean Amen Corner?'

'That's it, missus.'

'I'm on me way. I'll go down there an' tell them daft coppers they got the wrong one. Poor little thing, she ain't a bad gal, it's a cryin' shame!'

Mrs Taylor's eyes gleamed at the pleasing prospect of doing a public service and getting a good story out of it at the same time. She'd show that old scumbag up for what she was!

It had taken Maud Ling half the night to run Harry Drover to earth. She had first gone to Battersea, alarming his parents by appearing on the doorstep of

8 Falcon Terrace, and then she'd had to make her way on foot to Clapton in the north-east and enquire of some rather seedy looking characters where she would find the Salvation Army College. When she got there it took all her tears and pleadings to have young Mr Drover woken up and brought to the office at such an hour.

As soon as he saw her, Harry knew that he was being summoned on the Lord's business, though at first he questioned Maud as to whether Mabel herself had sent for him. 'She wanted nothin' more to do with me, Miss Ling,' he said seriously. 'She made it absolutely clear that our friendship was over. Yer heard what she said to me at the Hodgeses' weddin' – and yer could tell she meant it. I can't force meself on her if she don't want me.'

Maud's own personal grief, her weariness and lack of sustenance had brought her to the limits of her endurance. She lost her temper with Drover. 'For Christ's sake, ain't yer got no sense at *all*?' she shouted at him. 'Or are yer goin' to be a bloody fool all yer life? Your poor Mabel's in a bad way, couldn't be worse, locked up in a police cell for doin' summat she never done – so shift yer arse over to Tootin' an' *do* somethin' for a gal 'oo's always loved yer, yer stupid ape!'

'But yer heard her *say* it, Miss Ling, she never wanted to see me again,' he protested.

Maud almost shrieked, 'Can't yer see she was *ashamed*? She was ashamed o' so many fings, Mabel was. First 'er poor muvver drahns 'erself 'cause she got the pox – yes, the *pox*, 'Arry,' she affirmed, seeing his shocked reaction. 'An' Mabel 'ad to 'ave 'er own blood tested for it, just fink o' *that*, an innocent gal like 'er. An' the farver must've 'ad it as well, the dirty bugger, an' *somebody* must've given 'im a push dahn them stairs, that's why poor little George 'ad to be shunted orf to Canada pretty sharpish to stop 'im tellin' what 'e knew. Only Gawd knows what Mabel's bin frough!'

'Oh, Miss Ling – oh, Maudie, are yer *sure* o' this?' gasped Harry, white-faced.

"Course I am, an' that ain't all – she's banged up now in a police cell for killin' my poor lady, when all the time it was 'er wicked ol' grandmuvver did it, made a pig's ear of it – and now there's me lady layin' dead – oh, me lady, me poor, dear lady, oh, *Gawd*!'

Maud had collapsed in a fresh storm of sobs and had been despatched to a women's shelter, while Harry, who had already hastily dressed, grabbed what little money he had with him and rushed out to the nearest Underground station which took him to Victoria. From here he got the first steam train out to Tooting Junction.

His mind reeling under the series of shocks that Maud Ling had thrown at him, Harry Drover nevertheless began to understand many circumstances that had previously been unexplained, particularly the apparent inconsistencies in Mabel's behaviour. It was after the death of her father that she had turned away from him and he now realised that it must have been the time when she had made the discovery of her parents' syphilis. And the reason for the sudden despatching of poor George to Canada now appeared all too obvious. Why on earth had he not been more sensitive, more discerning of the agony that both Mabel and Albert had suffered on account of George? He now remembered the pain in Albert's eyes at their last meeting when George was mentioned, and the edge to his voice when speaking of the parents' deaths – because of that horrible affliction that had driven Annie to end her life. Harry stifled a groan as he sat in the train, thinking of Mabel's lonely shame – and having to undergo a blood test for such a disease, his own sweet, innocent girl . . . and oh, he should have realised, he should have *guessed* that Jack Court's death had been more than an unfortunate accident.

Oh, Mabel, Mabel, forgive me, I've been a blind, stupid fool . . .

And now some lady was lying dead because of what Mabel's grandmother had done to her. Harry pictured Mimi Court on the day that he had accompanied Mabel to see her and recalled some of the things she had said. And not said. He had felt a peculiar revulsion towards her at the time, which he was sure Mabel shared.

Then it all fell into place and he understood. He knew. She was an abortionist. No wonder Albert had been unhappy about Mabel living in her house, under her domination.

Other passengers might have noticed Drover's pale face and the grim set of his mouth on that early morning journey. Yet as he drew near to his destination they might also have observed a softening of his features, a new light in his eyes. Apprehensive he might be, but there was something else: something more than anger, more than pity, more even than his determination to save the girl he loved; something that was almost akin to joy . . .

Mabel had no idea what time it was, only that a new day had begun. From the other cells came sounds of coughing, groaning and buckets being put to use.

The early July sun filtered through grimy high windows overlooking a basement area, and the gaslights were turned off. The ever-present jangling of keys was heard and more footsteps echoing along stone floors. From the outside world came the noise of bakers' vans and milk carts getting ready to go out on their rounds.

Upstairs at the front desk there was some sort of altercation going on between the duty officer, Sergeant Wragge, and a man demanding access to one of the women in custody, though it was too far away for Mabel to hear. In the end some sort of an agreement was reached and two pairs of footsteps made their way down to the cells. Mabel was crouched disconsolately on her mattress when she heard them approaching and bowed her head so as to hide her face from whoever might be passing the cell.

But the footsteps stopped at her door and the guard took out his key to unlock it. Had they come already to take her to the Magistrates' Court? What a sight she must look! She had not had a wash, her hair was uncombed, her clothes were creased and she felt nauseated, with an itching scalp and foul breath. She was at her very worst.

'Court? Are yer awake? Yer got a visitor.'

She heaved herself to her feet, shrinking back involuntarily from facing yet another figure of authority.

A quiet, gentle voice spoke her name: 'Mabel.'

Harry Drover's voice. But he couldn't be here, he was at Clapton College doing his training to be a full-time Salvation Army officer.

Yet the voice went on speaking: 'Dearest Mabel,

it's me, Harry. I been sent to yer. Will yer look at me, Mabel?'

Slowly as if in a dream – because this had to be a dream – she raised her head a little way. The dark uniform was a blur before her eyes. She felt her hand being taken and held.

'I'll leave yer with her, then, five minutes, all right?' said the guard, and she heard the door being relocked and the man's retreating steps.

But she was no longer alone in the cell. A familiar steadying hand supported her as she swayed slightly, and when she raised her head she saw her love standing before her, real and substantial, his brown eyes alight with joy at the sight of her. 'Harry,' she whispered. 'Is it really, really you, Harry?'

'Yes, yes, Mabel, it's me. Don't be afraid, dearest girl, give me yer hands to hold – oh, ye're so cold. God bless yer, me own dear Mabel, I'm that happy to set eyes on yer again!' His words trailed off with a sound that was halfway between a laugh and a sob.

She leaned towards him and he caught her in his arms. She felt the rough material of his jacket against her cheek and the warmth of his body enveloping her, reviving her drooping spirits, giving back hope, bringing life and love to her broken heart. This was no dream; this was her Harry indeed! 'I've been prayin',' she whispered. 'The Lord must've sent an angel to fetch yer.'

'Yes, Mabel, He did,' he told her quietly, for though the angel's message had been couched in very unbiblical language, he knew he would remain forever in debt to Maud Ling who had faced difficulty and danger to get to him. 'I been sent to yer, Mabel, and I shan't let yer send me away again, not ever.'

She clung to him blindly, instinctively, asking no more questions but only giving thanks for this miraculous change from darkest despair to joyous reunion with the man she loved. There would be time enough for explanations later; her prayer from the depths had been answered, a lifeline had been thrown to her and she held on to it with all her might.

As for Harry Drover, no words could describe his happiness. Just to hold her, to feel her living, breathing body close to him again after their long estrangement during which his love had never faltered, turned Amen Corner into a paradise. Here, in this gloomy cell, within sound and smell of fallen humanity all around them, his heart rejoiced and he thanked the Lord he served, happier than he had ever been since he and Mabel had first shyly declared their love. 'Ye're trembling, Mabel, let's sit down. Here, I'll take the stool and you sit on the bed and lean up against my shoulder.'

She obeyed and kneeling up on the lumpy mattress she laid her head on his shoulder, encircled in his right arm. Closing her eyes, she savoured the incredible fact of being together again, oblivious to all else.

When the guard came to fetch Harry, neither of them noticed him, and he stood regarding them for a minute before giving a shrug and walking away. The five minutes lengthened to fifteen before he returned. 'Time's up, I'm afraid, and Mrs Cheale's here to see to, er, Miss Court.'

'Don't worry, Mabel, I'll be waitin' for yer nearby.

I'll come to the Magistrates' Court with yer,' Harry assured her as he left.

Mrs Cheale raised her eyebrows. 'Got a good 'un there, gal, I'd 'ang on to 'im if I was you. Just the sight of a Sally Army uniform should do the trick an' get yer orf.' As she bustled around, she told Mabel that a strange woman was at the duty desk upstairs. 'Brought 'erself in, poor ol' soul, askin' to go in a cell. A case for Springfield Asylum if ever I saw one. Yer see all sorts 'ere, I'll tell yer!'

Presently the constable on duty with Sergeant Wragge came down to speak to Mabel. He looked rather amused. 'We got this old lady in, a Miss Lawton, lodges with yer grandmother and wants to see yer. Says she's got somethin' important to say, though she could be ravin'. Sergeant Wragge says ye're to come up to the custody office an' let her tell yer, only we'll sit in on it, right?'

'Miss Lawton!' cried Mabel. 'But she was questioned by a policeman yesterday and said—' She broke off, wondering if all the upheaval and anxiety had turned poor Ruth's brain. 'Can Mr Drover sit in on it, too?' she asked as she followed the constable upstairs. 'He's very good with people in distress.'

'Oh, I don't know about that, miss,' came the reply, but in fact Harry's uniform gained him admission under Wragge's watchful eye, provided that he stationed himself against the wall and kept silent.

With her black coat unbuttoned and her black silk hat set at a rakish angle on straggling grey hair, poor Miss Lawton made Mabel think of a bedraggled old bird. Eyes darting, she backed away when Mabel approached her. 'No, no, Mabel, I've found my courage and I've come to tell the truth!' she shrilled. Turning to the sergeant, she went on, 'This young woman is innocent, officer, completely innocent! She had *nothing* to do with Lady Stanley's death, nor any of the other clients who came to my sister for her services. *I've* known what went on, I've known for over thirty years, but Mabel had nothing to do with any of them, nothing at all!'

Mabel paled and did not dare to look at Harry. What was he about to hear?

'Just a minute, Miss Lawton, did yer say yer *sister*?' asked Wragge. 'D'ye mean Mrs Court, the missing person?'

'Yes, but she's not Mrs Court, she's Miss Prudence Lawton, my younger sister and I've never told a soul all these years. I promised I wouldn't, but not any more. No more! No longer!' Her eyes glittered as she looked around at the two policemen and Mabel, and in spite of her bizarre appearance there was a certain strength of purpose in her manner that Mabel had never seen before. Likewise her speech flowed freely: gone was the nervous stammer, the constant fidgeting with her hands. 'I owe it to Mabel, don't you see?' she continued. 'If anybody should be in a cell, let it be me! Oh, Mabel, I'm your aunt, your great-aunt, and you're my niece, and I've never been able to say it – to be what I am to you – please forgive me!'

She covered her face with her hands, and Mabel rose at once and went to her side. 'There now, Ruth – Aunt Ruth – don't cry,' she murmured, though feeling utterly bewildered. 'I ... I'm glad ye're my aunt, y'see, I've always wanted to be closer to yer.'

Another aunt she hadn't known she had – and Mimi not Mimi, but ... *who*?

'So yer sister's real name is Prudence Lawton, is that right?' asked the sergeant, writing in his note-book. 'Did yer say Court was her married name, then?'

'Oh, no, officer, she took the name Court after she had the boy, her son Jack. They were very good to her, the Masood family, and bought the house on Macaulay Road for her to bring up the child. The midwife who delivered Prudence took her on as an assistant and taught her midwifery – just as she's taught *you*, Mabel. They worked together for a short while, until Prudence started taking special clients – that was about the time that she took in our poor mother and me when we were without means. We were practically starving.'

Mabel trembled. The story which the police sergeant clearly found incomprehensible began to make sense to her. 'Yer mother, Ruth,' she said softly. 'Was she the old lady that my mother knew?'

'Yes, Mabel, that was my poor dear mother and your great-grandmother. A sweet and gentle soul who endured great humiliation all her life. Our father was a country clergyman, you see, and we grew up in a small village in Essex. But he was not – well, he was not what he should have been and there was trouble with a young woman, more than one, in fact, and it became a scandal. He had to leave the parish overnight and our mother was left with us two girls, quite penniless. We had to leave our home and go into lodgings. Prudence hated it and went off to London, and I stayed with mother. I made a little money with piano lessons, but mother never recov-ered, it was the strain, you see, her faculties deserted her and we had to move on from one place to another until there was nowhere else to go. We would've had to go to the workhouse if an old acquaintance hadn't told us about Prudence, known as Mrs Court and living as a widow with her son. She thought she'd left her old life behind and she wasn't pleased to see us when we turned up at Macaulay Road – but she took us in and kept us, only I had to promise never to say who we were. Thank God – oh, thank God that mother never knew how Prudence supported us all, though *I* knew, I *always* knew and never said a word. Jack never knew that I was his aunt, nor that my poor mother – *our* mother – was his own grandmother. We lived on sufferance all that time – my lips were sealed, you see.'

She paused and looked up pleadingly. It was the longest speech that Mabel had ever heard her make; usually she could barely string two sentences together.

It was at this moment that she caught sight of Harry and, disobeying the sergeant he stepped forward, placing his hands on her shoulders. 'Ye've been a dutiful daughter, Miss Lawton. What yer sister did was no responsibility o' yours, so don't blame yerself for it.'

'Mr Drover! You've come back to Mabel – and you know she's innocent, don't you?'

He nodded. 'Yes, Miss Lawton, I know.'

Sergeant Wragge was quite bemused and Mabel could only look on in astonishment. How did Harry know what Mrs Court did and why wasn't he thoroughly horrified by it? Or had he misunderstood?

Evidently not, because Miss Lawton went on confidingly, 'All those women who came to the house, and those Prudence went to visit in their own

410

homes – I knew about every single one, Mr Drover, and I used to pray for them. And do you know, Prudence never lost one, not until now. But Mabel had nothing to do with them.'

'Nothin' to do with these – abortions, yer mean?' asked Sergeant Wragge point-blank, thinking it was time he asserted his authority and made it clear what they were talking about.

Mabel winced, but Ruth answered him at once. 'Absolutely nothing, officer, I swear. She looked after the maternity cases in Tooting. Prudence never took on local women in trouble – her special clients paid her a hundred pounds, that's how she made her money. They were much wealthier than the ones Mabel attended.'

Mabel simply could not believe her ears. To hear the unmentionable openly talked about in a police custody office and Harry of all people listening – it was incredible.

And more incredible revelations were to come. Sergeant Wragge's curiosity had been aroused by what he had heard. 'This son of hers, Miss Lawton, this Jack Court,' he cut in. 'Didn't he get killed last year in an accident? Fell downstairs an' broke his skull if I remember. Was he her only, er, child?'

'That's right, officer, Prudence was barely twenty when Jack was born. His father was a gentleman, the son of a high official in the Indian Civil Service, received at Queen Victoria's court. The boy had been brought over to be educated in England when he met Prudence.'

The two policemen exchanged a grin and Mabel recalled the scene outside the coroner's court when Mimi had angrily rounded on Albert and told him that Jack's father had been a *prince among men*. An

Indian prince? She could just hear Albert laughing his head off at the very idea. Yet it would account for his swarthy appearance and Alice's and Daisy's dark-eyed beauty.

Ruth Lawton's shoulders suddenly drooped. She seemed drained of all energy and her face was grey with exhaustion. Wragge must have noticed too, for he closed his notebook and advised her to go home and rest.

'Home? I'll be moving into the Tooting Home from now on, officer – Prudence won't want me at 23 Macaulay Road after this. And do you know, I don't mind at all. I'm free for the first time in years. Free as air!' She beamed a seraphic smile upon them all.

'Take her down to the waiting room and get her a cup o' tea,' Wragge told the constable, standing up and looking embarrassed about returning Mabel to her cell. 'Though I dare say ye'll get off on account o' the lack of evidence against yer, miss, an' havin' the, er, captain as a character witness,' he added, assigning Drover a rank he had not yet attained. He stifled a yawn: it was time for Sergeant Whittaker to take over on the day shift.

They never saw the arrival of Mrs Taylor at the front desk, demanding to see Mabel and informing the constable that they had taken in the wrong Court.

'Yer can't see nobody,' he told her. 'There's been enough busybodies in an' out o' here already, it gets more like the Elephant an' Castle by the minute. Tell yer what, though, missus, yer can take that poor ol' lady 'ome.' He gestured to where Miss Lawton sat on a form, smiling dreamily to herself.

'What? Indeed I'll do no such thing! What a cheek, treatin' me as if I was no better than ol' Mother

412

Cheale!' spluttered the indignant midwife, sending
forth a spray of tiny drops of spit. She looked Miss
Lawton up and down. 'The poor ol' soul looks three
'alfpence short o' tuppence, anyway.' She stared
harder. ''Ere, I know where I've seen 'er. Don't she
lodge with that Court woman 'oo's 'opped it? Yeah,
that's 'er, name o' Lawton. Plays the pianna for the
ol' paupers in the Tootin' 'ome.'

'And Mrs Court's sister, so she says. If ye'd be
good enough to take her home, she'll tell yer the 'ole
story,' said the constable artfully.

'What? Oh, I see – well, all right, then, in that case.
I'm always ready to do anybody a good turn.' She
walked over to the old lady in sudden goodwill.
'You jus' come along o' me, dearie, an' I'll soon get
yer home. Well, I never!'

The officer from Lavender Hill station hardly
noticed the two women as he strode into the station
with new information. 'All right, Whittaker, yer can
let her go. The ol' man's called it off.'

When Mabel was once again let out of the cell and
taken upstairs to the office, she could scarcely take in
what was being said to her.

Harry, on the other hand, could hardly contain his
joyful relief. 'Ye're free, Mabel, ye're *free*, praise the
Lord!' he cried, impervious to Whittaker's angry
glare.

'B-but what about the magistrate?' faltered Mabel,
clinging to the edge of the desk as her knees turned
to water.

Disapproval was written all over Whittaker's surly
features as he reeled off the formalities of discharge
from police custody. 'I jus' *told* yer, Court, the case is
orf, all charges withdrawn, an' yer can go.'

'Doesn't Miss Court get any kind of apology for

413

bein' detained in a filthy cell for twelve hours?' demanded Harry.

'Why?' snorted Whittaker. 'Jus' 'cause the charges are dropped don't mean the crime ain't been committed. Lady Stanley's as dead as she was before, but 'er 'usband's pretendin' she died o' natural causes, so's to save a scandal. Not that everybody won't guess it was an abortion. Well, go on, then, I've signed yer discharge, what're yer waitin' for?'

But Mabel neither heard nor saw him. A buzzing in her ears drowned out all other sounds and a web of wavy black lines criss-crossed her vision, getting darker and thicker, blotting out the light.

Harry caught her in his arms as she fell.

Chapter Nineteen

'How're yer feelin' now, dearest? Fancy a cup o' tea or somethin'?'

Mabel opened her eyes and at first had the extraordinary sensation of being in bed with Harry beside her, but as she returned to full consciousness she found that she had been fast asleep on the sofa in Mimi Court's front parlour.

It was now midday and Harry was bending over her, his brown eyes full of tender concern. 'There's been a lot o' callers, Mabel, but I wouldn't let any of 'em disturb yer. There was a Mrs Hollis who left a note – here it is – she says yer can go an' stay with her if yer haven't anywhere to go, but—'

'Who? Oh ... oh yes, Mrs Hollis,' said Mabel, recalling the dawn birth in Furzedown Road. 'My little Anna Mabel's nearly a year old already.' She smiled. 'Mm-mm – that was a lovely sleep, Harry.' She yawned and stretched, unable to remember ever feeling so warm and safe and cherished, not since her earliest childhood and the shelter of her mother's arms. 'Where's Miss La—Aunt Ruth?' she asked, looking around.

'Packin' her clothes ready to go to the Tootin' Home. The vicar o' St Nicholas's church has put in a word for her and the Matron's got a place for her today.'

'*Today*? But the Tooting Home's a—'

'It's not a workhouse, but a place of refuge for the

415

aged poor of the parish, Mabel,' said Miss Lawton, coming into the room at that moment. She was pale and there were dark circles under her eyes, but her manner was composed, with just a little hint of anticipation. 'It will suit me very well, Mabel, and I've already met quite a few of the elderly folk through my musical afternoons there,' she continued. 'Prudence often said I'd end up in a private asylum at her expense, but she won't have to pay a penny to the Tooting Home.' She paused and added with a self-conscious little blush, 'As a matter of fact, the Matron says I'm just the sort of resident she prefers.'

'I'm sure you are, Aunt Ruth – but are yer *certain* ye'd be happy in there with all those poor old men and women?' asked Mabel doubtfully.

Ruth Lawton stood and regarded her niece with a smile of pure contentment. 'Much, much happier that I've ever been here, my dear. I shall be *free*, you see!'

'Will yer get a cab to take yer belongin's?'

'Yes, Mr Drover has kindly arranged one for three o'clock and says he'll come down with me,' replied the lady. 'And if you'll excuse me, Mabel, I'd better go and finish packing.'

When she had gone upstairs Harry turned to Mabel with a serious look. 'And what about *you*, Mabel dear? Yer know yer can't stay another night under this roof, not after what's happened.'

'I know, I know – I shouldn't've come here in the first place, it was just that – there was nowhere else for me to go, not after George had left.'

'Yer should've come to *me*, Mabel. I'd've found yer respectable lodgin's with a Salvation Army couple; I'd've helped yer, stood by yer, looked after yer – 'stead o' which yer ran away from me an' made us

416

both unhappy, refusin' to see me or answer me letters.'

There was a reproach, almost a sternness in his voice that made Mabel look up sharply, half afraid of what she might see; but there was only pity in his eyes.

For a while she sat in silence. There were things that had to be said, she knew, but how to begin? 'How did Maudie get to hear where I was, Harry? An' how did she find yer to let yer know?'

'She said somethin' about Sir Percy Stanley tellin' her about the trouble yer were in, an' then she spent half the night searchin' for me,' he answered gravely. 'Poor Maud, she's in bad enough trouble herself, now that her lady's gone. I'll be in her debt for life, an' if I can do anythin' to help her, I will.'

Mabel tried to picture the scene between him and Maudie: what her friend had told him about Lady Stanley – and Mimi Court. 'So that was how yer knew what Miss Lawton was talkin' about this mornin' at the station,' she said tentatively, fearing the answer.

He hesitated for a moment, as if debating within himself what he should reply. Placing his arm firmly round her shoulders he began to speak slowly and tenderly. 'Yes, Mabel, my dear, Maud told me about yer grandmother's business an' it tied up with what Albert hinted at when he came over to see me at Clapton in May.'

Mabel trembled. 'What *did* Albert tell yer then, Harry?'

'He gave me reason not to give up hope, Mabel. He didn't say it in so many words, but he ... he encouraged me to look ahead to some time in the future. An' he also said ye'd gone for an interview at Booth Street Poor Law infirmary.'

'Oh, yes, I start me trainin' on the first o' September,' she answered eagerly. 'That's only six weeks away, an' I thought I could stay here at Macaulay Road till then.'

'But yer were wrong, Mabel, weren't yer?' he pointed out. 'Look where it got yer! If the charges hadn't been dropped, ye'd've lost yer place at Booth Street *and* yer reputation as a nurse.'

Tarred with the same brush. The words came back to Mabel with sinister force. She sat up, jerking herself away from his arm. 'Oh, Albert was right, he was right! He said I'd made a big mistake, comin' here to live.'

'Yer made an even bigger mistake in turnin' away from *me*, Mabel,' said Harry soberly. 'If I'd only known what I know now – what Maud told me o' the troubles in yer family – I wouldn't've let yer keep me away. An' I won't ever let yer send me away again. We *love* each other, Mabel, we belong together, we have to share whatever befalls either of us, however long we have to wait to get married – can't yer *see* that?'

Mabel closed her eyes and let herself sink back against his shoulder. If he only knew all! 'An' yer don't believe I had anythin' to do with . . . with Lady Stanley or any o' my grandmother's special clients?' she whispered.

''Course not! What Mrs Court did for money was very wrong – wicked, in fact, destroyin' unborn children an' puttin' women's lives at risk, but it isn't for me to judge her or the women who went to her. *I* can't imagine what it must be like to be a poor girl in a desperate predicament. But o' *course* I know ye're innocent, Mabel, I didn't need Miss Lawton to tell me that. An' in just the same way—' He stopped speaking and put both arms around her before continuing in a low voice, 'An' in just the same way, dearest Mabel, yer weren't to blame for the trouble that came upon yer parents – the infection—'

Mabel stiffened in his arms and uttered an involuntary cry: '*No!*'

'Hush, my love. It was yer poor father's sin, not yer mother's or yours. And nor could yer help the way yer father died, however it was – whatever it was that poor George knew.'

'*Harry!*'

Mabel could not believe what she was hearing. All the secrets, all the hateful facts that had separated her from the man she loved, now being spoken openly and by Harry himself – and without any condemnation of those concerned, only sorrow and pity for all of them: Annie, Jack, Albert, George and herself. What sort of a man was this? Albert had teased him in the past, laughing at 'ol' 'Oly 'Arry, blowin' 'is trombone' – but Albert had known his true worth and appreciated him in a way that perhaps she had not. Not until now.

She tried to turn round in his arms to face him, but he thought she was trying to wriggle free from him, so tightened his hold. 'Oh, no, Mabel, I shan't ever let yer go again!'

'But . . . but aren't yer *shocked,* aren't yer *disgusted* by all ye've heard? Doesn't it make yer ashamed o' me?' she asked in genuine astonishment.

'What d'ye take me for, Mabel? It's made me *sad,* especially for your sake, but don't forget I'm a Salvation Army man and there i'n't much o' life we don't see. The only thing I hold against yer is the way yer treated us both, keepin' me away so's I couldn't share yer trouble. Though I was a fool not to 'ave understood better 'n I did,' he added with a little deprecating grimace. 'Oh, Mabel, Mabel!'

He relaxed his grip on her sufficiently to let her look into his face, at which she burst into tears, burying her face against his neck and the rough material of his tunic. 'I only – did it – for – for yer own good!' The words were almost hiccuped out between sobs.

'Oh, my own poor, silly Mabel,' he murmured, cradling her head as if soothing a child. 'My own beautiful girl, when I think o' what ye've had to bear o' the wrongs an' weaknesses of others, and you as pure an' innocent a lamb as ever was!'

She went on weeping, but there was a kind of blessed relief in the unrestrained flow of tears. Stroking her hair, his lips brushing the fair tendrils sticking to her forehead, he went on speaking softly as she quietened: 'But what's so wonderful to me is that it hasn't *touched* yer, Mabel, ye've been a light in the darkness o' this world – at Sorrel Street, at the Rescue, an' even here under yer grandmother's roof.' He smiled as a memory returned. 'D'ye know what I used to do, all this long time we've been apart? I've looked up at the night sky an' seen yer lovely face shinin' down on me like an angel. Yer can laugh if yer like, Mabel, but that's how I've always thought o' yer, time an' time again, when I was starvin' for a sight o' yer, an' yer wouldn't let me near. I've never stopped hopin' an' prayin', never stopped lovin' yer, Mabel, an' never will. An' now ye're in my arms again, real and livin', I'll never, ever let yer keep me away any more!'

As he stopped speaking she lifted her head and no

more words were needed. With the tears still wet on her cheeks Mabel yielded her mouth to his ardent kiss: a kiss that swept away all the misery of the past year, all her misapprehensions on a healing tide of love. Her arms went up around his neck and her hands locked behind his head, holding on, clinging to what she held most dear.

In that moment Harry Drover thought he need never again fear to lose Mabel. She was his for as long as they both lived.

Everybody seemed to have heard about Nurse Court's night in police custody, and anger against Mrs Court was loud and indignant. Gifts of money and food had arrived for Mabel, and offers of hospitality; she eagerly read the note from Mrs Hollis of Furzedown Road, offering her a room for as long as she needed accommodation.

It gradually became clear that the general condemnation of Mimi Court was more for abandoning Mabel rather than for her part in Lady Stanley's death.

'She's bin goin' to them society women for years an' chargin' 'em 'undreds, yet she wouldn't do nothin' to 'elp out that poor soul from Collier's Wood 'oo went an' poisoned 'erself,' declared Mrs Taylor. 'She could've at least sent 'er to ol' Dimmock on the Broadway – not that *I'd* ever recommend 'im,' she added hastily.

After Ruth Lawton had left for the Tooting Home, Harry returned to the subject that currently occupied his mind. 'So what are yer goin' to do, Mabel? Yer can't stay another night under this roof, 'cause I won't let yer,' he repeated firmly.

'I'll go down to Belhampton and see me aunts and

sisters,' she replied. 'Aunt Kate says she'll always keep a room for me at Pinehurst, and besides I want to see how Daisy's settlin'.'

Harry's face fell slightly. He had been going to suggest that she stayed with his parents in Battersea. Belhampton was thirty-five miles away and was a world he knew nothing about. 'Yer mean ye'll travel down there this evenin'?'

'Oh, no! I'll accept this invitation from the Hollises for two or three nights – that'll give me time to write to Aunt Kate. And I can go to see Aunt Ruth in the Tooting Home, to make sure she's happy there an' got everythin' she needs.' She frowned. 'The maids'll want payin' by the end o' the month, but I s'pose my grandmother'll turn up when she hears that the charges've been dropped, and—'

'And when that woman comes back ye're not to be here, Mabel. How many more times must I tell yer? If ye're goin' to stay with the Hollises, pack yer bags *now* an' I'll come down to Furzedown Road with yer, so's I can see for meself what sort o' people they are.' He spoke in a terse, proprietory tone that Mabel had not heard before.

'Er, all right, Harry, but there's really no need,' she said with a little shrug, surprised to discover how sweet it was to take orders from a man in authority.

Standing in spacious grounds and crowned with its clock tower, the Tooting Home for the Aged Poor was an impressive local landmark. Originally built as a college, it had been purchased at the turn of the century by the Wandsworth Board of Guardians to be a model home for deserving elderly people in distressed circumstances.

'And d'ye think yer made the right decision, Aunt Ruth? Do they treat yer well? An' feed yer?'

'Oh, Mabel, if you only knew how my life has changed! – the difference it's made to me!'

And indeed, Miss Lawton's whole appearance was evidence enough of her improved status. Mabel could understand why the Matron had been willing to secure a short-cut admission for a lady who was the ideal type of resident for the Tooting Home. Just as in spite of her odd black clothes and eccentric behaviour Miss Lawton had imparted an air of respectability to 23 Macaulay Road, which her sister had conspicuously lacked, so now her neatness of dress and gentle demeanour proclaimed a certain social standing. For the first time in her life Ruth Lawton found herself looked up to and extolled as an example to be followed.

'Matron says she's thankful to have a reliable pianist to accompany the morning and evening prayers,' she told Mabel with a shy smile. 'And some of the dear old people would have me playing for them morning and afternoon, every day!'

'Mind they don't take advantage o' yer, Aunt Ruth. Oh, I'm that *pleased* to see yer lookin' so well!' And aunt and niece exchanged a hug.

'And I'm just as pleased for *you*, Mabel dear, to know that Mr Drover's come back to you, such a fine young man in every way. He really loves you, Mabel – he deserves you.'

'I don't know if I deserve *him*, though, Aunt Ruth, but I'm really goin' to try to make him happy from now on.'

'Is he still in Tooting?'

'Oh, no, he's had to go back to college, but we're goin' to try to write to each other every day. I'm stayin' with the Hollises, whose little girl I delivered last year. But now I know that ye're all right here, I'll go to Belhampton for a week or two.'

Ruth Lawton nodded understandingly. 'Yes, you'll be wanting to see how little Daisy's getting on this time. Do give her my love, won't you?'

"Course I will. Oh, Aunt Ruth, we've been through a bad time, and poor Lady Stanley's dead – but things've worked out well for you an' me, haven't they?'

'Yes, Mabel, God's been very good to us.' And they hugged again, knowing that in escaping from the shadows of Macaulay Road they had both regained their self-esteem.

Aunt Kate answered Mabel's letter by return of post, extending a cordial invitation to stay at Pinehurst for as long as she pleased. It was therefore arranged that Mabel would stay until 29 August and return to the Hollises for three nights before commencing her training.

On the day before she left for Belhampton, Tooting gossip was humming with the news that Mrs Court had returned to her home in Macaulay Road with Elsie and was intent on discovering Mabel's whereabouts. 'But nobody'll tell the ol' witch where y'are, gal,' Mrs Taylor assured Mabel. 'In fact, nobody'll tell 'er nuffin' at all – she's been sent to Coventry, she 'as, an' serve 'er bloody well right!'

Mabel gave a shiver. She was not yet ready to face her grandmother and so told the highly delighted Mrs Taylor to let Mrs Court know that her grand-daughter had gone to her mother's relations at Belhampton.

'I'll tell 'er, Mabel, yer can rely on me – but not 'til after ye've boarded the train.'

'Mabel, Mabel!' Daisy ran forward to greet her sister as she stepped down from the train and Mabel's heart contracted as she held out her arms to gather up the excited little girl. Daisy seemed to have grown in two months, and was pink-cheeked and sun-tanned. She looked a picture in her frilly summer dress and sun bonnet, and was accompanied by Aunt Kate who explained that Alice was having a riding lesson at the Paddocks, so had been unable to come to the station. A manservant took Mabel's suitcase and the three of them walked up the leafy lane to Pinehurst where Aunt Nell had come over from Pear Tree Cottage to welcome her niece.

'You're in time for the summer fête on Saturday, Mabel!' Daisy told her. 'They're putting up coconut shies, an' the Paddocks are sending ponies to give rides. Aunt Nell's been baking lots of cakes, an' Lucy Drummond's brother's giving a Punch an' Judy show!'

Aunt Kate gently shushed her. 'Give Mabel a chance to rest and recover from the journey, dear,' she said, having been quite shocked by Mabel's appearance. 'My dear, you look dreadfully tired and you've lost weight. Have you been overworking?'

Mabel smiled and shook her head. 'I'm all right, Aunt, it's just been a bit busy lately on the district, that's all. Oh, it's so good to see all o' yer again – and Daisy looks ever so much better now, doesn't she?' And talks more like the Somertons, she thought to herself, conscious of a difference in her young sister that was more than just improvement in health and spirits. The nine-year-old had an easy self-confidence that had been lacking before. Daisy had in fact become a little lady, eager to show Mabel her new clothes, her kitten and the school exercise books proving her to be top of her class when school had closed for the summer holidays.

Mabel had made up her mind to say nothing of the recent events at Tooting and Mimi Court's name was not mentioned. The aunts already knew that their niece had left Macaulay Road and would be going to the Booth Street Poor Law infirmary on 1 September. She guessed that they had been talking about her future when Aunt Nell glanced at her sister and spoke for them both that same evening after dinner.

'Haven't you ever thought of leaving London, Mabel, with all its sad memories? You could get just as good a training at Winchester and we could see you so much more often.'

'But my fiancé lives in London, Aunt Nell,' answered Mabel simply.

'And do you really intend to join the Salvation Army?' asked Mrs Somerton with another quick look at Miss Chalcott.

'Yes, certainly, when I'm trained as a nurse an' Harry's a servin' officer. An' then when we're married I'll work with children in need o' care, just like I've always wanted to,' said Mabel, her eyes noticeably brightening.

'When shall we have the pleasure of meeting Mr Drover?' asked Aunt Kate.

'Well, er, he says he'd like to come down here to take me back to London at the end o' me visit,' Mabel confided with shy eagerness.

'Oh, very good! Please write and ask him to come for an overnight stay, so that we can all meet him and get to know him,' replied Aunt Kate at once.

'Oh, thank yer, Aunt, thank yer! I know he'd love that – it's really very good o' yer!' said Mabel gratefully. She was still a little in awe of her aunts and did not take anything for granted.

As the sunny days went by she found herself missing Harry more and more, and not only Harry: in a strange and unexpected way she missed the south London streets she had known all her life, so far removed from the well-ordered lives of her country-bred aunts who would not have understood how anybody could prefer the kind of life that their poor sister had embraced, to her cost.

The church summer fête illustrated for Mabel the essential differences between their lives and hers. It took place on a warm, sunny Saturday, and people seemed to stream in from miles around to admire the gaily decorated stalls, the home produce from garden and kitchen, and the various entertainments on the rectory lawn. The aunts were busy on the cake stall, and Mabel walked between Daisy and her inseparable friend Lucy Drummond who wanted to try everything. The three of them watched and applauded the Punch and Judy show operated by the eldest Drummond boy, Cedric, and a college friend of his.

'They're both crazy with love for Alice,' remarked Daisy conversationally and indeed, Alice Court at sixteen had become an acknowledged beauty, parading with her parasol between two girl companions and lowering her dark eyes demurely when young men looked at her, as they frequently did. She returned Mabel's smile rather coolly when they passed each other.

'There's papa!' cried Lucy. 'Papa, please may we have a strawberry ice?'

The Reverend Mr Drummond drew a quick breath at finding himself face to face with Mabel. 'Good afternoon, Miss Court. I trust you are enjoying your visit to Miss Chalcott?'

'Er, yes, Mr Drummond, thank yer,' replied Mabel, feeling tongue-tied.

'My wife and I are particularly fond of your sister Daisy.' He smiled.

'Thank yer, Mr Drummond. I like Lucy, too.'

'Please, Papa, may we have a strawberry ice? And Miss Court, may she have one, too?' pleaded Lucy, jumping up and down.

When the rector obligingly bought three ice cream cones, Mrs Drummond fluttered over to them, all lilac silk and condescension, with a wide-brimmed flowery hat. 'How nice to meet you, Miss Court! You must come to the rectory for tea one day, and meet Lucy's brothers and sisters.' She glanced up at her husband and took hold of his arm. 'If you'll excuse us, Miss Court, the rector needs a word with the churchwardens – good afternoon!' And she firmly led her husband away from the tired-looking girl with the jarring London accent, the very sight of whom seemed to have such an odd effect on him.

Mabel watched them retreating across the grass, reflecting that her own mother might have been in that woman's place. Anna-Maria, his first love ... 'Come on, Daisy, let's have our ices before they melt!' she said and proceeded to lick hers with relish. Catching sight of her, Alice hastily changed direction and walked as far away as possible. Heavens, she thought, what *must* the Drummonds think of her sister's manners?

The four weeks passed swiftly and there was no

doubt that Mabel's looks and general health were improved by the fresh air and country fare. She divided her time between the two houses, roaming the summer fields with Daisy and sharing reminiscences with her. She had saved all of George's scrappy letters to show her sisters, though Alice was usually otherwise engaged; she had become absorbed into Belhampton society, where her looks and ladylike airs gained her many invitations. She did not care to be reminded of Sorrel Street.

The arrival of Harry's letters was always the highlight of Mabel's days and not many went by without hearing from him. To her relief and thankfulness, he sent her news of Maudie Ling, who was still at the women's shelter where she had been sent after she had despatched Harry to go and rescue Mabel from police custody. 'They kept her on as a domestic servant and she helps in the kitchen,' he wrote. 'I hear that she cheers the poor women with her good humour so pray, dear Mabel, that the Lord is making a change in her life. Who knows what she may become? Praise the Lord for His goodness.'

Mabel found it difficult to envisage Maudie in the role of Salvationist, but she was grateful for news of her old friend and to know that she was safe, at least. She hoped that Harry would bring more news of her when he came down to stay at Pinehurst.

Pinehurst. The fine, solidly built Victorian home where the three Chalcott sisters had grown up and which was now so large for one single lady. Mabel's imagination filled it with children in need of love and care: the unwanted babies, the orphans, the neglected victims of drink, disease, poverty and all the social evils that turn children into waifs and strays. How she would love to open her arms and her heart to receive them under its sheltering roof!

On the evening before Harry Drover was expected, Mabel's aunts tried once more to persuade her not to return to London and a Poor Law infirmary training. 'If you're not planning to marry this young man for three years, you could have a much better life here in the country, Mabel,' said Aunt Kate. 'Country families are always looking out for reliable nursery maids and you could care for children in the comfort of a country house – and with all found, you'd be able to save all of your wages. Elinor and I think you should consider it.'

Mabel's reaction was one of bewilderment at their complete failure to understand her. 'What?' she cried. 'Don't yer see, Aunt Kate, I want to work with *poor* children, not rich ones! It's somethin' I've always wanted to do, ever since I first started takin' children to school when their mothers were ill or havin' babies. My first job was at the Babies Mission, an' I saw how some o' them little mites lived – one o' my friends begged on the streets with her baby brother 'cause their parents were always drunk. Then I worked at the Women's Rescue with babies that'd never know their own mothers. I used to pick 'em up out o' their cots an' try to comfort 'em when they cried. It nearly broke my heart.' She got up and paced the room while her aunts looked on in astonishment. 'Oh, can't yer understand?' she pleaded as tears spilled down her cheeks. 'I grew up poor, an' I *belong* with the poor, the children with nobody to love them. I've had a good rest here and ye've been very kind, but . . . but I couldn't possibly stay. Me life's in London with the man I'm goin' to marry one day. It's like a call I must answer, don't yer *see*?' She turned to face the two women, clasping her hands together. 'Alice is completely settled here and Daisy's happy bein' a Somerton. But I don't belong here – I must go back!'

For a minute there was silence, then Aunt Nell gave a long sigh. 'I think I understand you, Mabel. After all, you've seen so much more of . . . of another side of life than we have. You must do as you think best and I for one will support you.'

'And you know that you always have a home here if you need one,' added Kate quietly.

'Oh, I do, I *do*! And I'll always be grateful for what ye've done for us – for Anna-Maria, in lookin' after her children.'

Katherine Chalcott could not have asked for anything more.

'Mabel! Oh, my own dear girl!'

'Harry!'

Her heart leapt as he stepped down from the train and held her close for a moment. The very smell of his uniform jacket was sweet to her and to be in his arms again was bliss for them both. She had come alone to meet him and take him back to the house, which gave them a chance to talk as they walked, stopping every so often in the deserted lane to exchange a kiss. She told him of the conversation she had had with her aunts the previous evening.

'Yer don't know how relieved that makes me feel, Mabel. I been thinkin' that maybe ye'd want to settle in the country after all ye've been through.'

'Harry, how *could* yer? After all we've promised each other!'

'God bless yer, Mabel, I should've known ye'd

stick to what yer said ye'd do! Oh, and guess what news I got about a friend o' yours!'

'Maudie Ling?' she cried at once. 'Oh, what's happened to her? Tell me, tell me!'

'Got herself a place in service, up St John's Wood way – the woman took her on without references 'cause she'd been workin' for the Salvation Army. I'm sorry we've lost her, Mabel, but I've heard that it's a respectable family, so she'll be looked after.'

'Oh, that's wonderful news, Harry – an' don't yer see, it's all because she went to the trouble o' findin' yer an' sendin' yer to me – look how it's all worked out for her!'

'Yes, my love, I suppose it has.' Harry was not quite so confident that Maud had made a wise decision, but he kept his thoughts to himself.

Her aunts and uncle greeted him cordially, but it was Daisy who ran into his arms to be lifted up and hugged in mid-air, to her delight and his pleasure at such a show of approval from little Miss Somerton. He noticed a big change in Alice and told her that she had grown into a fine girl, at which she raised her dark eyebrows as if affronted by such familiarity.

Thomas Somerton went out of his way to make conversation easy at the table over the midday dinner and, when Harry refused a glass of wine, he was given lemonade without comment. Asked what he thought about Home Rule for Ireland, he said that surely the Irish should be granted what they wanted, it was their country, at which Somerton was highly amused and said that he should be in the Cabinet instead of the Salvation Army. Mabel glowed with pride, but her uncle was less satisfied by his views on a possible clash with a new industrialised and militaristic Germany.

Harry's reply was as prompt as it was serious: 'No country should ever go to war with another, Mr Somerton, and no government has the right to demand that men should shed each other's blood. It's against God's commandment.'

'But if one country is attacked by another, surely it has the right to defend itself?'

'If the British Empire's as mighty as we've all been told an' taught, I reckon Germany wouldn't dare take it on.'

'I just hope you're proved right, Mr Drover.' And Somerton wisely left it at that. Taken all round, Harry acquitted himself well with Mabel's relations, for as Aunt Nell confided to her sister, it was impossible *not* to like such a sincere, straightforward young man. And there was no doubt at all about his devotion to their niece.

On her return, Mabel went straight to the Tooting Home, accompanied by Harry. There they found her Aunt Ruth just as happy and contented as when last seen, and eager to hear about Daisy and the very different life she now led at Belhampton.

There was one question Mabel hesitated to ask, but knew she had to do so. 'Has Mrs Court – has yer sister been to see yer, Aunt Ruth?'

The old lady's expression was both sad and thoughtful. 'Yes, Mabel, she has been here. Somebody told her where I was, and she came and asked to speak with me alone.'

'Oh, good heavens, Aunt Ruth, this is what I've been afraid of – what did she say? What did she do to yer?' asked Mabel in dismay.

'Well, for a start, she didn't see me alone, Mabel.

433

Matron insisted on being present, because I'd told her that my sister might come and accuse me.'

'Oh, thank God. So what happened?'

'She tried to accuse me of breaking my promise to her, but I told her that her treatment of you released me from it. I said I'd borne a burden of deceit for too long, and that now at last I was free. And do you know, Mabel, she said she'd take me out of here and put me in a private home and pay for me.'

'*Did* she, Aunt Ruth? And what did yer say?'

'I thanked her and said I was happy here, and had no wish to go anywhere else.'

'And did yer forgive her, Miss Lawton?' asked Harry gently.

'Yes, Mr Drover, certainly I did. We have to forgive all injuries and wrongs, so as to live at peace with all people, according to the Lord's commandment. I asked her to forgive me, too.'

'Oh, Aunt Ruth, ye've helped me to make up me mind,' said Mabel, nodding. 'I shall have to go an' see her meself.'

'Then I shall come with yer,' said Harry Drover.

Chapter Twenty

Elsie answered the door to them and told them that Mrs Court was in the front parlour. 'She don't want no visitors nosin' round, but she'll see Mabel,' Elsie said, pointedly staring at Drover.

'Very well,' replied Mabel. 'You stay in the livin' room, Harry. Let me see her alone.'

He was reluctant. 'Then yer must leave the door ajar, Mabel, in case yer need me.'

As soon as Mabel set eyes on her grandmother she saw that she had been drinking. On the low table at her elbow was a half-empty bottle and a glass. She reached up for a second glass from the wall cabinet.

Mimi Court – Prudence Lawton – was a shadow of her former self. Her once plump features had sagged into fleshy pouches and the much-tinted hair was now almost white beneath a black lace cap.

Yet she rose to greet Mabel and they stood for a long moment without speaking, as if Mimi was weighing up her granddaughter. When she spoke it was with her company accent. 'So, Mabel – been to see ol' Miss Lawton at the Tooting Home, eh? How was she today?'

'Happier than I've ever known her, Grandmother – contented and peaceful.' Mabel could have added, *not living in fear any longer*, but she remembered Harry's reminder that she had not come to judge this woman, only to bid her farewell.

Mimi's eyes were wary. Since her return to

Macaulay Road she had immediately encountered active hostility from former acquaintances. She had become a target of open abuse from the likes of Mrs Taylor, who had shouted 'Scumbag!' at her in the street, and where there were not harsh words there were cold shoulders whenever she set foot out of doors. Shopkeepers who had once been deferential now showed no respect, and people stopped talking and stared at her when she approached. At one time Mimi Court would have stared them out and pulled herself through by sheer defiance, but now she felt too old and tired. And alone.

'So she's peaceful, is she? Senile, more like.'

Mabel did not answer. She could not help contrasting the different circumstances of the two sisters now, nearing the end of their lives, and to know which one was the happier.

Mimi poured out two glasses of port wine and pushed one towards Mabel. 'Well, sit down an' take a drink with me – go on.' She lowered herself into the armchair, while Mabel remained standing. 'Yer got over yer little adventure, then? Yer night in custody?'

'Thanks to Mr Drover and Miss Lawton, yes,' Mabel said quietly. 'It was the worst night o' me life, except when I lost me poor mother.'

Mimi held out her hands in a placatory gesture, palms up. 'Look, I'm sorry about that, Mabel, but it sounds as if yer got through it pretty well – very well, in fact. I'm proud o' yer.'

Mabel felt her indignation rising. 'I wouldn't've got through it if the charges hadn't been dropped,' she pointed out.

'Pooh! O' course they were dropped, I knew all along that ol' Sir Percy'd want to save his wife's name. My God, that girl was a fool if ever there was one. Had everythin' a woman could want, an' threw it all away for nothin'.'

'Whatever she was, she paid for it with her life,' said Mabel gravely.

A flicker of unease showed in Mimi's sharp brown eyes, now reddened by drink. 'What? Yes, well, it was the worse case I ever had, that was. And the last. I've finished with midwifery an' all that from now on. I should've stopped sooner, I 'aven't been on form since Jack went. Never lost a client all these years, though. Not until now.'

Mabel was silent. Her glass of wine stood untouched.

Mimi attempted a smile. 'Look, I know it was hard on yer, bein' taken in like that, but these things blow over, Mabel, an' don't I know it – been in a few tight corners in my time, an' come out of 'em with me good name intact and a good deal more besides. Now listen, I got plans for yer. Ye're nineteen now, yer got brains, ye're a good worker, in fact, I see a lot o' meself in yer, Mabel—' A faint sound like a cough or a choke came from beyond the door, but Mimi did not hear. 'Yer deserve a reward, Mabel. D' ye want to hear what I'm goin' to do?'

Mabel stood stock-still and expressionless.

'I'm goin' to pay for yer to train as a nurse at a good volunt'ry horspital, 'ow about that? Some-where like St George's or St Mary's. Ha! D'ye reckon ye'll be able to keep yer end up with them lady probationers? Yer money'll be as good as theirs!' She looked hard at Mabel, expecting a gasp of delight.

It had got to be said and Mabel was surprised at how calm she sounded. 'I've been appointed to start

437

trainin' on September the first at Booth Street Poor Law infirmary.'

It was Mimi who gasped. '*What*? A bloody workhouse out Lambeth way, nursin' the poorest, the lowest o' the low? Ye'd better write straight away an' tell 'em it's orf – ye're goin' to train at a proper 'orspital.' Her company accent was rapidly deserting her.

'No, Grandmother. I've *chosen* to train at a Poor Law infirmary. It's not a workhouse any more, it's been taken over an' there's a waitin' list for probationers.'

If she had slapped Mimi across the face it could hardly have been more of a shock. There was no question of persuasion or argument; this was total rejection and Mimi felt it as such. 'Ye're makin' the biggest mistake o' yer life, my girl. Ye're as bad as that ol' fool in the Tooting 'Ome, turnin' down a good offer.'

'My aunt chose right, Grandmother,' returned Mabel at once. 'She's happy now, she doesn't need any favours from yer, an' neither do I.'

Another slap in the face – and through the haze of wine, that word *aunt*. There was a pause. 'She's been talkin', then.'

'Yes, I told yer, she came to the police station and defended me against the charge of assistin' yer with ... what yer did. And it came out that yer were sisters, an' how yer took in yer own mother and sister without acknowledgin' them – an' I saw for meself how yer treated Aunt Ruth. But she's free o' yer now.'

Mimi made a choking sound, a grunt, as if she had received a physical blow. 'So that's what I get for takin' 'em in an' keepin' 'em for God knows 'ow

438

many years. I see. What else did she say? What other cats came flyin' out o' the bag?'

In for a penny, in for a pound. Mabel took a deep breath. 'That your name's not Court but Prudence Lawton – and my father's father was some kind o' civil servant from India.'

Mimi started and then gave a harsh, grating laugh. 'Oho! She told yer *that*, did she? An' about the good start in life I got for my Jack? Did she tell yer *that* as well?'

Mabel coloured, embarrassed by these revelations. 'She said the Masood family 'ud been very generous, but I'm really not interested in hearin' about that.'

'Oh, yes, you are! Everybody wants to know where they came from an' I'm goin' to tell yer, Mabel, so's yer can go an' tell yer Salvation Army man. An' yer *ought* to know, seein' as yer was so upset about them poor babies at the Rescue. Because I didn't part with *my* baby, Mabel, I brought 'im up on me own, an' struck an 'ard bargain for 'im! Hah!'

Again the deep, self-congratulatory chuckle as Mimi looked back on what she saw as her greatest triumph. In spite of herself Mabel was curious and waited half in dread of what she was to hear.

'Poor ol' Ruth. All 'er life she's envied me, 'cause I took after me father an' liked a bit of adventure, while she was a scared little thing, clingin' round 'er mother's skirts.' Mimi looked up suddenly with a question in her eyes. 'Did she tell yer what 'appened to our naughty father?'

'She said somethin' about a scandal, how yer all had to leave the parish where he was vicar,' muttered Mabel.

'That's right, an' that's when our paths divided, yer could say. When we had to leave in a hurry, I saw me chance to get away an' see a bit o' life. I couldn't bear to stay with those two, skimpin' an' scrapin' in cheap lodgin's, tryin' to stay respectable on next to nothin', so me an' me friend Sally Kent took ourselves off to London. We were both young an' not bad-lookin', an' I fell in with a seafarin' man from the East Indies, a good-looker with plenty o' money to spend. We lived well an' had a good time while it lasted – and Sally got a place in service, big 'ouse overlookin' Regent's Park, home o' Sir Sidney Horner, God rot 'im – Tory in ol' Disraeli's government, a crawler an' a lecher. It wasn't long before Sally caught 'is eye . . .' Mimi's mouth curled in bitter contempt as she remembered her unfortunate friend. ''Course, the next thing was 'Er Ladyship found Sally was three months gone, an' turned 'er out on the street without a penny. I swear it was Horner that ruined 'er, an' maybe 'Er Ladyship guessed what'd been goin' on, I don't know. But not every poor girl in Sally's case finds a Rescue 'ome, Mabel. Sally's spirit was broken an' she went the same way as yer mother – to the Thames.'

'Oh, my God.' Mabel closed her eyes, but could not banish the picture of the drowned face.

'Yes, yer can ooh an' ah, Mabel, but a lot of 'em goes that way. An' 'e got orf scot-free, the ol' goat. I remember it well, 'cause it was the same week I lost me own man. 'Is money ran out an' orf 'e went back to sea, said 'e'd be back but I 'adn't time to wait, I'd just found out I was in the same boat as Sally. It was a bad time all round, that spring of 1869.'

'Good heavens, Grandmother, so it was the sailor—' Mabel gave an involuntary gasp, thinking of Harry behind the door. Whatever else was he to hear about her origins?

Mimi did not answer directly. 'So, poor Sally was dead an' Horner was alive – but 'e 'ad it comin' to 'im, Mabel, oho! I saw me chance to get revenged for Sally an' do meself a bit o' good at the same time. Jus' before she left there, she tol' me that these bigwigs 'ad arrived from India, comin' to kowtow to the Queen, an' ol' Horner thought 'e'd worm 'is way in by offerin' 'em 'ospitality – let 'em stay at 'is place for the summer. So they moved in – Sir Akbar Masood an' 'is son Anwar, only a boy.'

'Masood!' whispered Mabel. 'Was that *him*, Grand-mother? The one who'd come over to be educated in England?'

Mimi laughed again. 'Oh, did Ruth tell yer that? Once she opened 'er mouth, she didn't know 'ow to shut it again, did she? Yes, Sir Akbar was well up in the Indian Civil Service at Hyderabad, spent 'is time 'obnobbin' with the Viceroy an' put on a big spread for the Prince o' Wales when HRH was on one of 'is state visits. Oh, yes, 'e was somebody, was ol' Akbar, an' 'e'd brought 'is eldest son over to try 'is luck at Cambridge – only 'e very nearly 'ad to turn tail an' go back in a hurry, Mabel, an all 'cause o' me!'

Mabel was both fascinated and repelled. She had been half expecting a tale of romance and doomed love; instead she was hearing about the daring exploits of a scheming maidservant.

'So there I was in poor Sally's place and Anwar was so easy – only seventeen, 'e was, as eager to learn as I was to teach. It was 'im first called me Mimi, an' I kept it, suited me better than Prudence. Ol' Horner was as smarmy as can be with 'em, bowin' an' scrapin', gettin' 'imself well in at court – there was me other name! – thought 'e was in line for the Cabinet an' all sorts o' favours. 'E never noticed me, Mabel, never 'ad an idea o' what I was plannin' for 'im!'

Mimi took another gulp of wine and let it roll over her tongue, licking her lips. A few drops spilled down the front of her gown. She looked up with an expression that was not so much a smile as a conspiratorial grin that made Mabel's blood run cold. 'That was a good time, gal. I used to creep into Anwar's room overlookin' the Park, an' wait for 'im. Those summer nights . . .' She sighed and her features softened a little at the far-off memory of the youthful visitor from the most exotic jewel of the Empire, he who had worshipped her young body. 'An' then, jus' as 'e was orf to Cambridge in the autumn, I sprung me little surprise on 'em. Told 'Er Ladyship I was three months, though I was gettin' on for five, an' said it was Anwar. What a to-do! I was no Sally Kent, I stood up there in front of ol' Horner an' said I wanted payin' off – or I'd kick up the biggest society scandal for 'alf a century. Said I'd go to the newspapers, I'd go to the city church they attended, I'd write to ol' Disraeli an' the Queen – remember I was a vicar's daughter, I'd been to school – an' said I'd let everybody know what'd been goin' on under Sir Sidney Horner's roof. I threatened to show 'em all up so's they'd never be able to 'old their 'eads up again – an' I *would*'ve done, an' all! They found out I wasn't bluffin' when I said I'd show the little dark baby to the world. Aha!' The brief tenderness had vanished, replaced by a mask of gloating vengeance.

'So – what happened in the end?' whispered Mabel.

'Well, they 'ad to pay up, o' course, for me to keep me mouth shut, an' I made sure I asked for double what ol' Sir Akbar offered. I reckon Sir Sidney must've gone 'alves with 'im, maybe 'e paid the lot – yer should've seen 'im, Mabel, *livid* with rage, I thought 'e was goin' to 'ave a stroke. But I stood me ground, an' walked away with enough o' the ready to buy this house an' give my Jack a good start. Aha, Mabel, yer father did well out o' them Masoods, considerin' I got 'im orf a Lascar sailor! Ol' Ruth didn't tell yer *that*, did she? Nobody knows that, Mabel, only me. An' now you.'

And Harry, thought Mabel. But by now she knew her fiancé well enough to know that such knowledge would make no difference to him.

'It wasn't easy, Mabel, none of it was easy, but I did it. I pulled it orf for my Jack.' Mimi's unfocused eyes gleamed for a moment and then darkened. 'An' now 'e's gone, too.' She put down the glass and raised her head. 'Listen, Mabel, I'm goin' to find a little place somewhere out in Surrey – Worcester Park or Carshalton or somewhere there's still a bit o' country. You shtay an' 'elp me move, be me comp-companion, get ev'rythin' after I've gone, you an' yer Shalvaton Army chap. Whaddya say? Don't go 'way, Mabel, gal – don't leave me all on me own.' Her recital had changed to maudlin pleading. Tears of self-pity welled in her eyes as she looked up at Mabel who stood still as a statue.

What do I feel for her now? she asked herself. Somewhere deep down in her heart she could find some pity for this unscrupulous woman whose blood ran in her own veins; but she felt no love for her, just as Mimi had shown no love for her own mother and sister, or for Mabel's mother. Or for Anwar Masood whose youthful passion she had used for her own ends. And even now she showed no remorse for what she had done.

But time and circumstance had caught up with her, and her triumphs were all in the past. Scorned by her neighbours and facing a loveless old age, she was making one last desperate effort to buy the contentment and peace of mind that her penniless sister possessed.

Mabel instinctively glanced towards the door, seeking Harry's presence and, although he could not see her, he sensed her need of him. He quietly slipped into the parlour to stand at her side and Mimi looked up blearily at them both.

'You tell 'er, Mr Drover, ye'll 'ave all me money an' 'ouse to live in, the pair o' yer. I'll buy yer a place yer can 'ave for 'omeless kids if yer want – that's what yer want, i'n't, Mabel? Only don't leave me on me own – stay with yer poor ol' gran'mother.'

Mabel steeled herself to face those imploring, frightened eyes. 'No, Grandmother. I have to start me trainin' on Monday. An' I don't want anythin' from yer.'

Mimi began to whimper. The tears spilled down her furrowed cheeks and her shoulders shook. It was not in Mabel's nature to cause suffering, however much deserved, nor was she to be the judge of this woman, now staring into a blank and empty void. So she put out a hand to touch one heaving shoulder. 'Goodbye, Grandmother. I hope things go well with yer move. I'll call Elsie to make yer a cup o' tea, shall I?'

'I'm takin' Mabel away now, she's been here long enough,' said Harry firmly, but added in a gentler tone, 'Remember it's never too late to make yer peace with God, Miss Lawton. No repentant sinner was

444

ever turned away from the mercy seat. I'll pray for yer.'

Mimi's expression was inscrutable, but Mabel suspected that Harry's well-intentioned words would be construed as insult added to injury. Without looking back, she let him lead her out of 23 Macaulay Road for the last time.

Epilogue

He is already waiting for her beside Lambeth Pier.

'Yer got away from college, then?' she says, her eyes lighting up.

"Course I did. I had to be with yer on this day of all days. Here, give me yer case. Did yer come up by train?'

'No, I got the tram. Let's walk by the river for a bit – I'm not due there till two. Oh, I'm that pleased to see yer, Harry! It isn't that I'm nervous or anything, but I've waited so long for this.'

They stand together on Bishop's Walk, looking downriver. The sky is a clear, clean blue, with only a hint of summer's end in the sunlight on the water, sending up a dappled reflection on the rusty ironwork of the bridge. Mabel's eyes are shining and Harry wants to share her happiness, so he firmly suppresses his own feelings about the next three years.

Three years. What changes may come, what unexpected events might occur by the time Mabel is qualified? He is certain only of the constancy of his love.

'I can't believe this Monday's really come at last, Harry, the first day of September! I've dreamt about it for so long – and there was that awful night at Amen Corner when I thought I'd lost everything – but now that it's actually *here*, I can't take it in! D'ye

realise that this time tomorrow I'll be a real probationer nurse in a cap an' apron, workin' on a ward,
lookin' after sick people!'

Harry smiles and says he knows how she feels. Big
Ben strikes the half-hour and they turn away from
the river to the Lambeth Road, to be engulfed
between retailers, public houses, coffee shops, milli-
ners, barbers and pawnbrokers; down the narrow
side streets they see aproned women at their front
doors and children playing on the paving stones.
Motor-driven delivery vans sound their horns and
horse-drawn brewers' drays clatter through the
streets; a wide farm cart piled high with bales of hay
goes trundling along to a stable yard.

All around her Mabel senses the teeming life of
London and her hand tightens on Harry's arm. 'This
is goin' to be my *home*, Harry, the place where I live.
I'll belong with these people.'

But when those three long years are up, ye'll
belong to *me*, God willin', he thinks to himself. At
twenty-two, halfway through his Salvation Army
training, he has few illusions about the lives of the
poor, the poverty and hardship that his Mabel is
about to encounter among the patients at Booth
Street Poor Law infirmary. She'll find them very
different from those at the Anti-Viv or the Bolingbroke.

They have arrived. Surrounded by a high stone
wall, the soot-blackened building looms up out of a
maze of intersecting streets, situated about halfway
between the Archbishop's Palace to the west and the
bottleneck of the Elephant and Castle to the east,
with trains rattling north and south to and from
Waterloo Station. Mabel looks up at the two rows of

rectangular sash windows and tries to picture the rows of beds behind them.

They are outside the front entrance. A young woman is standing nearby, holding a case.

'Looks a bit lost, doesn't she, Harry – d'ye think she's another new probationer?'

Mabel nods to the girl who smiles back uncertainly. They are about to speak when a white-painted ambulance turns into Booth Street and draws up beside two battered wooden doors set in the wall. A stretcher is taken out and a man is lying on it, wrapped in a grey blanket; the doors open and he is carried through. The doors bang shut and Mabel stares as if she could see through them.

'Who knows, Harry, I might see that poor man again tomorrow!'

He nods fondly, thinking of all the difficulties and disappointments, even dangers that this girl has come through in the three years since he has known her. Yet here she is, as fresh and hopeful as when they first met.

'That must be the nurses' hostel, see, over the other side, Harry,' she says, pointing to a four-storey block enclosed by the same high outer wall. It makes him think of an impregnable fortress and he turns down the corners of his mouth. Not much chance of snatching a goodnight kiss from a nurse imprisoned in a place like that . . .

A church clock chimes two and two more young women arrive at the front entrance, each accompanied by a carefully dressed older woman.

'Must be their mothers,' assumes Mabel, smiling again at the girl on her own. 'It's time, Harry,' she whispers. 'Thank yer – oh, thank yer for comin' to see me off – or rather to see me in! But now we'll have to say goodbye.'

'God bless yer an' keep yer safe for me, my own dearest girl,' he murmurs hastily and even though they're in broad daylight with bystanders watching, Mabel stands up on tiptoe to give him a quick kiss on the lips. He holds her briefly, then has to let her go.

'Dearest Harry – see yer soon as I can – I'll let yer know how I get on!'

'Don't forget to, Mabel, will yer?' The note of anxiety is reflected in his eyes.

'As if I would!'

She takes her case and joins the other three new girls. They push open the doors leading into the entrance hall.

His eyes follow her, his lips moving silently as the door closes. 'Mind yer come back to me, Mabel – oh, my love, come back to me.'

The door opens again and Mabel reappears just for a moment. She holds up her hand and touches her lips and her heart.

He has his answer.